THE
WRATH

**Also available from
Gena Showalter**

GENA SHOWALTER

THE
WRATH

CANARY STREET PRESS

**CANARY
STREET
PRESS™**

Recycling programs
for this product may
not exist in your area.

ISBN-13: 978-1-335-42490-7

The Wrath

Canary Street Press
22 Adelaide St. West, 41st Floor
Toronto, Ontario M5H 4E3, Canada
CanaryStPress.com

Printed in U.S.A.

To Jane Ladling. Not once did you complain when Jill Monroe and I left you in "utter peril." All so I could work on *The Wrath*. Okay, so perhaps there's a slight chance you maybe possibly did complain once. Perhaps five or ten or more times, but no higher than twentyish.

To Conrad Ryan. Not once did you threaten to arrest me when I took a wee bit longer than originally planned, keeping you in quote, unquote agony. Did you need to write me the ticket though? No. But I love you anyway.

To Jill Monroe and Naomi Lane. Because.

PROLOGUE

Excerpted from *The Book of Stars*
Author unknown
Warning: Living text subject to change

They are ancient warriors, evil to the core and loyal only to one another. Known as the Astra Planeta, Wandering Stars, Warlords of the Skies—the beginning of the end—they travel from world to world, wiping out enemy armies. Drawn to war, they turn even the smallest skirmish into a bloodbath.

To glimpse these brutes is to greet your death.

Having no moral compass, they kill without mercy, steal without qualm, and destroy without guilt. Their aim is simple, their goal fixed. Earn a mystical blessing to experience victory for the next five hundred years. A necessity in their endless war with Erebus the Deathless, for without this benediction, the Astra automatically acquire a curse. Five hundred years of utter defeat.—Page 1

★ ★ ★

The time has come to renew the blessing. One after the other, each of the nine will undergo an impossible task. Three have proven successful; the fourth must now demonstrate his worth. A merciless soldier, Azar the Memory Keeper recalls everything—except his own follies.

To win his challenge, he must face Lorelei the Incomparable, a perplexing goddess of desire. The charge is this: Resurrect her, then kill her all over again. But first he must face her husband, Rathbone the Only, a treacherous king of the Underworld who will stop at nothing to protect his beloved.

What will happen when these two powerful foes lock horns over a chosen female?—Page 12,847

Eons ago

Thunder boomed and lightning flashed in a storm-blackened sky. Rathbone the Only removed his helmet, uncaring as violent winds pelted icy rain in his face. His blood-soaked hair whipped, obscuring his vision. He wiped his eyes, but the image before him never altered.

Lorelei the Incomparable, goddess of desire and his beloved bride, lay on the field of slaughter, motionless atop a pile of slain demons and their assortment of severed parts. Her crystalline irises stared at nothing. Her perfect lips remained parted with a silent scream. A drenched sable mane stuck to ashen skin, molding to exquisite features able to inspire lust in all who gazed upon her. But....

Something with claws had ripped open her chest and plucked out her heart.

Rathbone couldn't bring himself to accept...hoped... "Lore!"

Though he'd fought on the front lines for twenty-one straight days and nights without wavering, there'd been no one strong enough to fell him. Here, he dropped to his knees, his armor clanking. His weapons rolled from a once iron grip.

With a shaky hand, he gently caressed Lore's glacial cheek. "Wake up, sweetness. I need you."

They had plans. Toast his victory with a glass of ambrosia and make love. An adored custom. But nothing changed. Lore didn't regrow a heart, as a deity of her capability should. She didn't smile with delight and coil her arms around him, the way he so desperately longed. Didn't tell him not to worry because she was soon to make his dreams come true.

"Wake up!" he bellowed, his voice hollow and broken. "Your king has issued a command." They had agreed. He would fight until achieving victory, and they would rule this Underworld kingdom together. Mere minutes ago, that victory had finally come. This was to be a time of celebration, not devastation. "I completed step one of our plan. You *must* wake."

Minutes passed in silence. The storm continued to rage, but she never revived, never responded.

Tears scorched his cheeks, mixing with freezing raindrops. His precious wife couldn't be dead. She was the mate chosen for him by fate, and he *required* her. He'd accepted it at their first meeting when she'd oh so sweetly requested his aid.

"Lore. Please," he croaked. "You must return to me."

Still nothing.

A roar brewed deep in his chest, grief attempting to tear its way free of his insides. What had happened? Why had she come to the combat zone? She might be a goddess of desire, born with incredible power, but she was a gentle soul. Afraid of blood. Terrified of blades. She should be tucked away in the safety of their hideout, awaiting his summons.

"I'm sorry, Rath." Hades, King of the Dead, patted and squeezed his shoulder. "She's gone."

Rathbone didn't spare the sovereign a glance. He loved the sovereign like a father and even owed the male his life, but Lore wasn't a subject they could discuss without coming to blows.

"You aren't sorry." He gathered the beauty close, her limp body hanging in his arms. "You hate her." His jaw clenched. *Hated.*

"True. But I love you."

That, he knew. Again and again, Hades had proven the truth of his claim. Though Rathbone's mother had considered him a great disappointment, the King of the Dead had seen something special in him. Hades took him under his smoky wing and spent centuries training him to be a soldier without equal. Today, that training had paid off. After a gruesome year-long war, Rathbone won the right to rule the kingdom neighboring Hades's. The Realm of Agonies.

Rathbone had lost much along the way. Soldiers. A fortune. His moral compass. *But I will not lose my mate.* "I committed the vilest deeds to defeat the former king," he rasped. A famed warrior named Styx. "His land is now my land. The palace he built is mine to lay at the feet of my wife, *so that is what I will do.*" Rathbone's volume grew until his speech overshadowed the newest clap of thunder.

Hades swiped his fingers over an increasingly frustrated expression. "You wed her, yet you maintain a stable of one hundred mistresses. Why is this lone female so important?"

"You answered yourself. They are my mistresses. She is my queen." No one mattered more.

Lore was the one who'd encouraged Rathbone to establish the stable in the first place. As an ancient, she understood the customs of the gods in a manner he did not. Deities of their ilk kept paramours, she'd said, and a warrior of his renown should enjoy more than most.

Was any female more perfect?

"You cannot bring her back to life," Hades said, giving his shoulder another pat, "but in time you'll recover from her loss."

Bring her back. The words echoed inside Rathbone's head. Yes! He could do it. The ancients possessed a way, and Lore had taught him how as a just in case.

"Give me your chisel," he commanded. The King of the Dead was never without one; Hades relished carving his initials into the bones of his enemies.

The sovereign frowned at him. "Why?"

"I will etch the Song of Life into her bones." Rathbone kissed Lore's brow before easing her to the rain-soaked pile of dead demons. Instinct demanded he teleport her somewhere safer, drier, and cleaner, but she'd told him location mattered. Death screeched its evil at him here, so here was where he must respond. "We'll be together again, sweetness. I'll give you more time—then I'll give you the world. I swear it."

"Rathbone—"

"You won't change my mind about this." He ripped the neckline of her gown, and the gauzy pink material split down the middle, revealing pale, slender curves he wanted healed *now*. The quicker he began, the better. But once he started, he couldn't pause until he'd carved the last word of the song into the final bone. To pause was to ensure eternal death.

Since he would allow nothing to halt him, her return was guaranteed.

"You're a fool if you do this," Hades warned. "The Greeks are tricksters by nature. I should know! *You* should know. I guarantee she's toying with you. See past your pride and rejoice that you're free. Move on."

Rathbone pressed his tongue to the roof of his mouth. "You've never loved a female the way I love mine—"

"You comprehend nothing of my past, boy!" It was the first show of anger directed Rathbone's way in centuries.

"Perhaps not," he corrected, "but it's obvious *you* do not comprehend the depths of my pain. Otherwise you'd understand the impossibility of moving on. Now, give me your chisel."

Hades huffed with disgust but tossed the tool to the ground, just within reach. "Very well. I'll let you continue. You are insolent, and you could use the life lesson. Just know your regret is assured. And, though I refuse to watch you throw away your future for a female you were using as a surrogate mother, I'll take great delight in laughing in your face when you realize the error of your ways." That said, the king stalked off.

"I've never used Lore as a surrogate mother," Rathbone snarled at the king's retreating back.

The male didn't turn or slow. He simply lifted a hand with his middle finger extended.

With a huff of his own, Rathbone focused on the current task and palmed a dagger.

Inhaling and exhaling a deep breath, he braced for what came next...

Begin.

He cut into Lore. As quickly and seamlessly as possible, he freed bone after bone. Taking apart the female he loved broke something inside him, but he didn't stop. They *would* be together again. Soon.

He would allow nothing less.

1

Present day

Rathbone tossed the liver he held into a bucket and wiped his bloody hands on his apron. All the while, the vampire strapped to a bed of stone sobbed. Of course, the blood-drinker's chest cavity currently gaped open, displaying what remained of his vital organs, so the tears weren't exactly a shocker.

They occupied a cell in Rathbone's dungeon. Moans of pain and misery echoed from every direction, creating the perfect soundtrack. The only downside? A grotesque, metallic scent saturated the damp, chilly air.

"Please," the vampire cried. "I swear to you, I'm not a spy."

"Why did I catch you spying then?"

"You didn't—I swear on the life of my beloved. I got lost. Was searching for—"

"Be quiet or I'll remove your tongue," Rathbone warned. He'd heard enough excuses and lies.

The male blubbered a few seconds more before going silent. "May I go now?" a third person asked.

Rathbone didn't bother to face the visitor who'd dared interrupt the torture session half an hour ago. There was no need. Mystical eyes known as mátia covered his body, granting him a three-hundred-and-sixty-degree view. Less apparel meant cataloging more details.

Today, he'd opted to go without a shirt. Since the apron strings hid little, he was able to observe the cell from every angle. Each element registered in unison, crafting a three-dimensional picture in his head.

A fae prince stood near the exit. Well, the spirit of a fae prince. The mystical defenses surrounding the Realm of Agonies prevented anyone from teleporting in without a special key. In fact, if someone attempted it, their spirit was ripped from their body, bound with enchanted chains, and whisked straight to Rathbone. If they tried to walk in, they had to first overcome countless traps.

The vampire had walked. The prince had gambled with teleportation. Both were suffering because of their choice.

"Let's recap what you've told me so far," Rathbone said to the fae, his tone casual. He reached for a crimson-stained dagger on the wheeled cart at his side, sending the vampire into another round of sobs. "Your name is Bogart. You are the consort of a harpy, and you've come from her land, Harpina. Three months ago, nine warlords invaded the realm, slaughtered the males in their path and temporarily incapacitated the females. You would've died, too, but a harpy-oracle, also known as a harpacle, visited you days before and told you what to do during an invasion, even providing you with a blueprint to escape. Now the warlords and harpies are allies, working together to defeat Erebus Phantom. As payment for her kind deed, the harpy-oracle asked you to deliver this message to me. She has seen where the rest of my wife resides. For the right price, she'll spill every detail. Do I understand you correctly?"

"You understand," the prince confirmed with a sharp dip of his pointed chin. Despite the manacles around his wrists, he waited at attention, as a good soldier should, showing no reaction to Rathbone's gruesome activities.

"Help me, Bogart. Please." The wounded vampire struggled against his bonds. "I'm innocent! I would never spy on the King of Agonies! I'm not a fool."

Rathbone cut out the immortal's tongue, as promised. A fresh howl of pain morphed into a choking fit. He tossed the muscular organ in the bucket. "Tell me more about the harpy-oracle," he commanded the fae, replacing the dagger with a scalpel. He'd used a different weapon for each removal. So far he thought he preferred the ice pick. But he might change his mind. He had sixty-four other weapons to utilize. "Every detail."

"Her name is Neeka the Unwanted. She's half harpy, half oracle, as I previously stated, and all sex appeal. Her addition, not mine. She instructed me to tell you she's the owner and operator of Greater than Greatest at Finding Stuff. She also mentioned the vampire, who is indeed a spy. He came on behalf of the Astra, and he's a herald of their newest task." A pause. Then, "I'll be honest. Neeka might not be entirely sane. Immediately after she explained the situation, I asked her a question, but she'd already forgotten who I was and what she'd said. She threatened to castrate me."

Neeka the Unwanted. Not a name familiar to Rathbone. Had this harpacle spoken true or lied? For that matter, had this prince spoken true or lied? In the Underworld, you could trust no one at any time. Including yourself.

"Despite this supposed insanity," he said, "you decided to do as she requested, three months late, putting your life in my hands because...?"

"I owed her, and I always pay my debts. But I'm not late. She told me when to come."

Yes, but why would any oracle worth her salt summon an enraged King of Agonies to her doorstep? And that was exactly what she'd done with this stunt. Rathbone would be in her face before sunset. If he wasn't convinced of her authenticity and talents, she would die on his table like thousands of others.

He didn't like being reminded of his only failure.

The scalpel bent in his grip as memories assailed him. In a split second of time, he remembered how, all those centuries ago, he'd etched the Song of Life into Lore's bones, one after the other. How innumerable demons had surrounded him while he'd chiseled, not to stop him or launch an attack, as he'd expected, but to wait. Each time he'd completed a bone, a small contingent of the creatures had collected it and fled, laughing. Because they'd known the consequences, just as he had. Rathbone couldn't resurrect his wife until the pieces were reunited.

Back then, he'd been forced to allow the thefts. Having begun the Song, he couldn't pause his task without slaying Lore for good. In the end, he'd retained only the last bone he'd etched. The others, he'd soon learned, had been sold to the highest bidders.

Familiar fury bubbled, but he tamped it down. During the ensuing centuries, Rathbone had tracked the missing pieces to distant worlds, removed them from inside immortals and various creatures, found them buried underground and hidden in mazes. Now he required only six. A clavicle, an ilium, two metatarsals, the left femur, and her skull.

Though he'd never ceased his search, thousands of years had passed since he'd heard the slightest rumor about the goddess. Suddenly this Neeka could deliver everything he lacked?

A lie. Surely.

"You may go," he told the fae. "You've passed on your message." And assured the harpy-oracle's apprehension. "If you return, I'll kill you. Then I'll collect everyone you love and kill them too. Eventually. No telling how many years I'll keep your consort in my stable first."

For dramatic effect, he shoved the crooked scalpel into the vampire's heart. The ensuing screams provided the perfect amount of extra. Rathbone's specialty.

As the fae's spirit was yanked from the cell and restored to his body, wherever that happened to be, the blood-drinker regrew his tongue. Excellent.

Rathbone grabbed a pocket saw. Though he tried to focus on the newest remodel of the vampire's mouth, his thoughts continually returned to the harpy-oracle. He might not know her, but he'd heard of the Astra Planeta. Nine sky gods who did in fact wage war against Erebus Phantom, a death god. Their rivalry rekindled every five hundred years. According to legend, the combatants followed the same pattern for each conflict. The Astra invaded a new world, subjugated its people, and completed a series of impossible tasks while Erebus worked to defeat them.

What if the vampire had come from the Astra's camp, as advertised? A spy sent ahead of a new task involving Lore.

"If you pass out before you answer my remaining questions," he said when the male grew too weak to shout, "things will be worse when you awaken. That, I promise you."

Too late. The prisoner went quiet, sagging into unconsciousness.

Anger blended with impatience, singeing deep. Rathbone dropped his newest weapon on the tray, metal clattering against metal. If he couldn't get answers from the vampire, he might as well visit the harpy-oracle sooner rather than later.

He geared to flash to Harpina, intending to hunt her down. A prickle on his nape bolted him in place. Another intrusion was imminent. Who dared approach him this time?

A spirit wearing a long robe the color of pitch appeared beside the door, exactly where the fae had stood, his wrists also bound by chains. Disheveled white curls framed a pale face with thick black brows, ebony irises, and a large, hooked nose.

Well, well. Erebus Phantom himself.

Curious, Rathbone stood, wiped his hands on the apron, and pivoted to face his newest guest. His casual expression endured, revealing nothing of his emotions. Another specialty. He'd learned early: anything other than total confidence invited more problems.

"May I help you?" he asked with a deceptively pleasant tone.

"You may. But first, introductions should be made. I am Erebus the Deathless, son of Chaos the Abyss. And you are Rathbone the Only, son of Argus the All-Seeing."

"Thank you for the reminder I didn't need. I assure you, I haven't forgotten who I am or who helped conceive me." Most beings tended to identify him based on his accomplishments rather than his sire, a notorious being he'd never met. A true shapeshifter like Rathbone, able to shift into anything or anyone. Argus had been covered in mátia, too. A reason he was chosen to serve as a bodyguard for Hera, queen of the Greeks and Rathbone's mother.

From what he'd pieced together, Hera had slept with Argus, hoping to spawn an army of protectors just like him. She'd gotten pregnant, as intended, but thanks to her jealous husband things hadn't progressed as she'd probably envisioned. Her withered crone's heart hadn't helped matters, either.

"Very well. I'll skip the pleasantries and platitudes. I come bearing news." Erebus spread his arms as far as the shackles allowed, seemingly unconcerned by his captivity. "Soon, an Astra Planeta named Azar the Memory Keeper will be given thirty days to resurrect and murder your beloved Lore. The survival and ascension of all Astra depend on his triumph. As you can imagine, Azar will cross any line to succeed."

The Astra Planeta again. Motions clipped, Rathbone removed his apron, giving the mátia an unrestricted view of his guest.

"Let me guess. You are a kind, benevolent being here to aid my quest to ensure Lore's well-being."

"I'm honest enough to admit I'm neither kind nor benevolent," the god replied with a cunning grin. "But. I'm certain we can aid each other. I seek to destroy the Astra Planeta, after all, and you wish to obtain revenge against the one who killed your wife the first time...who just happens to be Azar. As you can see, our end goals are aligned."

Rathbone arched a brow. "If you expect me to believe you or assume I need your assistance, you prove only your stupidity." This wasn't the first accusation to come forth against the supposed assassin. Those who wished to manipulate him into trouncing their enemies used to reach out daily. The claims had stopped when he consistently exterminated everyone involved, including the messengers.

"Oh, no," Erebus said with a shake of his head. "I would assume nothing about you or anyone else. I *know* you need my assistance. I've glimpsed a myriad of futures and without me, your darling Lore meets her ultimate end one way or another. And I don't expect you to trust me—yet. That will come. Consider this a token of my good faith."

Cunning smile reemerging, Erebus tossed something small and white in Rathbone's direction. As it soared through the air, it slipped from the spirit realm into the natural, becoming solid. He caught it and jolted, his breath hitching. In his palm rested a metatarsal with a swirling *X* chiseled in its center. The smallest mark of the Song of Life. Not a fake, either. Every cell in his body vibrated with welcome, as if a part of him had come home at long last.

"During your war with the Astra, I can be of further use to you," Erebus said, confident. "How much further is up to you. For now, I'll leave you with a nugget about your future. Once the warlords are officially informed of your involvement, Azar will pay you a visit. You will give chase. One day, you'll notice your wife's face tattooed on his body. When you do, don't allow yourself to stare. You'll become trapped in the memory of her death, and Azar will end *you*."

"Or the memory proves your involvement." Always a possibility. "You fear me too much to take me on."

Erebus chuckled. "Fear you, puppy? No. Heed my warning or don't. Until we speak again, great king." The god bowed at the waist then vanished by choice rather than force.

Rathbone's mátia remained glued to the tiny bone resting in the palm of his hand. After all these centuries. For too long, his life had been a puzzle missing pieces: incomplete. Now...

One step closer.

Deep in the tattered remains of his heart, hope sparked anew. To bring Lore back...to finally taste vengeance for her death... He would do *anything*.

A sense of urgency bloomed. Rathbone closed his fingers around the precious bone and flashed to his secret room. A doorless chamber beneath his palace, with bejeweled walls, colorful tapestries, and ornate adornments collected across the ages. Two golden thrones perched upon a round dais. A his and hers. Lore's remains were preternaturally anchored to her seat, bathed in eternal torchlight.

The moisture in his mouth dried as he lowered to his knees and set the metatarsal in its proper place, completing her right foot. Oh, the satisfaction...

Trembling, he petted her femur. "Forgive me for the delay, sweetness." How he missed her gentle nature and even gentler touch. "Today marks a new day for us." If any of what Erebus had said was true, the Astra named Azar was soon to die screaming.

Craving answers, Rathbone flashed to Harpina. Not to find Neeka, but to seek out this Azar. To observe and study. Having visited the land upon occasion, he had only to picture the palace to materialize inside it. He shifted his appearance mid teleport, arriving as a tattered book in the royal library.

A crowd of harpies stalked the aisles. As intended, none noticed him. Few beings ever did when he took an inanimate form. He looked and listened, hunting his prey. Flashing deeper into the palace, he transformed into whatever fit the aesthetic. A forgotten dagger. An oval mirror on the wall. An at-home guillotine. Eventually, his search proved fruitful. He caught whispered conversations about a "sexy slice of man beef," which ultimately led him to the Memory Keeper's private bedroom. Antique furnishings had been pushed against the walls to make space for gym equipment.

On the mantel in the shape of a cat figurine, Rathbone studied the object of his interest. A big man. Black and bearded. Azar wore a short-sleeved T-shirt, hiding any tattoos that decorated his torso. Different faces marked his arms. Those images moved, jumping from one location to another. None belonged to the unrivaled Lore.

Incredible power radiated from the Astra, creating a force field of some sort. He bench pressed over six tons at a speed almost too swift to track. Under his breath, he rasped, "Forget. Forget. Forget."

Forget what? And how can I exploit the information?

Suddenly the Astra erupted from the bench, a tri-pronged dagger in each hand. He scanned the room, the tattoos on his arms freezing in place. Utter calm and icy determination overtook him.

Never, in all Rathbone's days, had he beheld sharper focus on another warrior. No doubt this soldier cataloged every detail around him, large and small.

Azar's gaze shot to the cat figurine and narrowed.

He senses me? Shock punched Rathbone. No one sensed him. Now, he simmered with indecision. Stay or go?

Better question: Had the Memory Keeper killed Lore or not? Would he come for her once her bones were reunited?

As the Astra stalked closer to Rathbone, vines of resolve pierced centuries of disappointment and frustration, growing thicker, harsher, bringing a new purpose to his existence. Suddenly, his objective became clear. Protect the bones he owned, whatever the cost, and locate the rest, finally gifting his kingdom with its queen. Then, in homage, lay Lore's killer at her feet.

He refused to team up with Erebus, regardless of the god's astonishing gift. The Deathless's treachery was too well-known. But the harpy-oracle, Neeka… She was a mystery. A possibility.

Was she an ally worth having? He would find out. Perhaps she despised the Astra for what they'd done to her people and her world. Maybe she'd seen the future and opted to side with the winner. Whatever the reason for contacting Rathbone…

He would dig into her life, hunt her down, and force a face-to-face.

2

Neeka the Unwanted, harpy-oracle extraordinaire, gold star entrepreneur, and all-around genius, thank you, glanced at the ex-husband who despised her. She couldn't blame him for his sentiment, considering she had murdered him on three separate occasions. Though she only accepted blame for the first death. Her version of a divorce. It wasn't her fault the Phoenix lord continually rose from the dead.

Presently, she occupied a small cage in Ahdán's travel tent. He perched in front of her, sharpening a blade. His (failed) attempt at intimidation.

"Why are you looking at me as if I betrayed you?" he asked. "Especially considering the violence you've employed to kill me."

Neeka listened to Ahdán with her eyes, reading his lips. At the age of five, enemies raided her camp, and a soldier stabbed her in both ears. Too young to repair the damage, she was rendered deaf for eternity. "Give me another dose of your toxin, and you'll die before the sun sets."

Earlier, he'd injected her with a horrible poison meant to change her species to his. It was the fourth dose he'd administered since they'd exchanged marriage vows several years ago, and each new inoculation had triggered a worse reaction than the last. Sweat still poured over her too-hot skin, soaking her bra and panties, her only garments, yet her teeth chattered from cold. Her bones ached, her muscles throbbed, and her nerve endings sizzled.

No matter an immortal's origins, they required ten doses of the toxin to facilitate a total transformation to Phoenix. If they survived the injections themselves. Most victims died at the halfway point. Even those like Neeka, with Phoenix in their ancestry.

"Where is your thanks?" he asked. "I'm helping you reach your full potential."

Ha! "You care nothing about my potential." Ahdán didn't even like her. He sought to create a mate too terrified to defy him. A good little sex robot, willing to be used and abused at his convenience. "You care about my ability to survive your flames, nothing more." An upside of the transformation, yes. That, and the ability to revive from death as he did. But. As soon as she could withstand his fire without burning to ash, he planned to bed her. With or without her approval.

Wait. Should she seek to withstand his flames? Had she foreseen her own death and now worked to protect herself?

Was that why she'd permitted her own capture? And she'd absolutely permitted it. She'd been tucked safe and secure inside a secret realm only a rare few could access. Which meant something enticed her to leave and place herself in her ex's crosshairs.

Neeka searched her (amazingly brilliant!) mind for answers but couldn't resurrect the tale of her imprisonment. Beyond this particular interlude, her thoughts were blankish, as if she'd dropped into the middle of a story without reading the back blurb. A common occurrence for her, and one of the many disadvantages of being the world's most magnificent seer.

At different points throughout any given day, her mind tired of jumping from present to future to past then back to present or future, and she short-circuited, her memory erased. Most times temporarily. Sometimes permanently.

She hadn't always been this way, able to see forward and backward, round and round. It started after Ahdán dispensed the first dose of toxin, inadvertently torching a barrier to the ability. The best she could do now was piece together any fragments of information available.

As Ahdán droned on, she sighed. No clues there. He merely spouted complaints about her less than stellar qualities. As if she had any!

Ignore the twinge of doubt.

She tuned him out by looking away and examined her surroundings. A traditional battlefield marquee with an open floor plan, vintage cloth walls, and an all-natural, dirt-packed floor. Very last century. Former tortures had left their mark, staining the material with splatters of crimson. The air carried notes of rust and iron. It was nice and all, but again, but very last season.

Hmm. Did the words written in marker on her forearm mean anything? *He-licks-her.* Other than the obvious.

Think! The last thing she remembered was snuggling in bed, alone, always alone, reading a how-to guide for making better jewelry. A new passion. If males refused to notice her greatness and bestow gifts, she would perform the honor herself.

Well, whatever the reason for allowing her capture, the reward must've outweighed the risk.

When the tiny wings between her shoulder blades vibrated, she returned her gaze to the Phoenix. Ugh. He was mid-tantrum, banging his weapon against the cage bars.

"Pay attention to me."

Neeka couldn't hear his voice, but dang if she didn't feel his whine with her entire being.

"Sure thing." She winced, as if sorry for him. "But first, you gotta become more interesting. Go ahead. I'm waiting."

He scowled, and she blew him a kiss. "Your harpy friend. Taliyah. She never should've taught you to speak. You're much prettier silent."

"You're hideous at all times." Though, granted, on the outside, Ahdán wowed with model-worthy features and a body bulging with brawn. Too bad he sucked.

She hadn't forgotten why she'd married the sadistic brute. Save Taliyah's sister from having to contend with his evil and empty his royal treasury. Assassinating him had been a wonderful bonus.

Ahdán pressed the tip of his blade into his index finger, drawing a bead of blood. "Your pain will be my pleasure, wife."

She yawned. "Do you get delivery out here? This girl could use a bite."

Most harpies adored anything fried or sweet. Not Neeka. She always jonesed for veggies. A constant source of humiliation throughout her childhood. Maybe because she'd been so sickly. Just one more aspect of her life that had made her different.

"Maybe a drink?" she added. "Your tears on the rocks, shaken not stirred."

Blue flames crackled over his pale locks. Aw, did his inability to intimidate her sting a bit?

"To start, I'll remove your eyes." He stood, putting his loin cloth on display. A *rising* loin cloth. "I'll ensure you can't grow new ones."

She smiled at him. "Know that I'll enjoy what comes next." Wait. She would? Why? What came next? Had Past Neeka set her up for success?

"Wife, you won't be enjoying anything ever again. I'll ensure that, too."

"I'm not your wife. Not any longer. Our connection ended with your first death."

The corners of his mouth curved in a cruel grin. "You will *always* be mine."

Biceps rippling, he opened the cage door and reached inside. Just before contact, he jerked. His spine contorted to an odd angle and his chin tilted upward, his mouth opening wide, making him look as if he were howling.

What the—ah. Okay. The tip of a spear extended past his teeth, rivers of crimson streaming over his bottom lip. He twitched once, twice, before going limp, expelling a final breath.

The male responsible for the Phoenix's latest death tossed the body aside, as if it weighed nothing, granting her visual access to his leer-worthy physique. *Hellooo, man candy!* He was a giant, almost double the other warrior's size in both height and brawn. And he was hot. Not handsome. Hot. Amazingly so. He had thick black hair, crimson skin, and exaggerated features. Aggression emanated from him. The kind that boldly proclaimed: *Bow or break.*

Meow. If she cared about dating, and she didn't, nope, not her, he might—might!—be her type. He wore black leathers and combat boots, but no shirt. Thank goodness! Look at the wealth of eye tattoos that littered his chest. Such a peculiar choice of ink—Neeka yelped. Those tattoos *blinked*. They even scanned the area as if they were truly able to see. Maybe they were. Some stared straight at her, making her wings quiver with delight.

When his (real) black diamond eyes fixed on her, she gulped. The intensity!

A cluster-ball of information rolled from a shadowy corner of her mind, handing out tidbits of information like Halloween treats. He was McBoney. Or rather, Rathbone the Only, King of Agonies. A shapeshifter and spy without equal. Closest friend of Hades, the King of the Dead. Known as a royal playboy who lacked morals and boundaries, with a fearsome temper.

He wasn't someone Neeka had ever interacted with and yet, she had a niggle...

Him. He was the reason she had allowed Ahdán to lock her up. She sensed it.

Say yes. Whatever Red proposes, say yes. But—

"Yes!" she blurted out. Then the thought completed. *Don't be too eager.* Oh. Right. *Not too eager. Got it.* "But also no," she added, batting her lashes at him.

Brow furrowed, he canted his head and deepened his study of her. "You are Neeka the Unwanted, from the Eagleshield clan, but part of the Skyhawk clan. Owner of Greater than Greatest at Finding Stuff, and the oracle who left me a crumb trail of clues to this location. Yes?"

Mmm. The way he mouthed every word sent shivers spilling over her spine. She almost forgot how much she hated her moniker. "Yep. That's me. I can do it, too. I can find anything, anywhere, at any time. Except sometimes. And other times, too."

He pursed his lips, the only soft thing about him, with a bottom plumper than the top. "I'm told you can return my wife to me."

"You're hitched? Bummer." Not for her, of course. She didn't care about dating, remember? "I know a ton of harpies who would've handed you the keys to their orgasm and let you take it for a spin."

He double blinked. Like, every set of eyes double blinked. Then those tattooed, living irises stared at her, hard, and she kind of wanted to preen or shrink into herself. She wasn't sure which.

Frowning, he spread his arms and announced, "I am Rathbone the Only, King of Agonies."

Nailed it! The Realm of Agonies was one of ten kingdoms in the Underworld and a place of incredible wealth. And, yes, okay, probably tons of agonies, too. "Be honest. Did you or did you not pierce your junk because you lost a bet with Hades? Rumors have flown for ages, and I've got my money on maybe."

He and his eyes gave another of those double blinks. "You sent a messenger to me, claiming to know where the rest of my wife is located. You said I can utilize your services for the right price."

What did he mean, the rest of his wife? "Hmm. That *does* sound like me." If only the memory would surface.

A muscle contracted in his jaw. "Is this your attempt to negotiate a higher fee?"

"Maybe? Gotta be honest. That sounds like me, too."

"Very well." He didn't mask the threat in his expression as he stated, "I'm happy to present you with a deal you cannot refuse."

Good thing she planned to say yes. Eventually. "I'm intrigued. Tell me more."

"I'd rather show you." He reached inside the cage and clasped her hand, surprisingly gentle as he aided her exit.

The scent of exotic spices and juniper berries instantly enveloped her. A rich, intoxicating aroma she savored. Oh, wow. It might come from him. Eager to confirm, she stepped closer, buried her nose in the hollow of his neck, and inhaled. Mmm. Definitely him.

Great! Now she kind of wanted to stick him on a shelf, shove a wick down his throat, and burn him candle-style.

She peered up at him. "You could be bottled and sold for millions."

He offered no comment. Just flashed her to a new location. From the Phoenix lord's dungeon to a throne room, where precious gems glittered on the walls in swirling, colorful patterns, white flames danced atop torches, and a gold-veined marble floor gleamed.

She gawked at the opulence. But, um, the chamber possessed no doors. Not a single escape hatch in sight.

Trepidation prickled her nape. A prison for someone like Neeka who couldn't teleport.

"Help a girl out and tell me what I'm supposed to see," she said, ready to vacate the place ASAP.

to me. Suddenly I'll know the answer to your every dilemma, and you'll be oh, so glad you waited. All the reviews I've written agree. My customer service is matchless."

"I'll give you three days."

"And yet I'll take as many as I need."

"Not good enough. I must put her back together quickly."

"That doesn't change my timetable."

"Then we are unable to reach a deal, and annihilation is back on the table."

"No problem—for me." She faked nonchalance. Because what else could she do? "Your failure to reanimate your wife costs me nothing." Or everything? That niggle… "Do you validate parking, or should I pilfer from your coffers on my way out?"

Tick, tick, tick. "What makes you worth such a risk?" he grated.

Got him. Confidence restored, she asked, "What *doesn't* make me worth the risk? In all the planets in all the galaxies, there's only one other being capable of unearthing anything anywhere, and it's my mother." Grenwich the Great, a harpy-Phoenix born with extraordinary tracking abilities. "She won't charge you as much as I do, but she'll judge you every minute of every day, and she won't be shy with her commentary. If that's your thing, go for it."

He appeared thoughtful.

Ugh. *Maybe I don't "got him."* Neeka almost stomped her foot. If he fired her and hired her mother…

He slashed a hand through the air. "We'll revisit the timing issue. Right now, I wish to hear of your dealings with the Astra Planeta."

Whoa, whoa, whoa. Rathbone was mixed up with the Astra? That was a problem. Taliyah, the harpy General as well as Neeka's best friend, had recently married the Astra's smokeshow of a Commander, forever linking their two species. Though Neeka was the world's best oracle—*suck it, Grenwich!*—she was a harpy first. Her loyalty belonged to T-bone and the Astra, not some ultrasexy Hellboy who might or might not sport a Prince Albert.

The Astra were gonna owe her so big if she had to walk away from a paycheck like Rathbone's. Except...

Neeka was supposed to say yes to the king. Her pre-knowledge insisted. She felt it with every fiber of her being. The longer she remained in Rathbone's presence, the clearer the sensation became.

Whatever proved necessary, she must, must, must help him find his wife's bones. The survival of the harpies depended on it.

Wait. It did?

Yes! The realization burrowed deep, and there was no arguing. For her, it was Rathbone or bust. But. The fact that the Underworld king had mentioned the warlords after displaying such urgency could mean only one thing...

She swallowed a groan. "The warlords search for your wife's bones, too." Most likely they sought the female for their next blessing task. The timing fit.

"I'm not sure—yet," he replied. "I'll learn the answer soon enough."

Neeka refused to lie and say she despised the males. Why complicate an already complicated situation with an outright falsehood? Rather, she offered the truth with misdirection. "You're going to pay me to screw over those who invaded my home world? Do I sign on the dotted line now or later?"

He looked disappointed in her. "Do you think I failed to do my research while hunting for you? Harpies and Astra are allies."

Careful. "Most are, yes. Some aren't." Also truth. But. He *was* supposed to be an amazing spy. He'd probably discovered the identity of her best friend, the Commander's wife. Better Neeka switch tracks. "In case you're wondering, I ain't no hater. I'm an ally full stop."

He did another of those double blinks. "Why sign on my dotted line then?"

Here goes another dose of honesty. "I can't shake the impression that you're the one I'm supposed to aid." She rubbed the spot between her breasts, where the knowledge burned. A familiar sensation. "If I override a knowing, bad things will happen." Maybe not at first but eventually.

The real conundrum: Being unable to explain her choice to the Astra or Taliyah. Whom she would *not* be betraying, by the way. Somehow, she'd find a way to help them, too, without alerting Rathbone. In fact, aiding Mr. Red was the only way to stay in the know and benefit her friends. But. Neeka didn't need mystical foresight to understand her friends would consider her new partnership a huge betrayal. And because she'd have to pretend to side with Rathbone to keep his suspicions under wraps, she'd probably be labeled a traitor. At least until the truth came to light.

Oh, how that would hurt. Just not enough to alter her course. Besides, emotions were fleeting and always subject to change.

"Your assurance does nothing to assuage my misgivings," Rathbone said without a shift in his expression. "If I agree to hire you, you won't leave my realm unless we are together, and you will have no contact with the Astra."

"I'm good with that." Especially the stay together part. Ahdán would revive in the coming days and recommence his quest. He existed for nothing else. "So." She spread her arms. "Do we have a deal or not?"

Rathbone stared at her, silent.

Neeka held her breath. Impatience warred with uncertainty as seconds ticked into minutes.

Petting Skeletoria's arm, he finally nodded. "We do."

Relief washed through her, and she grinned. "Congrats! You've got yourself a world-class partner. Let the adventure begin!"

3

Rathbone studied the oracle he'd hired, unsure what to make of her. A curious creature. Forgetful but intelligent. Vague but also blunt. Brave enough to admit a connection to the Astra, but cunning enough to try to hide the information at first. Maddening. Sexy. Not quite sane, as advertised. Nothing seemed to intimidate her.

Whistling under her breath, she skipped around the room, touching this, poking that. The scent of sugared cherries and sweet almonds trailed her, soon infecting his every breath with its delightfulness. He hated it!

What he hated more was sprouting wood schoolboy style anytime she neared. A spontaneous reaction he hadn't experienced in centuries. But then, the fae prince had mentioned Neeka's appeal. Something she had in spades. Flawless dark skin complemented bright amber eyes, curly black hair, and the most adorable indentation in the center of her chin. A red bra and matching panties flaunted a lush, hourglass figure.

Why had she written *he-licks-her* on her arm? To torment him? Because now, no matter how valiant his efforts, Rathbone couldn't stop imagining licking her.

Was she the answer to his dilemma? Would she find the rest of his goddess, succeeding where he had failed? If so, he might consider adding Neeka the Unwanted to his stable. Mistress number one hundred and one. At least until he ceased reacting to her. Or not. He preferred his females less vexatious.

"This is how you familiarize yourself with my vibe?" he asked as she traced her blunt-tipped fingernails over a row of cushioned chairs lining the back wall.

She didn't respond. Instead, she jumped on a chairback, rose to her tiptoes and waved her fingers over a spear of eternal torchlight. Somehow, she remained perfectly balanced.

Annoyance frayed already razed nerves, pouring petrol on the inferno of impatience burning in his gut. "Have you sensed anything yet?"

Again, there was no response. She didn't even bother to glance in his direction. Unacceptable! He would tolerate many things from this female, but allow her to ignore him? No.

Rathbone flashed over, kicked the legs of the chair out from under her, and caught her as she fell. With a shriek, she sank her nails into his shoulders, clinging to him as she darted her gaze in every direction, on the hunt for a threat.

He expected a slap as soon as her alarm wore off. A dagger to the throat perhaps. Harpies were recognized by their violent tempers and gift for dishing instant payback. But this warrioress merely gazed up at him, as if he'd ripped off the head of her favorite doll.

"You did that on purpose," she accused.

"Yes," he responded without guilt. He'd paid a high price for his crown, and he demanded to be treated with the respect his position deserved. "When I ask you a question, you will give an immediate response." He didn't bother with an "or else." She would do what he demanded, and that was that.

How could the King of Agonies allow anything less?

She smiled sweetly, baring tiny harpy fangs. "Just so you know, the first startle is free. The second will cost you dearly."

Enjoying the feel of her far too much, he dumped her on her feet and stepped back. "You expect another ambush then? Have you no plans to protect yourself?" Was she without self-defense training?

"If you desire answers from me," she said, pushing the words through clenched teeth, "make sure I see your lips." She tapped her ears. "These don't work."

She was deaf? He closed his eyes for a moment, battling shame and yes, guilt. She must've experienced a catastrophic injury before the ability to heal lightning-fast immortalized her.

Forging ahead, he explained, "Things will go smoother if you keep your attention on me." Considering how well he was paying her, she owed him that and more.

"Cater to your every selfish whim. Got it." She faked a grin and batted her lashes. "But you should get real fascinating real fast, or my mind will wander, and it won't be my fault." Aaand yes, she skipped off to study a tapestry depicting his final battle against Styx. "Is this you? I bet it's you. Be honest. You executed its creator for depicting you as a red marshmallow man, didn't you? Oh! Did we just discover your superhero name? The Marshmallow Man. Cherry Marshmallow?"

This must be retribution for the chair. Because he in no way resembled a marshmallow.

Stiffer than a board, Rathbone flashed in front of her to guarantee she read his lips. "I'll grant you a fourth payment—an unspecified boon—if you find at least one of Lore's bones *today*. Proof to me you possess the skills you bragged about."

"Well. Consider me properly motivated," she replied with a genuine grin, far superior to the fake. She hooked her arm through his, acting as if she hung on his every word. "Take me to dinner and tell me more about you and your lady love. I learn better when I'm fed."

How was he supposed to deal with a being like her? Cave in? He had to cave in, didn't he? "Are you a typical harpy, only able to eat what you steal or earn, or you sicken?" She struck him as more of a flighty seer than a bloodthirsty murderess.

"I am. So be a dear and explain how I'll be earning each of my six daily meals and assortment of snacks."

"By breathing." For now, she was the most important person in his life.

"That I can do."

He flashed her to his private dining room. A massive space consumed by a long table piled high with both sweet and savory dishes. The spread remained available twenty-four seven, the dishes exchanged every hour and always the right temperature. A mystical amenity already in place when he'd overtaken the kingdom.

"In contrast," he added once he'd gained her attention, "if you fail to procure my property, I'll unleash my wrath upon your loved ones. My bucket is hungry for entrails."

"I thought we'd already agreed to that." Neeka dismissed him to "ooh" and "aah" over the dishes as she loaded a plate. Munching on steamed broccoli, she claimed the spot at the head of the table. "My compliments to the chef."

With a sigh, Rathbone picked her up, set her in the adjacent seat, and plopped into the vacated chair.

She continued eating, unbothered. "I can't help but notice we're alone here. Where are your servants and subjects?"

"Their loyalty belonged to the previous sovereign, so I killed them."

"And you couldn't find anyone willing to work for you after that? Weird."

"My wife will select our servants." Also, he'd been busy assisting Hades the past few centuries. The other king had warred with Lucifer, a hell prince currently impaled and in lock up, guarded by winged warriors known as Sent Ones.

"As far as excuses go, it's threadbare at best. You were too lazy, admit it." She devoured a spear of asparagus. "So? Delight me with the story of your romance with Skeletoria. Help me understand the fairy-tale romantasy I'm soon to rekindle."

A harsh rebuke reached the edge of his tongue. For the sake of the partnership, Rathbone swallowed it. "Her name is Lore. Lorelei the Incomparable. She's a goddess of desire." He tapped a claw tip against his empty plate. *Clink, clink, clink.* "I will permit many leniencies with you, oracle, but not this. Not disrespect to my wife. Consider this a solo warning. Next time I act."

"Ten-four," Neeka replied with a jaunty salute. "Only say nice things about the nasty bag of bones. Don't worry. I've got it plugged into ole faithful now."

He swiped his tongue over an incisor. "Lore is my everything. My fated." No use trying to pretend otherwise. Let this female comprehend the depths of his feelings. His willingness to cross any line, no matter how objectionable, to accomplish his goal. "I won't compromise her well-being."

The oracle shrugged, unimpressed. "As long as your check is good, so are my services. Now, then. Tell me the important stuff. Explain your meet cute."

What an odd, exasperating creature. "We met the same as anyone else, I suppose. I visited the Realm of Agonies to decide whether to contend for it or not." Back then, he'd been a fresh-faced soldier full of determination and dreams. "She belonged to the former king. I took her from him, then claimed his lands as my own." From the beginning, Rathbone had striven to prove himself worthy of the gentle beauty. To be the male honored to pamper her as she deserved. She had rewarded him well for it.

Having spent his childhood hidden on a distant planet, raised by servants, he'd longed for family of his own. His mother had deigned to visit him upon occasion, but only to compare him unfavorably to the father who hadn't wanted him. With Lore, Rathbone had gotten his wish, and it had been far superior to anything he'd imagined.

"And then?" Neeka encouraged.

"And then someone killed her." Someone he had yet to identify. Unless Erebus had told the truth. When Lore awoke, she would explain what happened, and Rathbone would proceed accordingly. "After I revive her, we'll rule this kingdom together."

"You're right." Neeka popped a bite of squash into her mouth. "Your story is the same as everyone else's. There's no pizzazz. Nothing to regale your future brats with—yet. Thankfully, I'm on the case. And because I'm such a giver, I'm gonna gift you with a freebie and spice things up. By the time I'm done, you'll have the grandest tale to ever grand!"

A ridiculous claim undeserving of a response. "What do you know of love stories? Do you have a companion?"

"Nope. Well, yes and nope." She hiked her shoulders. "A few years ago, I married the Phoenix you just poled. I filed for divorce by killing him, but he re-alived, as he always re-alives, and injected me with the turning toxin."

Rathbone frowned. Harpies didn't do divorce. Not with their consorts. "Why did you wed him if he isn't your fated?" What was *her* meet cute?

"Well, my father is an oracle and he told me I'd find my consort in the flames. Since I owed a friend a favor, I decided to pay up and be a hero at the same time, taking her sister's place at the wedding. I hoped Ahdán was my Inferno Man. He wasn't."

Rathbone detected a note of sadness. Like any good king of the Underworld, he pounced on a perceived weakness. "Help me bring my wife to life, and I will slay the Phoenix again and again until he stays dead. Consider it another bonus." His suspicious nature forced him to add, "But if ever you betray me..." Several of his mátia opened, glaring at her. So far, she hadn't shown a hint of fear concerning his promises. But she would. "Lest you think I'm someone willing to forgive the slightest duplicity—" He whipped out his arm and caught her by the wrist.

Flash. They materialized in the foyer of his dungeon. Voted *the* destination to avoid when visiting the Underworld for three centuries running. The scent of blood and terror lingered on the walls. Which made sense. Every partition was built from the remains of previous guests.

"Understand me," he announced. Around them, immortal beings of varying species were chained to different torture devices, begging for help. Moans of anguish and desperation provided the chorus. "This is what happens to those who work against me. And do you know who works against me, oracle? Anyone who isn't working with me."

Neeka traversed a wide hallway minus her host, exploring the luxurious but abandoned palace. She must have gotten trapped in her own little world after their side trip to the dungeon. Now, she had no idea where she was or when and how she'd lost the guy.

Such a curious fellow. He had all kinds of extra flavor. Her favorite kind of immortal. They kept things interesting. Add in Rathbone's überprotective streak and unwavering determination to guard what belonged to him, and he skirted the edge of perfect.

She came upon a spacious sitting room with velvet settees, porcelain side tables, and portraits of the Crimson King contorted in the most ridiculous poses while wearing next to nothing. A smile bloomed as she examined each masterpiece.

Pretty sure she recognized the artistic style, she checked out the artist's signature. Madame Anya. Yep. Sure enough. Neeka snickered. Anya, goddess of anarchy, was a party buddy. Anya loved to gift her "artwork" to anyone who miffed her. That Rathbone displayed the collection, rather than burn it, spoke of a delightful sense of humor Neeka appreciated. An unexpected trait from a hardened warrior who enjoyed dishing threats.

What would he say if she demanded *his* kingdom as payment? Because dang. The gem-covered walls in his secret throne room extended here, and they were totally to die for. So sparkly!

He might actually agree, considering he was head over heels, fallen into the abyss obsessed with a skeleton he planned to resurrect.

Strangely enough, Neeka was maybe kinda sorta envious of the corpse. Oh, to be loved in such a way. Thanks to Grenwich's chosen moniker, Neeka herself was forever cursed to be, well, unwanted. Her lack of male companionship had nothing to do with her personality, she was certain of it. She slapped!

Though she'd lived for centuries, her first official "date" was her wedding. No one else had ever asked her out or accepted an invite when she'd done the asking. In fact, the only romantic encounters she'd experienced were the nights she'd thrown herself at a guy, practically begging for affection. Many had taken her up on the offer. Too many. Before each instance, she'd hoped against hope that her fate had changed. That she had scored an adoring significant other. But the guys had bailed immediately after nailing her, energizing her secret insecurities and activating pure devastation. Nowadays, she admired gorgeous males from afar and pretended she appreciated being single. Sometimes she even believed it.

And okay, yes, her lonesome, loathsome past might possibly be the real reason she'd jumped at the opportunity to marry Ahdán. More so than her father's prediction. Neeka couldn't not seize the chance to belong. To be part of a couple. United until death. She sighed dreamily. Then she glowered. As soon as she'd had her first conversation with the Phoenix, she'd realized he intended to chain her to his bed, whether she agreed or not. Without hesitation, she'd proceeded with the original plan: take the place of his long-promised bride, steal his money, and remove his head. Exactly what he'd deserved.

But enough about Ahdán the Ash Bringer. Better to focus on the King of Agonies and a job well done. Winning that open-ended boon and impressing Rathbone with her skill by finding the biggest and best bone right off the bat was a must. Just boom, *Look at me, I'm amazing. Now pay up.*

Piece of cake! Mmm. Cake. Carrot. Without frosting. Or any other ingredients. She moistened her lips.

No, no. Concentrate. Despite Rathbone's possible beef with the Astra, Neeka's instincts sang. Aiding Red Ranger was right. Necessary for harpykind. And really, she maybe kinda liked him so far. Steadfast loyalty was another rare, ultrasexy quality she greatly appreciated.

So. Time to earn more for a single job than Grenwich ever had. A bonus in itself! Neeka rubbed her hands together, mind whirling. If she were the skull of an ancient goddess of desire, where would she hide?

A tap on the shoulder startled her. Heart thudding, she spun. A stony-faced Rathbone towered mere inches away. He held a gorgeous diamond necklace with stones almost as big as her fist.

"This is for you," he said, waving the jewelry in front of her face.

Neeka snatched and donned the jewelry before he had a chance to change his mind. Before she registered how sensual his strong red fingers with their sharp black claws looked clutching the delicate gems. Before she got smart and thought things through.

As she traced her fingertips over the cool stones dangling from her neck, her thoughts caught up with her actions. Big mistake, accepting his bribe. He'd tested her, nothing more. Just as she sought to learn him, he sought to learn her. Now he knew the truth. Like most harpies, she wasn't immune to the pretty pretties.

Might as well take this all the way home and reveal her raging possessiveness, too. "This is mine. If you attempt to steal it, you'll lose a hand, at least eight eyes, and every piercing you may or may not possess." What belonged to her belonged to her. Always. No exceptions.

"They are mátia. The eyes," he replied easily.

Feeling a bit revengeful, she winced and added, "Great. But, um, do me a favor and remind me of two supersmall, minor details. Who are you, and what am I doing here?"

His mouth floundered open and closed.

She imagined choking sounds were leaving him and elbowed his abdomen. "Just teasing, Red Riding Wood. Or maybe Red Riding Woody. Professor Seesalot? We can always revisit Cherry Marshmallow."

"I prefer results," he grated.

"That's a terrible nickname. But fine. Let's see if I'm comfortable enough to tune my antenna into your future." She focused inward and—*boom!* A vision formed in a burst of color, and she gasped. "Lore's skull waits at the bottom of an ocean!"

In her head, Neeka saw it so clearly. Lavender sand peppered with colorful coral. A school of polka-dot fish with horns. Two mermaids swam nearby, scrutinizing the symbols etched into the cranium.

Rathbone clutched Neeka's shoulders and gave a rough shake. "Which ocean? In which world? What era, oracle? Tell me!"

"I don't know, okay?" she grumbled. "Dang. Take it easy, gorilla grip. It's not as though there's a sign that reads Atlantis, six miles east of the queen's stable."

"Atlantis?"

One second she occupied a sitting room with lavish furnishings, the next she stood outside, warmed by a beam of bright golden sunlight. Before her, clear purple water lapped at moss-covered rocks. Behind her, lush trees stretched for miles, split by a pink waterfall spilling over an azure crystal cliff.

He'd brought her to the entrance of the fabled land.

"I didn't mean we should visit—oh, never mind." For all she knew, she *had* meant they should visit. What if her subconscious led them here on purpose? Besides, they were here. Might as well check things out.

One *You Impressed Him* award coming up!

"If you are wrong...do not be wrong." Tension radiated from his taut frame. "Do hold your breath."

What! "Don't you dare take me—" Frigid water engulfed her. Thankfully, Neeka complied with his instruction and didn't inhale any liquid. Still. A quick burst of panicked flailing ended when Rathbone jerked her close.

Mmm. His muscles felt good doused in water.

As they scanned the area, strands of his semi longish hair twined with hers. A lovely, mesmerizing sight she enjoyed far too much. But oh, how she adored seeing something of hers connected to someone else.

She forced herself to look away. Her gaze snagged on iridescent mermaid tails. Bingo! She tapped Rathbone and pointed.

The king flashed her again. They reappeared between the mermaids. He elbowed both females aside without hesitation, reached out with his free hand, and snatched the skull.

Awe lit his features. Triumph pulsed from him. He flashed a third time, whisking Neeka to the doorless throne room. They dripped icy water all over the marble floor.

"You owe me a boon," she said after sucking in a mouthful of air.

"It's yours with my compliments." He released her, bounded up the dais steps and approached the smaller throne, where he dropped to his knees. Determination converted into supreme satisfaction as he slowly, reverently, anchored the skull in its proper place.

Just like that, Neeka toppled straight into a new vision. Images blasted her mind, each a tornado of revelation. She viewed the harpy throne room, with Lore's golden seat affixed in the center, ripped from its former residence. Saw the gloriously handsome Astra named Azar kneel before the skeleton as Rathbone had done and adhere the final piece into place. Watched as muscle and skin developed, a gorgeous brunette with baby blues and pale skin appearing. She was naked.

The goddess smiled slowly and stretched, and oh, wow. No wonder Rathbone was obsessed. The chick oozed raw sex appeal.

The remaining Astra and their harpy consorts observed the proceedings with trepidation, while Erebus bubbled over with glee.

Rathbone stood among the group—in chains. There was no sign of Neeka. Why?

The freshly formed beauty smiled at her audience. "Hello, Rathbone. Chains suit you." Her smile grew as she addressed the others. "Azar is my puppet, and soon, the rest of you will be food." She soaked up their reactions. Everything from rage to uncertainty. "Let's give them a preview of the feats to come, Azar. Bow before me."

The masses quieted, awaiting the warlord's reaction. Expecting him to erupt.

But Azar sank to his knees. "Do not do this," he whispered to the goddess. "Please, do not." Dark irises beseeched her.

For the briefest blip, Lore seemed to soften. Then she snapped, "No one asked for your commentary."

Rathbone fought his confinement, shouting, "I love you! There's got to be another way. Please."

"Shut up," Lore muttered, rubbing her temples. "Just shut up. I can't concentrate, and I need to concentrate." Glaring at Azar, she demanded, "Cut out his tongue."

The Astra rose, crossed the distance, and obeyed, then returned to toss the tongue at her feet.

Ouch.

"That's better," the goddess breathed out. "Only a few minutes remain until your defeat is assured. We'll wait out the clock before I continue with the festivities." And yet, less than sixty seconds later, she crooked her finger at the Astra. "Azar."

He stiffened. "You want your kiss now."

"Why not? I'm bored."

"It didn't have to be this way." He lunged, cupping her nape with bloody hands and melding his lips to hers. She froze, as if stunned. Then she kissed him back. The two feasted on each other as if they'd waited lifetimes for the chance, and they'd never get another.

Ultimately, he recoiled. But he didn't move away. He studied his hands. His glittering palms. The same shimmer covered her cheeks.

Neeka gasped with shock. Stardust! Something an Astra produced for his fated mate, and only his fated mate. But Lore belonged to Rathbone.

Didn't she?

The goddess scowled at the Astra before kicking him in the chest. "Don't do that again."

"You are... mine," he croaked.

"Why are you hesitating, Azar?" the Astra Commander shouted. "Kill her!"

Azar paid his leader no heed. Fisting and unfisting his hands, he kept a hungry gaze on the goddess. "You are mine," he repeated with authority. And warning.

"I am my own," she said, rising and sauntering past him. "You know what? There's less than a minute left. I think I'll go ahead and jump to the finale."

The Astra watched their comrade do nothing to the goddess, now utterly shellshocked. A panting Rathbone watched her, obviously gutted.

"I've waited so long for this." Lore stopped several feet from the crowd and smiled again, unabashed by her nudity. "But I don't think you're going to enjoy what happens next."

They shouted protests. She spread her arms, tilted her head toward the ceiling, and released a blood-curdling scream.

Shadows exploded from her being. Hundreds of them. They flew across the room, taking shape. Small, disproportionate monsters with spindly arms and legs, scales, and razor-sharp teeth. A glowing gold circle ringed their pupils. They solidified midair and surrounded the audience. Then, they feasted, devouring warriors and harpies alike. Everyone but Erebus.

The Deathless laughed, clapping as Astra and harpies died in agony. And the shadows weren't even done. They flew out of the throne room, ravenous for their next meal.

The vision cut off, and Neeka recoiled with horror.

As reality replaced the future, she shuddered. No wonder she'd sensed the end of harpykind.

Pressing a hand to her churning belly, she struggled to catch her breath and meet her companion's gaze. To tell him what she'd seen or not? Surely he would realize the importance of preventing such a catastrophic outcome.

He towered in front of her, glaring with the intensity of a thousand suns. "What did you see? Tell me."

Instinct shouted, *Admit nothing!* The man who'd spent many a millennium searching for his dismembered wife wouldn't trust a warning issued by an oracle linked to his enemy. But he would be incensed enough to fire her, perhaps literally, preventing said oracle from sabotaging his efforts so she could change the future. And she must change the future.

Not an impossible task. Alter this and that, and you also altered your fate. But what this? What that?

Neeka raised her chin. At least she knew her endgame: Stop the regeneration of the goddess. To do that, she had two choices. Prevent the acquisition of the four remaining bones, leading Rathbone *and* the Astra on a wild goose chase. Or disappear the skeleton altogether. Whichever proved easiest.

If ever the king discovered her true motives…

No. He wouldn't. She was smart enough to stay fifty—twenty-five...ten...at least one or two—steps ahead of him at all times. No big deal.

A humorless laugh escaped.

"Oracle," Rathbone grated, gripping her shoulders. "What. Did. You. See?"

Thinking fast, she muttered, "The coming friction with the Astra Planeta. So many died. Or die." Oh, how they were going to hate her. Far more than she'd realized. But now she knew why she'd needed to say yes to Rathbone, what danger threatened her beloved people, and what she must do to save the day.

"If you're afraid...don't be afraid," he commanded. "I won't allow the warlords to harm you."

He assumed she feared? Neeka wrenched from his clasp. "How dare you, you...you...swine!" Why, the nerve of this male! "I have out-partied a wolf, survived a round of hot box with a dragon, and won a staring contest against Medusa. I fear nothing! Visions tire me out, that's all. I require rest. *R.E.S.T.*" Not that she would indulge. Harpies didn't sleep near anyone but a consort. Their fated mate. The only male in existence able to calm their rages. Among other things.

"Very well. You may rest for one night." He craned his neck to stare at Skeletoria, his expression glazing with adoration once again. "By the way, you did an adequate job today."

"I know." Wait. Had she read his lips wrong because she watched him in profile, or had he used the description 'adequate'? Oh, the very suggestion burned. "I did an amazing job. Five-star. Ten even!"

He hiked his shoulders without looking away from his obsession. "Go. Select a room. We'll start again in the morning."

She narrowed her lids. "Yes. We will." Just not the way he supposed.

Tonight, she considered her options. Tomorrow the sabotage began.

4

As the sun rose on the Realm of Agonies, Rathbone shut the book he'd been reading. The only bit of history he'd found on the Astra. He turned off the mortal soap opera he'd left playing in the background, stored his secret stash of chocolate chip cookies in a nightstand drawer, and stalked to his dresser to pour himself a glass of ambrosia to hopefully subdue the wild energy crackling inside him.

He changed his mind while standing there, as he always changed his mind whenever he wished to imbibe. Drink from the "victory decanter" before Lore's resurrection? No. Not until they could toast their future.

Soon...

Anticipation pricked him. Only four bones to go. Three if the oracle had another vision today.

The oracle. In an instant, other thoughts of Neeka intruded. Unwanted thoughts, and the very reason for his inability to settle.

Was this how she'd gotten her moniker? By stealing into a man's imagination and compelling him to picture her *doing things*. Like talking nonsense while sinking to her knees and slowly opening his fly?

His anticipation sharpened. Rathbone rubbed a tight spot in the center of his chest. Like a fool, he craved another dose of the oracle and her illogical conversations. There was something a little off about her, and it was a lot addicting.

What had she done overnight? Because she certainly hadn't stayed in a bedroom and rested. He'd sensed her presence in every chamber of the palace and even outside in the garden maze. The urge to spy had been strong. Too strong. But anytime he'd caved and flashed to her location, she'd already moved on.

He stomped to his bathroom, disrobed, and entered the shower stall. As hot water rained over him, he decided he'd gone too long without visiting his stable. A travesty he would rectify today. Yes. Good plan. Once he'd burned off this excess energy, he could focus on what mattered. Lore's resurrection. Fortifying the mystical defenses surrounding his kingdom. Returning to Harpina to observe the Astra Planeta. If Erebus's prediction proves correct, Azar the Memory Keeper would visit the Realm of Agonies any day.

Neeka might be willing to offer insight about him and the others. Perhaps Rathbone should speak with her before he visited the stable.

His blood heated, and he scowled. With more force than necessary, he grabbed a towel from its hook, ripping the material, and flashed to his dresser. He opened the top drawer, where stacks of leathers were folded, then dried off as he contemplated which pair to wear. Brown-black, jet black, or pitch black? Appearance mattered when you faced a foe. Had nothing to do with looking his best for his new employee.

"After some top-notch oracling last night, I've decided to accept the position as your royal matchmaker," Neeka announced, barging into his bedroom. She held a notepad and pen, scribbling thoughts. "We can discuss the increase in my pay later."

Rathbone stiffened. He had yet to don a stitch of clothing, and she'd dared—dared!—to invade his private space without permission? A rebuke barreled to the tip of his tongue, only to die a swift death.

Desire stole his breath. She might be chaos walking, but she was also the loveliest creature he'd beheld in centuries.

Curly dark hair spilled from a messy bun. Long lashes cast shadows over high cheekbones. A straight nose led to lush red lips.

Not by any stretch of the imagination could this female be referred to as a quote, unquote surrogate mother. If anything, Neeka was the babysitter who planned to throw a party as soon as Mom took off. And Rathbone dug it.

She stunned in a blue tank top with the words *Trust Me, I'm a Professional* haphazardly embroidered in the center, as if she'd done the needlework herself. While blindfolded. Tiny yellow shorts displayed her lithe long legs to perfection. Multiple pieces of jewelry adorned her throat and wrists. Necklaces and bracelets she must've found in trunks throughout the palace. Not a surprise. Harpies loved thieving trinkets. They were also, supposedly, quite fastidious, yet this one was streaked with dirt from head to toe.

"Why are you so dirty?" he asked.

Never glancing up from the notepad, she said, "There's no need to sing my praises. I know my brilliance is boundless. Also, I'm not using my boon for this. You're going to accept because it's the right thing to do."

What? That made no—ah. Obviously, she hadn't heard him and jabbered on, expecting him to listen. He required her attention if they were to have a two-sided conversation. But even as she traipsed deeper into his room, she remained utterly absorbed by that notepad. Did she plan to ignore him the whole time? While he was naked? He snorted. *Good luck with that.* He was a large male. Huge. And growing. Impossible to miss.

"Well?" she demanded, finally pausing to glance at him. "Are you going to sing my praises or not?"

He stood in place, allowing her to drink her fill. Except, she didn't drink her fill. She didn't even sip. Her attention remained fixed on his lips as she awaited his reply.

Irritation budded. "You said there's no need for praise."

"And there isn't," she replied, a schoolteacher admonishing a naughty student. "But you should still do it when it's warranted. That's only polite."

Did she seriously not notice his massive erection? Not care enough to discover whether he was pierced? "You're right," he grated. "It's only polite to praise something when warranted." Like the metal-laden battering ram between his legs!

Mumbling about errant employees, he yanked on a pair of black leathers, struggled with the straining zipper, and stomped his feet into his best combat boots. The mátia on his chest watched the oracle without blinking. Not. A. Single. Reaction. From. Her.

Irritation sharpening, he flashed to his closet, tugged a T-shirt from a hanger, and returned to his spot near the dresser.

"Why are you so dirty?" he repeated as he jerked the material over his shirt.

"I was hoping you'd tell me."

Did she truly not recall or was she faking to hide her activities? He might desire her, but his trust in her remained shaky at best.

She moved her gaze over his room, her mouth forming a small O. Awe radiated from her. "Oh, Rathboner. Your chamber is incredible."

Pleasure puffed his chest. Until he clocked what she'd done to his name. He scowled. Then he shrugged. As far as nicknames went, it wasn't bad.

"After seeing the rest of the house, I expected plain ole ordinary luxury, not pure class and sophistication," she said.

While he'd left the rest of the palace mostly untouched, saving the bulk of rooms for Lore, he'd designed this spacious suite with his wife in mind. Each piece of furniture was molded from solid gold. On the walls, gemstones created a dizzying mosaic, mimicking the secret throne room. Sheer, wispy curtains welcomed a cool, salty breeze from an open balcony, inviting the sounds of a rushing river.

"Your room is only missing a Rath Boned original by Anya," Neeka added. "You should stage your favorite over the mantel."

Noticed his gallery, had she? "I hung them to remind myself to kill Anya as soon as my schedule clears."

Neeka snorted. "Lie! You love them."

Fine. She wasn't wrong. He'd felt indignant at first, but whenever he'd looked deeper, he'd encountered amusement. Maybe even satisfaction. He was a wee bit vain—a trait he took great pride in—but beautiful artwork was beautiful artwork. Ultimately, he'd decided to save the collection for Lore's enjoyment, too.

"Do *you* have a favorite?" he asked.

"Oh, yes. The one of you riding a circus bear with curling pink ribbons streaming from your hair. As well as all the others. Plus the one Anya hasn't painted yet. Oh, Rathbone. Wait till you see it!"

The way she seemed to melt over the idea...

He growled.

"Hold up. Stop everything." Neeka rubbed her temple. "My instinct is flaring."

Was she having a vision? He went still.

A cunning gleam glistened in her gorgeous amber eyes. "I'm supposed to move in here, and you're supposed to move out. Yep. That's what my instinct is demanding, I'm sure of it." She winced at him. "Sorry, Majesty, but you'll have to bunk somewhere else for a while."

Hardly. "Stay in here if you wish, but I won't be budging."

"Excellent idea. We'll stick together like glue and talk more about my unparalleled matchmaking. Are you game to hear about your brand-new love interest?"

His irritation returned with thorns. "I have a queen." And multiple side pieces. "I have no need for another." Except, maybe, one. He was still debating the wisdom of the idea.

"Wrong." Neeka jumped on his bed, uncaring about the filth she deposited on his sheets. "You lost your queen. Until you revive her, you're single and ready to tingle."

He pressed his tongue to the roof of his mouth.

"Why do you think she's yours, anyway?" the oracle asked, curious.

His hackles flared. "Because she is," he snapped. How he detested this topic. A sore spot for centuries. "I know because I know, and that's good enough." Unlike the Astra Planeta, who called their fated ones 'gravitas,' he didn't produce stardust. A phenomenon he envied. He didn't inject a claiming venom with his bite, like vampires, either, or imprint in the manner of shifters.

"News flash. Truth is truth, regardless of your opinion."

He worked his jaw, unable to refute her words.

"I'll be brutally honestish with you, Red Herring. I've got to connect with your love story to score another vision. To get the ball rolling, let me see you in action with someone else. Nope, don't say no. Check it. I'm setting you up with a nice living lady. A nymph who's a real showstopper with a never-ending party in her pants and a ninety-seven percent chance of restarting your dead libido."

Dead libi—"Get naked, and I'll show you how alive my libido is," he roared. "I keep the concubines in my stable well satisfied."

Her brows furrowed. "What, are you a big, bad slab of man

meat who's gotta be dipped in special sauce on the regular or you shrivel up?"

Rather than stomp over and yank her into his arms, he flashed to the chamber used to store garments for every occasion, collected a long-sleeve shirt and a pair of sweatpants, then returned to the oracle.

"Shower and wear these," he said as soon as her gaze landed on him. "Consider them your official uniform."

When she continued to stare at him with expectation, disregarding his commands, he dropped the clothes at the foot of the bed, clasped her hips, and lifted her from the mattress. The second the softness of her skin registered, an image played inside his head. Neeka, naked. Rathbone, kissing his way up her spread legs.

A harsher growl brewed in his chest.

As he set her on her feet, she dropped the notepad and pen, and cupped his shoulders for balance. "Neeka," he snapped. "Speak."

"I think I misread your lips." Glittering amber eyes framed by spiky black lashes watched him with earnest entreaty. "I'm certain you didn't tell me you maintain a stable full of concubines."

"Would you prefer I call them lovers?" he asked, and yes, there might've been a tinge of defensiveness in his tone. He released her and stepped back. "Or paramours, perhaps?"

Disappointment spread over her expression. "Wow. Just when you think you know a guy, boom, you discover he's a low-down cheater."

He popped his jaw. "Mere minutes ago, you tried to set me up with a nymph," he reminded her with gritted teeth.

"Yes, but that was before I knew you lacked any sense of loyalty."

A muscle jumped in his jaw. It was going to be a common occurrence in her presence, he was certain of it. "I'm not cheating. Lore helped me pick half the stable's members."

Neeka pretended to have a heart attack. "You opened the stable of unfaithfulness while she lived? Oh, your poor concubines. Do they know they're placeholder bangs?" She fluffed her hair. "*My* male will want me and only me, and that's a fact. Not that I'm ever gonna couple up. Nope. Not me. Not ever. I've got better things to do."

Why so determined to remain alone? And why *did* he desire other women despite being wed to a fated wife? Why had Lore encouraged it rather than keeping him all to herself, as Neeka intended to do with her consort?

Rathbone ground his teeth. The last two questions had the same obvious answer. Because they were gods, their thoughts on a higher level than those of a common immortal. So why did his nerves remain pricked?

"While you did your top-notch oracling," he grated, "did you happen to locate another bone?"

"No, but I'm on the cusp, probably. I just need to connect with your love story, as previously mentioned." Twisting a fallen lock of hair around her finger, she batted that thick fan of lashes at him. "About your stable—"

"No more talk of the stable. I want results."

"Sure, sure," she muttered, sliding her gaze from him, effectively ending the conversation. "Oh! How wonderful."

She skipped across the room to trace an anatomically correct heart hidden within the wall mosaic he'd designed and mounted himself. Another of his romantic gestures.

Watching her elegant fingers graze the image drew another growl from him. *What is she doing to me?*

Neeka turned to waggle her brows in his direction. "My kingdom must have this pattern in every room, or I'll revolt."

She liked his work that much? Something warm and soft unfurled in his chest. He opened his mouth to respond, only to remain quiet when he sensed the impending arrival of an ally.

Since he acknowledged a single ally, he pivoted toward the door, awaiting Hades's entrance.

The other king materialized in the open frame, wearing a perfectly tailored three-piece suit.

"Hello, Uncle," he said. Though he'd never tried to hide their familial connection, few beings recognized it. Fewer still knew Hera, Hades's sister, had birthed Rathbone. She'd never cared enough to claim him publicly.

His lungs squeezed.

"Don't 'hello uncle' me. You have five seconds to—" Hades noticed Neeka and went quiet. When his dark gaze returned to Rathbone, he arched a brow in question.

The sovereign's appearance hadn't changed a bit over the centuries. But then, neither had Rathbone's. In disposition, however, they'd both transformed. While Hades had mellowed, his temper becoming harder to prick, Rathbone had graduated from an eager youth desperate to prove himself worthy of his royal status to a warrior assured of his power.

"I hired her," he explained.

"And she agreed to be hired?" Hades asked with a chiding tone. "Willingly?"

"She did," Neeka responded, whirling away to dig through Rathbone's sock drawer. "Even though she's being discussed as if she isn't in the room, an activity sure to set her nerves—and therefore your lives—on edge."

Rathbone tracked her with his gaze, ensnared by the gracefulness of her movements as she aimed for his desk to rifle through a stack of papers. By the mystery she presented. The challenge.

"Have you forgotten I'm here, *Nephew*?"

He blinked with surprise. Yes, he had. "I can guess. Come. I'll show you what you wish to see."

He removed his shirt, freeing the mátia, which immediately jerked to the oracle. Rathbone tossed the material into the hamper near her thigh. He trusted Hades, despite the male's hatred of Lore, but that wasn't a reason to relax his guard.

Or he tried to toss the material in the hamper. Neeka caught the garment without facing him, brought the cloth to her nose and sniffed, humming with delight.

Hot, frothing desire gripped him.

"This is humiliating," Hades muttered. "For you."

"Come," Rathbone repeated. Scowling, he flashed to his special throne room.

His uncle appeared in the center of the room, dark gaze zooming to the remains. His lips curled in a cold smile. "Two other bones are in play, after all. And one is the skull, no less." He raised an invisible champagne glass. "Kudos to you." The dryness of his timbre belied his words.

"Resign yourself. She's coming to life. Soon."

The King of the Dead strode to the throne and attempted to lift Lore's hand. He proved unsuccessful; exactly as he'd proven unsuccessful in the past, each piece adhered with an unbreakable enchantment. He released a noise of disgust. "Remind me why I like you again."

"Because I'm extralikable. And family. And because I spy for you whenever you ask nicely."

"Yes, but I miss the days when you obeyed without hesitation or question." The royal performed his version of a pout before adjusting a spiked ring on his finger. "I'm supposed to deliver a message from Taliyah Skyhawk, the harpy General, who just happens to be Neeka's best friend."

A fact Rathbone had learned during his search for the oracle. Had she tried to hide the information, he definitely probably would've locked her in his dungeon rather than hire her. "Let me guess. If I hurt the girl, I'll suffer."

A negligent shrug as Hades descended the dais, returning to his side. "Something like that," the other male said.

"For now, I guard her with my life. She is—" Ravenous sexual hunger clawed at Rathbone, stealing his thoughts. It was a sensation one female caused.

Confused, he returned his gaze to the throne. His jaw dropped. There, standing between the golden seats, stood Lore, wringing her fingers.

Did he truly see her? Or was she nothing more than a mirage?

Inside him, hope flared. "Lore?"

She gazed upon Rathbone as if he were the sole male in existence. A soft smile bloomed even as a lone tear slid down her cheek. "Hello, my love," she rasped. "There's much we need to discuss."

Her lilting voice filled his ears for the first time in centuries, and he jolted. Mirage or not, she was here. Lore was here. With him. A swell of anticipation proved stronger than any pain he'd suffered since her loss, destroying centuries of apathy in seconds.

He croaked, "Leave us, Hades. Now."

"Trust me, I'd rather be anywhere else. I'll go and smooth things over with Taliyah. But you and I *will* speak again." With that, Hades vanished.

Rathbone barely registered the male's statements. Eight long strides brought him to his beloved mate. "Are you truly before me?" He reached up, intending to cup her exquisite face. His fingers misted through her, and a roar of fury sped along his tongue. He *needed* to feel her. Recalling how much the slightest display of anger frightened her, however, he clamped his teeth, so only choking sounds escaped. "Are you real?"

"I'm here. I'm real." She offered him another smile, even as a second tear descended.

The sight shredded him. "Do not cry, beauty. Whatever's wrong, I'll make it better."

Watery baby blues pleaded with him. "Then you must act quickly, my darling. Time is running out."

5

Happy to be alone, Neeka stripped down to her diamond necklace and rushed through a cold shower. Using Big Red's assortment of products didn't help douse the fire raging through her. Worse, the scent of spiced juniper berries added fuel to the flames.

She might need a total memory wipe to cool off. How else could she forget a naked Rathbone and the colossal red rocket he'd pointed in her direction. He was pierced from tip to base, exactly as rumors claimed. *Ribbed for a woman's pleasure.*

The air grew thick yet steamy, making breathing more difficult. How she'd stopped herself from gawking at the prehistoric beast and his mighty club, she wasn't sure. She only knew her heartbeat had yet to slow.

As she rinsed soap from her skin, her gaze caught on her forearm, where she'd scripted *he-licks-her.* What did it mean? To let Rathbone lick *her?* Because okay, if Past Neeka insisted. Present Neeka owed the girl big time for scoring this job assignment.

But. That couldn't be right. Neeka did not, would not, could not, should not ever mess around with a so-called married guy. Even though he wasn't technically married.

Was he?

Upon emerging from the massive stall, she doctored the clothing he'd provided, cutting wing slits in her new shirt, and turning the sweatpants into shorts more miniscule than the last pair.

As she dressed, she directed her thoughts to things that mattered. Why had she been so dirty? She thought she remembered digging somewhere for something, but where and for what? Why? And dang it, how had her scheme to distract him with another lover and avert disaster failed so miserably?

She'd intended to convince Rathbone to date around. To form an attachment to a non-evil immortal. Someone exceptional, so he'd cease longing for Lore. At least long enough for Neeka to cobble together a better plan. But nooo. He maintained a stable filled with well-satisfied mistresses, proving a new love interest wasn't the answer to her dilemma. And they *were* well-satisfied, weren't they? She bet they spent hours in comas of bliss.

Ignore the envy. What was she supposed to do now? Besides finish her search of his bedroom to learn more about him. No witnesses meant no reason not to do it.

In a blaze of motion, she browsed the contents of his other drawers, opened trunks, and scanned any new document she came across. Well. He owned a wealth of boxer briefs decorated with wild prints. From cartoon animals to smiling cupcakes and stick people. But he'd never worn a single pair, as evidenced by the tags he had yet to remove. He collected house slippers with animal faces, ate cookies in bed, printed pages from romance novels, and watched human dramas as evidenced by the shows recorded on his TV.

What a surprising, complicated male. Merciless killer, ruthless king, devoted husband with multiple lovers, collector of the most amazing underwear, closet romantic, and sweet tooth aficionado. Color Neeka fascinated. And disappointed. He'd lost serious sex appeal points with that stable confession. If he were her male—which he wasn't—but if he was—which he would never be—she would insist on fidelity.

Go to him!

The command thundered inside her head, making her spine shoot ramrod straight. When the inner warning blasted a second time, her wings buzzed, and she dropped the briefs she hadn't realized she'd carried.

Urgency acted as a lashing whip. Where had he gone? She raced for the door only to grind to a stop mid-way. Playing hide-and-seek would waste time she didn't have. There was no reason to physically chase him down when her father had taught her how to merge her inner eye with someone else's outer ones. A skill known as Peering. It was something anyone could do with practice, not just an oracle.

The act required a boatload of energy she didn't wish to expend right now, but honestly, it was her best option. *So much at stake...*

Decision made. Shutting her lids, she let her stream of consciousness flow from her being and slip through the palace, on the hunt for Rathbone. His essence drew her down, down, down...

Hmm. Though Neeka used every trick in her playbook, she failed to merge with him. Mental blockades and barriers abounded. Unwilling to give up, she persevered, slithering around, searching for the slightest crack in his defenses. Oh, oh, oh. Was that a fissure? She approached slowly, then contorted this way and that to push through. Pain wracked her until...*click*.

Relief drizzled over her as Rathbone's perception became hers. And oh, wow. This was how he and his many eyes—err, mátia viewed the world? There'd be no sneaking up on him, that was for sure. He saw absolutely everything. Specks of dust.

The slightest flicker of torchlight. The barest slither of a shadow. No detail was too infinitesimal.

She took stock. He occupied his special throne room. Wait. Shock punched Neeka. The dark-haired beauty from her vision. Lore. She was here. Alive. No, in spirit form.

The king prowled a circle around the goddess, desperate to make contact. He swiped out his arm once, twice, attempting to clasp her to no avail. Growls rumbled in his chest—Neeka felt the vibration in her own chest and marveled anew. She'd connected with other immortals in the past, but never to this extent. Never so attuned to someone's reactions.

Lore sobbed, and he halted with a curse, giving Neeka a chance to better study her new nemesis.

Hmm. The crying goddess might lack the zest of the cold, sinister killer she'd seen in the vision, but the two bore the same face and come-hither vibe. Goodness gracious, did Lore exude a come-hither vibe.

In seconds, Neeka was panting. She might just climb the next man she came across. Even Big Red.

"Please," the goddess sobbed, and Neeka gasped again. She could hear through Rathbone's ears! The first sound she'd detected in forever. "My killer's name is Azar. He bought my skull eons ago, and he's carted me from world to world ever since. Until yesterday, when he cast me into the sea."

"The Astra," Rathbone snapped, and oh, his voice! Deep and rough. Hard and tough. *Magnificent.* A caress to each of Neeka's cells.

Warm shivers deluged her spine. Of apprehension, not attraction. Obviously. No doubt he planned to unleash his wrath against his enemy ASAP. Would he expect Neeka's aid? Or fire her if she didn't produce another bone today?

"Why rid himself of your skull if he requires the entire skeleton?" he demanded of Lore. "There must be a reason."

"Azar wanted you to find me." Fat tears left pink trails on the goddess's pale cheeks. "He's using the skull to track me, intending to steal everything you've collected."

"He might learn your location, but he'll reach you." The vow smoldered with rage, causing the goddess to cry harder.

"He won't stop, Rathbone. Every five hundred years, he and his brethren must complete the vilest of tasks. It's how they earn a victory blessing. He murdered me for a task, and he hopes to repeat his success. Tell me you'll do whatever it takes to save me, and I'll believe you. There's no one stronger than my male."

"I will do whatever it takes," the king snarled. "Anything. Everything."

Oh, yeah. He planned to launch an attack. Aggression flooded Neeka's body. Her own, as well as the excess spilling from Rathbone. Any male in such an agitated state would absolutely fire his oracle for a failure to produce.

She couldn't let that happen. For the time being, she required unfettered access to him and Lore. Was the goddess an evil vessel for shadow monsters or an unwitting victim?

Dang it, either way, good ole Neeks had to go and make herself invaluable to the king once again. Presenting him with a second bone should showcase her astounding ability and prove her unparalleled worth. Not to mention the ferocity of her fake loyalty to him.

Yes, it was a risky move, but it kept her in the game. Also, there'd be three bones left. More than enough to stop Lore. On the other hand, the move wasn't that risky, considering Neeka planned to destroy the entire skeleton before the final bone was found.

The smallest spark of guilt flickered. Rathbone would be devastated by the outcome. But he wouldn't die in the digestive track of a shadow creature. Perhaps he'd one day come to terms with the tradeoff and thank her.

"I miss you so desperately, my darling. Tell me you love me," Lore beseeched.

"I love you," the king echoed with gusto, making Neeka's pulse leap with longing. "I will bring you back." He came to an abrupt standstill in front of the goddess. "Azar cannot have you," he reiterated. "I won't stop until he's dead, and you are fully restored."

Her tears ceased flowing at long last, a glint of hope flaring in the goddess's innocent baby blues. "I know. You're too strong and cunning to fail."

"I am."

Hmm. Was she sincere, or pandering to an alpha male's ego?

With an unsteady hand, Rathbone reached out, mimicking the motions to wipe the moisture from his wife's cheeks. He was just so gentle with her. So reverent. And the contact, though intangible, rocked Neeka's world. Her longing magnified, overshadowed only by envy. Never, in all her days, had a man touched her with such tender concern.

"Never forget you are my one and only." The goddess began to fade, and he stiffened, clearly not ready to let her go.

One and only. Rathbone the Only. Had Lore given him his moniker?

"Where are you going?" he demanded. "Stay with me."

"I can't stop this," Lore told him, tearing up again. "I'll strengthen as fast as I can and return. Nothing will keep me from you, my...." A second later, she was gone.

Denial exploded from the royal. He dropped to his knees and yanked at hanks of his hair, a mate pushed past his limit. Even Neeka teared up. His devastation hurt her on a gut-level, and sympathy welled. The day she'd admitted nothing she said or did would ever win her mother's approval, she'd exhibited a similar reaction.

As a tendril of weakness coiled around her spine, signaling the end of their connection, she moaned. *Not ready to leave him.*

The weakness paid no attention to her desires, spreading quickly and escalating. Her vision of the throne room dulled...

Her eyelids popped open, and she scanned her surroundings. Rathbone's bedroom. She stood halfway to the exit, the same spot as before. Though darkness was falling over her mind, she took a step forward. If she could just make it to headquarters—the room where she'd set up shop, storing everything she'd confiscated from other chambers—she could sleep off this feebleness and return to the king refreshed.

But her knees buckled with her second step, and she toppled, out cold before she hit the floor.

Rathbone exploded to his feet and drove his fist into a wall, gemstones raining to the floor. Dust plumed the air. Seeing Lore after all this time…hearing her lyrical voice, being unable to hold her…

Bellowing a curse, he punched the wall again. And again. Her presence—and subsequent disappearance—triggered an avalanche of sensations. From the burn of fury to the icy cold born of unshakable determination, to the sharp ache of unquenchable lust his goddess always inspired. The need to hunt her down and drag her back proved fiercest. But even he, with his incredible power, couldn't extract a spirit from an unseen realm.

There must be something he could do.

The oracle! Yes. She would know.

Rathbone teleported to his bedroom, where he'd left her. "Neeka," he shouted, ready to tear the palace apart if she'd wandered off. He scanned the room, jerking the second he spotted her. She sprawled on the floor, unconscious, her cheek cushioned by a pair of his underwear. Blood trickled from a cut in her lips.

Flash. He crouched at her side, his heart thudding as he checked her vitals. Not great, but not terrible, either. He gathered her close, an action guaranteed to wake an unmated harpy from slumber. But it didn't rouse her. She remained as limp as a noodle.

His stomach knotted. Was she worse off than suspected? What

happened? He carried her to his bed, gently placed her over the comforter. The cut on her lip hadn't mended in the slightest bit. She wasn't healing.

Why wasn't she healing?

He couldn't stand by and do nothing when blood—harpy medicine—flowed through his veins. Rathbone raked a claw through his palm, uncaring of the sting. A nice pool of crimson welled. He pried open her mouth with his uninjured hand and poured the liquid down her throat.

Yes, in his research he'd learned harpies were particular about who they fed from. He didn't care about that either. She might not even realize he'd gone this route.

The cut on her lip healed in a matter of seconds.

He heaved a relieved breath. See? Worth it. "Neeka. Oracle. Harpy." As gently as possible, he clasped her shoulder and shook. "Wake up."

She didn't. Because when did she ever do what he asked? But she did smack her lips and mutter "Five more minutes, T-bone."

Relief bombarded him. Whatever had happened, she was on the mend. But who was T-bone?

He looked over the rest of her. More shoulder length black curls had escaped the bun, tendrils curling over the pillow. She wore the T-shirt he'd provided. The hem had ridden up, revealing a circle of rubies around her navel. She wore the sweatpants, too, but she'd hacked off most of the fabric, leaving her glorious legs on display. Chocolate chip cookie dust stuck to her fingertips. Had she searched his room and eaten his snacks during his absence? Well of course she had. What harpy wouldn't?

He tried to walk away, but more and more mátia zoomed to her navel, ensnared. The fact that his blood now flowed through her body...

Muscles turned to tempered steel, and he rumbled with undeniable desire. She wasn't responsible for his reaction of course. Lore was. Being in the goddess's presence always left him ravenous for physical release. A reason he'd agreed to open the stable in the first place.

Focus! He launched into a swift pace beside the bed and worked to sort through everything he'd learned today. Lore's spirit was bound to her skull. He should have guessed. Should've tried harder to locate it. Should've saved her from the Astra sooner.

Guilt and shame scorched Rathbone. She'd cried. Cried! A goddess with a heart as pure as hers should only ever laugh.

From now on, nothing would sidetrack him from Lore's reanimation. Finally, king and queen would get to enjoy their later.

Well, maybe he'd let himself be a little sidetracked. Death awaited the Astra who'd dared take what Rathbone loved most—a warlord who planned to do so again. Revenge demanded its due.

A satisfying but flawed strategy. If he went after the Astra first, he'd all but hand the warlord victory. As he'd learned from his war with Styx, defeating other gods required patience, undivided attention, and unending resources. Attempting to defeat harpies, allies to the Astra, at the same time only complicated matters further.

To acquire everything Rathbone desired, he must see to Lore's safety before he launched his attack against the Astra.

As soon as Neeka awoke, Rathbone would demand she find another bone. If she couldn't, he would lock her in his dungeon, where she'd remain until she complied. Their easy comradery was over.

A soft moan rose from her. Strung as tight as a bow, he flashed to the oracle's side, ready to explain his plan of action.

"The elephant is wearing the wrong tutu," she muttered.

What dreams danced inside her complicated mind? They must be as chaotic and nonsensical as the female herself. He wouldn't doubt if unicorns frolicked among the tutu-wearing elephants, eating cotton candy while brandishing blood-soaked machetes.

Rathbone sat beside her and traced a fingertip along her jaw-line. "Neeka. Enough lazing. Wake."

Slowly she pried open her eyelids. Rich amber irises ringed by a darker brown found him, glazed by the vestiges of sleep. A soft smile played at the corners of her mouth. "Hmmm. I taste good."

The sight of her knotted his stomach all over again, but not with concern. Not this time. At least she made no mention of the blood.

"Did you know you eat chocolate chip cookies in bed?" she asked, stretching.

"I do," he admitted. No one else knew about his secret obsession, not even Lore.

"I prefer celery," she admitted in such a grave tone he couldn't help but smile in turn.

"What do the elephants prefer?"

"Elephants?" Her brows drew together, and she blinked rapidly. "I'm in bed. I slept. Near you." She jolted upright. "How dare you invade my space!"

"Your space?" Anger replaced the sense of whimsy, reminding him of his purpose. He stood, saying, "You have one hour to find the next bone. Things are different now."

"Yeah, yeah. I know," she grumbled. "Lore is back in town."

"How did you—"

She tapped her temple. "Oracle, remember?"

"You had a vision? That's why you passed out?"

"Yes and no. Look," she said before he could insist on an explanation. "I get it, no need for a speech. If I fail you, you're gonna go merciless villain on me. Prison cell. Chains. The works. But do us both a favor and chill out. I'll do my duty, okay? As promised, I always sometimes come through."

"Do it quickly," he insisted.

Neeka peered up at him, all innocence. "You're as surly as a bear roused early from hibernation. How am I supposed to operate under these conditions?"

He balled his hands. Was she playing him? Secretly driving him to insanity to aid the Astra? After all, she had summoned Rathbone to her doorstep. Even if she claimed not to remember.

But either way, what choice did he have but to roll with her methods? She got results. Anything else could be dealt with later.

"You will remain by my side," he grated as pleasantly as he was able, "but you will be silent unless you have a vision."

He took her hand, tugged her to her feet, and flashed her to the vampire's cell in the dungeon. Perhaps the bloodsucker knew how Azar planned to trace the skull's location, perhaps not. But by the end of the session, Rathbone would have an answer one way or another.

The male's chest wound had closed, shielding his new internal organs. He lay on the stone gurney, still bound by chains. Wide awake, he cried, "Please don't hurt me."

Releasing Neeka, Rathbone stalked to the table scattered with his tools. "I have new information, greater determination, and boiling menace. Before I finish with you, you *will* tell me what I wish to know."

"Uh, Red Dragon. I'm not having a vision or anything, but this is a moment you'll want me to speak, I'm certain of it." The oracle raised her hand, as if seeking permission to go on. "If you'd be so kind as to allow me the honors…"

Neeka skipped over without permission, as guileless as she was carnal. His insides clenched. She jumped onto the stone, straddled the vampire, and smiled sweetly at him—before shoving her fingers into his eye sockets. Her victim bowed his back and unleashed an agonized scream.

Rathbone bent to put his face in front of hers. "What are you doing?" And okay, yes, he was a little in awe of her right now. Such a cruel act from such a delicate-looking female…

Was there anything sweeter?

"I'm digging around in his past," she explained. "Among other things. Believe it or not, this is the easiest way to establish the necessary bond to acquire the answers you seek. And yes, I expect to be in the running for Employee of the Day."

The vampire bucked and sobbed, thick red blood running down his cheeks.

Neeka closed her lids to concentrate. Different emotions played over her features. Confusion. Interest. Amusement. Anger. Resignation. She tsk-tsked. "Oh, Mr. Vamp. Off Santa's good boy list you go. What a naughty, naughty boy."

"Tell me," Rathbone demanded, his curiosity caught. Not that she heard him. He reached over to gently squeeze her shoulder.

"Okay, here's the lowdown," she said, understanding his gesture. "He's a spy for the Memory Keeper. But you already knew that. While he doesn't know how Azar is tracking Lore—that *is* what you're wondering, right?—he's learned a ton of stuff about you and your kingdom. He's been cataloguing everything, in fact. Determining the measurements of the bedrooms by the pattern of your footsteps. Listening to whispers. Studying your strengths and weaknesses."

"Funny," Rathbone deadpanned for the vampire's benefit, even as curses bellowed in his head. "I have no weaknesses."

"Azar can access the vampire's memory remotely," she continued. "He's already watched your previous interactions, I'd bet my life on it. Well, maybe not my life, but definitely yours."

The vampire went quiet and stilled, as if the pain had never truly bothered him. A startling change. Rathbone huffed with indignation. What else had the soldier lied about?

Neeka opened her eyes and plucked her fingers free. "That's it. That's all I got."

"Harpies and Astra are allies, oracle," the blood-drinker stated, seeming genuinely confused. Of course, he'd seemed genuinely frightened only moments ago. "Why are you doing this?"

She hiked her shoulders, saying, "Because I have a payday. Why else?"

Greedy wench. The exact opposite of Lore, who'd only ever demanded his body. So why did this female intrigue him?

Rathbone scrubbed a hand over his face. He wasn't used to bewilderment. Or admiring someone other than his mate or his uncle. Could he trust the oracle?

One thing he discerned as absolute fact. "The vampire dies *now*." He swiped a jagged stake from the table. "The Memory Keeper will learn the depths of loss." *As I have.* "This is only the start."

"Nope." The oracle hopped to the floor and wiped her hands on the waist of Rathbone's leathers. "He lives."

Still worked up after Lore's visit—surely—he hardened, straining his zipper in a matter of seconds.

Neeka noticed his erection at long last and did a double-take. "Um. You... I... Um. I realize my desire to spare him arouses you. Err, arouses your suspicions. About my loyalties. You probably think I'm a spy like the vamp." She ran her bottom lip between her teeth, her stare morphing into a leer. Tone noticeably throatier, she said, "Let me clear things up. I'm what you call a working girl grinding hard—very hard—for a paycheck. Congrats on having such an impressive meat stick, by the way."

He nearly choked on his tongue. The heat growing in his cheeks had nothing to do with being flustered. "Yes. Well. Nothing you say will convince me to spare the prisoner."

"Not even if my instinct tells me he's valuable to us? That we'll need him in the future." And still she stared.

His grip on the stake constricted. *Think!* There was something he must point out. An inconsistency that bothered him...

When he stepped back, putting a little distance between them, his synapsis began firing again. He gritted out, "Your instinct seems to kick in when you aren't getting your way."

All innocence, she batted her lashes. "So you noticed the co-incidence, too?"

Did nothing intimidate her? He reached out with his free hand to pinch her chin. "Have you forgotten what happens to those who betray me?"

"I have not." Far from intimidated, she stepped into him, rubbing her chest against his. Then she took things further and clasped his face. An intimate action no one but Lore had dared attempt in…ever. But he allowed it with the oracle because—just because. She traced her thumbs over the rise of his cheeks and asked, "Do you really think I'd risk my payday?"

"I don't know." He stroked his thumb into her indentation. "How greedy are you?"

Rub… "The greediest," she rasped. "I like things. Crave them."

He almost dropped the weapon and palmed her backside to rock into her. His shaft *needed* pressure.

Desperate to end this conversation before he did something he couldn't take back, Rathbone snapped, "Very well. The vampire may live. For now." He tossed the stake and flashed the oracle to the throne room. If she must connect with his love story to spark a vision, so be it. Anything to return his focus where it belonged.

"Get comfortable," he snapped. "We aren't leaving this room until you learn the location of a bone or die trying."

6

Azar the Memory Keeper opened his eyes, severing his connection to the vampire. Different thoughts and emotions piled on top of each other. Too many to sort now. Or ever. The pile was one of countless others, a collection amassed over eons. They didn't matter for the time being. He must speak with his Commander.

Able to telepathically communicate with all Astra, he requested a face-to-face. —*There's been a development.*—

Roc responded immediately. —*Conference room in five.*—

Azar strode into his bathroom and stood at the sink. He examined his reflection. Tension pulled his skin taut. His lips remained set in a grim line. He was a man wrecked by torment, and it showed.

"Forget," he commanded as the foulest of his recollections vied for attention, relentless. "Do not carry your regrets to the meeting with the Commander."

Roc's position deserved Azar's full attention and respect. But he didn't forget. He couldn't. At least he succeeded in pushing the secret into a dark corridor of his mind.

At the four-minute-and-fifty-eight-second mark, he flashed to the conference room.

The open space provided a long table with ten oversized chairs. The Commander sat at the end, reading over a stack of papers. Even sedentary, he was a tower of strength with cropped dark hair, eyes of gold and gray, and skin heavily marked by *alevala*—moving soul stains that mimicked tattoos and trapped onlookers inside the memories responsible for their application.

Azar was surprised to find the male alone. Since his twenty-first wedding—a long, weird story—he'd rarely left his wife's side.

Roc didn't glance up as he stated, "Speak."

"The oracle, Neeka, has betrayed us." Azar had never met the female, but he'd seen her hanging around the General, Roc's beloved wife. The two were supposedly best friends.

The studying ceased, the Commander going as still as a statue. He flipped up a blazing gaze, locking on Azar. "Explain."

Roc was a male of few words. Like all Astra, he was a child of a war god, bought, raised, and trained by Chaos, Ruler of the Abyss. Each warlord possessed the ability to create—and destroy—entire worlds.

But Azar wielded an ability his brothers-by-circumstance did not. Total recall. No detail escaped his notice.

"She aids Rathbone, King of Agonies." Someone Azar had never met but knew all about. "I'm confident he's the warrior Erebus will pit against us next. Me, specifically."

Every five hundred years, Erebus the Deathless, father of phantoms, issued a challenge the Astra could not refuse. A single impossible task for each warlord. If even one warlord lost or forfeited, the entire army received a catastrophic curse: defeat with no hope of triumph.

The newest round of challenges had kicked off three months, two weeks and six days ago. Three Astra had passed their tasks, with a fourth set to begin anytime. They used to go in order of rank. But things were different now. They weren't just fighting to circumvent a curse; they labored to ascend. A supernatural process that would instantly download more power and new abilities into them. Enough to make them equals with a being like Chaos.

For the first time, Erebus got to choose the order and plot the tasks. No one knew what fresh horrors loomed. And the god would inflict horrors. The worst of the worst. He owned the Blade of Destiny, a mysterious weapon able to mystically open doors into the many variations of the future.

Seeing the end from the beginning provided a distinct advantage. But. Despite the alteration in procedure, the Astra had still won those three battles. The Blade had failed to show Erebus what their gravitas did to help them achieve victory. A fatal flaw. Unless the Deathless had lost on purpose. Always a possibility. A male who enjoyed doling out misery upon misery wouldn't want the war to end until he'd wrung out the last drop of happiness from his opponents.

"Hmm." Roc compressed his lips into a thin line. He leaned back in his chair and linked his fingers over his middle, deep in thought.

Azar had begun to suspect Rathbone's involvement after Erebus delivered a message via phantoms. Mindless beings able to assume a ghostly or tangible form. Bound to the will of their creator, they did as Erebus instructed without deviation.

Before Azar had slain them, they'd repeated a riddle over and over again. *She is heartless, he is blinded, and you are screwed.*

Azar had guessed they spoke of Lore the Incomparable. A thorn in his side lacking a heart both emotionally and physically.

Beads of sweat trickled from his brow. *Don't go down that path. Not now.* Hopefully not ever. *Forget, forget, forget.*

"Go on," Roc intoned.

Deep breath in, out. "As you are aware, I sent my best spy to Rathbone's kingdom. Khalid allowed himself to be caught and tortured to acquire a mental blueprint of the palace. He pretended to pass out when Erebus visited. Rathbone returned soon after with Neeka in tow." Azar explained what he'd heard and saw through his connection to the soldier.

Roc's expression grew darker. "Why would the oracle betray her own kind?"

"According to her, a payday."

"Hmm," the Commander repeated. He ran his tongue over perfect teeth. "Taliyah trusts her, and I trust Taliyah. Neeka must have been under duress. Pretending to be on board to aid us in some way."

"Perhaps." Azar summoned specific memories to the fore of his mind. A complicated process but also a boon for remembering every detail of every moment. He replayed the few times he'd spotted the harpy-oracle, cataloging her expressions and mannerisms. "But not likely," he advised. "She's more formidable than other harpies. From what I gather of her character, no one can make her do anything she doesn't wish to do. Not even the Underworld king."

The Commander scrubbed a hand over his mouth. "Rathbone's wife. Her bones. Tell me everything."

"That's easy, considering I know little." *Careful.* "She is Lorelei the Incomparable, a goddess of desire who left Olympus for uncertain reasons. Too many rumors claim too many things. From jealous wives, to besotted males, to legions she's supposedly deceived. After I removed her heart, Rathbone etched the Song of Life into her bones, but demons stole and sold them. He has regathered all but four."

"And now you believe you'll be tasked with finding those bones to…what? Revive her yourself to kill her again?"

"Yes."

Another "hmm" rose from the male. After a brief silence, Roc's shoulder rolled in, and he heaved a sigh. "This couldn't come at a worse time. Taliyah has been in a magnificent mood." The grumble in his tone almost roused a chuckle from Azar. Almost. "She and her sisters are competing to see who can out romance their consort, so *I* have been in a magnificent mood."

Consort. Something Azar never wished to become. Relationships weren't his thing. He sometimes used sex to distract himself from the past, but honestly, each encounter was the same as any other. Nothing special. Another memory to retain.

He returned to the subject that mattered. The coming task. "What would you like me to do?"

"I don't know yet. We're missing something. Why did Erebus choose this female for you? Is there a possibility she's your gravita?"

"No." Azar refused to think along those lines. *Not her. Anyone but her.*

Roc stared at him, hard, and he struggled to maintain a neutral expression. "The Deathless put Taliyah in my path. Ophelia in Halo's, and Blythe in Roux's. All fated mates. Why deviate from pattern now?"

"To throw us off." *She isn't mine. She isn't!*

Heavy, oppressive silence before, "Until we're given the official task, send more spies to the Realm of Agonies and Olympus. Learn everything you can. I'll speak with Taliyah about Neeka."

Azar nodded, certain he'd gotten the better end of this deal. The harpy General had a mean streak—and the power to back it up. But then, she was a daughter of Erebus. When she rampaged, things broke eternally. Even the strongest of wills.

As protective as she was of her friends and her people, she might not believe the news about the oracle. She might even attempt to save the girl, interfering with Azar's task.

No wonder he preferred biddable females. Something Lore would never be.

He told his Commander, "It shall be done."

★ ★ ★

How long must I languish here?

Neeka sprawled on the cold marble floor, idly tapping mani-
cured nails and gazing up at an ornate ceiling painted to resem-
ble a morning sky, with a variety of beings at play. This wasn't
a position she normally adopted in front of others. Her wings
were trapped, suppressing her immortal strength, but dang. She
was so exhausted she almost used her precious boon to flee this
now hated throne room.

Excluding her brief spell of unconsciousness, she hadn't slept
a wink in ages. Before she'd met Red, the sexiest king in history, with his intoxicating scent and smoldering stare, constant
mental gymnastics had kept her awake and drained.

He perched upon his seat, gazing adoringly at Lore's remains.
Something he'd done for the past twelve hours.

Twelve. Two more than ten. Eleven hours and fifty-nine
minutes more than Neeka's patience could bear.

Again and again, he'd issued a request for the goddess to return. Had the female deigned to respond? Not. Even. Once. It
would've been sad if it weren't so hellish.

His unhealthy obsession with a (potential) incubator of shadow
monsters had to end. Thankfully, it might be dulling a wee bit,
despite current evidence to the contrary. A couple times today,
he'd sprung wood for Neeka. He'd also bantered with her. Had
even acquiesced to her request and caressed her chin as if he
were handling a valuable vase. And the way he'd looked at her...

Warm shivers brought a smile to her lips. He and his mátia
had absolutely *devoured* her. That had to mean something.

Obviously, she didn't reciprocate his attraction. Not in the
slightest. She wasn't a fool. But an idea percolated...

What if she seduced him, luring him away from the goddess?
Sure, Neeka hadn't cranked up the heat for a guy in centuries.
And yeah, okay, her skills were rusty at best, as proven by the fact
that she'd never won more than a quickie. But again, what if?

She traced a fingertip over the words on her arm. *He-licks-her.* Had Past Neeka given Future Neeka permission to accept the king's kisses?

Wait. *He-licks-her. Helikser. Elikser.* Realization struck, stealing her breath. Elixir! That. That was the solution to her dilemma. *Excellent job, Past Neeka!*

According to ancient rumors, there was an enchanted substance able to create a bond stronger than that of fated mates. If Neeka located a vial of it, she could win Rathbone from Lore. He would reject the bones, letting the goddess fade into the ether of memory, preventing the destruction of harpykind.

Although, yes, Azar would still lose his task, earning a curse for the Astra Planeta and a blessing for Erebus the Deathless, who would ascend and acquire more power. Not the most amazing ending.

Fine! It was lackluster at best. And yet, with it a glimmer of hope remained. The Astra could slumber for a half millennium, as they'd done after previous defeats, except this time, harpies would guard them. Then, when they awoke, the warlords could defeat Erebus. It'd be tougher to do, but not impossible.

Neeka probed her intuition, on a quest for any red flags. A sense of danger bloomed, but what was new? Danger awaited her on every path. Until a better solution popped up...

I'm going for it. Decided, she relaxed and stretched her arms over her head, then shifted to her side. Her gaze landed on Rathbone for the thousandth time—she gasped, her eyes widening. Uh, he and his eyes were no longer focused on the goddess. He stared at Neeka. And he was smoldering again.

Dang, he gave good smolder. His red skin darkened, as if actual coals burned beneath the surface. Embers crackled in the mátia.

A tremor traveled from head to toe. She slid her gaze down his body, an action suddenly as necessary as oxygen. All those muscles. Another raging hard-on...

She fanned her overheating cheeks. Rathbone the Only was a total snack cake.

"Something on your mind, majesty?" she breathed out, sitting up. "Feel free to share with the rest of the class."

"Change clothes and have a vision," he growled. "I told you we weren't leaving this room until you did, and I meant it."

Okay, that was so not what she'd expected him to say. Why did he care so much about her outfits? She gave herself a once-over, confusion mounting. The shirt and shorts covered all her personal bits. There were no bloodstains. No embroidered message, either, because she hadn't had the tools to sew a new one, but even still, his command made no sense.

"Where am I supposed to find these so-called clothes?" she demanded.

He waved his hand and a garment appeared at her feet. "I'm sure you'll find something if you search," he replied with the driest of dry tones.

Ugh. A long-sleeve, floor-length robe. She would rather die.

Neeka climbed to her feet and anchored her hands on her hips. With a little sass—okay, a lot of sass—she told him, "I will possibly consider thinking about considering wearing such a travesty of fashion, oh great one, after my boss issues my first paycheck. Go ahead and scattered my slain enemies at my feet."

"A royal oracle should be covered from neck to toe."

Uh... "Where did you pick up *that* gem?"

"Myself." His gaze slid over her, burning hotter. "I am the only variable that matters in this situation."

Wait. "Are you demanding I cover-up because you can't stop getting steamed for good ole Neeks, no matter how much you try?"

His scowl sharpened enough to cut through steel. "Did you forget I spoke with Lore after spending centuries apart?"

Ouch. Bigtime rejection. *Always unwanted.* Why did no one ever see her potential? "First, I'm not wearing the robe. My outfit is perfect. Almost perfect. It lacks bracelets and anklets and rings to match my necklace. Hint, hint. Second, I can't force a vision." Not often. "Third, I'm unsure what else I planned to say."

He gripped the arms of his throne, his knuckles slowly turning white. "Oracle."

Uh-oh. He was gearing up to dish a power lecture, guaranteed. She rubbed her temples as if she were receiving an incoming telepathic message. "Hold up. My instinct is flaring."

His breath seemed to hitch.

"Oh, goodness. You're not going to like this, but you must close your stable. Yes, yes. That's what I'm sensing. It's for the good of the mission. If you don't do it, bad things will happen. Terrible things! The worst."

His scowl deepened. "You seek to punish me, nothing more."

Wrong. She'd meant what she'd said. This was for the good of the mission. *Her* mission. The acquisition of the elixir. Let him continue to harden with thoughts of his precious Lore. At some point, he would desire another outlet. The more he needed sex, the more he might turn to the smoking hot harpy-oracle he claimed he didn't want.

His torment was a bonus.

As cold as ice, she stated, "Go ahead. Take the chance."

Several beats passed in terse silence. Finally he stood, waves of tension pulsing from him. He motioned her closer. "I will do as you've suggested, but this won't end well for you. That, I promise."

7

Everything about the oracle bothered Rathbone. From her stimulating conversations to her unpredictability to the innate sensuality of her movements, to her luscious curves and intoxicating scent. That unique mix of sugared cherries and sweet almonds filled his nose with every inhalation, fogging his head. The fact that she had pulled his attention from his mate added to his irritation greatly. Lore's lack of appearance didn't help matters.

Where was she? Shouldn't a powerful goddess recover her strength quicker?

Did she watch him without his knowledge? Sleep? What, what?

Neeka sauntered over, every step sparking a new fantasy. Taking her against a wall. On the floor. His throne. *Lore's* throne. Beads of sweat broke out on his forehead. What was this oracle doing to him?

"Whatever you're thinking," she said, waggling her brows, "I'm a fan."

"I'm thinking I should've hired your mother," he retorted, offering his hand.

She flinched before accepting, and guilt sparked. When the softness of her skin pressed against his calluses, he nearly drew back. Too good!

He, a mighty king of the Underworld, considered retreat an option?

Grinding his molars, he flashed to his stable. A smaller palace than his own, filled with precious stones, fine tapestries, and hand-carved furnishings. He materialized at the entrance of the indoor pool, where many scantily clad females lounged and chatted. Vampires, shifters of every faction, gorgons, sorceresses, Amazons, banshees, a Phoenix, elves, griffins, and even a centaur. Because why not? No harpies or oracles, though. Not that it mattered. The females came in a variety of different shapes, sizes, and colors.

Incense burned from wall sconces, scenting the air, yet still he smelled only Neeka. He liberated his hand from hers. And not in retreat! They'd reached their destination, that was all. There was no need to maintain contact.

His concubines spotted him, and squeals of delight rang out. Females jumped to their feet and rushed toward him, hoping to be part of the group he took to bed.

"Stay where you are," he commanded, and they froze midway. He knew Neeka watched his profile, reading his lips. He felt the heat of her gaze. "Until further notice, I won't be visiting you. Unless I decide to kill my oracle for failure to keep her end of our bargain. If that's the case, I'll return tomorrow."

Unabashed, Neeka waved. "Hi. I'm his oracle. What he meant to say was this. Congrats! You've shed two hundred and fifty pounds of unfaithfulness. Go enjoy happy lives."

Rathbone popped his jaw.

An assortment of reactions came forth, but no one dared utter a word of complaint. He paid them too well.

Neeka fixed her attention on him. "Quick question for the good of the mission, so you can't refuse to answer. Is this how you treat everyone you bed, including Lore? All ferocious and demanding and such?"

He narrowed his eyes. "I wasn't *not* like this." Why?

"Stay where you are," she mocked, flexing her biceps. "Dude. You're losing cool points by the bucketload."

He lifted his chin. "Lore enjoyed it." Like the concubines, she'd never complained. Had only ever praised him for his strength. Exactly what he expected from his mate.

"By. The. Bucketload," Neeka repeated with a shake of her head. "No consort of mine is ordering me around, especially while he's banging other chicks. I'll be his one and only, and he'll be mine, and that's that."

Something cracked inside his chest. To his amazement, yearning leaked out. To be so desired by his female that she refused to share him with others...

Perhaps he should shut the stable permanently, as Neeka suggested, and be faithful to Lore. Or at least give the concept a test run.

It wasn't a repulsive idea.

He peered at Neeka, his curiosity snagged. "You also told me you weren't interested in acquiring a mate," he reminded her.

"And I'm still not. I was speaking metaphorically. Anyway. Instead of setting you up with a great gal you don't deserve," she prattled on, unabashed, "I'll sign you up for my class, How Not To Be a Tool."

"Shouldn't you excel in a subject before you teach it?"

Rather than erupt, as anticipated, she canted her head, pensive. Then she shrugged. "You're right. Guess you're doomed to live the rest of your endless life in as is condition. Poor thing.

My apologies." When she patted his cheek and sighed mournfully, there was no stopping his show of amusement.

He snorted. Then he did the unthinkable. He smiled. With amusement.

Gasps of shock reverberated. Recalling their audience, he scowled.

The concubines were gaping at him, as if he'd sprouted a second head. So Rathbone had never argued with them. So he usually arrived on edge, took the first handful of women to reach him, and flashed off as soon as he finished. So what.

He snaked an arm around Neeka's waist and teleported her to his private beach. His thinking spot, where salt and majestic orclilies fragranced a warm breeze. The pink sands, blue coral, and purple waters always provided a slap of reality. Things could be worse.

"Find the next bone," he commanded, releasing the oracle. "My patience is running out."

"Ten-four." She saluted him before turning, tearing off her shoes and socks, then stepping into the lapping ocean waves. "Just gonna get my relax on to help speed the process along."

The sun adored her, deepening the rich hues of her skin.

He stood in place, the mátia riveted as she kicked the water, dancing in the sand, and skipped rocks. She moved with abandon, somehow both graceful and awkward, uncaring about the opinion of observers. She simply did what she pleased, when she pleased.

Must be nice. What Rathbone wouldn't give to not worry about his dead wife or vengeance. To just be.

Eventually, Neeka tired and rejoined him. "What if I need twenty-four hours of patience?" she asked. "Will you agree or go Neanderthal?"

Having a deadline mollified him. "I'll grant your request. But those hours will cost you."

Amber irises glittered with a combination of dread and playfulness. "What is it you seek?"

"The unspecified boon I owe becomes null and void."

"What!" She stomped her foot. "But that's my favorite part of the fee. Pick something else. Your price is too high."

"Pay the higher price or prove you place no value on your request." He crossed his arms over his chest. "How much is your life worth to you, Neeka the Unwanted?"

"Oh!" Scowling, she scooped water and threw the droplets at his chest. "That is the most logical thing I've ever heard, and I'm furious with you. Furious!"

"Do you agree to my terms?"

"Considering I'm irreplaceable to me, yes. I'll pay. Twenty-four hours for me, no unspecified boon for you. With the caveat that I obtain two unspecified boons if I find the same number of bones during this twenty-four-hour period." Smirking at him, as if she'd discovered some sort of loophole, she added, "How much do you value your Lore, King Reddy Locks?"

That smirk looked good on her. Good enough to eat. His gaze dipped, sliding over her entire body. In fact, there were lots of places to dine. "Using my own question against me. A bold move I admire. You deserve a reward, so… You've got a deal."

She beamed at him, soaking up the praise, and his chest squeezed. How did she draw such stalwart reactions from him?

What would it be like to kiss her? A woman who longed for her one and only. Who would demand he forsake all others on her behalf.

No reason to start his monogamy test run until later. "Since you forced me to close my stable, you should—"

"Uh-oh," she interjected with a moan. "Looks like your dream is about to come true. Incoming vision…" Her eyelids slid shut, and she rubbed her temple.

A vision about Lore? Heart leaping, Rathbone gripped the oracle's shoulders. "Tell me!"

"I see…" Her frown deepened. "You, sitting at a long, formal dining table. Demons fill the other chairs. They hold forks and knives, and chortle with glee. A pretty blonde is chained to a wall. She's sobbing quietly. There's a warlock strapped to the table. You cut him open. While he screams, you serve his organs to your guests."

Neeka saw into the past too? A surprise. Most oracles swung one way or the other, not both.

Rathbone wasn't sure how he felt about this. Already she considered him less "cool." How much had her opinion lowered with this vision?

He waited for her to refocus before he explained. "The blonde was a member of the stable. She and the warlock attempted to kill me, and their treachery did not go unpunished. I killed her as soon as the party disbanded." He'd meant what he'd told the oracle their first day together. If you didn't work with him, you worked against him and paid the price.

"But inviting demons to dinner?" Neeka shuddered. "Really, Rathbone. They're the worst of the worst."

Agreed. "I poisoned the warlock before I severed him. My guests died in agony, I promise you." A boast he hadn't shared with Lore. To safeguard her delicate sensibilities, he'd always hid the carnage of war.

Laughing, Neeka shook a fist in the air. "Brilliant, tricky boss. Tell me more."

The crack in his chest spread. This female understood and appreciated his efforts to defeat his enemies, no matter the cost.

Or she pretended.

Rathbone stiffened, a bitter taste coating his tongue. He'd wondered if the Astra had sent her to spy. What if they'd commissioned her with his distraction as well? Neeka the Unwanted was a little too perfect for him.

Better to keep her at a distance. "Come. We must go somewhere else." Anywhere else. Out of the sun and away from the water, the temptation she presented should lessen.

Rathbone linked his fingers with hers and flashed to the royal garden—no, she stunned among the thorny roses. And she was peering up at him with wide eyes, clinging to his hand.

Forget distance. He would take her mouth and—

A growl scraped his throat. He didn't understand the intensity and speed of his reaction to her. And what was this new, terrible sensation growing inside him? This…calm. As if everything was right, nothing missing, nothing broken. Even though so much was missing and nearly everything was broken. How was a king supposed to get anything done feeling like this? He hated it. And loved it. What did it mean?

With the question, tension returned. Ah. Excellent. His normal condition. The familiar. Exactly what he was used to experiencing every minute of every day.

He flashed the oracle to his bedroom, a location they'd utilized before. Surely he'd have no problem thinking—no again. Things were different now. He imagined Neeka splayed across his mattress, demanding he pleasure her and her alone, and he cut off a groan.

When he geared to flash to an icy tundra, she wrenched from his hold. "This is where we part, Scarlet Storm," she said, backing away.

"We stay together, remember?" The words burst from him. "I recall hearing something about you sticking to me like glue."

"Obviously, I meant we stay together every minute but bedtime. Now, good night, sir." Looking anywhere but him, she pretended to tip an invisible hat, then spun, revealing the small, translucent wings that protruded from slits she'd cut in the shirt. Those adorable wings buzzed rapidly as she sped from the chamber.

Rathbone almost followed. But what would he do when he caught her?

He worked his jaw and returned to the hidden throne room. Still no sign of Lore. Could nothing go right for him today?

"Lore," he called, being sure to gentle his tone. "Show yourself. We have much to discuss." A minute passed. Then another. Silence reigned.

He pressed his tongue to the roof of his mouth, plopped into his throne, and drummed his fingers against the golden arms. Right back where he'd started.

Seemed he had to make a choice between A and B. Spend his evening waiting on his mate or spy on his too-sexy oracle to discern her intentions. Decisions, decisions.

Neeka sat on the floor of her palace headquarters. A spacious suite as far from Rathbone's as possible. She'd propped a large oval mirror against the wall in front of her. Behind her, on the other side of the chamber, logs burned in the hearth, warming the air. With her legs bent at the knees, she contorted this way and that, painting her toenails. The glittery blue polish really made her feet pop.

"Is the possibility of losing my best friend's trust worth this hassle?" she muttered in a secret language she'd invented as a child. "No. So, as soon as I'm done here, I'll hunt her down and explain things."

"Okay, but she'll die in the digestive tract of a shadow monster." Her reflection replied in the same language, and Neeka didn't have to read her lips. Her voice filled her head.

"Fine. I'll stand down." Reflection was right. There were times to bare all and times to keep quiet. A premature revelation could be the death knell of Neeka's scheme. "Even Taliyah, with her brilliant mind and cunning strategies, isn't ready to learn the truth."

"Exactly. Now that that's settled, forget your dilemma and rest. You look haggard. Which means I look haggard. Which is unacceptable. I'm a total babe."

"You're a total pain, that's what you are."

"But you love me anyway."

She sighed. "I really do."

"So prove it and obey. Rest."

"Sure thing. Next week. Maybe. But probably not." Whether her companion was a long-term figment of her imagination or a living extension of her being, she didn't know and didn't care. They'd been bosom buddies ever since her mother's first murder attempt.

It happened soon after Neeka lost her hearing. According to Mother Dearest, little Neeks had become an embarrassment. Too weak to prevent a soldier from harming her, then too feeble to heal.

To be honest, the rejection had hurt more than the injuries. But now wasn't the time for childhood regrets. *Focus up.* She had a doomed future to circumvent and all.

"A plan of action is more important than a nap." A jaw-cracking yawn followed her words. "Rathbone is preparing for the arrival of his dead wife. He's determined. Brilliant me promised him results in twenty-four hours. But I gotta snag the elixir as well. A necessary tool to free him from Skeletoria's clutches." With a sigh, she capped the polish. Leaning forward, she blew on her toenails. "That's why I'm consulting you, my preferred semi-expert in matters of everything and nothing."

"Okay. Here's your plan, each step fully vetted. First, stop lusting for the king. Second, don't attempt to seduce him. Third, forget the elixir. Finally, find a way to give the bag of bones to the Astra. If they know about the shadow monsters, they'll take precautions."

And risk ending up on Rathbone's dinner table, served to demons as a delicious appetizer? No, thank you. "Blame him for the lusting, not me. He's the trifecta of masculine carnality. Tall, broad-shouldered, and stacked with muscle. And he smells good. And his skin is warm. Plus, you've seen the way he smolders when he looks at me, right? How's a girl supposed to ignore that? And get this. He recently twined his fingers with mine."

For centuries, she'd witnessed couples holding hands with linked fingers, and she'd envied them greatly. This marked her first personal experience with such a phenomenon. How right the world had felt. As if the past, present, and future had aligned to reveal the true meaning of perfection. As if the worst of her struggles had been worth it to get her to that special moment.

But it wasn't a special moment to Rathbone. He preferred a twenty-minute boner garage. No doubt he hoped to use her for an occasional bang now that his stable was closed for maintenance. And that was his loss. Neeka had a lot of pent-up affection to give, if ever she decided to jeopardize her heart. And she just might, now that she'd experienced the joy of hand holding. To belong to her man...

Pay the higher price or prove you place no value on your request.

A sentiment that applied to every avenue of life. How much was a forever relationship worth to her?

"Find a way to heed me, I'm begging you," her companion pleaded. "Aligning with the red one isn't smart. He's a bad bet. Trust me on this. Have I ever steered you wrong?"

"I honestly don't remember." This wasn't one of her smarter days. Different visions of the past, present, and future were knocking on her mental door, seeking entrance. A cluster too plentiful to deal with without passing out. Holding them at bay as they seeped out one by one required a distraction. Hence Miss Reflection. "Have you?"

She shrugged. "Maybe? I'm drawing a blank, too."

Yeah. That tracked. "Well, I agree he's a bad bet." Forget his infatuation with Momma Shadow. If they dated, he would treat Neeka the same way he'd treated his concubines. A convenience to dispose of the moment he got his nut. "Good thing I'm not seeking a future with him. Only a future, period. Which brings me back to the elixir. How do I find it while earning my keep? There's gotta be a way to accomplish both simultaneously."

Rathbone—wait. Her foresight tingled at the exact moment her reflection froze. Someone had just encroached upon her territory. Except, as she straightened and scanned, she found no evidence of an intruder.

Hmm. *Something's different.* Searching, searching… There. The stuffed teddy bear on the mantle. She didn't recall seeing it as she'd hauled her pilfered goods into the room. Had she forgotten it, or had the king materialized it the same way he'd materialized the robe, eager to observe her on some kind of nanny cam?

Nanny cam. Definitely. A hint of exotic spices and juniper berries laced the air.

Well, how dare he spy on her while she plotted to betray him!

This required swift action. Neeka stood and stretched, acting totally normal. Whistling, she skipped to the mantle—and swiped up the bear.

"Ah-ha! Do not monitor me again, Wrath Boned," she growled in the animal's face. Then she tossed the toy into the crackling hearth and watched with glee as it burned beyond recognition.

But. Hmm. It wasn't satisfaction that flooded her. Her brows drew together. What *was* that? Regret? Had she *liked* being observed by Rathbone?

No, no, absolutely not. But maybe a little? Not that it mattered. She shook her head—the answer to both her problems smacked her, as if it had fallen from a top shelf in her mind. Neeka jumped up and down, excited. Of course! Nova, the Astra home world, harbored the mythical Hall of Secrets. From what she'd gathered by eavesdropping on the warlords, the solution to every problem floated there, ready to be plucked from thin air.

There would be lots and lots of guards. Probably boobytraps, too. No doubt the reason she'd sensed danger whenever she'd considered the elixir. But no matter. A girl did what a girl had to do.

One unbreakable bond, coming up.

8

As the morning sun rose, Rathbone shed his last patch of charred flesh. He'd spent the night recovering from his tangle with Neeka's hearth. His mood was...not great. The oracle had detected him faster than Azar. Swift enough to catch Rathbone off guard. A world-rocking first, and something he should've anticipated.

She was a seer. Though he doubted she'd realized the truth. That he was the bear, and the bear was him. Why attempt to murder the male responsible for your "payday"?

Next time, he would be more discreet. And there would be a next time. She'd mumbled words in a language foreign to him, and he wished to know to whom she'd spoken. He hadn't seen anyone, but the lack meant nothing. Astra could speak telepathically.

If she communicated with the warlords...with Azar...

Frothing with fury, Rathbone rose from bed, showered, and selected a pair of leathers but no shirt. Better to watch her every move.

He halfway expected the flighty beauty to barge into his bedroom before he finished buttoning the pants. That she didn't, even though he paused repeatedly, only worsened his mood. Twelve hours remained on her twenty-four-hour clock. If she failed to find a bone and he must remove one of hers to prove a point, so be it. What he refused to do, no matter how much she provoked him? Allow her strange appeal to affect his body.

Lore was now his "one and only." Something he craved more with every second that passed. They deserved a chance to become an indestructible unit. Would she appear today?

Eager to see her, he flashed to their throne room. The underground sanctuary was fortified in a thousand different ways, surrounded by enough traps to stop a hundred immortal armies at once. *No one* entered without his permission.

"Lore," he called, stalking toward her throne. His combat boots thumped against the marble floor, creating an audible heartbeat. "Show yourself, my sweet." A command as much as an entreaty.

This budding desire for Neeka would fade as soon as his wife appeared. He was certain of it.

The barest outline of Lore's form developed near the royal dais. Fresh tears cascaded down her pale cheeks as she reached for him.

Chest tight, he raced closer. Too late. She vanished as he ascended the top of the platform. A curse exploded from him.

Would the addition of the next bone increase her strength, allowing her to stay for longer periods? There was only one way to find out.

Determined, Rathbone flashed to Neeka's chosen bedroom. No oracle, yet her incredible scent lingered. He compressed his lips. Ignoring an internal cloudburst of heat, he tuned his ears to sounds arising throughout the palace. There. Muttering in the kitchen.

He appeared at the entrance and scanned. Spotting her, Rathbone blinked, thunderstruck. The oracle had piled her curls into a tower of elaborate braids. A beaded bustier barely covered her breasts. Matching underwear and transparent pantaloons displayed the rest of her luscious curves. The sheer half mask hanging from her nose to her chin hid nothing while accentuating everything. Crystals dangled over her forehead, mimicking bangs. Golden armbands circled each of her biceps.

He scrubbed a hand over his mouth. She faced his direction, but she hadn't noticed him yet. Too busy kicking the refrigerator door closed while balancing multiple dishes in her arms and mumbling, "This is mine. All mine. I've earned every bite by breathing. Scarlet Fury said so. So Imma power up and get down to bees wax. Yes sir. That's what I'm gonna do."

Perhaps she'd spoken to herself yesterday?

To gain her attention, he flipped the kitchen light switch twice.

"Fried and dipped in sugar!" she shrieked as she dropped the dishes. Glass shattered, food spilling in every direction. Her gaze flipped up. Pressing a hand over her heart, she frowned. "Oh. Hello, Rathbone."

Lust punched his midsection. Because she'd spoken his name with those red, red lips? A reaction he didn't understand and refused to explore.

"What did you choose to eat?" A ridiculous question, but he didn't snatch it back. The refrigerator produced whatever the opener wished. At his dinner table, she'd loaded her plate with every dish but had only consumed the vegetables.

"That's none of your business," she rushed out, punting as many morsels as possible under the counter.

"Everything is my business."

"What are you doing here?" The color in her cheeks darkened. "Our meeting isn't scheduled for another one to six hours, depending on when I decide to pencil you in."

He flashed closer and looked over the food, confusion sprouting. Vegetables again. Very much *not* fried or sugared.

"A plain, vegetable medley? Squash. Asparagus. Broccoli. So many carrots."

"The butter and salt are invisible. Did you ever think of that?" The defensiveness in her tone doubled his confusion and even sparked amusement.

A shocking turn, considering his present mood.

She stepped over the mess, approaching the counter where an overstuffed backpack waited. Planning an extended trip without him?

He flicked his tongue over an incisor. "If you intend to escape me—"

"I'm not intending anything of the sort," she interjected. "You see my outfit, yes? Clearly, I'm ready for our next mission."

Tension seeped from his muscles. "What does your outfit have to do with our task?" He didn't allow himself the luxury of giving her curves a more thorough examination. His frayed control might snap.

"Only everything," she said, spreading her arms. "You'll carry the backpack, obviously. Your life depends on it... I think. I have a feeling."

"Explain."

"Well, the pack is stuffed with the essentials, and you've got the brawn."

"I didn't mean—never mind. Explain why you're dressed so..."

"Provocatively?" she asked, fluffing her hair. "Thank you for noticing."

As if any male in existence had the power to do anything *but* notice.

"I've found a bone. Well, almost." She shifted on her sandaled feet. "I've perceived our starting place. A world called No—"

She went quiet. Her brow furrowed, and she canted her head. "Uh-oh. Trouble comes."

A world called No? Never heard of it. And what trouble? He sensed no approach.

Azar materialized directly behind Neeka.

Shocked, Rathbone palmed a dagger. The warlord wasn't bound, injured, or in spirit form. Somehow, he'd bypassed the defenses and flashed in.

Bombs of fury detonated inside Rathbone. *The—Astra—will—pay.*

He launched forward. Azar slung arms around Neeka and yanked her against him, pinning her wings and using her as a shield. He rested the tips of his black claws against her throat.

Rathbone froze, his fury flaming into pure rage.

The warlord's cold expression never altered. "She belongs to us," he proclaimed in his deep voice. "Come for her at your peril."

Rathbone prepared to do murder. He glanced at the oracle to reassure her, certain he'd see tears.

She sighed, decisively not terrified or even upset. "Can we do the throne room trash talk another day, boys? I'm currently all booked up." How bored she sounded.

"No trash talk," Azar said to Rathbone, "merely truth. Give me Lore's bones, and I'll allow you both to live."

Rathbone palmed a second dagger, saying, "I will enjoy killing you."

Save Neeka, gut Astra. He advanced, an attack strategy forming. If the oracle was harmed in the process, he'd fix it. But the pair vanished.

He worked his jaw. Neeka had provided him with her new location at least. A throne room. In Harpina, no doubt, where a trap must await him. Not that he cared.

Flash. Rathbone materialized as thread on a tapestry he remembered seeing hanging above the royal dais, giving him a full view of the chamber and everyone in it. A dark-haired, shirtless male with moving tattoos sat on a throne next to a pale beauty dressed in black leather. General Taliyah. In the center of the room, Azar kept Neeka before him, maintaining a loose choke hold, while seven other warlords stood in a half circle behind them. The infamous Astra Planeta.

Rathbone swallowed his emotions and focused. Erebus had spoken true. Azar had visited, and Rathbone had given chase. But he didn't need the god or the oracle to explain his next move. *The warlords die. The General, too.*

"Let her go," Taliyah demanded. "She isn't our enemy."

The words purchased a reprieve for her. Rathbone would merely inflict injuries upon her in the coming melee.

There was a beat of hesitation as Azar awaited his leader's instruction.

Roc nodded. "Let her go."

The warlord lifted his arms, freeing Neeka, who smoothed the wrinkles from her garments.

"I hate to get kidnapped and run, but I've got errands."

"Tell Roc your plan," Taliyah ordered. "How you were held hostage by a hell king and pretended to aid him to protect yourself."

"Uh, you want me to lie to your consort?" The oracle shook her head, as if astonished. "Wow, Tal. Wow. If I were him and you weren't so hot, I might lock you up and throw away the key. Or give you a very good spanking. Meow." She pawed at the air.

Rathbone jerked. She'd told the truth? She aided him without reservation?

Shock radiated from each of the Astra, but it quickly morphed into anger. Azar took another step back from the oracle, as if he didn't trust himself to be within striking distance. It was then, that moment, that Rathbone received an unobstructed view of the male's chest. He went still, not even breathing. As Erebus predicted, Lore's lovely face took up prime real estate in the center of the Astra's chest.

Two urges consumed Rathbone with equal measure. To stare, and to attack. The ensuing tug-of-war left him momentarily immobilized. Then the image jumped to a new spot, nearly wrenching a roar from the deepest depths of his being, giving away his location. He chased the ink with his gaze even as he recalled Erebus's warning. To peer at the image for a prolonged period would cause him to lose himself in the memory of her death.

Impatience whipped him. He needed to see what happened. Had wondered for centuries. And yet, now wasn't the time. There was too much at stake. Neeka's survival topped the list. Rathbone still needed her.

Though it cost him layers of sanity, he looked away.

Taliyah white-knuckled the arms of her throne as she leaned forward. "You are *not* helping the King of Agonies."

"Except I am," Neeka said. "And I'm actually late for our next appointment." She checked a wristwatch she wasn't wearing. "If someone would be so kind as to flash me to his side?"

The General thrust out an arm, blocking Roc, who'd made to stand. "Rathbone is our enemy, Neeks. The next blessing task has been issued. Azar is to gather the bones of the hell king's queen, reassemble her to bring her to life, then kill her."

Taliyah's words fueled Rathbone's rage. He boiled over with it, the tapestry sure to burst into flames. Forget mercy. No reprieve for the General.

"Too bad, so sad," the oracle proclaimed. "I'm not gonna let the Astra succeed."

She—what? Rathbone settled as satisfaction appeased the worst of the rage. Chosen over friends and allies. An undeniable honor.

Several Astra reached for weapons. Azar unsheathed a scythe.

Rathbone barely contained his snarls.

Taliyah gaped at the oracle. "Is the Underworld baddie your consort or something? Is that why you're doing this?"

"What? Mr. Red? A consort?" Neeka choked on her tongue. "Are you high right now? His fated mate is the same bag of bones everyone's so hot to trot for, remember? I'm the girl who refuses to settle for anything less than the total devotion and adoration I deserve. I'm in this for the payday."

Did she protest too much? Did the oracle, perhaps, desire him?

The other woman's mouth floundered open and closed. "Who are you?"

"I'll pay you double to aid us," Roc grated.

"Sorry, Rocky," Neeka replied, breezy, "but you can't afford my rates."

Hmm. What did she believe Rathbone provided that these warlords didn't? He'd promised a treasure, a kingdom of her own, the death of her enemies, and a review. Possibly an open-ended boon or two. Things these powerful gods could easily give her as well.

Perhaps she *did* desire Rathbone. He almost smiled.

Azar adjusted his grip on his blade. Considering striking without permission?

Rathbone tensed to flash—only to go still yet again. In a blaze of motion, the oracle unsheathed a hidden blade and struck, removing Azar's hand. The warrior hissed as blood spurted from the severed artery.

"Whooo-whooo," she called, collecting the severed appendage and pumping it toward the ceiling. "What a souvenir!"

Roc and Taliyah jumped up. With an abundance of scowls and growls, the Astra closed in on Neeka. Done waiting, Rathbone teleported, landing beside her. He slung an arm around her waist and tried not to notice the tantalizing heat of her body. The sweetness of her scent. Unimportant details during battle.

"She belongs to *me*," he snarled, flashing to *his* throne room.

He released her as soon as they landed, ready to defend and slaughter.

Would the Astra follow? Could they? This chamber boasted far more defenses than the rest of his palace.

One minute passed. Two. No Astra. As furious and determined as they'd been, they would've followed if possible. Which meant they couldn't enter this specific location.

Excellent. Though it would cost him much needed energy, he would add the same fortifications to the rest of the palace.

"What took you so long?" Neeka demanded. The dripping hand of their enemy remained in her grip, an onyx ring glinting from the index finger.

He scanned for any sign of Lore. Not even the faintest outline. Rathbone gnashed his teeth. "Antagonizing me isn't wise."

"I wasn't antagonizing, I was complaining. There's a difference. Now, where were we before the interruption? Oh, yes." Grinning, she told him, "Get this. We're sneaking into Nova, home of the Astra. Well, no wonder I wanted this. I'm so brilliant." She removed the ring from Azar's finger and dropped the appendage. *Thud.* "Their planet wanders the galaxies, making it impossible to pinpoint an entrance without a key."

"I've been to Nova." Before the Astra moved in, the god Chaos had lived there. Hades and Chaos once had many dealings.

"Excellent. Give me a sec and I'll—" Her irises glazed over, and she went quiet.

Having a new vision? No better opportunity to fortify the palace then.

Dividing his attention between Neeka and his task, he added the necessary defenses. Because he and the kingdom were eternally bonded, each two parts of a whole, he altered the realm's blueprint in his mind. What he added here manifested in reality.

There went his hidden reserve of energy. The stockpile he used to heal instantly on a battlefield.

His everyday energy sprang a leak, depleting him further. Still he worked.

He was just finishing up when Neeka gasped and blinked.

"What did you see?" he demanded. Sweat dampened his skin. His limbs trembled.

Ashen, she looked anywhere but him. "No, thank you. This vision was personal, so I'm keeping it to myself."

That, he didn't like but understood. Rather than prod, using up more strength, he flashed to the kitchen, grabbed the backpack, and returned. "I expect results, harpy," he said after forcing her to face him.

"You always do." Her gaze dropped to his lips, and she licked her own.

Was the vision, perhaps, sexual in nature?

He offered her a slow grin and slid his arms around her, loving the way her breath caught. "Try to keep your mind on the mission, harpy."

She narrowed her eyes, as if she suspected what he suspected. "You, too, Majesty."

In a fantastic mood now, Rathbone flashed.

9

Focus. Forget the vision.

Shivering, Neeka stuffed the astounding images inside a mental box, then shoved that box into a dark corner of her mind. To be opened later. When she was alone. Sitting in an ice bath. The action failed to negate the wild mix of emotions whirling inside her. Triumph. Trepidation. Longing. So much longing.

She cast the shirtless Rathbone a swift glance and gulped. The bulging backpack hung from one of his broad shoulders. A thin sheen of sweat glistened on his wealth of glorious muscles. A handful of mátia continually scanned the area, seeking hidden foes. The others remained closed. Well, three kept watch over her, and she liked it far more than she should.

She did her best to take in the sights. They traversed the mean streets of Nova, a strange land both futuristic and ancient. Windowed tunnels connected towering buildings made of a shiny silver metal. An overgrowth of greenery climbed the walls.

Cobblestone paths intersected with sparkly, translucent roads, both teeming with a ginormous military force. Little wonder her sense of danger magnified with every step.

Turning a corner, they entered a bustling city square. The array of shopping centers doubled as a training ground. Soldiers congregated in each direction. She spotted vampires, shifters, gorgons, gargoyles, and banshees. Most were young, but all were learning to brandish different weapons. Older generations patrolled here and there alongside countless residents weaving in and out of various shops.

Many females were dressed as a sexual fantasy come to life, the same as Neeka. She blended in seamlessly; Rathbone did not. He earned speculative glances from anyone they passed. He was too big, too red, too unique, and dang it, too smoldery.

Thankfully, his distinctive appearance aided her endgame.

To succeed, she was gonna have to tick him off royally.

Might as well advance her pre-elixir seduction while she had the chance. Maybe he'd be so overcome with lust, he would forgive her for the event to come.

The mental box she'd just hidden burst open. Dang it! She'd forgotten to double and triple check the lock. A mini-movie played her mind.

Rathbone pinned her against a wall papered with flowers. He lowered his head and smashed his lips to hers, kissing the air from her lungs.

Kissing her. Neeka.

Not Lore.

And that wasn't all!

The picture morphed, revealing a naked Rathbone. *He stood in his bathroom doorway. Water dotted his lashes and cascaded along row after row of scarlet strength. He was hard, his piercings straining. The mátia glittered with desperate need as they watched a clothed Neeka.*

He stalked toward her...

In the present, real Rathbone shook her. "Why are you panting, oracle?" he asked as soon as she focused. He swiped out an arm, yanking her out of someone's path. Did he look ready to laugh?

Eek! Realizing she'd been staring at his lips, relying on him to act as her guide, she snapped, "I'm not panting. *You're* panting."

She forced her gaze straight ahead, ending the conversation. How soon till he kissed her?

Would they have sex?

A mewl of need escaped.

Would he ditch her immediately afterward?

She huffed with indignation. No future, no sex. But she could and should enjoy his seduction, yes? Maybe accept an orgasm or twenty. Otherwise, he'd grow suspicious of her motives.

"We're lost, aren't we?" Rathbone asked, frustration beginning to etch his expression.

Oops. She'd been staring at his mouth again. Not her fault. That lip-lock...

"We aren't lost. We're getting to know the world before we invade the palace." The imposing structure topped a steep mountain in the distance. "Trust the process, Rathbone-san."

"Trusting the process means trusting you."

"And you don't?" she asked, as if she was too dense to find the clues even with a miner's hat and a magnifying glass.

"I trust only myself."

Smart. "Not the oh, so charming Lore?"

"And Lore," he confirmed after a slight hesitation.

Oh, oh. What was this? Trouble in paradise? Perhaps splitting up the couple would be an easier chore than anticipated.

"Watch yourself." Rathbone's sinewy arm whipped out, snatching Neeka by the waist to thwart her collision with an opening door.

This is it! Her golden opportunity to pounce. Could she tempt the Scarlet Storm without the elixir or not?

Neeka used his shoulder as a prop and jumped up, rotating in the air and flinging her legs around his waist. He halted right there on the sidewalk, his gaze snapping to hers, and gripped her backside. His heat and strength enveloped her, and his enticing scent teased her nose.

Fire flashed in his irises as she molded her curves to his solid frame. Her breath caught. He was hard as steel.

"What are you doing, carrot?" As people darted around them, he kneaded her, making her heart pound in a frenzied rhythm the rest of her yearned to emulate.

Carrot? An endearing nickname just for her? What she wouldn't give to hear his tone! If it matched the hunger in his expression...

The most delicious aches bloomed. "What do you think I'm doing, Rathboner?"

His pupils dilated, one shade of black overtaking the other. A good sign, yes? She couldn't think past the incredible need sweeping through her. To move against him. To lick and bite and taste.

"I think you're playing with fire." His gaze dipped to her lips. "Do you want to burn?"

She ran her bottom lip between her teeth, tempted to *do things* to this male, and not just for the mission. "Who says I'm not already burning?"

He opened his mouth. Closed it. His eyelids narrowed. "You're flirting with me. Care to admit why?"

"How dare you," she said with mock affront, toying with the ends of his hair. "I'm flirting *well*." She was, wasn't she? "*You* admit it."

"Why?" he insisted, ignoring her demand. "I'm not your type. I'm taken."

"Are you though?" How he held her, his sensuous response, told a different story. Plus, she'd never forgotten the stardust Azar left on the goddess. Rathbone couldn't be the woman's mate. For all Neeka knew, he belonged to...someone else.

"I am," he insisted.

"Are you though?" she repeated. Before he could protest a second time, she brushed the tip of her nose against his and added, "Maybe I find you irresistible. Ever think of that?"

His lips softened. His inhalations shallowed, and his gaze hooded. "I did think of that."

Anticipation tingled across her nerve endings. He'd purred the words, hadn't he? "And...?"

"And." With a huff, he set her on her feet and severed contact. "We're here for a reason. Let's get it done." He stomped off, forcing her to follow.

Dang it, where had she gone wrong?

As she caught up, he adjusted his grip on the bulky bag and asked, "What's in this thing?"

Excellent question. She had yet to recall. "Can you not handle it? Poor baby." Faking sympathy, she reached for the strap. "Give it to me. The all-powerful harpy will save the day, as usual."

He angled, preventing contact. A little too quickly? "I can handle anything you toss at me, carrot."

Her special nickname! She groaned. Already it was her kryptonite. Wait. "Do you even like carrots?"

"I do now." Had he grumbled those words? He looked like he'd grumbled.

A group of soldiers passed them, and she snapped back to business. Showtime!

Most of the males were too busy perusing Rathbone to notice her. But some did. After giving them a practiced deer in headlights look, she ducked her head, as if too intimidated to maintain eye contact, then she stopped in the middle of the busy pathway.

Rathbone backtracked. "Have you seen enough of the world?" he asked as citizens blazed past them. He frowned when she clasped his shoulders and corrected his stance. Perfect. "May I flash us closer to the palace now?"

"Did I forget to tell you? You won't be flashing for a while." She offered him her cheeriest smile. "The metal won't let you."

His frown deepened. "What metal?"

A nanosecond later, a spear whizzed through the air and embedded in his heart. He stumbled, the backpack slipping from his shoulder. Onlookers gasped or screamed and dashed off.

Amid the throes of shock, Rathbone glanced down at his injury. The thin beam protruded from both sides of his torso. "You orchestrated this?"

"Yes, and you're very welcome." She beamed at him.

When he attempted to remove the weapon, spikes popped from the shaft, holding the missile in place. Blood several shades darker than his gorgeous skin trickled from the wound.

"The metal prevents teleportation of any kind," she explained. "I know, I know. I should've given you a little more warning." For her own plan to work, she'd needed an excuse to leave his side. "If it helps, there's a second spear headed your way."

As promised, another lance whistled between them, about to nail its mark. He ducked just in time, yanking her down with him. As he glided to his feet, he grabbed the pack and tossed her over his uninjured shoulder. Then he bounded onward, heading away from those who'd threatened his life.

Laughter escaped her as the taut globes of his backside bounced directly in front of her face. She'd expected this, but man, she hadn't anticipated enjoying the ride so much. What a view!

"Is now a good time to mention the supertroopers are following us?" she asked casually. Unable to see his lips, she could only assume he'd answered with an affirmation. "Don't worry. When they catch up, I'll do the talking and save the day."

A growl left him; she felt its vibration. Picking up the pace, he wove through the buildings, beings, and bushes in his path.

Laughing anew, she slapped his hot-buttered buns as if they were bongo drums. "Faster, faster!"

Rathbone turned a corner, hit an invisible wall, and ricocheted. Or rather, the end of the spear hit the wall, punching deeper into his chest and shoving him backward. The ensuing pulsation shattered every bone in her body. Her laughter died as searing pain wrenched a scream from her throat.

He must have experienced similar injuries. His knees buckled and down they went, hitting the ground with a hard thud. Well, well. The spearhead was clearly a detonation device.

Armed warriors closed in around them, their weapons glinting in the light. Rathbone fought to stand, fierce determination in his eyes. Her vision blurred, the gloom of unconsciousness infiltrating more and more of her mind. Still, she clocked the moment Cerise Ironclaw comprehended the hopelessness of the situation. Carmine Stormfury? No, still wrong. Whatever. He slanted his body in front of Neeka's, acting as a formidable barrier against any attack.

He was only protecting his investment, but her foolish heart didn't understand that. The organ skipped a beat.

She dragged her dulling gaze to the soldiers, almost regretting what came next.

"Who are you?" the tallest of the males demanded. "How did you enter Nova? You do not belong here."

Showtime. "Help me," she cried. "Please! He abducted me. Held me captive. Help," she repeated weakly, just before her world went dark.

Neeka awoke in a soft but unfamiliar bed. She lifted her arms over her head and arched her spine as she gazed about. A mental spotlight switched on, illuminating specific memories. The trip to Nova. Being held in Rathbone's arms. Their capture.

I made it into the palace as hoped?

The room she occupied screamed "wealth" and "privilege." The vanity was made entirely of crystal. Each wall depicted a detailed and colorful mural featuring the birth of a star. A priceless array of precious gems studded the hearth. Purple velvet swathed a pair of rocking chairs. The extravagant desk appeared carved from an Enchanted Elm, the rarest of trees.

She eased into an upright position, surprised to experience zero pain. Totally healed already?

Movement caught her attention, and she craned her head, spotting a dragon shifter pacing near the foot of the bed, dressed in a similar getup to hers. Female dragons were praised for their incredible ferocity, though this one looked like a delicate snack and a half. Long silver hair flowed in stunning waves, the perfect complement to the blue swirls branded in her pale skin. Icy blue eyes possessed a serpent-like slit for pupils, with yellow glowing around their edges.

The female noticed her and skidded to a halt. "She has awakened," she called.

Neeka's nerves throbbed. Here it was. The moment of truth. Would her plan crash and burn?

An armed warrior with black hair and warm brown skin dressed in leather strode into the chamber. He, too, was a dragon shifter with slitted pupils and those telltale blue swirls etched into his flesh. While the lady appeared delicate, even fragile, his strength was on full display.

He stopped at the foot of the bed and met Neeka's gaze, his features revealing nothing of his thoughts. "I am Kanta, and the female is Rowan. You are?"

"Neeka, harpy extraordinaire, and dearest friend to your Commander's treasured wife, Taliyah." Fingers crossed she spoke true. Not that she feared he might confer with the Astra to confirm or deny her story. Not a chance. At least not until after her departure. The odds were stacked in her favor, anyway. The Astra believed those they left in charge could oversee the safety of the world without assistance. Otherwise, why leave? And there was no way Kanta would reach out for help; a warrior of his stature hated to make himself appear weak.

He absorbed the information she'd presented without a flicker of emotion, bowed to her, and said, "Rowan, fetch refreshments for our honored guest."

The female raced from the chamber without beheading him for forgetting to ask nicely. Weird.

Wait. "You believe me?" Neeka snapped her fingers. "Just like that? What if I'm tricking you for some unknown reason?"

"You are not. I'm able to detect lies." He pulled a pen from his pocket and handed it to her. "This is yours. We took it from you. I apologize."

Not a pen, but an ordinary red marker? Why had she brought this? "Thank you."

A nod of acknowledgement. "I'm pleased to tell you the male who abducted you is being held in the dungeon, where he will stay."

"Thank you," she repeated, and she meant it. Steps one and two of her plan achieved! She'd entered the impenetrable fortress without suspicion and neutralized Rathbone without endangering his life. Not much, anyway.

Now for step three. Finding the infamous Hall of Secrets without triggering an alarm. Someone somewhere in all the worlds had mentioned the location of the fabled elixir she sought, and she intended to listen to the conversation ASAP.

Rathbone was probably gonna be a wee bit miffed by the time she got around to step four—his rescue—but he would get over it as soon as she explained step five. Retrieving a bone. Which she would do, buying time to then fetch the elixir.

"—is he, and how did he enter Nova?" Kanta was asking as she refocused on his face.

Neeka guessed his first question. "He is Rathbone the Only, King of Agonies, and he possesses a key stolen from Azar the Memory Keeper." Because she'd been sure to stuff said ring into Rathbone's pocket soon after their arrival. "They're at war. Both males want me so bad, they keep thieving me away from each other. It's maddening, I tell you. Maddening!"

Finally, a reaction. Kanta stiffened, scales momentary growing over his skin. A sign of pure rage. "No harm will come to you here. We will guard you with our lives, I swear it."

So he wasn't going to protest? Nor tell her how his internal lie detector assured him there was no way two such amazing warriors were fighting over her? Well. She shimmied her shoulders and raised her chin. "I accept your protection as my due."

The door opened and Rowan reentered, carrying a tray filled with covered dishes. The shifter set the food upon the desk.

"—make yourself at home here," Kanta was saying. Dang it, Neeka needed to do better about focusing. "You have earned the food simply by being our honored guest. If there's anything you require, Rowan is yours to command."

He understood her dietary restrictions. Nice. "After I eat, I'd love a tour," she announced, stuffing the marker in her pocket.

"Then a tour you shall have. See to it, Rowan." He offered a stiff nod, spun on his heel, and marched from the room.

Step three achieved!

Triumphant, Neeka kicked her legs over the side of the bed and stood. How about a quick nosh before diving into step four? Something told her she needed to store up energy while she had the chance.

Rubbing her hands together, she padded to the desk. Excitement swiftly downgraded to disappointment as she lifted the lids. Her shoulder rolled in. Corn dogs. Fried marshmallows. Fried cheese. Bologna salad sprinkled with candied crackers.

There was no way she could choke down any of this. Her stomach prechurned with sickness. "This is...definitely food."

Rowan wrung her fingers. "We have few harpies here, but I encountered many of your kind before my move to Nova. I remembered your preferences well, yes?"

"Oh, yes," Neeka said, trying to filter the disgust from her tone. Her kind loved this stuff. Why couldn't she? "But you know what? I should probably let the meal rest before I dive in."

That was a thing, right? "Kanta promised me that tour, and I'm eager to begin. How about it?"

"Of course." The shifter smiled, eyes of molten gold and ice blue crackling with excitement. "Prepare to be amazed! The Astra have filled this home with the most amazing treasures from across the galaxies."

"It pays to steal from the planets you conquer, I guess." Had Roc not fallen in love with Taliyah, harpy treasures would fill these halls, too. Not that Neeka was resentful or anything. Fair was fair, and the Astra had defeated the harpies in battle. Though their win wasn't assured against Neeka herself.

She linked her arm with her tour guide's. "Show me."

Rowan led her into a wide hallway, pointing out this and that. Neeka retreated inside her mind, probing for a specific knowing.

Ah, there you are. As subtly as possible, she herded the other woman in the proper direction. Finally, they stood before a closed red door.

"Oh, no! How did we get here?" A tremor shook the shifter. "We must leave. Only the Astra are permitted in this area."

Neeka looked left, right, up, down, and behind. No one else stood nearby. Not even a single guard. It was like her enemy *wanted* her to do this. "Sorry, hon, but I'm going in." *Find the elixir, save the worlds.* "You're not."

Knowing it had to be done, she struck, driving her claws into the gentle woman's chest, and ripping out her still beating heart. The shifter toppled, out for the count.

"Hate me now, thank me later," she said, dropping the organ and patting Rowan's cheek, accidentally depositing streaks of red. In a few hours, the too-gentle dragon would wake up with a brand-new organ and inner defenses she'd desperately needed. "Leave them better than you find them, that's what I always say."

Neeka latched onto the doorknob and twisted. The hinges glided as smooth as oil. No lock? Oh, yeah, the Astra definitely wanted her to do this.

She slipped into a hallway without furnishings or decorations. Just plain white walls peppered with multiple doors.

Huh. What was— A wave of whispers bypassed her ears and slammed into her mind. She sucked in a breath. So many! Too many. They barraged her awareness, the cacophony enough to drive her to her knees. She smashed her palms over her ears, but it didn't help. The volume only increased.

Determination turned her insides to stone. No cluster of conversations was gonna keep her down. Gritting her teeth, she lumbered to her feet and pressed on. *Find the elixir and a bone. Save the worlds.*

The noises ceased abruptly, and she heaved with relief. Sweet peace and quiet reigned. Then, she sensed it. The whispers hadn't vanished; they'd congregated. Now they spun and spun in front of her, some peeling back, others drawing closer together. Spinning. Shrinking. Swelling…

The constellation exploded, going off like a Fourth of July firecracker. A brutal pain erupted in her temples. Warm liquid seeped from her ducts and ran down her cheeks. Her knees buckled once again, and she dropped. But bit by bit, she absorbed new nuggets of information. Oooh. What was this? A *recipe* for the elixir? Even better than a location!

As she continued downloading information, a familiar blanket began to cover her mind, attempting to hide the information. Everything she was learning.

No, no, no. She couldn't forget. This was far too important. Neeka crawled forward…stumbled to her feet…and raced to the door, escaping the room. The final whisper cut off before reaching its end. *If you wish to save everyone, Neeka, you need only—*

Need only what?

Panting, she collapsed next to the dragon shifter, who was already halfway healed. With no other options, Neeka whipped out the marker—no wonder she'd brought it!—adjusted her clothing, and began writing the elixir's recipe on her skin.

As soon as she finished, she wrote the shocker she'd heard about Lore's missing femur. But she only managed to etch *M, I, R* before the information vanished beneath the blanket.

Argh! Time to find Rathbone and blow this joint before she forgot anything else.

10

Searing fury consumed Rathbone. Some he directed at the treacherous harpy-oracle who betrayed him to save herself. Most he focused on himself for allowing her to distract him at such a critical point in his war with the Astra. He'd ignored the danger, more intrigued by his companion. Eager to maintain their connection and hear whatever colorful thing she would say next.

Something a newly monogamous male shouldn't do. A mated male, especially. And he *was* mated, despite Neeka's inference. He wasn't a fool; he hadn't chosen the wrong eternal lover. The fact that he couldn't conquer his heightened awareness of the oracle meant something else.

So sexual tension vibrated in his marrow, even now. So his muscles remained hard as rocks. So he craved the perfidious beauty responsible for his capture. So what.

With a brutal yank, he removed the spear from his chest at last. The spearhead ejected shrapnel on its way out. Blood gushed as the wound knit back together, sealing that shrapnel inside him. A process slower than usual. His reservoir of energy had yet to replenish.

He attempted to flash. To shift forms. Both failures. Rathbone pursed his lips. No reason to wonder over the lack; Neeka had warned him. The shards. They floated through his bloodstream, damaging everything they encountered.

He'd have to escape the old-fashioned way.

Reclined in a corner, Rathbone scanned his cell. A seven-by-seven prison with walls made from a solid black substance he'd never encountered. There were no windows, bars, or doors. A fleet of small metal bugs lined the ceiling, their round bellies glowing, providing the only source of light.

Anytime he stood, those bugs descended to flay his flesh from his bones in a matter of seconds. Not that he cared. He'd learned to overlook physical pain long ago. But he stayed put, expecting a visitor at any moment. An interrogator who would demand answers. Why had he come? What did he plan? Had he brought others with him? He preferred to start the way he intended to finish: intact.

A disturbance in the air alerted him to an incoming presence. He didn't bother shifting into a better position before a dragon shifter materialized on the other side of the chamber, Neeka's backpack dangling from his shoulder.

Rathbone sized up his visitor in a snap. A leader with centuries of brutal battles under his belt. An elder, judging by the number and size of azure markings embedded in his skin. Powerful, with an affinity for more than the creation of fire.

"I am Kanta. There's no reason to introduce yourself. Neeka updated me."

She did, did she? Rathbone bit his tongue, tasting blood. "You in charge or are you merely a lackey?"

"Today, I am the decider of your destiny." Kanta tossed the pack to the floor, out of Rathbone's immediate reach. A heavy thunk sounded as the zipper gaped open. "Why do you carry a bag filled with pink rocks?"

Rocks were the "essentials?" *You've got to be kidding me.* He glanced over. Sure enough, a pile of fist-size, pink rocks weighed down the material.

His fury burned a thousand degrees hotter.

"Nothing to say?" Kanta asked.

Tone as casual as he could manage, he said, "I'm quirky like that."

A light flared in the shifter's eyes, there and gone. At the same time, Rathbone's feet caught fire, disintegrating in the blue flames. Anguishing pain wracked him, but not by word or deed did he reveal it.

He flashed his teeth, displaying an amused smile as his feet regrew gradually. "No way you're in charge of this realm while the Astra play whipped househusbands in Harpina. I've gotten hotter watching Golden Girls."

The dragon's nostrils flared. Rathbone expected a thorough head to toe roasting. With impressive restraint, his visitor controlled his temper, seconds ticking by without the start of another inferno.

Kanta rolled his shoulders and popped his neck. "You push me on purpose, and I am unsure why. But I will find out." He withdrew a thin, half-moon blade from a hidden sheath on the side of his leathers. "A cut from this weapon cannot heal."

Rathbone arched a brow. "Are you waiting for an engraved invitation? Start."

Whoosh. The blade sliced through his jugular and returned to the dragon. Blood spurted from the wound, spraying over the floor, the pack, and even the walls. Though his flesh didn't knit together as swiftly as usual, it did knit together, earning a confused frown from the other male.

Another toss. Another slice. More spurting blood. Yet again,

Rathbone healed. He flashed his teeth with another smile. "Clearly you've never fought a King of the Underworld."

"You have tricks. This is good to know. I do as well." Kanta withdrew something resembling an ice pick from a second pocket. "This little gem—" He went quiet as the room rumbled.

High-pitched squeaks rang out as the pack shook. A second later, a handful of blood-splattered rocks erupted from the opening.

His jaw dropped. Not rocks, after all. Small, round creatures with beady eyes, sharp teeth, and sharper claws. Half glommed onto Kanta, ripping through his torso, and there was nothing the dragon could do to stop them. The other half went after the metal bugs.

In a matter of minutes, the warrior lay motionless on the floor and the bugs were no more. Darkness filled the cell. Not that it mattered. Rathbone possessed excellent night vision.

He leaped to brand-new feet, prepared to fight. The creatures jumped on him and—they were kissing him? Rathbone froze. What was even happening right now?

"Good beasties," he crooned, uncertain what else to do. "Daddy is ready to leave this room. Help him?"

Trilling with excitement, they slinked off and focused on the walls, clawing and chewing through the stone. As the hole grew larger, the beasties shrank, leaving layers of dust in their wake. Would they disappear altogether?

A worthy sacrifice.

As they pressed on, he gathered Kanta's weapons. The boomerang. The ice pick. Several daggers. He stuffed everything inside the pack and noticed a multitude of rocks remained. What had brought the others to life? The violence? His blood? A stern lecture from Neeka before she'd stuffed them in the bag?

Speaking of the oracle, his searing fury ticked down a level. A small level.

The beasties reached the other side of the wall before whittling away to nothing.

The hole they'd created was big enough for Rathbone. Excellent. He crouched to his knees, ready to start crawling.

Neeka stuck her head through the breach, her amber gaze searching. She beamed a smile when she spotted him. With a cheery tone, she said, "Hey, Wrath Boned. Surprised to see me?"

A bolt of pure desire pierced his chest. "Yes," he hissed.

"Well, that's rude," she replied with a pout. "As if I would fail to facilitate our escape. You're welcome. Again."

He longed to grab and shake her. Yearned to kiss the breath from her lungs. "You have some explaining to do." He shoved himself through the hole, urging her backward. "You can talk on the go."

"I knew this was our only means of survival, you see," Neeka said, completing her explanation. Hopefully she'd made sense. She struggled to think as she led Rathbone through a series of secret passages hidden throughout the Astraian palace.

The mental blanket had slowed its descent, but it wasn't stopping. She lost more memories by the minute. In fact, she expected a total reset soon. Which sucked so hard. The things she'd heard had begun to unravel…things past, present, and future, spoken by countless immortals. Mysteries best left undiscovered. Nonsense. Meaningless gossip. Crimes. Love affairs. Riddles and complex puzzles certain to break her brain for good. Secrets, secrets, secrets.

Rathbone squeezed her hand, and she jerked into focus, realizing she'd nearly walked into a closed door. Right. Concentrate on their escape, allowing instinct to guide her. She definitely shouldn't think about their intertwined fingers. Or his callouses. And heat. And scent. Had she moaned?

She'd moaned, hadn't she? To mask it, she said, "I sense we

won't face any opposition on our way out. A reason to celebrate with spontaneous noises."

They reached a shadowy alcove, and Rathbone yanked her against him, spinning her so that they faced each other. Eyes narrowing to thin slits, he maneuvered her against a wall.

"Let's pause." He pinched her chin, resting his thumb in the indentation to ensure she read his lips. "Tell me if I understand you correctly. You happily sacrificed my wellbeing to get inside this palace."

She nodded, unabashed. "So far so good."

"And you chose not to warn me beforehand because..."

"Maybe I didn't think you had the acting chops. Think about it. If you'd known the truth, there was no way you could've convincingly pretended to be upset about your capture."

He flashed his teeth. "That is the most illogical—" His nostrils flared with the force of his next breath. "With Lore on the line, I can do anything."

"Wrong. With Lore on the line, you're a total liability," she accused, trying not to pant. He just...he felt so good. Hunger for him sharpened, becoming an ache. Or rather, joining hundreds of others.

"Did you acquire a bone?" As if he sensed her weakness, he kicked her legs apart and edged closer, his heat coiling around all those aching places.

Careful, careful. "Not yet." Might as well advance her cause. Neeka traced her clawtips up his chest. The mátia closed, as if savoring her touch. How utterly *divine.* "I need a piece of information first."

"What information?"

"Exactly. But if all goes according to plan, we'll have your precious bone by the end of the day." She pricked the hammering pulse in his neck, then licked her lips when she spotted a drop of blood. "Unless..."

He leaned closer, the warmth of his breath fanning her cheek. "Unless what?"

"What if—and I'm totally speaking hypothetically here—we *don't* search for it?" Her heart raced. *Taking a big chance here…* "We take a little break. Flash to Earth. Spend a few days forgetting about dead goddesses and brutal Astra, and do a little self-care. You can tell me your turn ons, and I can show you mine." She would recover from the mental blanketing in style, without the pressure of a mission, and maybe win him to her side in the process.

His pupils exploded over his irises. "Is this what you were pondering moments ago?"

"Don't talk. Think." Slowly, languidly, she gyrated against him. "Better yet, feel."

A growl rumbled in his chest. He rocked his hips with her next rotation, rubbing his erection between her legs. Her breath caught. He was pure steel.

This male had needs, and those needs were focused squarely on Neeka.

"When you decide about our self-care," she said, daring to nip at his bottom lip, "Kiss me once for yes and twice for no."

His head lowered, and she went still.

He was going to do it? He was going to kiss her? Trembling, she leaned forward to meet him halfway. At the last second, he clasped and lifted her hand to kiss her knuckles twice.

"I'll allow you to live. This time," he said, releasing her and backing off. "If you decide to fake another betrayal, you will notify me first. Any other action will be considered an actual betrayal. I'll proceed accordingly."

Ignoring her crushing disappointment, she offered a jaunty salute. "Sir, yes, sir."

This encounter wasn't a total loss at least. He'd made a move. He'd even taken a beat to consider her suggestion. For now, that was enough. Baby steps still got you to the finish line.

"You shouldn't complain, Captain Crimson. Look how far my methods have gotten us. News flash. This oracle gets things done."

Features blank, he motioned to the hall. "Lead the way."

Fine. "Just so you know, stress causes impotence."

"I'm not—never mind. Get moving."

She marched on, and he kept pace behind her.

They snaked around a corner, approaching the final door. A towering iron gate that should lead to an uninhabited forest. Instinct insisted the forest was the only route off this planet alive. Almost there...

She reached for the knob—argh! No movement. "Locked."

Rathbone threw his body into the block with such force, the hinges exploded and metal bent. He helped her through the jagged entrance.

As they ventured into a cool, sweet-smelling woodland, a familiar pang cut through her temples. Her steps lagged, resignation acting as a shackle connected to a boulder. Oh, yeah. Her mind would blank in a matter of minutes. The mental blanket had just breached her most recent set of memories.

"Let's slow the pace a little," she said. "Did I mention I'm ninety-six percent certain we'll make it to our destination without opposition?"

Rathbone maintained the lead, but he did dial down his speed. He angled his face toward hers, saying, "Tell me about the rocks."

She didn't mean to, but she grabbed his hand and linked their fingers, craving contact. Needing it. Usually, she faced her problems alone. How nice to have a partner for once. "They're grimlings, and I dug them from your garden." Oh! Finally! An answer rather than a question. The information ran from the falling blanket, escaping her mouth. "I sensed them and knew they would aid our escape. And they didn't attack you because your blood is their blood."

She scanned ahead, hoping to cobble together a clear, easily explainable plan for him to follow once she checked out. Trees abounded in every direction, their limbs heavy with beautiful purple flowers. Poisonous? Lush, dewy bushes lined a dirt path. The very path they currently traversed. But she spotted no foot or paw prints to indicate a safer route. No insects flew about, either. A definite sign of trouble.

Should she and Rathbone veer? But where? When? *Think, think!*

Another pang erupted in her temples, light beginning to wane. "Listen, Red. I'm about to pass out."

"Are you injured?" he demanded, slamming to a halt. She must not have answered swiftly enough, because he maneuvered her body this way and that, on the hunt for wounds.

"Mental overload," she explained, clasping his wrists. "My mind is gonna reset, and there's nothing I can do to stop it. Don't take it personally, but I might not remember you when I awaken. And don't think my little nap means you're a contestant in Mr. Neeka's Consort or anything. I'm not your typical harpy, and this won't be a typical rest."

His lids slitted. "You will remember me, and I'll hear no more on the subject." He swooped her off her feet and into his muscular arms, clutching her against his chest and stalking forward.

Oh, wow, this she liked more than the hand hold.

Neeka rested her head on his shoulder for a moment, saying, "If I attack you, don't strike back. Use my safe phrase—*You're right, and I'm wrong.* It's the only way to calm me down."

"Oracle—"

"No. Just listen. When you come across the starways—" Starways? Oh! Oh! The information she'd searched for earlier suddenly dawned. Doors into other worlds, and the only way home. "Whatever you do, avoid the red ones. And the pink, orange, yellow, blue, and green ones."

Teeth clenched, he said, "Perhaps you should tell me an *acceptable* color."

Another pang hit, far stronger than the others. More light extinguished, and she cringed, certain only seconds remained. "This next part involves Lore's bone. Do not, under any circumstances—" Total darkness descended, and Neeka sagged into unconsciousness.

11

"Do not what?" Rathbone demanded. Of course, no response was forthcoming. Neeka was too busy resting peacefully in his arms.

Anger burned inside him, fueled by coals of desire he hadn't yet quashed. He strode on, unsure where to go and unable to concentrate on anything other than the female in his arms, who'd assured him there'd be no opposition.

Forget the bone for a minute. Something had changed between him and the oracle the moment she'd stuck her head through that hole in the wall and smiled at him.

No, the change had come before his imprisonment, when they'd traversed the streets of Nova and she'd climbed on him, broadcasting lust and vulnerability. A combination he intended to experience again. Soon.

Or not. He bit off a curse. Long-term loyalty mattered more than short-term pleasure.

Focus. They were trapped in an unfamiliar world more advanced than most. Despite Neeka assurance, he sensed aggression all around. He hadn't yet recharged, couldn't shift or flash, and he saw no evidence of a starway. Not that he knew what to look for. Any second, the oracle could awaken without her memory, complicating an already complicated situation.

Even with the grimlings and his newfound arsenal, Rathbone felt ill prepared for the task ahead. Getting home with a bone and a still breathing Neeka.

A disruption in the atmosphere sent a tingle across his nerve endings. He tensed, gazing left, right.

In a rush of motion, the forest came alive. Vines shot from every direction. Some stabbed pointed tips at him. Others endeavored to eat him in a series of gobbles, their snapping, thorn-filled mouths opening and closing. Flowers spit glowing spores, causing his next breath to scorch his lungs.

Dizziness overtook him. *No opposition, carrot?*

With the help of the mátia, Rathbone dodged each attack and dashed forward. Neeka remained cradled against his chest, her sleep undisturbed.

Up ahead, the land split in two, a crack widening as it spread across the dirt, heading straight for him. He jumped, clearing the fissure. Landing jarred him, but his gaze caught on a startling sight. A starway, no doubt. What Rathbone referred to as a threshold. A door between worlds or dimensions.

This particular threshold stood between two ivy-covered trees, an endless expanse of dark sky and glittering red stars filling it.

Now he knew what to track at least, so track he did. Rathbone diverged from the path, weaving through the forest. But as he bypassed starway after starway for being too pink, orange, yellow, blue, or green, his confidence flagged. What other color remained? He didn't—there! That one. Black with pinpricks of white. Except, as he veered closer, the trees beside it stretched out their limbs to create a barricade.

No matter. He settled Neeka over his shoulder, purposely cut his palm with a claw, then thrust his bleeding hand into the backpack to grab a grimling.

Without slowing his steps, he tossed the beastie at the limbs. In seconds, the creature created a hole in the wooden block just big enough for Rathbone to dive through.

As he soared, he adjusted his hold on Neeka, tucking her safely against his chest once again. Razor-sharp bark grazed his sides, peeling through layers of skin, poking mátia. Searing pain electrified as frigid cold registered. He collided with solid ground, leaving a crimson trail as he and his bundle rolled over a field of ice.

Icy rain pelted him as he leaped to his feet and took stock. New world. Dark and stormy. Miles of ice. No roads that he could see. The only discernible landmark was a mountain in the distance.

Very well. He'd go there. Mountains provided caves. Caves sometimes supplied provisions—and traps. Not that a trap could stop him from claiming the shelter as his own.

Several grimlings and two daggers had fallen from the bag as he'd rolled. He gathered them, alert. No signs of life. No protests from Neeka, either. She never even stirred.

Worried for her, he started forward, walking, running, sprinting. Amid the rain, wind, and hoarfrost, his concern magnified. His body heat, though fierce, wasn't enough to warm her. Her teeth chattered.

Relief deluged him when he reached the hoped-for cavern. It wasn't hidden or high, but accessible from the ground. Wondering what fresh hell awaited him, he hustled into the waiting darkness.

The spacious cavity appeared deserted save for two blanket-covered corpses. They huddled next to a makeshift fire pit teeming with ash. A stack of logs and pair of backpacks waited off to the side.

Nova citizens? Other escapees? Either way, this was a trap. Had to be.

Rathbone gently laid Neeka near a rocky wall and looked her over. The rain had deposited a sheet of ice on her skin. Blue tinged her lips, and her teeth no longer chattered. He needed to get her warm fast.

Remaining on alert, he hauled a stack of logs to the pit. After cleaning his palms of any trace of blood, he struck two unawakened grimlings together, using them to start a fire. If someone or thing was going to attack, he and his companion might as well be warm.

As the wood burned, he inhaled deep, testing the smoke in case poison laced the bark. Clean. After tossing the frozen corpses outside and making sure they stayed dead, he brushed off the blanket, picked up Neeka, and carried her over, laying her upon the soft, dry fabric.

"I'm getting you out of these wet clothes for your own good, oracle. Harpy. Carrot." He didn't know what to call her in a situation like this. "I'd prefer you wake up and tell me you'll do it on your own."

No response. Very well. He stripped her out of the wet garments, save for her underwear. *Do not look. Do not.*

As he stripped himself, the mátia zoomed to her, and there was no stopping them. He traced his tongue over his teeth. *Sexy female.* The gemstones around her navel glinted in the firelight. And the scarlet lace...

Wait. Words covered her thigh in permanent marker. He frowned as he read.

19 drops Deadpool
1 tsp minced dirt snake
8 PB&J eggs

½ tbsp fried Lot Us
Stir with arrowhead
Drink and bake

A recipe? For what?

A mystery for later. Rathbone rifled through the former guests' backpacks and confiscated a coil of wire. With deft fingers, he rigged a clothesline and hung his and Neeka's damp garments.

"I hope you're ready for me." He lay beside the oracle and pulled her on top of him, chest to chest, then wrapped his arms around her, surrounding her with his body heat. Before long, her chill faded. Warmth overtook the entire hideaway, leaving him damp with sweat.

She shivered, rocking against him, and Rathbone hissed. He fought to keep his mind centered, doing his best not to notice the perfect fit of her lush curves, the sublime glide of her soft skin, or the heady scent of sugared cherries and sweet almonds.

An impossible battle. He noticed everything. And craved more.

Guilt racked him. *Think of Lore, soon to return.* His mate deserved his devotion, considering he planned to demand hers. Would she give it?

Irritation joined the guilt as he recalled his earlier conversation with the oracle. She'd asked if he trusted his wife.

For the first time in forever, he'd remembered rumors he'd heard when he'd moved into the palace after Lore's death. Whispers about her dealings with Styx. How she hadn't been his prisoner, but his puppeteer. It was one of the reasons he'd killed the servants.

Not once in their relationship had Rathbone noted any evidence to support the outrageous claim. There was no one sweeter or gentler than his Lore. She was tenderness and light. Necessary ingredients for his life. She wasn't some bold warrior woman who sometimes forgot his name and rarely made sense. Who teased and tempted him with her wit at every opportunity, making him laugh and growl in equal measure.

As Neeka snuggled deeper into his hollows, getting comfortable, he measured his breaths. When she released a throaty moan, he decided she was warm enough. Time to search for a way off this planet. But as he shifted, intending to rise, she opened her eyes and jerked upright, dislodging his arms.

Their gazes met. Anticipation unfurled, a spring ready to pounce. She had better remember him. Or else. "Hello, Neeka."

Neeka tried to make sense of her current reality. "You are Rathbone, King of Agonies."

"I am," he replied without an emotional inflection.

"I'm draped over you, almost naked." And a lot too cozy for her peace of mind. "Since I haven't said yes to a guy in eight centuries, Imma need to hear your explanation for this situation in the next five seconds, so I can decide how to kill you."

Firelight danced over his face as he double blinked. "Eight centuries? Without sex?"

That was his takeaway? "Four. Three." *Think, think.* What had happened? "Two. One and a half."

He narrowed black diamond eyes. "You told me this might happen. I didn't wish to believe you, but here we are." Inhale. Exhale. He ran his tongue over straight white teeth. "I'm wrong, and you're right. That is your safe phrase."

Dang. That did sound like her. But there was only one reason she'd abandon her no nooky rule and seek to protect a male from her wrath...

Had she found her consort at last?

Vulnerability softened her tension. "Well, then." She cleared her throat and, though stiff, settled atop him. "This is your second chance to make an awe-inspiring first impression. Don't blow it." *Please.* "Are we dating?"

"We are... partners," he said.

What did that mean? He *was* her type. Not traditionally handsome, but better. Arresting. Intense. Rough. And don't even get her started on the massive body all but incinerating her.

The fact that he was naked and growing bigger by the second left her breathless.

"You obviously—very obviously—want me." Her heart leaped. *And he's still growing. My, my, my.* Hat tip to his DNA. Wait. She dug her claws into his chest, suddenly uncertain despite the mounting evidence. "You want me, no one else?"

His expression softened, as if he'd just realized something embarrassing about her, and oh, she longed to bury her face in the hollow of his neck. To hide. To cuddle closer.

"I do want you," he confessed.

Well, then. She relaxed over him, getting more comfortable. "Do you want me for longer than a night?"

A slight vibration petted her from the inside. Had he groaned? "Much longer."

Ooh. Maybe things were too new to label. "Tell me more about us. My impression of you is improving."

He didn't take the bait. But he did reach up and smooth a lock of hair behind her ear. "Do you recall how you ended up with your moniker?"

The action, coupled with the question, coming on the heels of his amazing confession, so startled her, she blurted the truth. "My mother. It was her way of punishing me for failing to stop her foe from stabbing me in the ears during an invasion. Well, one of the ways." Her head ached as she pushed back the memories. "I was five."

The corners of his mouth turned down. "She blamed you for not overcoming a grown warrior's attack?" He waited for her nod of confirmation to add, "You were a child."

"But also a harpy with two years of training at her side." Neeka would give anything to hear his voice. Was it as deep and husky as she suspected? "She lost her consort that day." Not Neeka's father, who still lived. He'd stopped wanting anything to do with her, too. Push, push, push. "My weakness contributed to her sudden lack of a family. Someone had to pay."

"Yes. The soldiers. You were a child," Rathbone repeated, his dark eyes glittering with menace. He traced his fingertips along the ridges of her spine, gentle, so gentle. When his fingertips brushed the edge of her wings, she moaned with delight.

"Remember the part about me being a harpy? That matters. I'm also the daughter of a harpy-Phoenix and a master oracle. Greatness is built in my DNA. I should've done better."

He pressed a soft kiss into her brow. "Young Rathbone would've adored avenging young Neeka. He knows what it's like to be despised by a parent."

"Oh?"

"I tell people I'm Rathbone the Only because I'm the last one standing on a battlefield. The truth is, my mother dubbed me If Only. If only I was as strong as my father. If only I were faster, smarter, more skilled."

"Oh, my sweet baby." Neeka poured herself over him then, offering comfort of her own. No wonder people coupled up. Did anything compare to this? "How did you get rid of the *if*?"

"I referred to myself as the Only so often, others eventually did the same."

Hmm. Maybe she could borrow his play. Drop the "un" and become Neeka the Wanted. Yes, she liked this idea.

"Let's talk more about you," he suggested, so eager she got a little giddy.

"I think we should kiss to help me remember our association." Yes! Kiss. She *needed* to taste him.

A mix of longing and regret flashed over his expression, confusing her. Why regret?

With the reflexes of a jungle cat, he flipped her to her back, pinning her to the blanket and staring down at her. "There's something I must confess." His gaze dropped to her lips. He gulped, his Adam's apple bobbing. "We are..." His gaze dropped again and lingered.

"Go on," she rasped, slithering under him. She ran her hands up his spectacular chest, adoring the silken peaks and hollows. "We are still fighting our attraction to each other? In the middle of an intense negotiation about our relationship?"

He flattened his palms near her temples, fiercer by the second. "I don't know what we are doing."

"Let me help you figure it out." Spreading her legs, she contoured her body to his, becoming a cradle for him. With her knees bent at his waist, she rocked her hips and moaned with delight. So good!

His breaths seemed to roughen. He flicked the tip of his tongue over an incisor. "You were sent to kill me with pleasure, admit it."

"Pleasure. Mmm, yes. Gimme." Unwilling to wait a second longer, she lifted her head and mashed her lips into his.

As he opened for her, she thrust her tongue past his teeth. Oh! He was hot. An intoxicating inferno. And his taste. A decadent blend of sweet wine and spices. But...

He didn't kiss her back. Not at first. "Rathbone," she pleaded.

With a growl she felt in her bones, he met the next thrust of her tongue with one of his own, feeding her the passion she craved. As he claimed her with possessive strokes, he plumped her breasts. She couldn't think. Fragmented words erupted on repeat inside her head. *Yes. More. Please.*

Desire proved unrelenting. Hunger more so. They were the only two people in the universe. Neeka and her ravenous beast. A ruthless warrior who acted as if he was devouring his first meal in centuries. She thrilled, overwhelmed with—

He wrenched free without warning, drawing a groan from deep within her.

Panting, he rushed out, "My body will hate me for doing

this, but it's what is best for you. Neeka...carrot... I'm mated." Infinitely tender, he caressed his fingers over her cheekbone. "I hired you to find Lore's bones, so I can bring her to life. We ended up in an ice world. You were freezing and needed my body heat to warm."

"Shh, shh. Give me—" She ceased writhing. Wait. What? Her stomach twisted. Mate, he'd said. He was fated to be with someone else? He wasn't Neeka's consort, and he didn't intend to keep her? *Always unwanted.*

She gathered her defenses and spat, "Okay, I'm done."

When he remained in place, silent, she attempted to shove him off. With her wings pinned, she lacked the strength. Unacceptable!

"I will do another count," she snapped. "If you haven't moved by the time I finish, you're dead. One."

She struck, going for his throat. He didn't want her? Fine! But he shouldn't have kissed her as if she held the air he required for survival.

Regret radiated from him as he caught her wrist. Holding tight, he told her, "I wish things were different."

"Lie!" Why did people always say that? "If you wished things were different, you'd do something different."

He flinched.

"But that's okay," she said, going for a breezy. "I'm not mad. Not about that. You haven't thanked me for your rescue. You've only complained."

"Thank you?" He sputtered. "Where is *mine*?"

As if. Leveling her most patronizing mien on him, she said, "Rathbone, you're alive because I've kept you that way. And I don't need my memories to know that. It's common sense."

After a few seconds, he huffed, puffed, and glided to his feet. Neeka exhaled with great relief, *not* dejection.

Motions jerky, he stuffed his legs into a pair of leathers he ripped from a cord and strapped on combat boots. "We can go home as soon as you to cut metal shards from my body. They prevent me from transporting us."

She stood and dressed in the remaining clothes without a care. Yep, no doubt about it. Zero cares. There were plenty of other thousand-eyed fish in the sea.

"Well?" he demanded. "Will you do it?"

With a cheery if brittle smile, she told him, "Slice into you? Happily."

Okay, so, maybe she had a slight care.

He gripped her chin, forcing her to peer up at him. This seemed so familiar. Had they argued like this before?

A memory hovered at the edge of her mind...

With fire and brimstone in his dark irises, he said, "You are the most—" He stopped himself. "If I wasn't—" Again he stopped. His lids slitted anew. His breathing turned choppy.

Her heart pounded against her ribs. "Just say it, whatever it is."

His lips peeled away from his teeth. "I don't know what I want to say," he roared. She *knew* he roared. The vibration traveled over the ground, through her and—wait. Something approached. Something big.

Rathbone must have realized it, too. He released her, his gaze darting.

As if they'd been partners forever, they grabbed as many weapons as possible and pressed against each other, back-to-back. He watched the rear of the cavern, and she observed the mouth. Until a massive boulder fell into the opening. Bye, bye light. Sheets of dust plumed the air, and she coughed.

"I have a prediction." She gagged when the putrid scent of decay assaulted her nose. Another vibration started up, this one a bone-rattler. "We're about to engage in a battle to the death."

12

Expecting Nova to be running like a well-oiled machine, with no problems or disturbances of any kind, Azar appeared in his home world. His strategy was simple. Speak with the warrior he'd left in charge, visit the Hall of Secrets, and learn more about his opponents. Instead, he discovered nothing *but* disturbances.

An unusually large number of soldiers congregated in the foyer, filling the area and surrounding Kanta, the male in charge.

What happened?

"Take your wolves north," the dragon shifter shouted. "Send yours south. Yours east. Yours west. Put your vampires in every room of the catacombs. Set your Amazons loose in the forest."

In that moment, Azar knew. The Underworld king and his oracle had visited.

He grunted. *My mistake.* He'd assumed Rathbone would be as easy to manage as before, when Azar's blessing task had revolved around Lore's original death. Then he'd had only to await the perfect chance to strike—when her husband and protector was busy winning a kingdom. Why wasn't he there now, protecting it?

Azar should've known this go-round would be different. Lore's demise had transformed him as well as Rathbone. Change brought, well, change.

Do not think of the goddess yet. Forget.

"Forget," he echoed. But he forgot nothing. He never had, never would. That was his curse. To see his great shames and mistakes play in Technicolor detail for the rest of eternity.

Kanta noticed him and paused for a beat, momentarily disconcerted. Then the dragon shifter kicked into leadership mode again, completing his litany of orders. When he finished, he joined Azar.

"Tell me," Azar demanded.

Fury grew in him as the other male outlined the events of the invasion. He balled his hands into fists. The oracle had made it inside the Hall of Secrets. What had she learned?

"The blame is mine," Kanta said, raising his chin and squaring his shoulders. "I trusted her word."

"No, you trusted your instincts, and I cannot fault you for it." The shifter possessed the innate talent to detect truth and lies. The fact that Neeka tricked him meant she believed her own lies, or she wielded an ability greater than his. "I, too, made a critical error with the female." Though Azar had already regrown his severed hand, the sting of humiliation had yet to lessen. "Continue on. Alert me when you find their trail." He didn't await a response. Knowing the shifter obeyed without question, Azar marched off.

Anyone in his path moved out of his way fast. He could've flashed to the Hall, but he required the extra minutes of foot travel to prepare himself for what was to come: an onslaught of voices soon to join the others. A permanent part of his life, no matter how terrible.

Had he known he would be forced to kill Lore a second time, he might've done this ages ago.

When he reached the red door, tension gouged him. A strike more crushing than those delivered by any enemy. Considering he and his Astra brothers had fought and conquered every species currently living in Nova, he'd overcome a wealth of powerful foes. Kanta was an excellent example. The shifter was able to torch entire cities in a matter of minutes, summon smoke storms and control others with his voice, and yet, Azar had defeated the male on the field of battle. He might have lost limbs in the process, but he'd still rather do that than this.

Deep breath in. Out. Azar turned the knob and entered the Hall. The flood of voices crashed into him, and he wavered on his feet. Fighting to stand, he crossed from one end of the corridor to the other. He struggled to keep his thoughts centered on Rathbone, Lore, and Neeka and block out the rest of the chatter. The more stalwart his focus, the faster he would draw information featuring the trio.

One whisper merged into another, his ears twitching each time he identified the objects of his study.

I don't care what she's calling herself. That's her. Jezebel the Destroyer. I know it. I served in her temple as a child, and I've never forgotten her wretched face.

As soon as he finishes carving a bone, take it. You'll be unable to destroy even the smallest fragment, so you will sell some and hide others. Convince me you understand your mission.

If he's anything like his father, his greatest strength and weakness are the same—his eyes. Blind him, and you can do whatever you wish to him.

You wed her. Now you own her. Give her the remaining doses at once. If she dies, she dies. If she survives, she'll be able to withstand your fire at last and you can bed her anytime you wish.

She ruined me! Built me up then tore me down. She'll do the same to him. I just have to outlast him.

When he learns about the child—

A hard rap echoed from the walls. Azar jerked and spun toward the source. Clarity came. Someone stood on the other side of the red door. Only Kanta would dare. Meaning Rathbone and Neeka had been found.

Dizzy from information overload, Azar wiped the sweat from his brow and hurried from the enclosure. He tried to blank his mind and failed. What he'd heard...

What was true and what was a lie someone told someone else? What mattered, what didn't? At least he'd recognized two of the voices. The male who'd commanded demons to take the bones and the king who'd considered himself ruined. Erebus, who still lived, and Styx, who didn't.

The tidbit about Jezebel disturbed Azar. Jezebel was a goddess of passion and treachery. A malevolent seducer who left destruction and devastation in her wake. He'd never met her, but he'd certainly heard tales. A lover of legions, a stealer of spouses, and worst of all parasites. After empowering a partner, she syphoned every drop of strength so subtly, they never suspected what had transpired until it was too late.

Was Lore actually Jezebel? She definitely fit the bill.

Deal with the king and his oracle, then figure it out.

Once the block closed behind him, Azar croaked, "Tell me."

"They made it through a starway," Kanta replied, his tone stiff. "You'll find them on Moonides."

"Moonides." He blinked with surprise. "Then they're already dead."

Nothing—no vision, premonition, or warning—could have prepared Neeka for what happened next. As she moved to Rathbone's side, two daggers in hand, a giant white spider with cottony fur, ten yellow eyes, and ten spike-tipped legs creeped over the ceiling in slo-mo. A thick, putrid substance oozed from a mouthful of fangs.

Her wings buzzed with aggression. The creature was something usually only seen in nightmares.

A word drifted through her mind, and she shuddered. "I think this is a zombider."

"It is," Rathbone said when she chanced a glance at his lips.

"If I know me, and I do, I told you not to enter the cave until we figured out a way to kill the disgusting zombider."

"You told me nothing. You passed out."

Oh. Well. "My bad. So. Have you ever fought one of these?" Would her daggers do any damage to such a colossal beast?

"Never. But I've heard of them, and I know a single bite can spread the infection to immortals."

Temporarily, she hoped. Surely their immortality would cleanse them. Uncertainty seared her sternum. "Do me a favor and don't die." Otherwise, she'd be stuck in this world until another flasher showed up.

"Same, oracle. Same."

As if he cared.

The thought must have fueled the memories that waited at the fringe of her mind; finally they pushed front and center, and she gasped. The elixir. Her attempted seduction of Rathbone. The Hall of Secrets. Lore and her disastrous endgame. Everyone Neeka loved dying if something wasn't changed.

Any lingering resentment she harbored toward Rathbone faded. They'd kissed. That lip-lock, brief as it had been, was progress. He might not want to want her, but want her he did. At least periodically.

Lowering, the zombider blocked an entrance to the spacious tunnel that stretched behind it. The only way out. It didn't attack, but paused to look over Neeka and Rathbone, no doubt preparing its dinner menu. First his liver, then her kidney, then a hunk of both their brain matter.

Instinct shouted, *Strike!*

With a war cry, Neeka tossed a dagger.

The blade sank into the creature's eye, and it opened wide its mouth. Releasing a high-pitched shriek? Must be. Rathbone cringed while Neeka's eardrums throbbed.

As dizziness assailed her, two spiked legs swiped through the air at a blurring speed. She went high as Rathbone went low.

Ding, ding, ding. The battle was on. The zombider lunged, attempting another swipe while chomping those fangs at Neeka. The perceived weak link? Irritation guided the launch of her second dagger, cutting through another eye, creating enough of a distraction to allow Rathbone to slice off a spindly leg. The loss didn't slow the beast.

Tiny white bugs scrambled from the wound and jumped on Neeka.

"Ahhh!" she shouted as they skittered over her skin. Pain fogged her vision, but she flung them off and stomped on each. "Drive it back, and I'll go for the bone." Wait. What? There was a bone here?

Her gaze shot to Rathbone. "There's a bone here?" he echoed, grabbing a fiery log from the pit, and advancing on the creature with strikes of his own.

"Oh, yeah. Did I forget to mention that, too?" She followed him, amazed by his skill. The effortless way he alternated between offense and defense. His speed surpassed even the zombider's. When he struck, he struck hard and sure, never missing.

Releasing a series of awful clicks and calls, the creature scurried up and down the rocky walls. Rathbone didn't back off.

Bone, bone, where was the bone? She scanned the darkness. There. As Rathbone fought on, she ducked and dodged and rushed forward until she reached the ledge of an enormous pit.

Down, down, down, she peered, finding thousands of bones in a mammoth pile. All that remained of the creature's former meals. Her stomach twisted. So many pieces. How was she supposed to find Lore's?

Wait. Did she see an outline of the goddess, frantically waving her over?

Neeka almost turned away. What if she pretended she couldn't find anything in this mess? Better yet, what if she destroyed it altogether, ending both the king's and the Astra's quests here and now?

Could she destroy it? Something she'd heard in the Hall probed her recollection…

Realization hit, and she moaned. Dang it! The Song of Life rendered the bones indestructible.

Very well. She'd brought Rathbone here to keep herself in the game, buy time, and re-earn the boon. Maybe fortify his trust in the process. She would stick with her current plan and fetch the clavicle.

Clavicle? That's what she'd found? Neeka dove into the pile and made her way to Lore, who radiated desperation.

The female's mouth moved at top speed, as if she was spewing her sentences. Neeka caught the words *dig deep*. Rather than watch the goddess's lips for clarity, she got busy tossing and burrowing to find the object of her desire. Her wings flapped. Her biceps protested. Running out of options—oh! A clavicle with markings. She snatched it up and began her climb to the top of the pile, dagger at the ready.

Lore remained in place, not following the piece of herself. When Neeka saluted her with a middle finger, the other woman's mask of desperation slipped the slightest bit, revealing a hint of cold hatred.

Well, well, well. The evil monstress lurked in there, after all.

Neeka blew her a kiss and bounded from the pit, more determined to save her world than ever. She catalogued the current situation.

The flames on Rathbone's log had died, so there was nothing to keep the creature at bay. No, the beautiful king was forced to fend off slash after slash, fighting to avoid injury.

"I've got it, so you owe me a boon," Neeka called, waving the clavicle to draw the creature's attention her way. But the zombider spun and swiped at her faster than she expected, catching her off guard. She jumped back, whooshing into the pit once more, losing her grip on her remaining weapon and the bone.

Rathbone raced to shield her as the zombider rushed over. At the last second, the king angled his body, catching that piece of Lore before it clattered into the pile, leaving Neeka to crash. She lost her breath upon impact, stunned her into immobility.

That...that...jerk! She'd lowered her standards and allowed him to kiss her, and this was the thanks she got?

The zombider took advantage of her position, ramming a spike through her shoulder and pinning her down. Oh, the pain! Her back bowed, and she shrieked.

Just as a black film sprouted over her vision, Rathbone cut his way out of the creature's chest. Out of. As if he'd flashed inside it. Guts and other things spilled over Neeka and the pile.

The zombider collapsed on top of her, sinking its fangs into her throat just before releasing its final breath. Another shriek barreled past her lips. No, no, no! Its venom. Her future. No!

Rathbone worked as fast as inhumanly possible, freeing her from the teeth as well as the dead weight. With a gentleness she resented, he collected her in his arms and carted her from the pit. By the time they reached the cave's entrance, where they'd begun, she could see again.

"Let me go," she demanded. When he refused, she beat her fists against his shoulders. How dare he act chivalrous after choosing a stupid bone over her very life.

Tears welled, and she struggled to blink them back.

"Are you crying?" he demanded, gripping her chin. He flinched before glowering. "You stop that immediately!"

"What? Me? Cry?" She hit him harder. "I hope your intestines rot and exit from your mouth! The zombider toxin has obviously affected my eyes. Shut up!"

He laid her down on the blanket, near the fire, still so gentle. Looking her over, he asked, "How do you feel?"

"How do you think I feel?" she snapped. "You're the first one I'm eating when I turn." How long did she have? Was she soon to hunger for living flesh? Would she rot and reek?

"You aren't turning." He scrubbed a hand over his face. "You told me the Phoenix lord injected you with his toxin. How many doses have you received?"

Thinking about slaying her so she'd come back healed? "Only four. Not enough," she grated. "No one has ever made the transition before receiving the tenth dose, so don't you dare kill me. Even if I show signs of zombieism. You can't. Because I'm calling in my boon." It galled her to use it so quickly, and for this, a travesty of injustice he had caused. "You will give me a chance to recover. If you trust nothing else, trust this. Without me, you will never enjoy a true happily-ever-after." Because Lore's shadow monsters would eat him!

"I'm not giving you a chance to recover, I'm demanding you do it." He balled and unballed his hands. "If we can return to my palace, I can aid you. Are you able to remove the metal shards?"

"Oh, I'll remove those shards all right. With pleasure." Never had she looked forward to injuring someone more.

Though her head swam and her stomach pitched, and all she wanted to do was lie back down and curl into a fetal ball, she lumbered to her feet.

Rathbone knelt in front of her and pointed to where he suspected the different pieces of metal were lodged. It took immense effort to concentrate on the task but somehow, she clawed and sliced and dug out the obstacles to her ticket home. Well, not *home* home. Her temporary HQ. The zombider's toxin soon began to heat, cooking her from the inside and out. Reminded her of the Phoenix venom on steroids.

By the time she removed the last shard, sweat soaked her. "There. Done," she said, breathing now a chore. She wiped her bloody hands on his skin. "Let's—" A flash of movement drew her attention to the left. Except, no one had materialized. Had she glimpsed the future? "Someone comes."

A blink and a half later, Azar appeared. Their gazes clashed, and he narrowed his eyes.

Rathbone jumped to his feet while scooping Neeka into his arms.

"She was bitten." The Astra withdrew a dagger. "She dies first."

"Touch her, and I'll make you watch Nova burn." Rathbone teleported Neeka to her bedroom. He laid her upon the comforter, saying, "The Astra won't interrupt your healing. Before we left, I fortified the palace defenses."

"Good for you," she muttered, panting as a wave of pain swept in. She so didn't want him to see her like this. "Now, get out of my room. You've done enough damage for one day."

13

Rathbone remained beside the oracle's bed, guilt a barb in his conscience, slicing into inner wounds he hadn't known he still possessed. They'd been buried too deep. Until now.

You've done enough damage. Words his mother had spewed anytime she'd deigned to visit him. She'd also spouted classics like "you ruin everything" and "why can't you do anything right?"

As a youth, he'd shriveled inside, longing to earn her approval. Not once had he succeeded. Always she'd found fault with his efforts. In turn, he'd lashed out at the servants responsible for his upkeep and quickly became a spoiled terror. Until Hades, Rathbone hadn't received a single word of encouragement or praise from another living soul.

He rubbed his knuckles between his pectorals. With his uncle's help, he'd come to understand the problem had been with Hera, not himself. But Rathbone couldn't blame his mother for his current situation. He alone had hurt Neeka. And he'd hurt her far worse than the zombider. That, he saw so clearly.

He shouldn't care. She was an employee, nothing more. But he cared.

Blood coated her shirt near where she'd been bitten and stabbed. White crust surrounded the punctures, the centers raw and oozing. Her usually vibrant skin dulled. Red rimmed her irises, and blue tinged her lips. Agony etched each lovely feature.

When he'd chosen to save the bone rather than Neeka, he'd been in the heat of battle, acting on old instincts. He might have, perhaps, possibly made a grave error that would haunt him for eternity. Hearing the oracle scream…seeing her writhe in anguish…watching her realize he'd jeopardized her life when he'd had the power to save it…

Rathbone hung his head, an invisible dagger twisting mercilessly in his chest. "What can I do to help you?" he croaked.

"You can leave," she snapped. "I'm not sure how many other ways I can convey the message. Exit. Vanish. Flash onto a pole."

The barb cut ever-deeper. "Forgive me, and I'll double your payday." He would give her anything she desired.

"I don't want double. Now, take your balls and go play with someone else. I won't buy you new ones if I'm forced to break the tiny pair you've got."

He blinked. The one who'd gone toe to toe with the Astra Planeta to score a payday now despised Rathbone so much, she turned down double?

"I'll fetch a healer," he rushed out, an old, familiar desperation taking hold. He didn't wait for her response but flashed to Hades's palace.

The sovereign wasn't in the throne room. Or the war room. Or the barracks. Or his bedroom.

A splash sounded from the bathroom.

Rathbone flashed inside. Hades lounged in the bathtub with a nymph on each arm. The trio hadn't gotten to the main event, but they were gearing up for it. A huge ornate mirror hung directly over them, reflecting even the smallest undulation. *The* mirror. Hades's greatest treasure. A cursed goddess resided behind the glass.

Hades, being Hades, perceived Rathbone's presence and opened one eye, pausing to say, "You stink, and I'm busy."

The females began to gag. "Are those...intestines dangling from your ear?"

They ran from the bath, water sloshing over the rim.

"The oracle requires a healer experienced with zombider bites," he told the male. "Your very best."

Hades arched a brow at him. "That's a tall order. One you'll have to pay for. The usual fee will do."

"Yes, yes. A Spy On the Enemy coupon, to be redeemed at an interval of your choosing." He pushed the words past clenched teeth. Rathbone might be family, but that didn't mean he received a discount.

"I'll have the good doc sent to your front door in—"

"Now," he interjected.

Another sigh. "Now," Hades agreed. "You've grown into an annoying adult. Anyone ever tell you that?"

"Often. Hurry." Already impatient, Rathbone flashed to his palace's entryway. He counted the seconds. When no one appeared at the fifteen second mark, he geared up to return to Hades. With knives. Just before he acted, the healer arrived. A fae with a medical bag in hand and a note pinned to his tunic. That note read, *You owe me. H.*

Not bothering with a discussion, Rathbone flashed the male to Neeka. She hadn't left the bed, and her condition had worsened. A white cottony substance rimmed her mouth. Her eyes were fully bloodshot.

"I told you to leave," she shrieked, thrashing atop the mattress. "Why are you still here? I want you out! The other guy can stay, though." She released a hollow laugh. "You brought drugs, right?"

"What happened?" The fae set the bag at the foot of the bed and dug inside.

"Zombider bite," Rathbone grated.

The healer reared back, the bag falling to the floor, the contents spilling out. "You must chain her, or we must leave. If she bites us—"

"She won't," Neeka snapped. "Unlike foolish kings, I prefer quality to quantity."

Rathbone took the insult as his due and nodded, echoing, "She won't. Now, make her feel better."

Terror radiated from the paling healer. "She'll either expunge the toxin or she won't. We'll know the answer by nightfall. But we shouldn't be here. We should leave."

"Make her. Feel better. Now." Rathbone rolled his shoulders, adapting a battlefield stance. "Her bite isn't the ending you should fear."

"Y-yes. Better." Agitated and jumpy, the fae inched toward the bed once more. He gathered his scattered medications, then selected a syringe and a vial of gray liquid. Took several tries to make the needle sink past the vial's cap, but he succeeded.

His trembling intensified the closer he got to Neeka. He stuck her in the arm as quickly as possible, leaping back when she hissed at him.

"Nothing's happening," she burst out, slurring the words. "I don't...you can't... don't you dare look at me, Rath..." Her lids slid shut, her head lulling to the side. Her body went lax.

A small bud of relief flowered. Asleep, she felt no pain.

Rathbone drew in a heavy breath. She'd wanted him to leave. Fine. But he would return.

"You will wait in the room next door," he told the fae. "If she wakes, you will administer another dose. And just so you know, I'll sense each time you enter. Harm her in the slightest way—I suggest you do not harm her. Your treatment is tied to hers." He deposited the male in the other room, then flashed to his private bathroom for a shower.

As the scorching water poured over him, washing away evidence of the battle, his thoughts remained on Neeka. He was responsible for her condition. The fact that he'd let her get hurt after he'd pinned her to the blanket and ravaged her mouth for a too-short stolen moment...

After the staggering sense of finding a key to his lock...

After she'd bantered with him in a candid exchange, letting layers of sarcasm and flippant disregard peel away to reveal her vulnerable core, revealing her inner turmoil...

Just as his mother left him with festering wounds, her mother inflicted irreparable harm. Neeka had trusted him with the knowledge. *And with a single decision, I rejected her.*

The guilt shredded him. He needed to make it up to her, but would she let him? She must. She wanted him. Badly.

She might hate him now, but she'd been unable to get enough of him before. He hadn't forgotten the swift increase of her heartbeat, or the shallowness of her breaths. Or the fever flush that had radiated from her skin. Or how the sight and feel of her had elicited such intense desire, he'd felt drunk with it.

From the second their lips met, pleasure had frayed any semblance of self-control. How he'd managed to gather the strength to stop the kiss, he wasn't sure. Now, that uncertainty haunted him. He shouldn't feel this strongly for anyone but Lore. That he did...

What did it mean?

Rathbone emerged from the shower stall, dried off, and dressed in a clean pair of leathers. He retrieved the clavicle and flashed to the secret throne room, where Lore paced beside her throne, waiting for him.

For the first time, he wasn't hit with a punch of frenzied lust at the sight of her. Because he was already frenzied by another female?

"There you are," she said, and promptly burst into tears.

"No crying," he said, doing his best to school his annoyance. Before their separation, even days ago, her upset had gutted him. Now he wished only to return to his oracle and never, ever see *her* cry again. "I come with a gift." He held up the clavicle, showing the goddess the treasure as he approached.

She barely acknowledged the offering. "I can't *not* cry. I'm so afraid you've tired of waiting for me and chosen another female as your forever queen. Tell me you haven't."

He worked his jaw. Did Lore care nothing about the price paid to retrieve this newest bone? No appreciation for the efforts made on her behalf?

"How can you think this?" he demanded. "Much has been lost for you."

"Did the harpy not inform you?" She wrapped her arms around her middle. "I was there in the pit. I saw the horror on your face when she was bitten."

Neeka hadn't told him of the encounter, no. But then, she'd been a little too busy trying to survive. "I thought you must remain near the skull."

"Not anymore. I'm strong enough to latch onto any bone." Gliding closer, she added, "About the oracle."

"Why does my relationship with her concern you? You have always encouraged me to keep a stable." Unlike Neeka, who would insist he dismantle it permanently.

Despite the harshness of his tone, Lore dried her tears and offered him a shaky smile. "That's right. I have." She wiped the moisture from her cheeks with swift swipes. "You are the most wonderful male in existence, and your happiness matters more to me than anything."

So different from the criticisms he'd heard from Hera, and now Neeka. He should thank Lore for always seeing the best in him.

"Is she one of your lovers?" Lore asked, peeking at him from beneath her lashes.

"She isn't." But she could've been. Rather than snap the bone into place, he shoved it into his pocket with a little too much force. "She's the oracle I hired to help me put you back together."

"Because you love me," Lore said, rewarding him with a smile.

"Yes," he rasped. And yet...

What was this strange emotion working through the innermost passages in his mind? With a harsher tone than intended, he said, "I will be disbanding the stable, never to reopen." He pulled the trigger, then and there. With or without Lore's approval, he was done spending himself with concubines. "I'm willing to flash there now. With the bone in my pocket, you can follow me and bear witness."

Her smile fell. "Why would you do this? Darling, there's no cause for such a drastic measure. I know you're a god in his prime, and you have needs. And I delight when you delight, so of course I want you to be with whomever you wish, whenever you wish it. Except the oracle. There's something about her. I think she secretly plots against us."

He pressed his tongue to the roof of his mouth. "Her, I keep. She's the first being to aid my quest."

New tears gathered at the corners of Lore's eyes. Her bottom lip bowed in a pout. "You're upset with me."

Yes, he was, but he didn't know why. So she had no problem sharing him. So what? There were worse problems.

"I'm sorry," she rushed out. "It's just so hard, being trapped in this form. Especially when I believe the oracle hopes to win you away from me for nefarious reasons, and I yearn only to protect you."

His brain provided a mental picture of the female in question doing as accused and attempting to win his affections. He saw Neeka, naked in bed, beckoning him closer. The female equivalent of lightning in a bottle.

Every muscle in his body hardened, and guilt stabbed him anew. "Only three bones are needed." The words were minced against his teeth. "You'll be in my arms soon." Then, his confusion would end. Surely.

Gliding closer, she reached for him the way she used to do. Though her fingers ghosted through him, she remained at his side, petting his chest. "There's nothing I desire more than becoming tangible and being with you. I've missed you so much, my love. More than I can ever express." All silk and velvet, she purred into his ear. "Why don't you sit in your throne while I list everything I adore about you, hmm?"

Something she'd done many times in the past. Today, he had no interest. Curiosity was blooming. "Come. Behold." He flashed to the sitting room with his portraits.

Lore appeared a second later. She gazed around and gasped. "Who dared disrespect you in such a manner?"

Well. Not the reaction he'd anticipated.

"There's something else," he muttered. He flashed to his bedroom, and once again, she appeared seconds later. "What do you notice in here?"

She peered here and there, then smiled at him. "This is beautiful, and I'm excited to share it with you." Gliding forward with the grace of a gazelle, she soared through the open doors that led to the balcony. The soft, smoky breeze from the River Styx blew in, scenting the air with burning sandalwood. "I'll love being out here with you, showcasing our love to the world."

"A circumstance I have envisioned many times," he intoned. Just not lately.

Her smile faded and she returned to him. "You're still upset with me?"

"No." He didn't know what he was. Disillusioned, perhaps?

Did they have anything in common? "Come." He teleported to the throne room and snapped the bone in place.

She appeared at his side, smiling again. "Will you sit and allow me to share my list now?"

Perhaps this was what he—they—needed. Intimacy. Connection. Fighting his longing to check on Neeka, whose room was above him, just to the right, he eased into his chair and gripped the armrests.

As Lore gazed at him dreamily, waxing poetic about his accomplishments, reminding him of the charming, sexy goddess he'd first married, his gaze cut to the ceiling. He struggled to sit still.

If Neeka failed to recover...

His entire body jerked at the thought. She would recover. No other outcome was acceptable.

Neeka awoke with a gasp. She sprawled in a ginormous bed, soaked in sweat but no longer burning up. Memories rose to the surface like bubbles in champagne, relief merging with anger. She'd survived the zombider toxin, no thanks to Rathbone, who had believed her when she'd spouted all that nonsense about wanting to be alone and actually left her alone. At least at first. How dare he!

The "healer" had merely raced in a few times, injected her with a sedative while begging her to recover, and raced out. Thankfully, the worst of her anguish had faded to a dull ache. Even better, the urge to munch on living flesh had vanished entirely.

A quick scan of the chamber proved she was riding solo. No healer, and no King of Agonies, the male who cared nothing for her well-being and everything for his results.

Well, dang. Her anger just brutally murdered her relief. Was he with Lore even now, thrilling over his newest acquisition? The one his nonprecious oracle almost died for?

Neeka pursed her lips. Well, no matter. This girl needed to get to work. She had harpies to rescue and all. The faster she fulfilled her mission, the sooner she could rid herself of the royal thorn in her side.

She eased into an upright position and rotated, letting her feet hang over the bed. Shadows crept behind the large bay window, heralding the arrival of night. The perfect opportunity to shine. She stood on trembly legs. Not yet ready for another visit from Dr. Jab Happy, she snuck to the bathroom on her tiptoes, turned the water to its hottest setting and stripped.

When her attention landed on her naked reflection in the full-length mirror, she cringed. Then she frowned. A series of words covered her body. "What did I write?"

"The elixir recipe," Reflection responded.

Oh! "I'm brilliant."

"Agreed."

She read the ingredients, details snapping into place.

Drops of Deadpool—water from the Azure Isles.

Ground dirt snakes—tree roots from Etheria.

PB&J eggs—seeds from a nest of bonded mythical birds in Warslasea.

Fried Lot Us—the ashes of a special lotus flower found only in Atrichi.

Arrowhead—the tip of an arrow once shot by Eros. Something she'd collected years ago, for reasons she hadn't understood until now. But, um, how was she supposed to acquire the rest of the items without alerting Rathbone to her purpose?

Mind whirling, Neeka blew her reflection a kiss and entered the spray of water. Though she meant to get in and out, the wet heat felt too amazing to ditch. As she scrubbed from top to bottom—thrice!—her bad mood evaporated, clarity whooshing to the rescue.

What was she doing, pouting? Had he broken her brain with his kiss before putting her life in danger? Yes. But she'd expected too much too fast from him. *Of course* Rathbone had chosen Lore. The goddess had spent more than a year with him, Neeka only days. And, really, she'd only just begun her seduction.

Conquests of any kind required extended time and repeated effort, especially when your skills were as rusty as hers.

Would she punish him for his stupidity? Absolutely. Plus interest. As any sane harpy would. But she also understood. And he *had* aided her recovery, despite her earlier refusal to admit it. He'd tried, anyway. He'd entered her bedroom anytime the healer had and stayed until she'd fallen into a drugged stupor. Those visits had been her favorite. He'd always traced his fingertips over her brow before he'd left. That was just as groundbreaking as the kiss. If not more so!

Spirits lighter, she lumbered from the enclosure. After toweling off, she entered the closet and picked through the garments she'd pilfered and stocked day one in the palace.

Today she required the perfect outfit for reupping a seduction. Maybe a halter top and jeans?

A scowling Taliyah appeared in front of her as she finished dressing. "You've got some serious explaining to do, young lady."

The sight of her friend caught her off guard. Gasping, wings flapping, she took a step toward the General. Well, the General's spirit, anyway, judging by the transparency of her form. Chains bound her wrists. Wait. The war! Neeka stilled.

"Are you role playing with Roc again?" she asked, feigning nonchalance. *Please don't hate me.*

Taliyah's pupils pulsed, expanding and contracting like a heartbeat. "Your new best friend has a mystical barricade around his kingdom not even the Astra can bypass—yet."

New best friend? Ha! "But you did it because you're stronger than them. Congrats! He's not my friend, best or otherwise, by the way. He's my current employer." And target.

Pulling unsuccessfully at the cuffs, her friend snarled, "Then you had better quit and hire on with me. The Astra are ready to take your head, and honestly, I'm not sure how much longer I can hold them off."

So, so badly Neeka wanted to share what she knew. This amazing woman had fought by her side for centuries, guarding her back, acting as her ears, too stubborn to buy into a cursed moniker. The mighty Taliyah had loved and supported her through thick and thin. But. In this case, sharing wasn't caring. Neeka's instinct hadn't altered. Now wasn't the juncture to spill; she'd do more harm than good. Besides, to succeed in her quest, she needed Rathbone's trust. The barest hint of betrayal could cost everyone everything.

She forced herself to shrug, even as the deepest parts of her cried, *Trust me.* "Well, keep at it and I'll consider thinking about giving you a cut of my earnings."

As Taliyah sputtered, an alert pinged in Neeka. She sensed the arrival of another intruder but...no one appeared. Wait. She'd never noticed the owl figurine on the shelf.

Like the stuffed teddy bear she'd thrown into the fire, it seemed to peer straight into her soul. Another hidden camera? Or was she missing something? In any case, this proved she must remain in character. Aka a greedy wench devoted to a payday. Even if she lost her only friend. Here and now, there was no way to comfort the other woman. To aid the Astra meant allowing Lore to be resurrected, and that Neeka couldn't do.

She swallowed the lump growing in her throat. Maybe this was the real curse of her moniker. Tasting friendship and losing it.

"What is he paying you?" Taliyah demanded.

"He offered double, but after our most recent adventure, I'm not settling for anything less than triple."

"Triple of what?" her friend said, pushing the question past clenched teeth. "Because I'll triple *that.*"

"Sorry, Tal, but I prefer being on the winning team." Her own.

Uh, had the porcelain owl just expanded its chest?

"Have you forgotten what's at stake?" Taliyah prowled two steps closer. "If a single Astra loses a blessing task, all Astra are cursed. Harpykind will share their fate!"

"Not true. The Astra will be cursed to lose every battle, yes, but harpies won't. We can act as their protectors and fight their battles for them." That would mean going head-to-head with Erebus, who would ascend, gaining more power, but so what? They'd overcome worse odds.

Yeah, she was digging this idea more and more.

"Tell me what you've seen of our future, at least," Taliyah demanded.

This, Neeka could do. In part. With a heaviness of heart she didn't even try to hide, she said, "Death. Lots and lots of death."

14

A male determined, Rathbone knocked on Neeka's bedroom door. He'd come to her with a foolproof plan lacking only a few minor details. Smooth things over with extravagant gifts stop getting hard at the mere sight of her, and find the remaining bones. It was the only honorable thing to do.

Honor wasn't something he normally aspired to achieve, but he was a desperate male willing to do desperate things to shed this wretched guilt. Plus, he owed her much. Regardless of his actions inside that cave, she continued to prove herself his staunchest ally.

Last night, when he'd perceived the harpy General's arrival, he'd flashed to the oracle, leaving Lore behind midsentence. Seeing Neeka up and well had flooded him with intense relief. When she'd chosen him over her best friend and allies, well, that relief had transformed into hope. She'd done it for payment, yes, but also, possibly, affection?

Just because Lore returned didn't mean Neeka's service to Rathbone had to end. He planned to unleash his wrath upon the Astra, and he would need an oracle. Yes, the Astra would be destined to lose every battle, making war a breeze. But as humans said, better safe than sorry.

Hinges whined as the door swung open. He braced. How would Neeka react to him?

How would *he* react to her?

His thoughts blanked. Sunlight turned her into a flawless tapestry of delights. Skin like dark silk. Eyes as pure as amber, outlined with kohl. Lips plumper and redder than cherries. Scent sweeter than usual.

"Yes? May I help you?" she asked. She'd changed clothes. Out of the halter and jeans and into comfy pajamas.

Muscles hardened, and blood burned. "We shall hang out, and you will get to know me better." Something she'd been eager to do to speed things along. "I have goodies to give you."

She canted her head, suspicious. "What kind of goodies?"

"The best kind." He clasped her hand, and teleported her to the dining room, where he'd arranged a feast. "You have earned every morsel. Enjoy."

"And the jewelry?" she asked, agog.

The reaction pleased him. He waved to encompass the array of dummies where pieces he'd acquired throughout the ages. "All yours. I'll have them delivered to your room after we—" she already zoomed over and collected several, securing them around her neck faster than a blink "—dine."

She opened her mouth to respond, then caught sight of the spread. Her eyes rounded. He'd gotten rid of anything sweet or fried and covered the table with vegetable and fruit dishes from the mortal world, Harpina, and his own kingdom. Some vegetables were cooked in butter, others in cream or broth or spices. Some were raw. The fruits were either boiled and mashed, mixed, or sliced and drenched in their own juices. He'd stood in front of the enchanted refrigerator for hours, different vegetarian cookbooks in hand. Not something he'd ever expected to do.

Appearing dazed, she tripped to the table, swiped up a carrot and bit into the end. Her eyes slid shut, rapture softening her features.

His muscles got harder, and his blood burned hotter. Perhaps she'd forgiven him?

"Go ahead," she said, motioning to him. "Do it."

"Do what?"

"Apologize." Peering at him with innocent expectation, she chomped another bite of carrot. "You're working up to it, but because I'm feeling so magnanimous, I thought I'd save you the agony of indecision and get us to the finish line so we can enjoy our meal. I mean, you did go to all this trouble so... Do it."

He pursed his lips. Rathbone had a lifetime policy: never admit to wrongdoing. Regret gave the other person power over you, providing directions to a wound they could poke and prod at their convenience. A lesson his mother had taught him well. But.

"I am sorry," he grated, expecting the words to taste foul. He blinked with surprise. They tasted right. He *was* sorry. Sorry she'd suffered. Sorry he'd endangered her life. Sorry he'd lost the easy camaraderie that had developed between them. "I'm sorry," he repeated. Much easier to say that time. "I am. I'm sorry. Very, very sorry."

"All right. I accept. Our beef is officially over."

He marveled as Neeka busied herself with the food, tasting everything and moaning. She'd truly forgiven him.

After she scooped her favorite dishes onto a plate and sat at the head of the table, he loaded a plate with the same items she'd selected and claimed the seat at her right.

Though he preferred meats and sweets, the first bite of something green wasn't terrible. "Did the healer aid you to your satisfaction or shall I kill him before I return him to Hades?"

"You borrowed him from the King of the Dead?" she asked.

"Borrowed implies I utilized his services free of charge. I assure you, I'll pay dearly."

She winced at him. "That sounds like a you problem. In case it wasn't clear, expenses never come out of my check."

He snorted. "I wouldn't dare."

Posture softening, she speared an apple wedge with her fork. "You said I could get to know you better. So. What do you admire most about Lore?"

"I will tell you." Reluctantly. "But in turn, you will answer questions for me." And he would absolutely, positively limit his questions to Neeka's process as an oracle. He was certain of it. Determined. Unwavering. "Do you agree?"

"Sure." Smiling, smirking really, she informed him, "I've now answered your first question, so you owe me an answer."

He would've laughed if his guts hadn't clenched. She was a female assured of her power yet still so soft and...he liked it. "I favored her gentle nature."

"Favored. Past tense?" Neeka asked, a brow arched. "Do you prefer something else nowadays? FYI, this is just an extension of my first question, so it doesn't count."

He pursed his lips, unsure how to respond. Yes, he still fancied Lore's gentle nature. But... His grip tightened on his silverware. Her lack of interest in monogamy bothered him. "As a child, I dreamed of experiencing such gentleness from another."

"Excellent misdirection, Your Majesty." Neeka saluted him with a glass of pineapple juice. "A wonderful way to avoid the subject you don't wish to discuss. Now I'm super curious about your childhood. Actually, I've been curious about your childhood ever since I learned we both have mommy issues."

Was that what he'd done? Misdirect? Or did some part of him hope to share the deepest aspects of his life and help her understand why he was how he was? No, that couldn't be it. He'd never desired to do such an irrational thing. Not even with Lore.

He tried to recall what kind of childhood the goddess had, but he wasn't sure they'd ever discussed it.

"Ask me whatever you desire—when it's your turn." He blinked as his words registered. That wasn't what he'd intended to say. Was it? He'd meant to guide Neeka to another line of thought. Yes? "Describe the characteristics of your desired kingdom." Again, not what he'd intended to say.

She deliberated for a moment and sighed. "I'm not sure what I want, honestly. I just know I'm supposed to rule someplace somewhere at some point." Moving corn kernels around her plate, she said, "It's probably a know-it-when-I-see-it situation. That's what happened after I got married and entered Phoenixia."

"Perhaps you can change things to suit your tastes after I take care of your ex. Free of charge," he offered and blinked. Had he actually spoken those three little words aloud? When she intended to demand triple his original payment?

No need to ponder his answer. Yes. Free of charge. Because Rathbone enjoyed her. She amused him. And frustrated him. But even still, some deep, hidden part of him needed to see her happy. This had nothing to do with nullifying the lord's claim on the oracle. Nothing at all.

"You already promised to murder my enemies as part of my payment," she said.

"Ah, but I'll keep killing this one until he stops rising."

"Really?" Neeka beamed at him, and Rathbone barely stopped himself from preening. "And what will you do if I pick your kingdom instead and give you the boot?"

"Wage war to win it back," he replied without heat. "I believe you intended to ask me about my childhood."

Neeka waved her fork in his direction. "You're doing this on purpose, aren't you? Hooking me with multiple lures to, what? Divide my focus? Well, it's working, you dirty sneak. I'm unsure which bait to gobble. No, you know what? I'm going with the childhood. Tell me everything!"

Her enthusiasm nearly drew a smile from him. "I was born in the heavens, my father a personal guard to Hera, who is my mother."

"Seriously?" The oracle popped a grape into her mouth. "This story just got more riveting. Do go on." She didn't say anything else upon discovering his link to a royal Greek, just shoveled more food into her mouth as if too captivated to risk a change of his mind.

"She kept me in a private realm, hidden from Zeus. Upon occasion, she visited me." The best and worst days of his existence. He remembered watching her with the mátia, longing for her to see something good in him. To praise him. To hold him. But she'd only ever found fault.

Why aren't you as fast as your father?
You aren't worth the trouble you've caused.
How I rue the day I conceived you.

"She wasn't fond of me." A muscle jumped in his jaw. "I trained to become her guard, but she was taken captive soon after my eighth birthday. A year later, Hades learned of my existence and came for me."

Sympathy softened Neeka's lovely features. "I'm sorry," she told him with a tone just as soft. "Well, I like young Rathbone already."

"What were you like as a child?"

"Sickly. The reason my mother disliked me from the beginning. Honestly, I think she latched onto the first excuse to execute me."

Needing to touch her, he slid a knuckle along her jaw. "Harpy children experience illness?"

"Not usually, but sometimes the different mix of species takes time to harmonize."

"Look at you now. Perfectly harmonized."

Neeka gifted him with a soft smile and leaned into his touch. The heat of her skin sent arcs of electricity through him.

"I once heard someone say parents know how to push our buttons because they're the ones who sewed them on," she said. "That might be why I prefer zippers."

He snorted, then frowned. A snort? From him? Amid such a serious topic?

Confused—not vulnerable, never vulnerable—he focused on the meal, eating the fruit off his plate. But every bite settled with the finesse of a lead ball. He thought the same might be true for her. She no longer ate with gusto but stared down at the remaining morsels.

He shouldn't have initiated this conversation. Something else had shifted between them. Something major. He just didn't know what it was or what it meant.

He—sensed a presence. "We're about to receive a visitor," Rathbone informed her, jumping to his feet. His chair slid behind him, scraping over the floor.

Neeka stood as well, clutching daggers he hadn't known she carried. Impressive.

Between one blink and the next, Erebus appeared in the doorway of the dining room, his spirit bound by chains once more.

"Enemy!" the oracle shouted, her adorable wings accelerating to warp speed.

"No need to attack," the god said with a patient smile. "I'm not staying long. Just thought you'd like to know the Astra have hired the Unwanted's mother to search for the remaining bones. She's homing in on one now."

Neeka went still and pale. "They did what now?"

Rathbone stiffened. "Anything else?"

"Oh, just a minor detail, nothing to concern your pretty head with," the god added, his tone casual. "But in less than an hour, the warlords will breach your new defenses and steal Lore."

15

Well. Talk about a mood ruiner. Neeka waited for Erebus to vanish before concentrating on Rathbone. Only seconds ago, her surprisingly nuanced king had displayed such heart-wrenching vulnerability, and yes, okay, he'd somehow cut her defenses like a hot knife through butter, reaching her ooey, gooey center. How she'd yearned to hug the boy he'd been and praise the man he'd become. Strong and determined. A warrior to his core.

Now? That warrior was not happy. Fury glittered in his irises. "You are my oracle," he said, a muscle jumping in his jaw. "Did he speak true?"

"Unfortunately, my senses indicate he did." Erebus lived to screw over the Astra. Allowing the nine to hijack Lore wasn't an option for him *or* Neeka. "Let's grab the goddess and hit the bricks."

Rathbone balled his hands. "I cannot just grab her. She's mystically bound to the throne, and the throne is mystically bound to the floor."

"Then we'll take the entire floor with us, buying me enough time to figure out a better solution." Neeka would tap into every brain cell and premonition she possessed.

He hesitated before offering a clipped nod. "Come. I wish to check the barricades I have in place to understand how they're going to do what they do so it never happens again."

He took her hand without waiting for a response. Blink. Suddenly they stood before a starway atop a snowcapped mountain. He stepped through it, tugging her behind him. They entered a—huh. A duplicate of his kingdom? They stood in the exact same spot as before but...not.

Her gaze darted from one terror to another. From this vantage point, she could see the entire realm. A ring of eternal fire acted as a boundary fence. The first obstacle to overcome. If someone managed to survive the flames, they'd come to a circle of slithering, thorny branches and snapping vines. Many immortals had perished there, their remains dangling from limbs. And just beyond that was a bubbling mote of acid where a school of monstrous fish swam.

If anyone managed to survive all that, there was a seemingly bottomless chasm to cross, a maze with disfigured dragon-like creatures lying in wait. No, not dragons. Gargoyles. A horrifying species she'd considered extinct.

Neeka's wings whirred as she recalled the occasion she and Taliyah had fought off an entire pack. They'd torn off two of her limbs and turned half of her organs into stone.

A cold rush of wind wrenched her from her thoughts. Locks of hair danced through the air. Hooking the strands behind her ears, she glided her gaze up Rathbone's body to read his lips. Maybe he'd already given the answer to her question, maybe not.

Her heartbeat thumped when she noted the mátia staring at her. Others scanned their surroundings. "What is this place?"

"The spiritual heart of the Kingdom of Agonies. And me."

His heart too? "One cannot exist without the other?"

"That's how every immortal kingdom operate. The word itself means a king's dominion, after all."

"But this...how are these defenses here, like this?" Why hadn't she seen them outside this otherworldly arena?

"As a man thinketh, so is he," he muttered, tightening his grip on her hand, as if he feared she would attempt to pull free.

Did he, maybe, derive comfort from her nearness, the way she derived comfort from his? Neeka inched even closer to him, until they pressed side by side. His heat enveloped her, blocking the chill. His scent filled her nose, fogging her head, making her too intoxicated to resist the urge to rest her head on his shoulder.

"Are you telling me you brought all this to life with your imagination?" She waved her free hand to encompass the entire horrorscape, that was part of him, the male. Why didn't the idea alarm her?

His chest puffed up the slightest bit. "I am, and I did. Anyone who attempts to enter physically must overcome every challenge, though they cannot see them. Those who flash are caught in a mystical trap." He pointed to the flames. No, to a spot above the flames, where the air shimmered with a glittering, jelly-like substance. "They are bound with chains when they pass through there."

Wow. The power Rathbone wielded, to create and fuel such magnificent defenses. Now she knew why Erebus and Taliyah had arrived bound.

Wait. "Do you sense every entry?" she asked.

"I do."

Well, well, well. Rathbone had absolutely, positively clocked Taliyah's arrival. Which meant he had absolutely, positively spied on Neeka via the owl figurine.

Tricky king. Could he get any cuter? Better question: Did he realize he'd lowered his head to nuzzle her cheek?

Uh-oh. She was nuzzling him right back. *Focus.* How would

the Astra come? Spiritually or physically? Maybe if she invented a brand-new obstacle?

Rathbone inhaled sharply and pointed. "They are here."

Neeka followed the line of his finger and swallowed a curse. Sure enough, the Astra gathered outside the ring of fire. All nine, decked for war. Spread out in a straight line, they wore huge helmets that caged their faces in teeth and fangs. Leather straps crisscrossed over muscular chests. Weapons abounded.

Radiating unshakable determination, they angled their stances to look up at her and Rathbone. Oh, yeah. They would totally bypass the barrier within the hour.

Her breath caught when Azar stepped forward, approaching the flames. He entered without pause. The others followed. Their helmets and clothing burned first. Then their skin bubbled, melting. Charring. Not once did they slow their gait. No, they continued gliding forward. Muscles and organs turned to ash until only bone remained. And still they kept walking. When their bones burned away, the particles blew backward, reforming outside the fire as fully healed—and madder—Astra.

They did it again and again, advancing a little farther each instance. No matter what pain they suffered, they refused to back down.

Though a hint of a solution teased her, Neeka couldn't quite grasp it. "Are we done here?"

Her companion didn't hesitate. Within a split second, they reached the throne room. Spirit Lore reclined in Rathbone's throne, drumming her fingers against the arms. The second the goddess spotted them, she vaulted to her feet. When she noticed the hand hold, she narrowed her eyes. Just for a moment. In a blink, she displayed only concern.

"Something has happened," she proclaimed softly, fluttering delicate fingers to her throat as she closed the distance. She took up residence beside Rathbone. "Azar comes for me, yes?"

"Yes."

Chest tightening, Neeka released him. During their meal, he'd shared bits and pieces of his past, comforted her as she shared some of hers, and kept her enraptured by his charm. How would he treat her in front of his queen?

"There's no need to fear," he instructed. He didn't reach for the goddess, at least. A thrill and a surprise. "I'm promised a solution."

Right. Neeka's cue. She had a sisterhood to save. Her new objective: Hide the bones from the Astra for good. If she could hide them from Rathbone, too, even better.

"Give me a few minutes to think." Neeka sprang into a swift pace, attempting to spark a vision. If she could see the end from the beginning, she could figure out how to get there. A trick that sometimes worked. Today? Not a blip.

Maybe she was still in recovery mode?

Argh! What she wouldn't give to stuff the goddess in her pocket and move on.

Hey! That wasn't a bad idea, actually. And it was doable. There was a harpy named Downsize Daisy. A loner who charged an exorbitant amount to morph an ex-boyfriend into a pint-size pocket rocket. The best revenge in town. Didn't Neeka have a gift certificate to redeem?

Could Daisy shrink the throne, with the floor attached? A big question in need of an immediate answer.

No doubt Neeka's request would be met with a stanch refusal, considering she was known as a traitor and all. To save harpykind, however, she was especially motivated to change the girl's mind.

"Okay, I have a plan," she announced, fixing her attention on Rathbone. "As previously suggested, you'll flash the throne and floor to a new location. A temporary fix. Once Mistress Skeletoria is secure, I have something more permanent in mind. To facilitate this, I need you to fetch a harpy, a second skeleton, a piece of paper, and a pen."

He fixed his attention on Neeka in turn, as if the glowering Lore no longer existed. "The Astra will never believe a common set of bones is—"

"Oh ye of little faith. I'm not going to trick them into believing the fake is Lore," Neeka interjected. "I can explain the plan and run out the clock, or you can help prevent a disaster. Please trust me when I say these supplies are absolutely mission critical."

He gave a stiff nod. "Very well. Will any harpy do?"

"Bring me the one known as Downsize Daisy. She's in Harpina…somewhere. Whatever you do, don't look her in the eyes while she's mad. Now go. Tick tock, tick tock." She gave the king a little shove. "Okay, bye."

He was frowning as he teleported, but still snubbing the goddess.

Lore's air of concern dissolved. "You won't steal him from me. He's mine."

"Is he though?" She hadn't forgotten the stardust Azar would leave on the goddess's skin.

The goddess notched her chin, a cold smile spreading. "Go ahead. Ask him."

What a snake! "You are rotten to the core, and he's not a fool. Not always."

"Darling, don't kid yourself. You hope he grows to hate me because you want him for yourself. You'd do anything to win him for yourself. But let's be honest. No one keeps the Unwanted for long."

Neeka flinched, every word a bullet. Win Rathbone for, like, forever? Hardly. Sure, she would never forget the incredible feel of his hard-won strength, demanding her body mold to his. And yes, she kind of loved the way his mátia watched her, as if there was no one else worth seeing. She also greatly enjoyed his scent. And his thoughtfulness. He'd provided a scrumptious meal without prodding. And okay, fine, she still admired his loyalty. If he hadn't been gaga for a dead woman, Neeka might have climbed aboard the Rathboner Express. But none of that meant she sought a happily-ever-after with the guy.

"You underestimate my appeal," she grated.

"And you overestimate it." Satisfaction glimmered in the goddess's crystalline eyes.

Pleased she'd struck a nerve? Hoping to shred Neeka's self-confidence so she'd back down? Ha! It was a trick as old as time, and good ole Neeks wasn't falling for it.

She levelled her shoulders and raised her chin. The King of Agonies didn't deserve to be saddled with this hideous creature. Starting today, Neeka would be cranking up the heat. Tomorrow, after this present danger passed, she would begin fetching the ingredients for the elixir. Breaking his tie to this monstress had just jumped to the top of her priorities list.

"I will take immense delight in luring him away from you. I'm already halfway to the finish line," she boasted. "He *loves* kissing me." He must. He'd practically eaten her face.

With a hiss, Lore jabbed a sharp nail in her chest. "You shouldn't cross me, oracle. You may see the future, but I control the will of my males. The slightest suggestion can make Rathbone your greatest enemy. He'll do to you what he did to the former king. Oversee the annihilation of everything you love."

"Joke's on you. He and I already agreed to that."

The other woman floundered for a response. Not used to being thwarted?

"Enjoy your last days with him, oracle. Your misery is assured."

Rathbone materialized with a screeching, bound, and blindfolded harpy in one arm, and a plastic skeleton in the other. He held the notepad and pen between his teeth. Wounds peppered his face, torso, and arms, each in the process of healing.

He looked between Lore and Neeka, and spit out both objects. "Why are you upset?"

Lore spoke up first. "The oracle admitted she intends to steal you from me by any means necessary." Pale and trembling, Lore wrapped her arms around herself, pretending to be frightened. "She's cruel, Rathbone. I can't be in her presence."

"Then leave," he stated, his tone unbending. "We'll handle things."

He defends me? To hide a wild surge of pleasure, Neeka busied herself with collecting the notepad and pen. She couldn't stop a peep at the goddess to gauge her reaction.

Lore dropped her jaw. "You allow an employee to disrespect your wife? Are you sure that's wise, my darling? While I recognize your incomparable strength, I worry your enemies will assume you're weak."

He narrowed his gaze, saying to Neeka. "Hurry along."

Not going to respond to Lore's insinuation? Was that good? Bad?

"Hey, Daisy," she said, focusing on what mattered. "Glad you could make it to our party. Listen, the big guy is gonna set you down. Don't try to psychokinesis us, all right? Instinct suggests we're going to be great friends, you and I. Plus, when we reach our next destination, I'll be making you an offer you can't refuse." Yes, she'd borrowed the phrasing from Rathbone. Why mess with a classic?

Daisy stopped fighting. Progress!

Neeka reached out and squeezed the king's shoulder, saying, "Put the skeleton on the larger throne, and be thinking of a safe place to flash a floor this size."

"I have decided on a spot already."

The second Rathbone released the harpy, she ripped off the blindfold, revealing narrowed brown eyes. "Why am I here?"

"We'll get to that." Neeka followed Rathbone up the dais. Once the fake skeleton occupied his seat, she arranged the limbs in the necessary position, wrote a note she stuck to a boney finger, and stepped back to admire her handiwork. "Sometimes I outdo myself."

Rathbone looked at what she'd done and scowled. "This was mission critical?"

"Um. Yeah. Isn't it great?"

He was still scowling as he took her hand and collected the other harpy. With a nod to a fading, fuming Lore, he said, "Appear to me when you can."

Flash.

Azar hurt all over, but not by word or deed did he betray his condition as he busted through the final layer of a mile-thick wall and marched into Rathbone's hidden throne room...where he discovered ruins and a single golden throne.

A plastic skeleton perched on it, one arm lifted, the middle finger extended. A piece of paper hung from that finger.

Azar read the nearly illegible text. *Roses are red, violets are blue. I forgot the next line, but oh how I adore defeating you.*

A growl brewed deep inside his chest. "Bring me the oracle's mother."

16

Rathbone teleported two harpies, the floor of the throne room and the throne itself to the catacombs of a subrealm in the Underworld known as the Realm of the Forgotten. A land Hades had purchased for times such as this. Rathbone had an open invitation to visit. Just being here should erase Rathbone, Neeka, Daisy, and perhaps even Lore from the mind of everyone but Hades, and anyone bearing a special tattoo to remember.

The problem was, Rathbone couldn't control the inner defenses or supernaturally sense intruders. And there was always a chance the Astra were immune to mental wipes. Even still, this was the safest place for their ragtag team during this short layover. Once they'd instituted the oracle's newest scheme, whatever it was, they'd go. He and Neeka had three bones to find.

Rathbone attempted to release her hand, a task that should've been easy. But his muscles proved stubborn and unwilling to obey, locking up.

He gritted his teeth and pried his fingers loose. When she clung to him, maintaining contact just a bit longer, he fought the urge to snatch her by the waist, yank her against him, and shout, "Mine!"

But she wasn't his.

"Now what?" he barked.

His sour mood did nothing to alter Neeka's air of calm. She smiled, saying, "Daisy, gril, let's chat about your future." She eased to the floor, getting comfortable, and patted the spot beside her.

Rathbone crossed his arms over his chest. Some of his mátia remained glued to the oracle, some stayed on the harpy, who hadn't made a move yet.

The female possessed shoulder-length black hair, a tan complexion, and plump curves. Sharp features gave her beauty a dangerous edge. He'd found her in a cottage miles from civilization, surrounded by forest and little else. Even animals and insects had avoided her.

Impatience got the better of him, and he prompted, "I suggest you hurry."

She bared her little fangs at him before plopping beside Neeka. "What?"

Rather than take offense, the oracle maintained her happy smile. "You've probably heard I'm a traitor to harpykind or some such semi-accurate nonsense. Maybe you've heard I seek to curse the Astra. Which is one hundred percent accurate almost."

"Yeah, I've heard." Zero emotion laced Daisy's tone. "And?"

"And I'm going to tell you something I haven't yet shared with the Rosy Menace." Her amber gaze darted to him, and he frowned. What hadn't she shared? "If the Astra succeed in their task, all of harpykind will be eaten by shadow monsters with gold rings around their irises. I've foreseen it."

Ah. Her unwavering support in the beginning made sense.

But shadow monsters with golden eye rings? What shadow monsters?

"Let's say I believe you," Daisy said. "What is it you think I can do to help?"

Neeka rubbed her hands together. "Get this. You're going to use your psychokinesis to shrink the throne with the floor, and place the entire atrocity in a small, protective orb."

Realization dawned, and he marveled. Such brilliance. The solution to his biggest problem, as promised. It was a plan he should've enacted ages ago. But then, most immortals who wielded a psychokinesis ability only moved objects with their mind. A rare few had the ability to manipulate an object's molecular structure.

"You will guarantee I'm able to undo the process at will," he told Daisy.

Neeka, who had focused on him to measure his reaction to her admission, heaved a sigh. "I guess I was so overcome by eye-feasting on you that I forgot to mention the orb will be bound to you and open at your command." Her gaze swung to Daisy. "If I'm picking up on correct details."

The harpy gave a stiff nod. "You are."

Eye-feasting? She admitted to liking the look of him? His chest puffed up. A conundrum he'd experienced often in her presence. "Will Lore's spirit be able to materialize while her bones are encased?"

"Yes. Or no." Neeka hiked her shoulders. "We'll find out together."

"But she won't be harmed?"

"Not unless we shatter the orb." Did she sound hopeful?

"My orbs are indestructible," Daisy bragged, and Neeka pursed her lips.

"Very well." He nodded. "We may proceed."

"Why would I even consider doing this?" Another demand from the harpy.

"Rathbone has an excellent payment plan," Neeka said, smiling so sweetly.

The corners of his lips twitched.

"You can pick between treasure, a kingdom to rule, or the death of an enemy. If you insist hard enough, he'll give you all three." Winking at him, she asked, "Isn't that right, Red Thunder?"

"No," he replied easily. "She'll do it, or I'll make her suffer in ways she cannot fathom."

Neeka rolled her eyes. "Dude. Have you learned nothing from me? Threats don't work with harpies."

"She's right," Daisy said, giving him a look of disgust.

Were the two adversaries ganging up on him?

Daisy arched a brow. "I don't want a treasure, don't need a kingdom, and I've already killed my enemies."

"Oh." The oracle turned pensive before brightening. "How about I give you what you desire most, then?"

"And what is that?"

"A glimpse at *your* future. My ability is back online, and I'm already picking up signals."

The harpy paled.

"That *is* what you've sought most of your life, isn't it?" Neeka insisted.

How he enjoyed watching her. Nothing intimidated her. Always she pushed ahead, toppling mountains and raising valleys as required.

Daisy gave a stiff nod. "I accept your payment. But I'm staying in this realm with you until I find new digs. The big guy compromised my cottage."

"Deal!" Neeka clapped and bounced, seeming genuinely thrilled. "Sister time! Our rooms will be side by side, and we'll do all night gab sessions."

Guess they were staying here longer than anticipated.

Cringing, the harpy stated, "I'll expect to be ignored at all hours of the day and night."

"No problem. You'll hardly know I'm there when I paint your nails and style your hair. And now that that's settled, we might as well get started." Neeka closed her lids, ending the conversation as only she could.

Daisy shifted. If she made a move to attack while the oracle was distracted...

Growling, Rathbone flashed over, taking up a post behind Neeka to stare the harpy down. He didn't care if he wasn't supposed to peer into the female's eyes. If she attempted to rearrange *his* molecular structure, well, let her try.

The harpy stared right back. But she didn't strike at him.

Neeka scrunched her brows, muttering, "Come on, come on. Show me what I want to see."

Having trouble? Rathbone cupped her shoulders. The contact startled her, but she relaxed as soon as he began massaging her tense muscles.

A moan escaped her, and she leaned into his touch. "Oh, yes. This is helping. If you stop, I just might ask Daisy to put a certain part of your anatomy in a small orb as well, if you know what I'm talking about." She paused, then loudly added, "I'm talking about your penis."

He fought a smile, even as heat poured through him, turning his veins into rivers of fire. In his lungs, air became steam. Sweat beaded his brow, and his zipper pulled taut.

He should walk away. Yes, he should.

But he didn't. This time, he didn't have the strength to let her go. Touching her felt right. It shifted things inside him. New things. Not purely sexual but wholly comforting. The massage continued.

His gaze slid to the throne, so close but so far. Did Lore's skull glare at him?

"Mmm," Neeka said, moaning again. "Don't stop. I'm almost there."

A groan rolled from the tip of his tongue. Those words…as seductive as the feel of her.

"Should I leave?" Daisy asked with a dry tone.

He glared at her.

"Oh, oh!" Neeka exclaimed. "I see you walking the shore of a peaceful stream. Water flows smoothly over golden rocks. Fish breech the surface, eager to glimpse you. Flowers bloom as you pass. Branches stretch in your direction."

The harpy jolted as if she'd been punched in the solar plexus.

"But…" Neeka's head tilted. Her expression pinched. "A glow is seeping from your pores. It's slight at first but is steadily intensifying. Oh. Oh, wow. It's bright. Too bright. Painfully bright." She sucked in a breath. "The light extinguishes as quickly as it sparked, and a shimmer of stars falls to the ground. I'm searching, but I can't find you anymore. You're gone, and there's no trace that you ever existed."

"So nothing I've done stops it from happening." The harpy's shoulders slumped. Her gaze darted to Rathbone. "Don't ask me any questions. I don't want to talk about it."

Neeka, who had no idea what the other female said, opened her eyes and straightened, gearing up to rapid-fire queries; he knew it, because he'd learned her. He trailed a knuckle along her nape, distracting her. Goose bumps rose over her flesh.

He wouldn't lean down and lick her there.

He wouldn't.

Daisy's morose countenance turned defiant. "Whatever," she said, standing. "Quick reminder. I'm a guest in your home, so you gotta protect me and deal with any baddies who show up. Agreed? Good. I'll be busy building a machine you're not gonna ask me anything about." She marched closer to the throne.

"Hey, Red." Neeka popped to her feet and jumped on him,

winding her legs around his waist. "You wanna talk about Lore's accusations against me?"

Instant, frothing desire consumed him. By sheer will alone, he kept a portion of his gazes on Daisy as he gripped Neeka's backside, saying, "There's no need. If you plan to steal me away, give it your best shot."

"You don't think I can succeed?" she asked, grazing the tip of her nose against his.

He savored the sweetness of the action. Her slight weight and soft curves. Her tantalizing fragrance. Her everything. "I think I would rather discuss the shadow monsters." A much safer topic. Because if ever a female *could* succeed in such an endeavor, it was this one.

Could a male be blessed with two fated mates? The very idea left him sputtering internally. Impossible!

"The monsters show up within minutes after Lore revives," Neeka said, cautious. "They eat harpies, Astra and even you, sparing only Erebus."

Hmm. A new type of phantom, perhaps? "I will research once we finish here."

"Silence," Daisy barked. "Let me concentrate."

He flashed his oracle in front of the harpy to better supervise the situation. Daisy stared at the throne, her dark eyes lightening, a glow rising from her flesh, growing brighter and brighter until spreading to the throne and the floor, wrapping around them from left to right, front to back. Everything but Rathbone and Neeka. The second the golden illumination covered every inch of gold and marble, the light exploded.

As soon as his eyes adjusted, he realized he stood upon a dirt floor, the marble gone. A small round orb waited where the throne had perched.

The harpy succeeded? Rathbone gave Neeka a swift peck before sitting her on her feet and—no, he stole another and another peck before finally flashing over to swipe up the little round ball. Any remaining tension drained as he studied the perfect translucent circle, a miniature throne room visible inside it, Lore's remains intact.

"So?" Daisy tossed her arms up. "Where's my room?"

Needing a moment to figure it out, Rathbone transported his companions to a sitting room upstairs.

"Hey! I know this place. I've been here." Neeka looked around, her eyes widening again. She gasped. "The wallpaper. How could I forget I'd seen it before?"

Pink, yellow, and blue flowers abounded. So what?

Her focus snapped to him, her pupils expanding in a show of desire. He went still. She had gotten hot for him? Because of wallpaper?

"You've been here?" he asked.

"Yes. In person and in…" Nervousness and anticipation molded her expression, making his chest ache. "A vision."

How interesting. He glanced at the wallpaper, then Neeka. The wallpaper. Neeka. She squirmed, and growls erupted in his throat, setting off a chain reaction. Hardening. Heat. *Need.* Everything flared anew. What had she seen to cause such a primal reaction?

Lowering his chin, he took a step toward her. *Will have her now and demand answers after.*

"Go on." Her cheeks flushed as she shooed him off, and he growled again. "Show Daisy where she's staying."

Daisy. Their audience. Right. Though his insides lathered, he retreated.

"When we're alone," Neeka continued, breathless, "we'll discuss the boon you owe me. I didn't find another bone, but I did save those you already possess. Don't worry, I'll make sure you enjoy what I demand."

She's greedy… for me? He barely stopped himself from rubbing his throbbing erection. Time apart might be wise. He could think. "What will you be doing while I'm gone?"

"Waiting eagerly." With the coyest of grins, she blew him a kiss. "Miss me."

He wasn't sure he'd be able to do anything else.

"You guys are embarrassing," Daisy muttered.

With more force than necessary, he stuffed the orb inside his pocket, grabbed the harpy by the arm, and flashed her to the farthest room in Hades's fortress.

"Behave," he said, stalking off. He'd forgo his 'betray me and suffer' speech for once. Right now...

He moderated his pace as he made his way to Neeka, who had all but admitted to wanting him for herself.

Why did she have to be so beautiful and soft? Smell so sweet. Rouse his smiles. Be so brilliant. Look at him as if she admired him as much as he admired her. His ever-increasing hunger for her complicated things. He should be strong enough to resist.

But.

He wasn't.

What would she demand as her boon? Sex? A dozen climaxes? His fingers flared and relaxed of their own accord. Whatever her request, he *must* do it. Honor demanded it.

Rationalizing to give yourself permission? Or thinking clearly for the first time in centuries? Rathbone didn't know and wasn't sure he cared anymore.

The doorway to his destination loomed ahead. He'd left Neeka in the sitting room with the mysterious wallpaper. Had her craving for him intensified?

Desperate to see her, he flashed inside. She was dashing from furniture to furniture, testing different poses, each more alluring than the last.

Beautiful vixen.

Her gaze landed on him, and she stilled halfway to the couch, mere feet away from him. He jolted as if hit by lightning.

Amused chagrin overtook her, until she noted the ferocity

banked in his features. Her lips formed a small O and all light-heartedness evaporated.

"What do you want?" he croaked.

Eyes hooding, she crooked her finger at him. "Come, give me a kiss."

"Merely a kiss?" He stood in place and breathed. In. Out. Her scent fogged his head. "Not more? The boon has no restrictions."

"Well, then," she said, her voice little more than a whisp. "Give me your very best kiss, and we'll see what happens from there."

Yes. He stalked closer. He would kiss her and strip her and give her such intense pleasure she only ever needed more of him—and then what?

The question stopped Rathbone in his tracks. What was he doing?

"You shouldn't tempt me like this." He *couldn't* have a second fated, which meant he would never be the one for Neeka.

Wonder and awe softened her stance. "I tempt you?"

"Beyond measure." Every muscle in his body hummed, the melody growing louder as he cataloged even the most miniscule of her reactions. From the sparkle in her amber irises, to the fever-flush spreading over her flawless skin, to her ragged exhalations. "But my situation hasn't changed."

She looked away for a moment, as if ending the conversation, and he nearly banged his chest and roared. Not done! Never done. Then she faced him with her chin raised. "That's not what my instinct tells me."

As much as he despised his next words, he uttered them. "You're wrong this time. Confusing instinct with desire." He hadn't spent centuries chasing Lore and his dream to give up now. But he couldn't, wouldn't stop this, either, if Neeka accepted what he offered. Temporary.

"Maybe," she allowed. "Either way, I want my kiss."

"You are sure?" Rathbone closed the remaining distance.

His heart thudded. "It won't change anything. You understand that, yes?"

Her chin rose another notch. "What if it changes everything?"

Proud harpy, determined oracle. Luscious female. "It won't."

"Or it will." She glided the tips of her claws up his chest, barely grazing his sensitive skin. "So what are you waiting for, Red? Pay up."

"I'll pay." He reached up and closed his fingers around a fistful of hair at her nape. For a long while, he peered down at her. "But you will, too."

"I know," she whispered, and he was helpless. "Please, Rath."

With a ragged groan, he swoped down to claim her lips with his own.

17

He wants me. Badly.

Reeling, Neeka wound her arms around her Scarlet King. This. This was her vision come to dazzling life, and reality far surpassed fantasy. From the moment he'd begun his massage, arousal had simmered in her blood, need for him growing.

Who was she kidding? Arousal had simmered long before the massage. And that was A-okay. For once, she wasn't a convenience her partner used but a femme fatale to be resisted, and she never wanted it to end. She longed to feel this warrior in every cell of her body. To be so consumed by his passion, there was nothing left but the memory of his touch.

He deepened the kiss, thrusting his tongue past her teeth, and demanding a response. Sensations erupted in different parts of her. Teasing swirls of pleasure. Endless coils of bliss. Heated flutters of rapture. Never had she ached so fiercely.

Every hard, possessive stroke was also soft and seeking. A total contradiction, and she couldn't get enough. Because how like Rathbone himself. There was no one more paradoxical. Married but single. Countless eyes able to detect the smallest speck of dirt while he remained blinded to the wiles of a goddess. Strong beyond imagining but sometimes putty in this oracle's hands. A good thing. Here, now, she was putty in his. Today, he'd made her feel like the most desired person in the world. Important to his well-being. As if she was alone no longer but part of a divine union.

I tempt you?

Beyond measure.

Intoxicated with feminine power, Neeka poured herself into every return lick. Oh, the taste of this warrior…the thrill…the *connection*. Not just a divine union but…meant to be?

Icy cold flash froze her blood. Meant to be…as in…no, no. No way, no how. Rathbone wasn't her consort. Yes, he was one of a kind. A veritable treasure trove of goodness who floated her boat, revved her engine, and lit her match. Not just intense but fervent. Not just determined but unshakable. Not just unusual but extraordinary. Everything she'd never let herself dream of having and a thousand things more.

But he wasn't consort material. He *wasn't*. She hadn't found him in flames, as her father had predicted. And, and, and…

Before she worked up a good panic about such a worrisome idea, he cupped her jaw, the heat of his skin searing hers. One of his thumbs found the indention in her chin, and boom. Instant calm. Immediate delight. He was shockingly gentle, as if she were as breakable as glass.

He lifted his head and stared at her, intense, his irises glowing with crimson fire—*all* of his irises. She stared back. They both panted. The savage hunger in his expression weakened her knees.

"Are we done?" she pouted, disappointed.

"I don't think we'll ever be done," he replied, and her knees almost buckled. Then he scowled, as if only then realizing what he'd said. "You are a very, very dangerous female. But worth every wound."

Those hot flutters migrated to her belly. "You want more of me?"

"Much more." He brushed the tip of his nose against hers. "You are a treasure."

She was? Well, of course she was. She was a harpy.

"And you are brilliant."

Her eyes widened. "Tell me something else you admire about me." *Please, please, don't sound as needy as I feel.*

The corners of his mouth curved with affection. "And commanding. You drive me to the brink of madness, but I find I am enjoying the ride."

Had the air just thickened?

"You crave more of me, don't you, carrot," he said, and oh, she wished she could hear his tone. Had he asked or insisted?

Either way... She was right. The kiss had changed everything. "Give it to me. You must. You owe back taxes on your boon." Nothing mattered but this male and this moment. Her needy, greedy body demanded assuaging.

"Let no one say the King of Agonies skirts his bills." Angling her head, he nipped her earlobe, then licked a path down her neck.

A moan escaped her. Upon reaching her thumping pulse, he growled; she felt the vibration. *Loved* the vibration. It unleashed the most delicious cascade of tremors. Waves of euphoria gave chase.

"Rathbone..." A plea. A groan.

Fisting the hair at her nape once again, he backed her into a wall. "I'll go slow. Exhibit unbreakable control."

Speaking to her or himself?

The second she reached the barrier, he returned his mouth to hers. A gentle brush of his lips. A firmer pressing. Their tongues twined together, as aggressive and wild as before, yet slower, just as he'd promised. A languid sampling to be savored—until he settled his hands on her hips, kicked her legs apart, and inserted his thigh between the gap, rubbing against her.

The pleasure! She bucked against him, then shot her gaze to his mouth. "Red."

"Slow," he insisted before she could demand more.

Shaking with need, she glided her palms over his abdomen. The eight-pack twitched, and she purred into his mouth. *I will have this male, even if it kills me...*

"Maybe *a little* faster?" she pleaded.

He gripped her backside and lifted her. Neeka wrapped her legs around him, locking her ankles.

"Is this fast enough for you?" He kneaded her breasts, and she rocked her hips. Moans escaped them both, the vibrations crashing together and reverberating, unleashing an endless stream of ecstasy.

"Red," she repeated. She bit his bottom lip, a slight nip, then licked away the sting. "Don't forget to pay interest."

The kiss turned frenzied, as if her greediness was fuel to his fire. Rathbone devoured her mouth, grinding his erection into her feminine softness. Need to need.

She mewled, meeting his tongue thrust for thrust. As she tunneled her fingers through his silken hair, grazing the tips of her claws across his scalp, those delicious reverberating rumbles increased in potency.

He shoved his hand into her pants, letting his fingers hover directly over her aching need, then wrenched up his head. Panting, he stared down at her. "I want inside you. Say yes."

She opened her mouth to agree—yes, yes, yes! A terrible premonition struck, killing the words. Fear bombs detonated, one after the other, and suddenly her heart raced for an entirely different reason, each eliciting a new reaction. A knotted stomach. A twisted gut, and ice glazed organs.

The day she had sex with Rathbone was the day her old life

burned and a new one rose from the ashes, with no bridge between them. For better or worse. She would never be the same, the damage irreparable.

It was a fate changing action.

The knotting, twisting, and icing worsened. Would he reject her immediately afterward? Treat her as a hired servant while catering to Lore?

Neeka wasn't ready to find out.

Worry issued a death rattle for any remaining desire. "I say no," she rasped. She needed to think.

"No," he echoed, his tone flat.

"The boon is satisfied."

"But we are not."

"I—I just remembered there's somewhere we need to be." Yes. The elixir. Her knockout punch. *Gather the ingredients, go from there.* She shimmed her legs from Rathbone, putting her feet on the floor.

Different emotions radiated from him. Confusion. Hurt. Anger. Confusion again. More hurt. Resolve.

Guilt slashed at her calm. And it shouldn't! None of those things meant he wished to keep her and forsake Lore. "The kiss didn't mean anything anyway, right?" Ugh. Did bitterness tinge her words?

He blanked his expression. "Right." Raising his chin, he loosened his hold on her. Stepped back.

Neeka pasted on a bright smile. "I know you're extra eager to find the missing bones. And guess what? Multiple locations are calling to me. If they're not in one, they're in another. So? Are you ready to embark upon another adventure, Ruddy Duddy?"

For the next three days, Rathbone flashed Neeka from world to world to world. A routine developed. The oracle spent her downtime dogging Daisy's every step, and Rathbone spent his researching shadow monsters with golden rings in their eyes, learning nothing. Any time he spent outside the library, he dogged *Neeka's* every step.

Bright and early each morning, the oracle barged into his bedroom—the chamber neighboring hers—announced the location that called to her the loudest, and he provided transport. They never kissed and rarely touched. Barely even spoke.

Like a pimply-faced teenager spurned by his first crush, Rathbone stewed. A humiliating development, but a development all the same. He craved more of the oracle. So much more. Their kiss was never far from his mind. How she'd clutched him, as if she couldn't pull him close enough. How she'd moved on him, rocking with more and more force, eager to get what she wanted—needed. How he'd clambered for harder and rougher, desperate to stake a claim he had no business making, all to slake a lust he couldn't shake. How he'd come so close to thrusting his fingers inside her honey.

Why had she pumped the brakes so suddenly? Why cultivate distance now? Her desire for him hadn't dulled.

Rathbone realized he was stroking the orb that hung from his neck. With a scowl, he returned his focus to his task: rowing the canoe Neeka insisted he build from scratch. Her instinct had *known* he needed to wield a hammer and nails to come out of this alive. But it hadn't been her instinct secretly leering at him while he chopped wood. No, that had been Neeka herself.

Would Neeka be receptive to becoming the sole member of his stable? Forever? It wasn't a perfect solution, but it had merit.

"What?" she demanded. "Why are you looking at me all..." She shivered, her eyelids hooding the way they'd done just before he'd kissed her. "Swoony."

Swoony? Rather than start a conversation he wasn't yet ready to finish, he said, "If we discover a bone today, I'll grant you an additional boon." The offer had nothing to do with hoping she'd seek another kiss. If they weren't navigating a mythical swamp, being swarmed and bitten by mutant bugs, they were crossing a desert as multiple suns melted the flesh from their bodies, or deep diving in putrid sludge. Enough was enough. If she happened to request more kisses, however, that was his burden to bear.

Today, they traversed a beautiful water world. Lavender waves stretched endlessly, light from a silver moon glinting off the surface. No fish swam about. No birds flew overhead. Actually, he sensed no life at all.

"And if we don't find a bone?" she asked, one brow arched.

"You'll grant *me* a boon." Hmm. He liked the sound of this.

"No fair," she said with a pout. "I wanted to risk nothing and gain everything."

He snorted. "I'm sure you did." As silence stretched between them, he continued rowing, trying not to glance her way. But one by one his mátia returned to her.

He would give anything to draw another ragged moan from those cherry lips.

"Very well," she huffed. "I agree to your terms. But know this. I'm open to anything but sex. Meaning penetration by your battering ram, just so we're clear."

A paddle snapped in his hand, half of it sinking below the surface before he registered what happened. A curse exploded from him.

"Such a silly butterfingers." Neeka tsked. "If you break the second one, we'll have to swim the remaining eight hundred and sixty-three miles."

Deep breath in, out. He placed the second paddle in his lap for safekeeping, uncaring about the water soaking his leathers. He cleared his throat, then asked, "Do you fear my…battering ram? I promise I'll be gentle—in the beginning."

She shifted in her seat, a flush spreading over her cheeks. Then she noticed the placement of his hand and frowned. At some point, he'd reached up to trace his fingers over the orb's smooth shell again.

Though she maintained her nonchalance, the sparkle in her lovely amber irises dulled. "Save your drilling for your goddess. My oracle senses tell me she's fine, by the way. If she isn't visiting you, it's because she's choosing not to. Think she's mad that you kissed me?"

"I don't know." *Had* Lore witnessed the kiss?

He expected a resurgence of guilt, but no. There was none to be found. "If she's upset, she'll learn to deal." Lore had advocated for a stable. If he opted to comply, she wasn't allowed to complain about the one he selected to occupy it.

He liked this idea. Neeka's need to be a male's one and only would be satisfied. She would belong to Rathbone alone—until she found her consort.

The second paddle snapped in half, but thankfully, both pieces remained in the boat. He swallowed another curse. If Neeka found her consort, she'd leave Rathbone in her dust, taking her delightful teasing and sexy greediness with her. This other male would receive her attention. Her kisses.

"That's very alpha of you." The beautiful oracle drew her legs closer to her chest and rested her elbows on her knees. "Tell me again how you'll defy your beloved wife to sleep with me but this time flex your biceps while you're talking."

She meant to shame him, he knew, but he did as suggested and flexed, assuming different power poses. Better to tease her than sulk about the future. "Go ahead. Eye-feast. You can't even help yourself."

A magical laugh left her, and she pressed her fingers over her mouth. His chest clenched. A familiar sensation now, and something only she elicited. A benefit he refused to part with.

Must earn another. "For my next trick, watch as I—" He went quiet when she moaned, her features contorting with pain.

"Carrot?" Rathbone demanded, on instant alert. Concern radiated from him. "What's wrong?"

She rubbed her temples. "Someone is attempting to Peer

through me. Don't worry. They won't breech my mental barricades. Plus, I can track them, following the breadcrumbs they've left behind."

"Peer?" he asked, but she'd already closed her eyes.

"I think I sense my mother," she muttered. "She's not an oracle, but my father taught her to Peer when he taught me. Why would she do this, though?"

Movement to his left. He swung his head in that direction, searching...there. In the distance, thick, dark smoke filled the air. It blocked out everything behind the two immortals who materialized, standing inside a boat of their own. Azar and the unfamiliar female at his side. A harpy who resembled Neeka. Both wore goggles.

"Got you!" Neeka exclaimed.

The smoke engulfed them, concealing their bodies before sweeping closer and closer to Rathbone's boat.

"Oh, no Azar did not," his oracle screeched, jumping to her feet.

A moment later, the smoke reached them. For the first time in Rathbone's existence, he couldn't see the world around him.

Fury and frustration converged. He heard a *whoosh* a nanosecond before a double-pronged spear cut through both of his eye sockets, throwing him into the water.

Lights out.

18

Okay. So. Neeka probably should've predicted this. But honestly? She'd been too wrapped up in her misery over Rathbone, plus her mission, and also too distracted by the Peer invader—who she now knew beyond a doubt was, in fact, her mother. And, yeah, okay, despite all that, she'd maybe, possibly been having too much fun bantering with the red king, who had surprised her at every turn. But, um, why hadn't he removed the spear, healed, and returned to the boat?

He could help her save the day from Azar and Grenwich.

"Couldn't defeat the One and Only on your own, Astra?" she called, feigning nonchalance. "You needed a hand? See what I did there?" With the obligatory harpy taunt delivered, she checked out of the conversation and dove into the water to find her partner.

The icy temperature shocked her system, and she gasped, swallowing a mouthful of sweet-tasting liquid. The very same liquid required for the elixir. No time to bottle the stuff. She'd have to wring nineteen drops from her clothes later. As her stomach churned, she searched the increasingly murky depths for her companion.

Despite stinging eyes, she focused long enough to pinpoint a stream of crimson. She followed it and jolted. There he was. Rathbone, but not.

Again and again, he shifted into other forms. And he did it in a blink, changing from one animal or inanimate object to another. From a black jaguar to the stuffed teddy bear she'd burned, to a house cat, to a diamond necklace, to a dog, to a dagger, to a snake, to a portrait, to a honey badger, to an ink pen.

She'd known he could shift into other beings, but she'd had no idea he also shifted into *things*. Such a tricky, tricky king. There'd been no nanny cam. Only the Only.

Why did this make him so much sexier?

Wings working overtime, she swam as fast as possible. Almost there… No matter his form, Rathbone continued to bleed. He wasn't healing. Or awake. He couldn't flash them to safety. Unless she forced the issue by Peering? Worth a shot.

The act would drain her, but better she pass out later than die with him now.

Catching up to him, Neeka wrapped him in the circle of her arms. His shifting ceased, thank goodness, and he remained in his original packaging. The spear was long gone, but his sockets were nothing but raw, hollow wounds.

Though her deflating lungs burned, she pinched Rathbone's nose and placed her lips over his, then blew what air she had left into his mouth. His chest rose, but he gave no other indication of life.

As she readied herself to Peer, trepidation tightened her throat, a boa constrictor she couldn't shake. Danger! Dreading what she'd find, she cast her gaze across the water. Blast it all! Azar was swimming toward her, a weapon clasped in each hand. His wicked grin heralded more trouble. Clearly, he expected to win this round.

What secrets had her mother imparted to him?

Neeka estimated she had less than a minute to facilitate a flash. As fast as possible, she closed her physical eyes, opened her inner one, and mystically reached for Rathbone. Unlike last time, he didn't resist. A mental door fell ajar upon her approach, making her entrance shockingly seamless. *Click.*

Suddenly, she heard the glug of water but saw nothing. Not their surroundings, and certainly not the Astra. Panic attempted to rise, but she rallied the strength to keep her attention on her goal: flashing. Could she do it using Rathbone's ability?

She pictured her destination of choice, hoping the warrior observed it too, whether he realized it or not. Then she mentally shouted, "Teleport! Now!"

Yes! The water vanished just as a sharp pain registered in her arm and chest. She and Rathbone landed on a hard floor with a harder thunk, impact abruptly severing their connection.

She blinked rapidly and sucked in oxygen. Air filled her lungs first. Light infiltrated her vision after.

A tide of relief crashed over her as she examined her surroundings. They'd made it to her secret hideaway in Harpina. A subrealm tucked inside another subrealm that was tucked inside her home world and forbidden to all Astra. Entering would be a declaration of war against their mentor, Chaos.

Knew I'd need this place one day. A few months ago, she'd completed a job for the enigmatic Chaos, father of Erebus as well as the powerful god who'd trained the Astra. As payment, she'd demanded this tiny biosphere with a private plunge bath and a pool house. She only wished she'd remembered it sooner.

A vibration drew her attention to Rathbone, who hadn't budged. He lay motionless, as if dead. She croaked a denial.

"You're going to be okay," she vowed.

He didn't switch forms again, but he hadn't started healing.

His eyes remained bloody sockets. His right bicep was in tatters. A gaping wound in his chest displayed his ribs.

Was the damage courtesy of Azar's daggers?

Neeka lumbered to shaky legs and tripped to the kitchen. She was weak but not drained, the effects of the Peer manageable. After retrieving a bowl, she removed and wrung her shirt. The water trapped between the fibers splashed into the container. Far more than nineteen drops. Excellent. That done, she rushed about, gathering supplies. Anything she thought she might need. Towels and rags. Salves. A bowl of fresh water. Scissors. Um, why did she have vials of Astra blood stored in the bathroom cabinet? Whatever. She placed everything near Rathbone and—

The lights turned on and off.

Gasping, she flipped up her gaze, finding Taliyah a few feet away, dressed for war in a typical harpy uniform: a metal breastplate with breast cups, a pleated leather miniskirt, arm and shin guards, and scuffed combat boots.

"About time you showed up," her friend said.

Neeka leaped to her feet once more, taking a protective post in front of the injured king. "How did you find me?"

"What? Like it's hard?" The General anchored her fists on her hips. "Now that he's out of commission, will you tell me what's really going on?"

Wait. "You trust me?"

"You seriously gotta ask? You are the marshmallow romantic who married a psychopath so my sister could stay with her consort. Of course I trust you."

But... "The last time we were together, you acted as if you hated me for my betrayal."

"Uh. Yeah. Why wouldn't I? I knew something major was happening and that you had a reason for pretending to be a traitor, so I played along, doing my part. Hey!" Taliyah frowned. "Did *you* not trust *me* to trust you?"

Uh... Hiding a wince, Neeka returned to her post and

crouched beside Rathbone. She caressed his chest, thrilling over each of his heart beats.

The lights flicked on and off again, the General's impatience getting the better of her. Neeka finally replied, "Why would I ever not trust you?" To her immense relief, instinct proclaimed, *Now is the time. Tell Taliyah.* "When you hear what I've got to say, you might understand."

The story flowed from her.

Black flooded Taliyah's eyes. A product of her phantom heritage. As a daughter of Erebus, she wielded the most amazing abilities. Neeka's top two faves? Ghosting inside of people and turning to mist.

Rocking on her heels, the General said, "So the Astra and harpykind will be destroyed if the warlords revive the goddess."

"Yep. They'll release Lore's evil power." Neeka removed the orb from Rathbone's neck and placed it around her own.   "I can't believe Azar will betray his brothers for such a heinous gravita," her friend said, her already pale skin growing pallid.

"I don't think he wants to, but she wields some kind of power over him."

"We need to tell Roc."

"No!" The denial exploded from her. "It's not time. The Astra aren't prepared to confront the truth, and they'll do something to mess up every good thing I've got going."

Taliyah scrubbed a hand over her face. "I can't lose Roc. I *won't*. And I won't allow my people to be extinguished."

"You think I will? Take my advice, and all will be well." At least, she hoped so. "I'm so close to changing things." She should have a new vision any day. "I just need a little more time."

"You've already made changes. I didn't know what was going on, as evidenced by Lore's success. Now I do."

"Good point." But was the change big enough to make a difference?

Taliyah kicked into a swift pace. "There must be a way to aid you."

Minutes passed, neither of them speaking. Neeka continued to doctor her patient without results. In fact, the more she attempted to help him, the more he bled, no matter how gentle she was. Frustration blended with fear and something she couldn't name. Sorrow? Guilt? What if he...died?

A barbed lump grew in her throat. The same way Taliyah refused to lose Roc, Neeka refused to lose Rathbone. Because she needed him to complete her assignment. Because—just because!

She faced her friend. "He is vital to my endgame. How do I save him?"

Taliyah came to a halt, blinked, and frowned. "You like him."

"Well, he's likable," she replied, a little defensive. Or a lot. Yeah, verging on a lot.

"Everyone who's met him would disagree. Just make it easier on us all and admit he's your consort."

"What? No!" Neeka sputtered for a moment. Rathbone, the male fashioned for her alone? The sole being able to calm the worst of her rages with his mere presence? Who made up for her past, enriched her present, and optimized her future? "What?" she repeated. "Stop being ridiculous. This is a serious matter."

"Or double down." With a calculated gleam in her ice-cold blues, Taliyah withdrew a dagger, sliced her palm, and marched over. As blood welled, she thrust out her hand. "Drink. If you vomit afterward, we'll know the truth."

Her stomach issued a new protest at the sight. Which meant nothing. Less than nothing. "No thanks. I know he's not my consort, and that's good enough for me. I mean, he's hot and all—" and a magnificent kisser, among other things "—but as I told you before, he already has a fated mate. But why won't he heal?"

"He can't. Not without the antidote. Azar used a toxin able to slay gods."

An inferno of fury blazed through Neeka, torching her composure. She stood slowly, grating, "I will *ruin* Azar."

"No, you won't. You will plot and scheme to save the Astra, ensuring Azar wins his task and defeats Lore before anyone dies, and I will get you the antidote. Agreed?"

No need to ponder. Taliyah wasn't a liar. If there was no other way to save Rathbone's life, Neeka's choice was made. "Agreed. Help me save the king, and I'll deliver a victory to the Astra."

Rathbone would hate her for it. More than if she destroyed Lore on her own. No alpha male thanked the person responsible for losing a second battle with their greatest enemy.

It wouldn't matter to him that he was gonna lose Lore anyway, even if the Astra failed. He would rage.

Would she find herself in his dungeon, strapped on one of his stone tables?

Maybe he'd forgive her. Eventually. Perhaps he'd even thank her. At some point, he had to see his lady love for what she was. Pure evil. Truth couldn't be hidden forever; it always found a way to shine. And yes, Neeka recognized the irony. Look at all the secrets she still kept from the male.

Taliyah nodded. "Give me an hour," she said just before she disappeared.

Neeka sank beside Rathbone and drew in a shaky breath. With a trembling hand, she smoothed wet hair from his damp brow. "Everything will be okay," she assured him.

His only response was a shiver of cold.

Careful of his injuries, she stretched out and curled her body against his, letting her heat wash over him. As she breathed him in, the world faded from her awareness. She braced, knowing what came next.

A vision overtook her mind.

She saw the harpy throne room. This time, Azar didn't have to add the final piece of the macabre puzzle that was Lore's skeleton. The dark-haired beauty was already flesh and blood. She perched in Taliyah's chair, wearing an evil queen ball gown, complete with an elaborate headdress dripping with diamonds.

Neeka's blood chilled as her heart nearly pounded its way free of her chest. *I failed.*

Azar knelt before her, head bowed. Lore petted his hair as the other Astra shouted protests. Taliyah stood among them. Grenwich and a handful of other harpies, too. And yes, Erebus was there, grinning as widely as before.

Hades acted as guard at Rathbone's side. The red king's fate hadn't changed. He remained chained to a wall.

He didn't struggle against his bonds at least. Oops. Spoke too soon. He erupted, fighting his captivity, bellowing, "Do not do this. Please do not do this. I love you!"

In real life, Neeka clutched him tighter. How she abhorred seeing this powerful male bound and helpless. But, um, love? He *loved* Lore, despite the evidence of her treachery? Or he lied to trick her into stopping?

The goddess glowered and snapped, "Shut him up. His bellowing is beyond irritating to my darling beasties." She rubbed a flat belly, as if she were pregnant. "I can't concentrate, and I need to concentrate."

Azar stood, unsheathed a dagger, stomped over and, after a savage fight, cut out Rathbone's tongue. For some reason, Hades allowed it.

A thousand protests bubbled inside Neeka.

The Memory Keeper returned to Lore, presenting the goddess with her prize.

"Marvelous. Marvelous indeed." Erebus widened his grin and clapped. "Do you want to proclaim me the winner of this task yet, or shall we continue?"

The remaining Astra went quiet with shock.

"That's better." Lore took the dagger Azar had used and licked the blood from the blade. Crimson smeared her cheek. A ghoulish sight, she stood slowly, almost chest to chest with Azar. "Oh, how I've longed for this day." She traced her fingers over his jaw. "Stop fighting your desire for me. Unleash it."

The Astra huffed and puffed, as if he wrestled with her command with all his strength. But in the end, he couldn't stop himself from obeying. Desire heated his eyes as he swooped in to kiss her.

"Mmm. That did it." She laughed as she pulled away, calling, "My sweet army. Come!"

Her laughter mutated into a scream as her head fell back, her body curved, and her feet lifted off the floor. She hovered there, nothing but a vessel as the shadow monsters burst from her abdomen. Wow. More than before. So many more. They swarmed the audience, attacking the Astra, Taliyah, Hades, and the chained Rathbone. Still no sign of Neeka herself. Chaos had vanished.

Though their group fought hard and dirty, the members were devoured until every trace of them vanished.

In reality, rigidity invaded her limbs. She might be dead in the future, but the vision chugged on. Erebus was the sole survivor of the feast.

"We did it," Lore grinned at him as the shadow beings surrounded him. "A war far easier than we anticipated."

The Deathless winked at her, evincing no hint of anxiety. "Which makes our victory sweeter."

Our victory? They worked together?

The vision dwindled to nothing, allowing the world to whoosh into focus once more. Neeka was panting, sweat drenched and crushed. She'd changed the future all right, just not for the better. Somehow, she'd made everything worse.

Rathbone had yet to move a muscle. Blood still leaked from his wounds. At least he survived these wounds. How else could he attend the ceremony and shout his love for Lore?

Obviously, Neeka hadn't utilized the elixir in this current fate. Thanks to their most recent trips, she'd already gathered the proper ingredients—items she carried around in a weapon sheath. With the acquisition of the water droplets, she now possessed everything. Was the elixir the answer to her dilemma?

There was only one way to find out. So, she would do it, no matter the cost. Once his obsession with Lore ended, they could collect and destroy the remaining bones. Along the way, Neeka could kill her mother. Not Azar, though; she'd promised Taliyah. But Mother Dearest was a hundred percent fair game. In fact, her death would mark another positive change.

There was a wrench in Neeka's plan, however. What if the General was right, and Rathbone was her consort?

Her breath hitched. He wasn't her consort, no way, no how. But he could be. But he wasn't. But he could be. But he wasn't, not while he loved another. Though there was always a chance, right?

If *Neeka* was his fated one, not Lore…if the goddess had tricked him into feeling what he felt, or would feel, which was a strong possibility… That meant Neeka would sever her own bond to the male when the two of them consumed the elixir, exchanging it for an artificial bond. She craved genuine, or nothing.

Was that the reason she'd forgone the elixir in the last vision?

Maybe she *wouldn't* do it, no matter the cost. There must be another way to win. What should she do, what should she do?

Taliyah appeared a few feet away, a vial in hand. She opened her mouth to speak but stayed quiet when she noticed Neeka's agitated condition. "No need to worry, Neeks. Your non-consort will heal, you have my word." She tossed the vial.

Neeka snatched the thing from the air, rasping, "Thank you." She didn't tell Taliyah what she'd seen as she poured the contents down Rathbone's throat. She'd thrown enough at her friend already.

Finally, his wounds began to heal, and Neeka sagged with

relief. He didn't awaken, but he did sag over the floor and sleep, tension seeping from him.

"See? My part of the bargain is complete," her friend said. "Now work on yours."

19

As excruciating pain downgraded to mere discomfort, Rathbone's thoughts unscrambled. A memory rose to the fore, carrying him back to the day he'd met Lore...

Eons ago
The Realm of Agonies

Shifted in the form of a common demon soldier, Rathbone led a chained and bloody Hades behind him. Sunlight shone all around, illuminating a thriving town square filled with torture chambers rentable by the hour, blood saloons, and houses of ill repute. Considering he was one of many carting a prisoner, he drew little attention despite his captive's notoriety. Helped that most residents were busy tormenting souls of the damned.

Pit fires raged here and there, casting flickering shadows and creating a revolting spectacle. Poor, unfortunate humans hung on spits, roasting inside the merciless inferno while bloodthirsty crowds jeered and cackled with glee. From all sides, agonizing screams pierced the air, assaulting Rathbone's ears. The acrid scent of smoldering spirits tainted the breeze, stinging his nostrils, nearly choking him with its bitterness.

From the sights, sounds, and smells, every aspect of the vile scene disgusted him. If he decided to be king of this realm, things would be different. Demons would be banished, and spirits would be liberated. To start.

"I think you're enjoying your role of captor a little too much," Hades said, his tone as dry as a desert.

"Just wanting to fit in with the locals," he responded, trying not to grin. He *was* enjoying his role a little too much, despite his disgust for his current form. The urge to claw through the scaly hide remained a constant itch in the back of his brain.

"Well? Is this the Underworld realm for you or not?"

Good question. He'd come here to scout. Unlike the other realms he'd visited, he hadn't rendered a decision in the first five minutes. The Realm of Horrors had been too cold, and the Realm of Falsities too dreary. But this…this he might like. Wide open spaces, warm breezes, and opulent structures. The buildings featured ornate gold finishes, glistening marble, and elaborate carvings. Especially the palace.

The colossal edifice perched atop a towering mountain peak, shimmering in the distance as though doused in starlight. A sight to behold, a beacon of radiance, and the picture of what had once been an unattainable dream. To claim this as his own, he must first eliminate its owner, King Styx.

Rathbone had never met the monarch, but rumors of his cruelty had spread far and wide. Once a merciful leader, he was said to have experienced a gradual metamorphosis, transforming into a ruthless tyrant for reasons unknown.

Killing him would be a pleasurable challenge. But… "I'm not sure," he told his uncle. Seven other Underworld kingdoms remained, and he should probably inspect them all. What if he preferred another?

The territory he selected was to be his forever home. His first home, really. Something he'd spent countless hours fantasizing about during his years in Aweland, the realm his mother had stashed him in to hide him from her husband. There, he'd suffered untold heartbreaks, unending self-recriminations, and bone-deep loneliness. The memories he carried with him needed replacing. A happier counterpart, at the very least.

"Is that Hades, the King of the Dead?" a demon called before whistling. "How'd you bag and tag him?"

"Easily," Rathbone returned without slowing his step, earning several guffaws.

"I might stab you in the genitals for that one," Hades muttered for his ears alone.

"How much do you want for him?" another demon shouted from the throng now congregating in front of a guillotine.

"Bring me your head, and I'll let you borrow him for an hour," Rathbone responded.

In a blink, another demon whipped out a sword, cut off the speaker's head, and raced Rathbone's direction with the abomination in hand. Ah, disloyalty at its finest. An all too common trait among the species, and something he despised with every fiber of his being. One of the many reasons he loved Hades. Those the King of the Dead loved, he protected, always staying true to his word. An honor reserved for few, and a luxury Rathbone hadn't experienced until meeting the other male.

"I meant *your* head," he corrected.

Another demon hurried over to decapitate the one holding the severed skull.

"My bad, I meant your head," he repeated, and the third demon died, too. The same process played out again and again, each demon dying before reaching him. "How long do you think this can go on?" he asked Hades between slayings.

"Not long enough. Looks like the fun is already slowing."

Sure enough, the fools finally caught on. At least fifty sets of narrowed red gazes settled on him.

"You're going to die for this," someone hissed.

Let them come. He could stand to blow a little steam before sneaking through the palace to spy on Styx. Rathbone wished to know if other rumors were true. Could the king recover from decapitation? If so, killing him wouldn't be easy. If Rathbone decided to do it, however, it would be done, regardless.

Of course, the male's death wouldn't end Rathbone's association with him. When an Underworld royal died, his body liquefied, soaking into the ground, bubbling up and growing into a river. A constant reminder of what used to be.

A commotion drew Rathbone's attention to the right. Soldiers and citizens jumped out of the path as a fury-crazed male wearing leather pants and a bejeweled crown dragged a bedraggled female at the end of a rope. Well, well. The infamous Styx in the flesh.

"Make way, make way," a demon shouted, marching ahead of the pair.

Hades and Rathbone were forgotten as everyone focused on the sovereign. Rathbone used the opportunity to study a potential foe. Not as big as expected but impressive all the same. Assured of his power, he mowed down anyone foolish enough to be in his path.

"Come one, come all," the announcer continued. "Watch our lord flog his once-favored concubine. Afterward, her organs will be served à la carte. Come one, come all."

Cheers resounded through the masses, salivating demons giving chase.

Rathbone turned his attention to the female, noting her features. Tangled sable hair, pale skin, and crystal blue eyes filled with tears. His chest clenched. A cut on her forehead dripped blood over one dainty cheek. Dirt streaked the rest of her. The imperfections did little to detract from her fragile beauty.

Her gaze darted, as if she searched for a rescuer. When she met Rathbone's stare for a mere heartbeat, desire struck him like a blow, snatching the air from his lungs. He stiffened as fierce yearning coursed through every nook and cranny of his body. In an instant, raw hunger threatened to whip him into a frenzy. A reaction he hadn't experienced since...ever. Yet it was the emotions that caught him off guard. Wonder. Hope. Desperation. Without a taste of this female, could he honestly claim to have lived at all?

Other males seemed to experience the same phenomenon. Aggression thickened the air. Growls blended with panting breaths. Many demons stroked themselves, uncaring who watched.

"I should speak with her," Rathbone said, all but foaming at the mouth for such an opportunity. "I have questions, and she could have answers."

"Yes, I'm sure that's the reason you must speak with her." Hades's tone dripped with wry humor. "Do us both a favor and walk away from this female."

The mere thought twisted his insides into knots. The strongest reaction he'd ever experienced in his lifetime. "Leave her in her tormentor's care? Your cruelty is showing, Uncle."

"I know. So why isn't yours? You don't have time for this."

True. Rathbone had one obsession and it was acquiring the perfect kingdom. But. He also didn't like seeing a female harmed.

His brow furrowed with confusion. He didn't? Since when?

"I can take a few minutes to save this poor creature," he stated.

"That so called poor creature doesn't need your help," Hades replied. "She's a Greek goddess of desire."

A goddess? Of desire? Rathbone peered at the prisoner with new eyes, riveted. A prize among prizes. The male who won a beauty such as her would be envied beyond measure.

She tripped over her own feet and fell, crashing into the cobblestone road. As merciless as the rumors suggested, Styx continued on, dragging her behind him. Though she fought to rise, she proved too weakened. Pained moans escaped her.

Hades shook his head, radiating pity. "Greek deities never leave something better than they found it. This female will wreck you."

Wreck him? Hardly. "*We* are Greek deities."

"Exactly. But fine. Go this route. I'll let you figure out the truth on your own."

Hands curling into fists, Rathbone struggled not to spring into action. *Hold.* Such unplanned impulsiveness could only lead to his downfall as well as hers. "Go to the palace. Learn what you can. I'll stay here with the king."

"The king. Right. I suppose these aren't needed anymore then." Hades yanked his arms apart, the chains breaking in two. With little effort, he tore through the metal wrist cuffs, one then the other. Rather than continuing to display his identity to the masses, he pulled his cloak's hood over his head, bathing his familiar face in shadows. "Just know you owe me extra for this. I expected a fun uncle-nephew day, a real bonding experience." He vanished.

Rathbone set off, too, following the royal procession to the town square, noting everything at once. From the number of demons present to the type of weapons hidden beneath their clothing.

Styx climbed atop a dais where a trio of torture devices waited. A stock, a chopping block, and a spiked pole. The sovereign strapped the female to the post.

"I don't deserve this," she cried, her tears spilling over her cheeks. The salty liquid mixed with the blood dripping from her brow to her chin. "I did nothing but tell you the truth, Styx. I don't love you the way you love me. I just want to leave. Why do you wish to keep me? Why won't you let me go?"

"She lies," the sovereign bellowed, slapping her. Growls brewed in Rathbone as blood trickled from a fresh cut on her lip. "She came to me. Bartered her body for my protection. I accepted, only to learn she's a traitor seeking to steal my kingdom for her own."

For several heartbeats, silence blanketed the land. Then someone laughed and others joined in. Everyone viewed his protests for what they were: a hollow attempt to appease his masculine pride. This fragile fluff steal a kingdom of the Underworld? Hardly.

A vein pulsed in the center of the king's forehead. With a rough huff, he snatched a cat-'o-nine-tails from a hook on the pole and whipped the demons in range of the dais. The collection of tethers slapped each soldier across the face, slicing through skin, scales, muscle, and even bone. High-pitched screams blended with a new round of laughter.

Styx stomped behind the female, who flinched and gagged at the gruesome sight before she scanned the crowd. Her crystalline gaze slipped over Rathbone once more only to snap back and widen. Did she sense his strength?

"Help me," she beseeched him. "Please."

Everything inside him screamed *yes!*

"Yo! Rathbone. Stop lazing, big guy, and wake up."

He frowned. That voice. Feminine, seeming to come from everywhere and nowhere at once. Familiar. Arousing. Embers of fire kindled.

"I don't want to die." The goddess struggled against her bonds, drawing his gaze yet again. And yet again, her plight snared him, his chest clenching. "I've never gotten to live."

He knew the feeling. *Must save her.*

"Give her to me," a demon demanded.

Others called out the same. A fight broke out around him, but he couldn't tear his gaze from the goddess.

Styx ignored the battle and prepared the whip for its next

strike—at the goddess. Sunlight illuminated every bruise and cut she'd already endured, now evident beneath the dirt and—Rathbone's brow furrowed. He did not spy a gleam of satisfaction in her eyes as she surveyed the chaos around her. Did he? No, of course he didn't. Terror etched her expression.

She needed protection. Saving.

Rathbone withdrew a blade. *Yes, I want this kingdom...and the female.* As strongly as he'd reacted to her, she *must* be his fated one.

"Come on, McMuscles. I'm being serious. Wake. Up." There it was again. The voice. Soft fingers seemed to brush over his face, yet no one stood before him. "We've got things to do. Stuff has happened, okay? I've learned much while you've been snoozing your life away."

Things to do? Yes. He must save the treasure bound to the pole before she died in anguish. But...he also didn't want to lose his connection to the speaker. Instinct demanded he claw his way to her, grab her, and claim her as his own, forcing all other males to admit an inescapable truth: *She belongs to me.*

He blinked and shook his head. *Belongs to me?* Was the brunette not his fated, after all?

"FYI," she said, "I'll give you ten more seconds to wakey, wakey on your own then I'll take a more direct route. Aka stabbing you until you fight me off. Ten. Nine. Eight. Oh, what the heck. Let's jump ahead. One."

He was torn between two desires, wanting to—Rathbone roared as a sharp pain erupted in his shoulder.

He jerked upright and opened his eyes. A dagger protruded from his shoulder. A fact he registered just before new memories flooded him. The ocean. The Astra and the fog. Agony. Falling. Water. Dying a thousand deaths without truly dying. The dream. Lore.

He drew in a ragged breath. So many revelations to unpack,

but Neeka currently straddled his thighs. Only one thought mattered. *Do not let her escape.*

"Oh, good, you're awake," she said, smiling as if she hadn't just knifed him in the shoulder.

He scowled at her. "Was that truly necessary?"

"Why else would I do it?" She rested her forearms on his pectorals and toyed with the ends of his hair. "You'll be happy to learn I've got a bead on the next bone, and ticked to hear my mother might get there first."

"Why did you injure me then?" he demanded, clasping her hips to lift her off but holding her close instead.

"Do you or do you not value speediness? Don't worry. I'll kiss your boo-boo and make it better." She bent her head and licked the pulse racing at the base of his neck, a good distance from his wound. "See? You're already healing."

He grew rock-hard in a blink. That soft brush of her lips. The gentleness. The dip in her voice. He only craved more.

As she straightened to meet his gaze, he noticed her eyelids had dipped, too. Better, her pupils expanded, eclipsing the vivid amber he'd come to lo—like.

Uncertainty pricked him, and he released the oracle to scrub a hand over his face.

"Guess playtime is over, huh?" With an exaggerated sigh, Neeka stood.

"Playtime never started," he grumbled. When he noticed her attire, his jaw went slack. Harpy perfection. Clad in a raven-hued gown, with a metal corset pushing her breasts skyward, she utterly stunned. The waist cinched in and the skirt billowed in free-flowing grace to kiss her ankles, with twin slits riding the length of each leg, parting with every movement she made. Bloodred stilettos hugged her feet, revealing toenails painted to match and igniting a brand-new foot fetish in him.

Had there ever been a creature more exquisite than her?

She'd pinned up her hair, displaying an elegant neck free of jewelry. He was glad. He had an unobstructed view of her racing pulse, every thump sparking a new burst of heat.

As he rose and took a step in her direction, needing...more, she hurried to a nearby coffee table to gather a stack of papers. "You're probably curious about everything that's been going on in the sixteen hours you've been asleep," she blurted out, looking anywhere but him, ensuring she couldn't read his replies.

He inhaled a deep breath. Exhaled slowly. Fisted and unfisted his hands. But take another step in her direction? No. She'd mentioned a bone. Lore, once the mate of his dreams.

His dream. *That's right.* He'd dreamed a memory. Meeting Lore. Until replaying their introduction, he'd forgotten the finer details. Hades's initial warning. Rathbone's estimation of Lore as a status symbol. The gleam of satisfaction he'd spotted in her eyes. Now that he knew her better, he couldn't brush it off. He'd viewed that same gleam every time he'd pleased her. But what did any of it mean?

Neeka's words penetrated his riotous thoughts, and shock pummeled him. The second she glanced his way, he asked, "I slept sixteen hours?" Truly?

"You did. Here's the rundown of what happened while you were out," she said. "I learned you're an omni-shapeshifter, so you can stop trying to hide it. And I'd kinda appreciate an explanation about why you haven't shifted into, oh, I don't know, an Astra, then snuck into their midst and killed them all?"

"I hate shifting into people," he grumbled, his insides bracing as if preparing to jump out of his skin. "I become the other person on a molecular level, which leaves a mark. But more than that, I need their blood to do it."

She gaped at him. "Are you saying you can access their thoughts and memories if you shift into their image?"

"I'm saying it messes with my head, leaving me feeling as if I'm me but not me, even when I return to my own skin." A weakness he rarely shared with others. Rarely? Ha! Try never.

Not even Hades knew. So why had Rathbone just handed the information to Neeka? "Why? Is there something you don't wish me to learn?"

Her features softened. "First, that sucks for you. It's hard enough being ourselves, yeah? Second, no. Read their minds if you wish."

That was why he'd done it. She got him. "I've enjoyed being myself lately," he admitted. Since meeting her. A fact he almost...feared.

"Yes. Well." She cleared her throat. "Moving on. Azar poisoned you, but I saved the day by acquiring the antidote. Yes, I've added an unnamed boon to your bill, and you *will* pay. I'll tell you what I want when I decide. Now, I'll give you fifteen minutes to clean up, then we're leaving this little paradise whether you're ready or not."

"I'll take however long I need, carrot." Which would be fifteen minutes, and not a second more. He scanned the paradise in question. An unfamiliar house with colorful walls, tons of windows, and bedazzled furnishings. Through the glass, he spied a lovely purple ocean lapping at pink sand. "Is this your home?"

"One of them."

He liked it. Felt comfortable here. Her personality shined through. Vivid, wild, and bright. It struck him as a place to rest and recharge, more of a home than the palace had ever been.

He rubbed the sudden ache in his sternum.

"Here. This is yours." Neeka reached into a pocket in her skirt, withdrew a small glowing orb, and tossed it in his direction.

Lore's hiding place. The ache worsened. He held his wife in his palm, yet he'd never felt less connected to her. Why? Why was he irritated by even the thought of dealing with her right now? Because of his doubts?

The same doubts Styx once displayed?

Had Styx spoken true regarding his dealings with Lore? Had

Rathbone misjudged her from the beginning, allowing desire to color his thoughts? Not just any desire, but a unique obsession a goddess of her class would have no trouble manufacturing, thereby convincing a young warrior he'd found his one and only...

But had he?

His gaze returned to Neeka.

"Well?" she prompted, shifting from one sexy foot to the other.

"Well what?" he demanded with more force than he'd intended. If Lore had tricked and betrayed him, rousing false desire inside him...

He ground his molars.

"Do you want the Astra to acquire a piece of your precious Lore, or are you the Wrath of Blood and Bones? Superhero name pending. Because that's what will happen if we're late for our very important date."

The mátia narrowed. "What date?"

She cringed, as if she felt sorry for him. "Lookit. I've been probing into the depths of my subconscious. Information hidden in shadows, visions I'd forgotten, tidbits left by the Hall of Secrets, that sort of thing. There's no easy way to tell you this, so Imma just blurt it." She paused to draw in a deep breath. Held it.

And held it.

"Neeka," he growled.

"Give me a second to center. Geez," she said, exhaling with force. "Okay, here goes." She drew in another deep breath, closed her eyes, and lobbed multiple balls of information at him. "Centuries ago, Hera hired a fae to join your stable, conceive her grandson, and bail on you. Congrats! It's a boy, and he somehow stopped aging at sixteen. His name is Maximus, and he's being kept in a world called Aweland. He's currently in possession of a bone, and we're going to steal it during his birthday party. You ready?"

20

"Do not stroke the ruby choker," Neeka muttered. "Do not."
She repeated the critically important mantra inside her mind
again and again, the words a lifeline to her sanity.

Head high, she ventured toward a Queen of Hearts–esque
garden behind a castle straight out of every fairy tale ever written. But dang it, the choker snaking around her neck seared her
skin—because the choker was Rathbone!

That's right. She wore the King of Agonies. He currently
pressed against her thumping pulse.

How she wished she could see his face and gauge his thoughts.
In the seconds after she'd made her big announcement about
his (alleged) son, he'd masked his features and said, "Wear me."
Then he'd shifted into the glorious piece of jewelry she'd cov-
eted with every fiber of her being. As soon as she'd donned him,
he'd teleported her to Aweland.

Clearly, he'd been here before, as he'd been to all the other realms they'd visited. Without a key, there was no other way to flash directly into a realm.

Dang it! She was stroking the choker. Besides being agonizingly aware of the sexy male strapped to her neck, she had to deal with a plague of mini-visions. For some reason, she kept seeing flashes of a younger Rathbone battling the fierce King Styx to save a sobbing Lore from a whipping.

The ferocity behind Red's every blow...he'd been a warrior possessed. Until he'd absconded with the goddess and reached safety. Then he'd become a besotted suitor, working hard to impress her. Presenting her with fresh flowers and jewelry. Massaging her, as he'd done for Neeka.

Her ribs drew tight. Knowing what she knew about his mother, she wondered if he'd attempted to buy the goddess's affections. Perhaps Neeka's mind showed her these tidbits as an alert. A *this is what you're up against* kind of thing.

Should she finally use the elixir?

She'd filled a fresh vial and strapped the little glass container to her garter. But every time she'd considered advancing her plan, she'd hesitated. What if Rathbone was her consort and she ruined everything?

She hated to admit it but...he could be. Her awareness of him continued to sharpen. Her desire to talk to him, to kiss him and touch him and ride him and cuddle him and eat carrots off his chest only ever magnified. Part of her longed to curl up in his embrace and let the rest of the world disappear while she napped. To pretend, just for a little while, that there were no obstacles in their way.

"Why don't you shift into my twin?" she muttered to him. "Being me on a molecular level has gotta be better than driving me to distraction during such an important mission. For goodness sake, Red, we're about to meet with your potential son."

The choker vibrated, sending an avalanche of tingles across

her nerve endings. Her belly fluttered, and her knees quaked. *Delicious.*

Gah! How was she supposed to function like this? "Is that your way of telling me there's nothing better than driving me to distraction?"

The next vibration wrenched a moan from her.

"I'll take that as a no," she muttered. "Now be a good boy. It's showtime."

Slapping on a smile, she approached a female dressed in a checkered Mad Hatter–type suit, minus a shirt, putting her ginormous bazongas on display. A top hat was pinned to her hair. An oversized bowtie complimented a jacket with floor-length tails. Judging by her pent-up-aggression vibe, she was a wolf-shifter. And bored. She held a clipboard, checking names against a lengthy guest list.

Behind her, the party raged. Groups of immortal females clustered together, drinking beer from cans and chatting, clearly pretending not to be as bored as the shifter. Everyone represented a topless character from *Alice in Wonderland*. No males were present. But then, Neeka had uncovered just enough information about the realm to know Hera, its owner, hadn't visited in centuries. Now Rathbone's somehow-eternally-sixteen-year-old son ruled the land, and he'd instituted a No Other Dudes law. And also topless Mondays. And Tuesdays, Wednesdays, Thursdays, Fridays, Saturdays, and Sundays.

Neeka stopped in front of Clipboard, who didn't bother glancing up as she intoned, "Name?"

"Blaze Champagne," Neeka stated, letting instinct guide her.

Clipboard looked up, exasperation evident. "Well, it's about time. You're only five minutes early, which means you're fifteen minutes late. The other strippers are already in their cages."

Cages? Neeka cast her gaze over the garden. Lush green bushes acted as walls, with flowering trees providing shade for

tables peppered with energy drinks, more beer, and all the fix-
ings for chili dogs and hot wings. "Um... I see no cages."

"Go past the bushes, through the maze, and to the right,"
Clipboard said. "And hurry! Trust me, you don't want His Hotness getting upset."

His Hotness? "Ten-four." She strutted forward, immediately
refocusing on Rathbone. "Your son sounds like a real tool, by
the way."

—*He might not be my child.*— Rathbone's rough and tumble
voice whispered through her head, and she yelped, drawing the
gaze of several attendees, all of whom eyed her with varying
degrees of pity.

"You can communicate telepathically in this form?" Dang it,
dang it, dang it! That was next-level intimacy and it unleashed
a more intense avalanche of tingles. This one left a trail of fire
in its wake. She sailed through an open arch between bushes.
"Why didn't you reply sooner?"

—*You can hear me?*— Shock saturated his words.

Guess he hadn't known. Which meant she was a first. An only.

Pride infiltrated her cells. Unless this was proof they were
maybe, could be, possibly inevitable? Brought together by destiny?

Ribs drawing tight again...

—*Hera paid a sorceress to allow my nanny and the military commander to communicate telepathically with me. Until you, I was never
able to reciprocate.*— His tone held notes of frustration and amusement.

"Am I your nanny or military commander in this scenario?
No, don't answer. We both know it's both. I promise I won't
use my position for personal gain. Other than a few times. A
couple dozen at most." Skipping now, she maneuvered through
the maze. Considering an endless parade of signs read "This
way" and "No, that way," she navigated with ease. "Since I'm
your overlord, as you just admitted, I insist we take this mo-

ment to discuss your thoughts and feelings. What if Maximus is, in fact, your child?"

—*I'll deal. But I expect my nanny to help me.*—

"Not your military commander? You're too macho to admit you secretly long to obey my every order?"

—*Yes, thank you for noticing.*—

The dry response extracted an unexpected laugh from her, and ushered in the most delightful waves of affection. She tried to make light of it, saying, "Rathbone made a funny." Adorable male.

A weary sigh drifted through her head. —*I don't know what to think or feel. So much has happened. Astra surprised me in my own home. I dreamed a memory that's made me question what I thought I knew, and learned I might have allowed a cold, calculating queen to raise a child I should have protected. Now I'm traversing the childhood home I despise with a female I crave far too much.*—

Neeka drew to a halt. What memory had he dreamed? What did he question? *This* was his childhood home? An amalgamation of fictional fantasy lands? Skipping over his "female I crave" confession was a herculean endeavor. For peace of mind, she did it and said, "I'd love to hear more about your childhood."

—*Hera wished me to become her personal guard, devoted to her protection. Loyal without reservation. But the trainers she entrusted with my care were too afraid of her to correct my mistakes, and servants catered to my every desire, unwilling to tell me no. Anytime she deigned to visit, I acted out, and she explained how thoroughly I disappointed her.*—

His matter-of-fact delivery broke Neeka's heart, but his trust in her helped weld it back together. He felt close enough to her—safe enough—to share painful glimpses of his past. The events that had shaped him into the steadfast male he was today.

Without thought, she reached up to stroke the ruby choker. "My sweet Red."

Rathbone's groan filled her head, and her blood heated. Perhaps they should focus on his craving, after all. Then a thought hit, bringing a boatload of fear, and she chilled in a hurry. He'd faced betrayal from his mother. Betrayal from his wife, not that he fully accepted it yet. Soon, he would face betrayal from Neeka. She'd told herself he would forgive her. But what if he didn't?

"There's nothing we can do with our past but learn from it, let it go, and grab hold of a better future," she offered, wrapping her fingers around the gemstones, as if they fought to get away. "We can't move forward if we're always looking back." Advice she should apply to her own life.

—*Are you trying to tell me something, carrot?*—

The beloved nickname, uttered so intimately, unleashed a hurricane of delicious sensation. Her knees quaked.

"I don't know," she admitted, starting forward. She drew up short when she cleared another arch and spied her new surroundings. Okay. Wow. Cages. They were scattered throughout a rose garden, dangling around a royal dais where a teenage boy reclined on a cushioned lounge, eating potato chips fed to him by a female dressed as a (topless) cat.

Though on the puny side, the boy possessed red skin and mátia. Not Rathbone's kid? Ha!

—*So I'm a father.*— Amazement, resignation, and regret dripped from each word.

"Oh, yeah. You're a father." But how had Maximus remained a teenager so long, without maturing mentally or emotionally? Because he absolutely had not matured. That was evident as he slapped a woman's butt cheek, snickered, and made a lewd hand gesture. "Do you see the mother?"

—*No. But I doubt she lives. Hera would've viewed her as a liability.*—

So they had no idea what kind of power and abilities the kid wielded outside of what he'd inherited from Rathbone. Well, no matter. "I'll be gentle with him," Neeka vowed.

The choker vibrated, making her feel as if she were being hugged.

Determined, she glided forward, stopping just in front of the dais. She caught Maximus's notice along the way, and he jolted upright with a scowl.

"You're wearing a top. Why are you wearing a top?" he grouched, brushing aside the next chip offering. "That's an offense worthy of death!"

"He's worse than a tool," she muttered.

—*But is he wrong?*—

She snorted. Another funny from Rathbone. Her lips curled in a smile.

"You find my wrath amusing, wench?" the kid sputtered.

Focus! Right. "Where's your Gam Gam, sport? Or a guardian? Whatever. Who's in charge here?"

"I am." Each of his dark eyes narrowed. "I'm Maximus the Dread, god of incredible power and might, with abilities your paltry mind cannot yet fathom, and you dare to question me?"

Neeka snickered with delight. Dude. Now a funny from the kid! The apple certainly didn't fall far from the tree. "Lookit, boy-o. You own a special bone, and I want it." Good. Blunt and to the point. "Give it to me, and we can have a tea together before I abduct you to another realm."

"I'll give you a special bone. It's right here." He grabbed his crotch. "So why don't you come take it like a good little girl?"

—*I don't know what to say except, meet young Rathbone.*—

She thought over the boy's offer, shrugged, and nodded. "Okay." Take the bone? Very well. "I accept your invitation."

—*You said you'd be gentle with him.*— Rathbone groaned the words.

"I tried my hardest and got nowhere," she whispered as she motored up the dais steps. "I know you await results, so I changed course. You're welcome."

—*Neeka. Carrot.*—

"I won't kill him, Wrath Boned. Honest!"

The punk's irritating smirk returned as she drew near, as if he'd won a great war.

The self-proclaimed King Hotness patted his thigh, expecting her to take a seat there. Instead, she canted her head, smiled— and punched him in the face. He flew from the lounge, crashing to the dais with a heavy thud. A pained groan left him. As blood spurted from his broken nose, the chip feeder rushed off.

"Now then," Neeka said with all the sweetness she could muster. "The bone I seek is an ilium with symbols carved throughout. You will give it to me. Your condition when we leave with it is up to you."

"You hit me. You hit me!" The boy scrambled to his feet, his mátia wide with astonishment. "You're going to pay so hard."

"Will I? Because I kinda feel like I earned a reward. Maybe I should do it again." Wings buzzing, Neeka leaped over the lounge and punched him again. Again, he flew backward, landing with a thud. She followed him over and pinned him down, pressing her knees deep into his shoulders. "Still feels like I earned a reward."

He struggled without success.

"Look, kid. Here's how things will progress. I'm going to break *your* bones every ten seconds you fail to hand over the one I seek."

—*I would rather you didn't.*—

"Fine!" she burst out for Rathbone's benefit. "I'll bruise you every twenty seconds."

"Guards! Guards!" Maximus increased his struggles. "You will die screaming."

"Now where have I heard that threat before?" Neeka raised her fist...

"Do not harm him," someone commanded behind them.

She punched the kid a third time before tossing a casual glance over her shoulder. The grandmother? Beautiful, with dark hair, pale skin, and vibrant blue eyes, wearing an ivory ball gown.

—*Hera*.— A growl sounded inside Neeka's head moments before Rathbone materialized at her side. Fury radiated from him.

This was Hera?

Hold up. Did he know Lore could totally pass for Hera's sister? "Oh, baby doll," Neeka whispered under her breath, "you really do have mommy issues that rival mine." No wonder he'd been clinging to a future with the female so staunchly.

Maximus ceased struggling. Neeka switched her attention to him just in time to see him mouth the words *My father*.

Her stomach churned, the urge to spank the little punk fading. Had he spent the bulk of his life wondering about his dad?

"He's so strong," the boy said, his expression reverent.

She sprang up, freeing him. He scrambled to his feet, his gaze remaining locked on Rathbone.

"You stole from me," Rathbone snarled at his mother, making *Neeka* shudder. Never had she encountered such loathing.

Hera lifted her nose higher in the air. "I'm surprised you found us, considering you are so consumed with your own life."

"I am so consumed?" The questions lashed from him. "Me?"

Neeka reached out to link her fingers with Rathbone's. He squeezed her, as if holding on for survival. She squeezed him right back.

"The clues were there," Hera said, her expression snippy. "It's not my fault you were unable to see them. As for the bone, you're too late. Earlier this morn, your companion's younger sister came with your wife to collect it."

Neeka's hackles flared. Younger sister? The nerve of this goddess! And oh! She hated, hated, hated that her mother had beaten her here.

Tension turned Rathbone into a pillar of stone. "I'll be taking the boy with me and undoing whatever was done to keep him this age."

"You won't." Hera smiled at him, as smug as Maximus had been. "Precautions have already been taken." A second later, everyone but Rathbone and Neeka vanished.

Rathbone remained statue still for several beats before cursing. He flashed her to his bedroom in the Realm of Agonies. Guess they were done with the Realm of the Forgotten. Which mattered because...she couldn't recall. Oh, well.

"I'll get him back, and I'll steal the bone from Grenwich," she promised. "I'll also find the remaining bones. She won't beat me again. In the meantime, we should probably talk about what happ—"

"I'm going to refortify the defenses," he interjected, keeping his gaze anywhere but on her. He said nothing more before flashing away, leaving her alone.

Knees knocking, she sank onto the edge of his bed. Poor Rathbone. So many shocks today. Almost dying. Learning he had a son. Losing said son. Temporarily misplacing a bone. Finding out his wife had helped his most hated enemy for reasons Neeka had already discerned. A new worry thrown on the mounting heap.

According to the visions, the goddess partnered with Erebus. Like the Astra, the Deathless desired Lore's resurrection. They hoped to kill her at the final ceremony, but the god intended for her to birth those hideous flesh-eaters. Ergo, Lore would do anything necessary to aid the Astra in their quest. *Should have guessed.*

Had Rathbone begun to accept the truth? Should she tell him everything? Was he ready to hear it?

What if he kicked her to the curb? She hadn't been part of the ceremony in either vision, so, something took her out of the game along the way.

Better to wait. To gain some assurances.

She withdrew the elixir from her garter, the thick liquid

swishing inside. The best assurance in town. Should she risk losing a genuine connection? Shouldn't she?

With the lives of harpies and Rathbone on the line, she should be willing to risk anything. So. Decision made. They would both drink and boom, their bond would solidify. He would be compelled to do whatever she asked.

Driven by instinct, she marched to the decanter of whiskey at the wet bar, unstopped the vial, and poured the contents inside. Trembling, she prepared two glasses…and drained one without thinking. Oops. The liquid burned going down. Burned hotter as it spread through the rest of her. Cells fizzed and popped. Well. There was no going back now. She'd ingested the elixir, and it couldn't be undone.

She refilled the glass, willing to ingest a second round when Rathbone enjoyed his first. Double the power, right? With nothing left to do, she sat at the edge of the bed and awaited his return.

How much time passed before he reappeared, she didn't know. But when he did, she was a mess of uncertainty. He was a mess, period, both sweaty and bloody. He spotted her, his mátia locking on her, noticed the waiting glass and scowled.

She licked her lips and proceeded full steam ahead. "Let's have a drink and discuss—"

"No drinks." He flashed over, grabbed the glass, and poured the contents into the decanter. "The Astra won't bypass my new traps. You're safe anywhere on the grounds. I'm taking a shower. Be gone when I exit." Poof. He disappeared.

Oookay. What just happened? This was more than an upset over today's events.

The urge to comfort him took center stage, and she remained. If he wanted her gone, he'd have to carry her out, and that was that.

Minutes that felt like hours passed. Finally, the door opened. She straightened with a snap, her heart thudding.

Her gaze found him. He stood in the doorway, naked. Water dotted his lashes and wet his scarlet skin, droplets cascading over his bulging muscles. His mátia focused on her, glinting with desperate need.

Her heart thudded faster, harder. She lost her breath.

"You should have left," he growled, stomping over to claim her parting lips with his own.

21

So many thoughts barraged Rathbone. His spoiled son, raised by a despised foe. Lore's partnership with the very enemy attempting to kill her. The lost bone. The comfort and torment of Neeka's presence. His undeniable desire for the oracle and no other. He'd never felt so raw or needed solace more.

He kissed his oracle with all the fervency seething inside him. She kissed him just as wildly, matching him stroke for stroke, grounding him in the moment. Addicting him to the wonder of her taste. The perfection of her scent. The delight of being wrapped in her arms. Her. Just her. Everything she brought to the table. Strength and cunning. Smiles and laughs. A shockingly tender heart. Such a zest for life.

Now, he burned. He was an inferno, and she was the never-ending supply of kindling. She lit an unquenchable fire so deep within him the flames consumed him from the inside out.

He rolled his tongue with hers, removed and tossed her metal breastplate. Before the heavy piece even hit the floor, he had her plump breasts in his hands. A groan of pleasure slipped from her, and he swallowed it. The sweetness of her whipped him into a frenzy.

This wasn't the same as other interludes, and he knew it. He ached worse, craved more, and cared nothing for the consequences. The danger of relying on someone else when he had yet to work through the box of unpinned grenades awaiting his attention.

What if…what if he'd made a mistake, and *Neeka* was his fated one? He'd told himself it was impossible, but was it?

The mere idea awoke a possessive beast inside him. It snarled and clawed, demanding its due. Her, only her. Him for her, and only him. No one else should hear these delicious noises she made. No other should hold and touch her like this. Rathbone the Only for Neeka.

He kissed her harder. Deeper. Desperate to leave his mark. Whatever she was to him, he—they—were done with their old ways of doing business. Pretending to be unaffected by each other. And he knew she'd pretended. Being draped on her neck today, he'd felt her pulse hammer with arousal. He'd also felt the heat of her silken skin and scented the fragrance of tart cherries and sweet almonds with every breath. He'd gotten locked in a constant cycle of arousal, too. Need her, calm himself. Need her, calm himself.

Now, his awareness of her reached new heights. *Despite* the windfall of truth that had been unleashed and the magnitude of events taking place around them. World-changing things he must deal with once he could think past the enigmatic beauty he longed to make scream in his bed.

Bed. Yes. Growling, Rathbone gripped Neeka by the waist and tossed her on the mattress. He covered her body with his before she ceased bouncing, pinning her with his weight. As she coiled her limbs around him, he let himself sink into her.

He sucked air between his teeth. Hardness pressed into softness, and it maddened him.

"I want you," he all but snarled, bracing on his elbows. Panting breaths left him. "All of you. Everything. Nothing held back."

Dark, luminous eyes met his, somehow confident yet vulnerable and so haunting he might see them in his dreams for the rest of eternity. "Why do you want me so much when you're in love with another?"

A muscle jumped in his jaw. "Let's not talk of her. There's only you and me in this bed."

She groaned, saying, "Dang you. That's a good answer." Softening against him, she moistened her lips. "I won't give you everything, but I will give you more. Remember, anything but the ultimate penetration."

"Very well." He would take whatever she offered and make it count.

Though the storm continued to whip inside him, Rathbone gently cupped her cheek and traced the pad of his thumb over the dip in her bottom lip. Her inhalation hitched. He lowered his head, kissed her brow, one eye then the other, then the bridge of her nose. The tip. She seemed to stop breathing entirely. Tremors rocked her against him. His? Hers? Both?

"Prepare yourself for *anything*," he commanded.

Her lids hooded. "Prepare *myself*?" Tendrils of curly black hair had escaped confinement and framed her face. "I'm supposed to do your job for you?" she teased, a siren he couldn't resist.

He gave her what must be a big bad wolf smile. "The oracle likes to play with her male. Noted."

The claim *her male* reverberated in his head, and it wasn't panic he experienced but satisfaction.

Their gazes met. Had she noticed his words?

With a ragged cry, Neeka lifted her head and claimed his lips. Oh, she'd noticed. She fisted his hair and thrust her tongue against his. Any gentleness in her had evaporated. Her ferocity sparked his, the kiss becoming frantic.

As she dragged her little harpy claws along his scalp, heat rushed over him. Thoughts dissolved one after the other. The hottest, sweetest desire raged. A potent blend of sensation, frenzy, and bliss.

Driven by primitive instinct, he slid his hands over her body. Learning her hollows. Kneading her peaks. Marveling. Her every curve dawned a revelation of rapture. And her reactions to his touch…

Guttural growls erupted from him. She responded with unabashed euphoria, moaning and writhing, urging him on and on and on. So on and on and on he went. And still the kiss continued. Still hands wandered. When he slipped his fingers beneath her panties, he thought he might never get enough.

Rathbone teased and tormented her until she gifted him with a string of ragged cries. As he slid a digit into her wetness, he licked her lips, her jaw, and ran her ear lobe between his teeth.

Eyes closed, panting and writhing as she chased his touch, she tilted her head, baring her vulnerable neck in offering. His chest clenched at the sight and feel of her. Pleasure in its purest form.

Heart a thunderous boom, he traced his tongue along her carotid, where hot blood rushed. When he reached the top of her transparent tank, truth spilled from him. "I don't think I'll have the strength to ever let you go."

She moaned and squirmed, sending his fingers deeper with their next inward glide. "I know you're talking, but I don't know what you're saying."

Good. He didn't want her to know. Not yet. He wasn't sure of her reaction—wasn't even sure of his own.

"Was it sexy, what you said?" She rocked her hips, straining the limits of his control. "I bet it was sexy."

"It was truth."

She chuckled, the soft sound washing over him. "There you go, talking without letting me know what you're saying."

"I'll make it up to you." He sucked her racing pulse. As she treated him to another exquisite moan, he pulled from her, climbed to his knees, and straddled her thighs. "Look at you," he said, and lapped at the honey coating his fingers.

Amber eyes dipped. Lips plumped from his kisses parted.

"You're staring," she said, half shy maiden, half enchanting temptress.

He took a long lick. "And sampling."

She slid a leg out from between his and pressed her booted foot against his pec. "Do I meet with your approval?"

"What do you think?" He lowered his hand to stroke his straining fly, the metal teeth soon to split.

Her gaze dropped. "Mmm," she cooed and nibbled on her bottom lip. "I think—" She gasped, confusing him. A second later, her irises turned glassy, and she peered far beyond him.

He frowned. "Neeka? Carrot?"

Silence greeted him. Was she having a vision? Not knowing what to do, he waited exactly as he was. One minute flowed into another, leaving him in a state of suspended agony. Finally, she blinked into focus, the exhilaration she'd evinced only moments before gone.

"We can steal the ilium from the Astra, but we must leave now," she stated, already wiggling out from under him.

"*Now* now?" he all but roared, nothing else registering.

"Oh, good. You didn't misunderstand." Appearing utterly unaffected by what they'd just done—and wouldn't be finishing—she jumped to her feet, righted her uniform, and held out her hand. The slight tremor nullified him somewhat. "Time is of the essence, and I've got to show you something before we confront the big bad."

"*I* am the big bad," he snapped, flashing to tower in front of her. "And I—you—" His hands fisted and unfisted. What did he mean to say? What, what?

She blinked up at him, vulnerable again. And yet, he also detected a thread of guilt. Why? "You *do* wish to fetch the bone, yes? You still plan to resurrect Lore?"

The stolen bone. His wife. The Song of Life. Neeka's warning computed at last, and he forced himself to nod. Because there were too many unknown variables. Because he needed the oracle far too much for it to be anything other than dangerous. Because he couldn't discern the truth concerning his forever queen until he brought Lore to life.

Neeka's shoulders shrank in the slightest bit, making his chest clench. "Thought so." She brightened up a second later, beaming a smile at him. "Shall we toast to the wisdom of your decision before we go then?"

"We shall not." He took her hand, twining their fingers. "Know this. I meant what I said. I want all of you. Long-term. I don't know what I feel for Lore. There's a chance she played and betrayed me, and if so, she will suffer the consequences."

The oracle softened, leaning into him, only to stiffen, straighten and pale. "We should go."

He'd stated his piece. Now he would give her time to think. "Where are we going?"

"Back to Harpina. Sorry, Ruby Fury, but you've got to do something you hate. And you aren't the only one! I'm moving into Roc's dungeon. But don't—"

"Worry," he interjected with a resolved sigh. "I know. You've got things covered."

Azar paced in front of the ilium that rested upon the dresser in his bedroom. His new tracker had collected the piece on his behalf. A situation he hadn't liked, but he couldn't deny the results. Even better, the female had a lead on the remaining bones.

"Show yourself, Lore." He knew she could appear wherever the smallest fragment of her skeletal system happened to be.

She did not show herself.

A mix of frustration and anger scratched at him. A familiar sensation when dealing with the goddess. She loved this game. Had enjoyed it since the beginning when he'd won her skull from a demon prince. Something Azar shouldn't have done. But he'd been unable to cease pondering the brave beauty he'd slain so ruthlessly. She'd gotten her hooks in him, and he'd been too much of a fool to see it.

He stomped with more force. "Show yourself. Now."

She didn't. Because Lore.

He'd read reports of Rathbone's dealings with Neeka, and there'd been mention of unnamed favors. Apparently, females responded to those. "Show yourself, and I will grant you a boon of your choosing, as long as it doesn't affect my task." He'd never lowered himself to bargain with anyone—until her.

As hoped, Lore materialized within seconds. Smirking. "Such an easy mark."

He ground to a halt. Well. He'd just discovered the downside to such negotiations. They worked.

"Oops, did I say that aloud?" she asked, turning and bending over. "I'm bad and should be spanked."

His hands balled into fists, as his blood boiled with things he didn't wish to name. Once, to torment him, she'd disrobed in his presence. Now, no matter how many layers of clothing she wore, he still saw her soft perfection on full display.

With everyone else, she pretended to be what they desired most. With Azar, she seemed to delight in revealing her inner evil. A punishment for overseeing her murder, he supposed.

Or maybe she worked with Erebus, his enemy. The male loved to toy with their emotions, leaving them in abject misery. Perhaps she pretended with Azar, too, giving him what he secretly desired. How frustrating it was to know everything and absolutely nothing at the same time.

"Are you Jezebel?" he asked.

"Maybe. Maybe not. Does it matter? Whatever name you call me, I'm still me."

Yes. Still loathsome. "Grenwich told me you assisted with the bone's acquisition. Tell me why," he commanded. "You know I plan to kill you again."

She pouted a little. "So no spanking then?"

His fists tightened, his knuckles threatening to crack. "Answer the question."

"Fine." Straightening, she said, "I did it because I wanted to. Obviously. Now, about that boon…"

"Half answers receive half boons," he grated.

"Oh, very well. I did it because I knew you wouldn't change your mind about bringing me to life. But Rathbone might. You should see the way he looks at his oracle. It's sickening, really."

"I could change my mind." He pushed the words through clenched teeth. He would never change his mind.

"Ha! When the time comes, you'll do whatever I command. You won't be able to help yourself."

Her unwavering confidence drew a panicked response from deep within him. "Forget," he demanded under his breath.

A tinkling laugh escaped her. "You can't forget what you did, and you know it. Eventually you'll have to face the truth. You won't be able to ignore the consequences of your past."

He fought to keep his mind focused solely on her. "Why aren't you upset? The red king has affections for another female, yet he is your fated." What did the goddess comprehend that Azar didn't?

"*Is* he my fated?" She sauntered over, halting mere inches away. "How can I be his…when I'm your gravita?" Her tone dropped to a husky whisper. "Can't you feel the connection between us, sweetness?"

The suggestion, and ridiculous endearment, went straight to his head, fogging his mind. What if they *were* fated? What if— he narrowed his eyes. "Your ability to influence the thoughts and emotions of others has strengthened."

"I know." She fluffed her hair. "Isn't it wonderful?"

"Even still," he continued, "you will never command me."

Her smile returned, only much wider. "We'll see."

Azar would have happily parted with an array of internal organs to reach into the spirit realm and throttle her. Lore was *not* his gravita. Deal with her for the rest of eternity? No. He might dream of her and hunger for her in ways he'd never hungered for another, but he truly believed walking into a firstone blade—the only weapon capable of ending him—was preferable to connecting his forever with hers. She would make an already miserable existence more so.

"Rathbone might change his mind, he might not," Azar stated. "I've been told trouble is soon to brew between the king and his oracle."

"Thanks for the information." Lore tilted her head, frowning with the barest hint of confusion. "But why tell me, thereby aiding *my* cause rather than your own?"

"I want you to know I will defeat you no matter the odds stacked against me. The moment you are tangible, I *will* strike, ending you for good."

She rolled her eyes. "Sorry, Astra, but I'll just revive yet again, thanks to the Song of Life. You won't be winning this."

He said nothing else. Because he understood what had to be done to end her permanently. And he would be doing it.

"By the way. I've decided on my boon." Simpering at him, she twirled a strand of dark hair around her finger. "After you bring me to life, but before the ceremony ends, you're going to kiss me—and mean it. I expect tongue, teeth, and heavy groping. Don't disappoint me, doll." With that, she vanished.

He bit back a bellow to demand her immediate return. Good

thing. Roc appeared in his bedroom, his customary scowl more pronounced than usual.

The Commander got straight to business. "We have captured the oracle, Neeka. She refuses to speak with anyone but you, and Taliyah refuses to let us rectify the situation with our customary methods. Therefore, you will question her. But I do not want the goddess's bone anywhere near her." He held out his hand, expectant. "I will take it for safekeeping."

22

What have I done? The question rolled through Neeka's mind as she sat in a dingy dungeon, waiting for Rathbone. Although, honestly, the answer seemed pretty apparent. She'd fallen into like with her Scarlet Thunder, taking a terrible situation and making it worse. A new specialty of hers.

Her reflection had nailed it. He was a bad bet, but she'd fallen anyway. She missed hearing his voice in her head. Missed *him*. Her feelings were engaged now, and that sucked on every level. She didn't even care that he was going to destroy her old life as soon as they had sex.

Bring it on. Some things needed torching.

See? Worse. He couldn't be her everything. No one could.

With a heavy sigh, she kicked out her legs and leaned against a bloodstained rock wall. The chains around her wrists and ankles rattled. Her cell's lone source of light came from a torch hanging outside the bars. It served as the sole source of warmth, too. Meaning, no warmth at all.

She hated being chilled. Or maybe the frigid temperature wasn't the problem. She'd been cold before with zero complaints. Neeka had a sinking suspicion her newfound disdain stemmed from being outside the heat radius of her partner.

Ugh. She was a fool, no ifs, ands, or buts about it. Kissing Rathbone? Loving the feel of his fingers inside her? Intending to do more? Practically begging for it before she did what the mission demanded and convinced him to drink the elixir? Oh, yeah. A straight-up fool. Add in a growing possessiveness and a need to protect him, even from herself, and she'd dug herself a hole from which she couldn't escape.

He'd never forgive her for her secrets, no matter how altruistic her intentions. If he couldn't forgive Lore, a goddess of desire he'd spent centuries chasing, what hope did the Unwanted have?

Neeka tossed a pebble across the concrete and dirt. Of course, this was always meant to be her fate. The gal tossed aside for whatever reason, left aching for what could have been.

She absolutely, positively could not kiss the King of Agonies a third time. Or a fourth. Especially not a fifth. Not until she'd explained the truth.

The moment had come. He was ready.

But was she?

He'd claimed he desired something long-term with her. But what was long-term to him? Did he still hope to keep Lore, too?

If only Neeka didn't admire him. And why, why, why did his every kiss and touch have to set her aflame? Why had she allowed Taliyah to fill her head with thoughts of accepting a consort? Here, now, Neeka could think of little else. Because the odds now skewed in Rathbone's favor.

Perhaps she'd take the General's advice and drink someone's blood. Just a few swallows. If she vomited, she'd prove Rathbone was hers. If not, she could stop weaving dreams of a happily-ever-after in a secret part of her soul.

A hard truth was better than soft ignorance, yes?

Roc appeared in the center of the cell, and Neeka quickly wiped thoughts of kisses and consorts from her mind. He offered her a smug smile, his dark eyes glittering with triumph. For a moment she kind of understood what her friend saw in the guy. Sexy! Except, this wasn't Roc but Rathbone. Big Red had shifted into the Commander, after she'd given him blood and busied the real one by turning herself in. Of course, the first thing real Roc had done was pin her wings, negating her immortal strength.

"You did it!" she said, jumping to her feet. "I never doubted you."

"As well you shouldn't. I'm amazing."

She couldn't hear his voice, but she knew it mimicked Roc's; Rathbone's mouth moved differently than usual. Stiffer. And okay, yeah, the transformation was kind of losing its appeal. If he became the people he portrayed, he might start to desire Taliyah, giving Neeka more competition to overcome.

"That you are," she agreed. "Because you're you. Capable of anything."

He straightened his shoulders, as if her praise had gone straight to his head. Holding out his hand, he showed her the ilium. "Azar didn't hesitate to part with his prize."

"Congrats. But you're feeling all right?" Worry coiled around her. "Your molecular makeup hasn't shifted so much you feel icky?"

"Icky?" One of his brows arched, amusement glittering in his odd irises. "The shift proved easier than ever, and I don't know why."

Ooh. That, she liked. "Maybe because you're more you than ever?" she asked, presenting her cuffed wrists. "Be a dear and free me, then get us the heck out of Dodge. I'm not a fan of my new metal. It makes me weak."

"With a mind like yours, carrot, you are never weak." He

hung the bone at his waist, clasped her wrist cuffs, and tugged her closer.

What a kind thing to say. Not entirely accurate but kind. "You… I…well." Deep breath in. Out. "As I was saying, we should go. I sense danger." Of course, she'd sensed danger before they'd arrived in Harpina, but that was neither here nor there.

He removed the shackles with ease and reached for the wing pinner.

A scowling Azar appeared, a dagger in each grip.

"My suspicions were correct. You are not my Commander," the warlord snarled. "Wherever you go, I will follow. Don't think you can hide in the Realm of the Forgotten. I have acquired a key."

A new ring graced his left thumb. "How'd you get it?"

"Hades gave one to Taliyah."

Rathbone thrust Neeka behind him when she geared to attack.

"You stole from my girl?" she shouted. Dang it! If she hadn't mooned over Rathbone's last comment to her, she would be free of the final restraint, and they'd be home already. But nooo. Her stupid feelings had to go and foil the perfect plan. Although, how Azar had known to acquire a key to the Realm of the Forgotten, she could only guess. Grenwich. Her mother must have tracked them there.

"I've wanted a go at you for a long time," Rathbone stated, palming daggers of his own.

"The feeling is mutual." In a blur of motion, the Astra swiped at him, each blade swinging in a different direction. A totally baller move Neeka planned to learn.

Rathbone dodged, shifting into some kind of prehistoric leopard as he sprang into a counterattack. As the two grappled with inconceivable savagery, she did everything in her power to ditch the stupid wing pinner. Weak as she was, she got nowhere fast. But maybe that wasn't such a bad thing? Despite the cramped quarters, neither male came close to her. Rathbone, her pretty kitty, continued to steer the violence as far from her as possible.

"Hurt him good, Red Rocket!" she called, certain she watched him with goo-goo eyes.

Both combatants landed blows. Arcs of crimson sprayed across the cell. Some hot droplets splattered on Neeka's skin. Medicine! Strength! Oh, how she needed strength…

Her mouth watered as she bent her head. The scent of exotic spices and juniper berries left her shivering with want. But… She sniffed, catching a hint of an unfamiliar fragrance. Azar's?

Ugh. A mix of bloods would only confuse matters more. If Azar's blood made her sick yet Rathbone's calmed her stomach, she'd learn nothing and wonder harder. Wasn't worth the risk.

Suddenly the bone Rathbone acquired clattered to the floor. The guys wrenched apart, reacting as if they'd heard an end-of-round bell. Her king shifted into his original packaging, and both opponents stared at the piece of Lore. Then they focused on each other. Well, *focused* was too mild a term. They warred with their eyes, two starving animals sealed inside an arena with a single slab of meat.

One…three…six heartbeats passed in suspended silence as Neeka contemplated her options, using her foresight to measure the odds of success. Dive for it? No. The flashers would beat her there. Throw herself at the Astra, allowing Rathbone to reclaim it? Yes. That. Not the most brilliant of plans but effective.

Before she made a move, however, Azar tossed a dagger—at her! He lunged, going for the bone, leaving Rathbone with a split-second choice. To her astonishment, he materialized directly in front of her. The blade sank into *his* chest but still she jolted. He'd saved her from a cut and a bit of pain instead of collecting a precious bone? Neeka's eyes widened. What did this mean?

Her knees knocked as he flashed again, going for the bone

next, but he was too late. Azar already had it in hand. The Astra backed up, smug.

She rushed to Rathbone's side, eager to read his lips.

"Big mistake, warlord," he stated as the males faced off once more.

"I won't fail my brothers or my task," Azar intoned. "I will take the rest of Lore's remains from you, revive her and end her for good. Nothing will stop me."

Rathbone arched a brow. "Are you sure you won't be too distracted?" Smiling coldly, he chanted, "Forget, forget, forget."

With a hiss, the warlord stepped forward. Disciplined to the core, he stopped himself midway. "You are an excellent spy. Noted. Whatever you think you've learned matters not. You'll be dead soon enough."

"Astra, I will eat your armies for breakfast and your comrades for lunch. You, I'll save for dessert."

Okay, trash talk time was over. "Time out, everyone." Neeka took a post between the pair, dodging Rathbone's arms as he attempted to grab her. "Let's get real for a sec. Imma be honest, okay? You're both fighting for a losing cause." The truth spilled from her at last. They needed to hear this.

Foresight whispered, *Yes! There's no better time.* They were both major players in this living rom-com—romantic tragedy?—and they were finally ready to hear what she had to say. Or somewhat ready. Mostly not ready at all. But it was a risk she must take, even if it meant losing everything she'd come to crave. Nothing else had changed the future for the better.

Now or never. "Lore is evil, and she plans to kill us all." There. The information was out there. No going back. "As soon as she comes to life, she is the one who unleashes the horde of ravenous shadow monsters with glowing golden rings in their eyes, who eat everyone but Erebus. She births them, and he cheers her on. They are lovers. Heck, he might even be the dad."

Azar glared at her. "I know Lore is evil. Once, she was called

Jezebel the Destroyer, her list of conquests legendary. But I'm onto your tricks now, oracle. You mix truth with lies. I've traversed countless realms, and I've never come across any such thing as shadow monsters able to eat gods."

"Maybe they're a new species."

He shook his head. "Grenwich warned me you'd weave some kind of tall tale to aid your male."

Wait. Grenwich wasn't an oracle. How had she known the future? Or had she simply taken precautions as a just in case?

Neeka balled her hands into fists and looked to Rathbone. He was as stiff as a board, aggression pouring from him. Ugh. Did he doubt her, too, or already hate her? Both?

"I'm telling the truth, the full truth, and nothing but the truth," she vowed, solemn. Though she couldn't blame either male for his suspicions. She'd brought this on herself. "Look. Why else would I seem to betray the General, a woman I dearly love? I'm doing everything I can to change the future and save us all, but so far I've proven unsuccessful."

"I choose to believe your actions rather than your words," Azar snapped. "To me, you are as treacherous as the goddess." He must have summoned the other Astra; they appeared behind him, one after the other.

Scowling now, Rathbone lunged, grabbed Neeka by the pinner, and teleported her—hmm. They were still in Harpina. A place called Last Stop Island, in the middle of the Broken Sea at least a hundred miles from civilization. A strong wind blustered, whipping tornados of sand through the air. Icy raindrops trickled from a cloudy gray sky.

Rathbone released her as if she were toxic and peered out at the choppy waves beating upon the shore. For a long while, neither of them spoke. Dismay began to fray her nerves. She wasn't going to enjoy what happened next.

"The Astra was right? You lied to aid me?"

She read his lips in profile, and she knew. He was deciding *her* consequences.

Hope withered inside of Neeka. But she squared her shoulders and marched onward, unwilling to backtrack. She'd chosen a path, and she would walk it out. Moving in front of him, she said, "I've never lied to you. I've always told the truth."

A muscle ticked beneath his eye. "Have you ever used truth to misdirect me?"

Raindrops splattered over her face, and she swiped them off. "Yes. Often. And I'm not sorry I did it, only sorry I hurt you. So very sorry."

A long while passed without a word from him.

"Say something," she beseeched.

He did. The death knell. "You've forced me to agree with my enemy. I cannot trust you. And if I cannot trust you, I cannot keep you."

Her heart and stomach traded places, both curdling. "In my defense—"

"You have no defense," he interjected.

Oh, but she did. "I'm trying to save our lives! That's the best defense there is."

"You're trying to save *harpy* lives, and you're doing it while scheming to cause the eternal death of someone I considered my fated." Absolute, utter rage glinted in his eyes.

A cold sweat beaded on her nape. "Not just harpy lives," she whispered, her wings buzzing beneath the pinner. "I've seen you die twice. No telling how many other times I've seen it and forgotten." In for a penny, in for a pound. "That's not all. I've attempted to use a mystical elixir to override your bond to Lore with a stronger bond to me." Keeping secrets hadn't done her any good. "You didn't drink it, though."

Rigidity descended over him. The kind of stillness that gripped a predator just before an attack. Again he lapsed into silence, which told her plenty.

Neeka flinched. They were over before they'd started, weren't they? "I won't beg you to forgive me." She'd tried that with her mother and gotten nowhere. "Do you believe me about Lore's evil at least? Or do you still want her?"

"What do my feelings for her matter? I don't want you," he snapped.

Ouch. That cut deeper than expected. Fighting a sudden well of tears, she clasped his shoulders, desperate for some kind of connection with him. More desperate to make him understand. "You know me, and I know you. You're strong and loyal, and when you aren't flaying my character, you're fun." *Do it. Tell him the rest.* "I doubt Lore is your fated because I think… I think you are mine. My consort."

He jolted as if she'd struck him. But he didn't speak.

"Rathbone—"

He shrugged her off, the finality of the action worse than any physical wound. "You didn't complete your job, so you won't receive your payday. If ever you approach me—don't approach me, harpy. You won't like what happens if you do." That said, he vanished, leaving her pinned and weaponless, fully vulnerable.

The fight drained from her, and hot tears gathered, stinging her eyes. Rejected. Again.

As if the storm had waited for her total defeat, it opened the clouds and deluged the beach with hail. She didn't move, just stood there, getting hit, bleeding inside and out. Another male had washed his hands of her. Granted, she'd contributed greatly to the demise of this particular relationship, but wasn't she worth a battle or two?

A harpy-mermaid pierced the surface of the water. The first of many. Neeka groaned. There were at least twenty with an assortment of sharks thrown in the midst. The army displayed unmistakable glee. They must sense her weakened state.

Harmaids despised harpies without tails. Or anyone. They were basically feral water cats with scales.

A vibration behind her. Rathbone? Hope sparked as Neeka spun.

She wilted. "Oh. It's you." Her mother sashayed through the island foliage, grinning. "Have you come to gloat or kill me?"

"Gloat," Grenwich said. She stopped at Neeka's side, but true to her word, she didn't strike. "I enjoy seeing you this miserable. Things will only get worse for you when I find the remaining bones."

Rathbone had left an invisible knife in Neeka's heart, and her mother just twisted it. "Lore's going to kill us all. You get that, yes?"

"As long as you die in defeat, I'll die happy."

Regret for what could have been joined the monsoon inside Neeka. More hurt. Frustration. Anger. For the first time in her remembrance, however, she experienced no shame and guilt. No more accepting punishment for a youthful foible.

"Get over yourself already. I was a child. You were an adult. Why didn't *you* protect me or your consort? Where is *your* blame?"

Her mother smiled coldly. An expression made all the more terrible as raindrops streamed down her cheeks in a mimic of tears. "I won't tell the Astra you're here. They'd collect you and lock you up again. I'm curious to learn who you'll go to for help, now that you've burned every bridge. Of course, you'll have to make it off the island without dying in the sea first."

23

Rathbone materialized in Hades's throne room. Empty. On the hunt, he flashed from room to room, startling any servants at work. Though they recognized him as a frequent guest with privileges few others were granted, all shrieked and raced off. No doubt his unchecked expression exposed the viciousness of his rage.

He found his uncle in the dining room, entertaining a bevy of beauties. The cursed mirror now graced a spot above the crackling hearth. There was never a time the merciless warrior didn't want the Goddess of Many Futures within his sights. Or her sights on him.

Without saying a word, Rathbone swung a fist, nailing the beast of a male in the mouth and knocking him out of his chair. A new chorus of shrieks. The females scrambled from the chamber.

Hades came to his feet slowly, waggling his jaw. A scarlet bead trickled from the seam of his lips. "I mean, it's not the worst greeting you've ever given me."

"Give me an outlet." In a single day, Rathbone's entire world had turned upside down and inside out. His oracle had betrayed him from the beginning. His dead wife might be worse than Hades predicted; she might be Jezebel the Destroyer, an ancient legend he knew through whispers. A bone remained with the Astra. Rathbone had a spoiled son who needed saving from a spoiled goddess. He couldn't stop thinking about Neeka's admission or the look of devastation she'd displayed before his departure from the island. Or the horrendous future she'd outlined.

She'd infiltrated every fiber of his being, becoming a part of him. Something only a fated one could do. Something not even Lore had managed. The goddess had obsessed him, but she'd never possessed him. Not like this. A detail as subtle as it was significant. But it couldn't mean Neeka was his. His true mate would never betray him like this.

"Ah. I see." A delighted gleam entered Hades's dark eyes. "Happy to say outlets are my specialty."

In a blink, the king was nothing but a tornado of black smoke whooshing Rathbone's way. A whirlwind of chaos, solidifying with every blow. But Rathbone was fast enough to land blows of his own. His mátia caught the slightest disturbance in the atmosphere.

They fought for hours, Rathbone unwilling to stop despite a plethora of broken bones and the many internal organs scattered across the floor. He didn't want to think beyond this battle. Didn't wish to exchange physical pain for emotional torment.

"If you don't start using your words as well as your claws," Hades said, kicking him the balls, "I'm taking my toys to someone else's sandbox."

Rathbone meant to remain silent. He had no desire to talk. But every detail burst from him, anyway, nothing left out. When he finished, he went still. Panting, bloody hands fisted, he hung his head. "What am I supposed to do?"

"Easy. Sell the orb to the Astra, let them deal with Lore's evil, and chain the oracle to your bed. I'll hunt down my great-nephew." Hades patted him on the shoulder. "You're welcome."

Rathbone ground his teeth. "I could be mistaken about Lore. Neeka could've lied to keep me to herself."

"You aren't. She didn't. Why would she?"

"Jealousy?" He rubbed his knuckles into the center of his chest. "You heard the part about being her consort, yes?"

"I did, but I chose to disregard it. My team needs an oracle willing to do anything to win, not a goddess attempting to smuggle a new breed of phantoms into existence."

Blink. "You think the creatures Neeka described are phantoms?"

"If not phantoms, demons. Lore is a goddess, and many of the Greeks reproduce on their own, the evil inside them becoming too much to contain. That's what happened with William."

William the Ever Randy. Hades's adopted son, and Rathbone's cousin. "It's difficult for me to reconcile this idea of Lore with the goddess I wed."

"Do it anyway," Hades intoned.

Rathbone scrubbed a hand over his face. "I must go," he muttered. He didn't wait for a reply but flashed to his not-so-secret throne room, where the plastic skeleton rested upon his throne, flipping the world the bird.

"There you are." Lore's voice filled the chamber. She materialized, stepping from thin air, and gliding toward him, her lovely features twisted with concern. "I've been so worried about you, my love."

The sight of her fueled his frustration and roused the worst of his speculations. How innocent she appeared. But was she? With every mátia riveted on her, he replied, "You don't believe I'm capable of protecting myself?"

His silky tone emboldened her when it should have elicited frighten. As her scent reached his nostrils, his body failed to react. There was no heating. No hardening. Suddenly, reconciling what he'd experienced with what he'd learned wasn't so difficult.

"Where have you been?" he asked. Would she lie?

Tears glistened in her baby blues. "Doing my best to aid you. I sensed a new piece of myself and rushed to gather as much information as possible. But I was too late. Hera had already gifted the bone to the Astra."

A plausible story. It made sense. So why wasn't Rathbone convinced? Because Neeka had planted doubts...or because the oracle had opened his mind to truth?

"Are you playing me, Lore? Or should I call you Jezebel?" The flat questions lacked emotion. "Did you play Styx?"

A horrified noise left her as she reared back. "How can you accuse me of such a thing?" Her eyes rounded. "You have sided with the oracle. D-do you not desire me anymore, Rathbone?"

He...didn't. There was nothing, no spark, no awareness, the sensual frenzy she once caused no longer stirring within him. The need to be near his ex-wife had vanished.

Ex. He considered Lore his ex, a part of his past rather than his present or future? He'd already accepted their end?

Relief seized him, and certainty solidified. Yes, he'd accepted their end. But did he judge her guilty of the crimes lobbed at her? Had she used him? Would she birth a new demon species?

"Whoever you are, whatever you've done," he offered softly, "that part of our relationship is over. If you are innocent, I'll bring you back, and you can live your life. If not..."

She wrapped her arms around herself, as if protecting an internal injury. "How can you hurt me this way?" she asked between sniffles. "Please don't allow the oracle's lies to sway you. She isn't trying to save the world but the Astra. I'm the one who loves you, dearest."

"Do you even know me?" he asked simply.

"Of course I know you! You're my king, and I'm your goddess. We belong to each other."

"I hate to interrupt such a heartfelt reunion," a familiar voice announced, "but some things cannot wait, and this is one of them."

Rathbone zoomed his gazes to Erebus, who stood bound and bleeding in the center of the room. The realm's new defenses had held.

Gasping, Lore whooshed behind Rathbone for safeguarding. So unlike Neeka, who would've tossed daggers as an icebreaker.

"Well, well. Hello, beauty. So nice to meet you." The other male smiled a hunter's smile and inclined his head in greeting before refocusing on Rathbone. "I've never steered you wrong, Majesty, and I won't do so now. You'll either believe me, or you won't. Succeed or fail. Ready? To defeat the Astra and save yourself, you must kill the oracle. Otherwise, she'll kill you."

Neeka crawled to shore and collapsed, dripping blood and water all over the crystal sands. Pain clouded her vision. She wheezed every breath. Her abdomen sported gaping wounds, and a leg ended in a gushing stump. She'd fed a shark her beautiful foot. A harmaid had lopped off two of her fingers.

She would've lost more if a kindly whale hadn't swallowed her whole and carried her a mile from shore, where he'd spit her out. Healing was impossible, considering she wore the wing pinner. As soon as it was removed and she drank a gallon of blood, she'd be as good as new. Probably gooder. Or better. Whatever. Oh, she hurt!

A nest of harpies came from every direction, reaching her in seconds. Gentle hands rolled her over and began patching her wounds.

She blinked rapidly, her sight clearing. Concerned expressions morphed to horror as her helpers registered her identity.

"Do you know who this is?" one said. "Neeka the Unwanted!"

"Traitor!"

"The General will want the honor of slaying her."

Yes, yes. Take her to the General. She tried to utter her agreement, but the words lodged in her throat.

Rough hands and sharp claws gripped her by the hair. She was dragged across the shore. Sand burned her wounds. Neeka persevered because what else could she do? Eventually, they reached the palace.

She darted her gaze over the growing crowd as her guards bragged about her capture.

"Death to Neeka!" the sisterhood chanted.

When the group parted, creating a gap, hope bloomed anew. Had Taliyah arrived?

The one holding her hair released her and stepped away, and Neeka's head smacked into the floor. A flare of pain. She groaned. Too weak to rise, she could only lie still as booted feet approached.

Azar crouched beside her, resting his forearms on his knees. "You've caused us nothing but trouble," he stated, "and if you were anyone else, you'd be dead already."

Again she tried to speak, but she suspected only garbled noises escaped. Blood followed on their heels. Lots and lots of blood. The liquid streamed from the corners of her mouth.

The Astra maneuvered her to a supine position before slicing his wrist. Skin split and crimson welled. He held the wound over her lips. Scorching blood dripped onto her tongue, sweet and strong. Power flooded her in a rush, amazing and wonderful and terrible.

Nooo! Neeka rolled to her side and vomited. Weakness returned and redoubled.

Well, here it was. Proof. Rathbone *was* her consort. Only his blood could heal her.

Why, why, why? Didn't fate understand they were incompatible? He was too serious, while she was a good time waiting to happen. The purveyor of unpredictable fun. She brought brilliance to her team, but he'd washed his hands of her, revealing himself to be a fool. He refused to admit their chemistry was combustible, and they were kind of amazing together. He nursed his very legitimate grudge and she, she… She sniffled. Despite everything, she still craved him.

"So. The Underworld king is your consort," Azar said.

She glared at his Adam's apple, hating him. Hating Rathbone. Hating herself. There was a zero-point-zero likelihood Rathbone would part with a single drop on her behalf.

A vibration cut into Neeka's thoughts. She searched for the source, seeing Taliyah. The General to the rescue!

"I've heard a disturbing rumor that had better not be true." Her friend shoved Azar aside and took his place, crouching beside her. She slitted her eyes. "A lot of people will die cursing my name if someone doesn't tell me what happened."

"I don't know what happened," Azar said, as calm as could be.

"Well, give her your blood." The General removed the pinner amid the Astra's protests.

Neeka's wings buzzed with relief before going limp.

"I did give her my blood," the Astra said. "She vomited."

Taliyah absorbed the information. "I was right. Rathbone is your consort. And he isn't here to aid you?"

Dang it! Neeka's tears resurged. The Red King might be the first consort in history not to want his harpy. But fine. Whatever. So he didn't want her. So what? She didn't want him, either. Not anymore.

Neeka was done setting herself up for rejection. Done with Rathbone. As of this moment, she'd washed her hands of him.

"Stay away from him," she croaked, careful to articulate each word. Ugh. Still protective of the guy. Such a fool!

"If you want to save him from my wrath," the General said,

putting pressure on the worst of Neeka's wounds to staunch the bleeding, "you'll have to strengthen and stop me."

"You cannot bring the King of Agonies here." Azar evinced incredulity. "What if he sent the oracle ahead with the express purpose of gaining entrance?"

"First of all, I can bring anyone I wish to *my* palace. Second, if that's the case, feel free to attack him at your leisure once my friend is healed."

A shockingly fierce battle growl left Neeka. Despite her weakness. Despite her disappointment in the king. She didn't want his blood. Didn't want his help or his presence. Didn't want anything to do with him ever again. No thank you.

Yet she said, "Stay. Away. From. Rathbone."

"Keep her alive," Taliyah commanded the Astra, ignoring her. "If she's dead when I return, you'll soon join her. That, I promise you."

24

Kill the oracle?

   Slay her?

   End her for good to save myself?

The questions played on a loop inside Rathbone's mind as he paced near the head of the River Styx. A desolate clearing where spontaneous fires sprayed from cracks in impacted soil. Trees no longer budded. The sky alternated between smoky and very smoky.

"Who am I supposed to believe?" he asked the former king. "Erebus or Neeka? He's never lied to me. She has." *Betray me once and lose everything you hold dear. Betray me twice...* "And what of Lore?" The ex-wife he must free or condemn. "Is she everything you claimed?"

Ripples moved through the water without the aid of wind, and he halted, halfway expecting an attack instead of an answer. A school of fish in a multitude of colors swam to the surface, drawing together, using their different colors to create a face. Styx. He laughed with glee.

Yeah, Rathbone deserved that. "Do you hate me more than you want her punished?"

The fish swam apart, then drew together again to spell the word *deciding*.

Once again, the fish parted and reassembled, showcasing another face—Neeka's. The placement of the red scales made her look as if she was splattered with blood. The words *dying won* floated beneath her.

His brow furrowed. "Dying won?"

More ripples through the water, as if Styx had just heaved his own sigh. Some of the fish traded places to turn *won* into *now*. *Dying now*.

Rathbone roared. Neeka, dying? *Get to her!* Without delay, he teleported to the island where he'd left her. He wasn't fond of the oracle, but he didn't want her dead, even to save himself.

Panic stirred when he found no sign of her. Lapping waves had washed away her footprints. His guts twisted. No need to go searching the rest of the island. She'd taken her chances in shark-infested waters to reach the harpy palace, hadn't she? And she'd done it while wearing a wing pinner he'd purposely left on her.

Air abandoned his lungs in a rush. She was supposed to stay here and consider the error of her ways!

He knew her. Should have realized... Neeka might not defend herself against emotional hurts, but she always met physical danger head-on.

He plowed a hand through his hair, his part in this whole debacle dawning. No wonder she hadn't told him the truth about her visions and goal. Look what he'd done. Add in his threats on day one and his continued habit of putting his quest above her life, and she'd had no other choice but to keep secrets.

She'd done the wise thing, and he'd punished her for it. Guilt attacked, ravaging his lungs.

Get to her. Rathbone stashed the orb and emerged on the other side of the sea. The usually crowded beach was deserted, not a single harpy nearby. Where had they all gone? And why?

On the hunt, he flashed his way to the palace. Searching, searching. Every common area was deserted, harpies nowhere to be found. Then he appeared in the overly crowded foyer, and the entire population seemed to be squeezed together, everyone speculating about "the Unwanted" and whether she was or was not a traitor.

Desperation drove him forward. He shoved his way through to the front—Horror nearly drilled him to his knees. Neeka sprawled on the floor, surrounded by a pool of blood; Azar stood nearby, his arms crossed over his middle as he stared off in the distance.

Claws extended from Rathbone's nails, rage using every other emotion as fuel. "Did you do this to her?"

Azar flipped up his gaze, spotted him, and shrugged. "From what I hear, *you* did."

Rathbone flinched as gasps sounded around him. Harpies backed away, chanting, "Fight, fight, fight."

He ignored them as he fixated on the oracle...she was so still. Too still. Shouts of denial echoed in his head. *Not again.* Neeka couldn't be dead. He needed her. The world needed her. She added so much flavor.

"Give her to me." Had her right index finger twitched? Hope bloomed into urgency, supercharging him. *Get to her!* She required his blood, and she required it *now.* "Hear me when I say nothing will stop me from leaving with that oracle."

"The only way you exit this palace is in pieces." Azar unsheathed two daggers.

Vibrating with aggression, he considered his options. Every second counted. Fighting the warlord—make that warlords. The other Astra materialized around them, creating a barrier, and it was clear they'd already been briefed on the situation. They spread their arms to block harpies while glaring at Rathbone.

Well. They'd made his decision for him. If the nine wished to battle, they would battle. But only as long as it took for Rathbone to reach his oracle. He needed only to touch her to teleport her to safety.

He braced to launch himself at his main opponent. Azar bowed up, ready to block. *Now!* Like an arrow, Rathbone shot forward—grinding to a halt when Taliyah appeared between them.

"Why weren't you where I expected you to be?" she demanded, shoving him toward Neeka. "Well, what are you waiting for? Medicate my girl. You're the only one who can."

He dove to his knees and reached for Neeka. At the same time, Azar dove for him, securing a metal cuff around his wrist. To prevent him from flashing?

He couldn't bring himself to care. Gently cupping Neeka's jaw, he tilted her face in his direction. Ice crystalized in his veins. A multitude of bruises, knots and gashes marred her.

"I will make you better." Another vow. Though she couldn't hear his promise. He'd tell her again when she was able to watch his lips. To see the truth in his eyes.

The Astra closed in, but Taliyah held out her arms, commanding, "No one touches him—yet."

Moaning, Neeka parted her lids and slowly focused on Rathbone. Between two heartbeats, she began pushing and kicking at him, fighting to create distance. All the while, she shook her head in denial, opening and closing her mouth. Choking noises left her.

A new realization struck, and he wanted to punch a wall. She attempted to deny him, preferring to suffer rather than accept his blood.

Sadness swept over him, pursued by an incredible sense of

loss. But let her go? No. Never. This harpy-oracle would drink his blood, one way or another.

He scraped a claw over his wrist and pressed the injured flesh to her lips. The head shaking, pushing and kicking intensified as she tried to dislodge him. Merciless, he held steady, his blood flowing into her mouth.

Any time he healed, he cut himself again and forced her to drink more. Each time, her strength increased.

"You will take what you need. Understand?" he intoned. "Why are you upset, anyway? I'm the one with a laundry list of grievances. Need I state the most obvious? Had you simply stayed put, you'd be just fine. Now, get better so you can explain how you're right, and I'm wrong."

Neeka ceased her struggles, but not her glare. She sank her claws into his flesh, now holding him in place, gulping faster and faster. Hoping to drain him? Good. Let her.

"Dude. Have you learned *nothing* about harpies?" Taliyah asked behind him. "Leaving us vulnerable to our enemies is an unpardonable crime. Taunting us afterward is the nail in your jockstrap."

"I know what I'm doing," he told the General, ignoring a fresh pang of guilt. "Finally."

The General's previous claim echoed. *Medicate my girl. You're the only one who can.*

Had someone fed the oracle blood and she'd vomited?

He pressed his tongue against his clamped teeth, his heart hammering. Possessiveness, yes, he felt it. Satisfaction, too.

Her bruises faded, and the cuts knitted together. A healthy glow returned to her skin.

When she bore no more injuries, she wrenched from him and popped to her feet. "How dare you! I didn't give you permission to save my life," she spat. Wet, ragged clothing hung from her newly healed form. "By the way, you aren't my consort. I renounce you. Renounce you I say!"

He waited, on edge, accepting her venting. Five seconds passed. Ten. Twenty. Forty. No sign of sickness. He almost rubbed his hands together with glee. He was, in fact, Neeka's consort. The warrior she needed above all others. The male she couldn't live without. And there was nothing she could do about it. No amount of renouncing would change the truth.

"I am your consort." His satisfaction spread, conquering new territory. "Your forever. And in the spirit of baring all, I've fed you my blood before. You were injured and sleeping and required healing."

Her eyelids slitted. "Astra, what are you waiting for? This Underworld outlaw endangered the well-being of your queen's favored assassin who is *not* a traitor. He deserves a lengthy stay in the dungeon. Alive. Mostly."

Rathbone smirked. "Desperate to keep me close, are you?"

She hissed at him.

"You heard the woman," Taliyah said, clapping her hands. "To the dungeon. Chop, chop."

The Commander heaved a sigh. "Lock him up."

For the time being, Rathbone wished to remain accessible to the oracle, in case she required another infusion of blood.

He kept as many mátia on her as possible as two males hauled him to his feet and led him away. He didn't protest their actions, but he did maneuver to turn, forcing the males to drag him backward.

She displayed cold disdain as she witnessed his departure, her head high and her shoulders squared.

"I understand your anger, carrot," he told her. "That's why I'm giving you twenty-four hours to visit me. Then I'll come to you. I can't promise I'll leave survivors."

Before he snaked around a corner, he thought he detected excitement in her eyes.

"You won't be going anywhere," Azar assured him. "When the Astra lock you up, you stay locked up."

"Ah, but you've never caged the King of Agonies. Trust me. When I want out, I'll get out." One way or another. Nothing would keep him from Neeka.

Nothing.

No, no, no! Rathbone couldn't be Neeka's consort. But he was. But he shouldn't be. But he was.

He wasn't someone she'd found in the flames. Unless her father's prophecy referred to the heat of adversity rather than actual fire. Or he'd lied about what he'd seen.

Argh! Neeka stomped around her old room, catching sight of her reflection as she passed the full-length mirror. The image made a motion, as if to say, *Well?* They were eager to converse about their new Rathbone-less future, but they had company. The General sat by the hearth, sharpening an array of daggers. Neeka was on house arrest until Taliyah convinced Roc of her trustworthiness.

Had Neeka changed the future at least?

Though she'd done her best to force a vision, she'd failed.

Dang Rathbone! He'd screwed up everything, showing up out of the blue, acting the hero. As if he wasn't the one who'd endangered her life in the first place! And the way he'd watched her when Azar and Halo escorted him out of the foyer, possessiveness seeping from his pores...

He had no right!

They were over. Utterly done. No hope for a second, third or fourth chance. Thanks, but no thanks. Rathbone might relish the idea of being her consort and receiving free oracle services for eternity, but he didn't like her. The bare minimum necessary for having a relationship with her.

Why did he wish to speak with her, anyway? There wasn't a good reason. But oh! Curiosity was getting the better of her.

No, no. She must stay strong. In fact, Neeka's next move was obvious. Find the remaining bones and protect those she loved.

If you wish to save everyone, Neeka, you need only—

The final words she'd heard in the Hall of Secrets whispered through her mind, a thorn in her side. She didn't recognize the voice, because ears. Had she spoken to the female directly? A past conversation she'd forgotten?

What else had the mysterious stranger said? What did Neeka need exactly?

Silly question. She needed Lore vaporized, that was what. "Did Azar find an orb when he searched Rathbone?" Guaranteed the Astra performed a thorough frisk before locking up the king and throwing away the key.

"Nope." The General continued swiping a blade against a stone. "Why?"

"That orb houses most of Lore's skeleton, and Rathbone is the key to open it." So what had he done with the thing? Pacing faster, she inquired, "You told Roc about Grenwich, yes? How she's willing to let both our people die to ensure I suffer."

"Yep."

When her friend offered nothing more, Neeka tossed up her hands. "What is with these one-word answers? Does Grenwich remain on the Astra's payroll or not?"

"Yep," Taliyah repeated, still sharpening. Swiping, swiping, back and forth. "Roc said the decision to work with her is Azar's, and the Memory Keeper is determined to keep her."

Dang it! "I hate the thought of her looking forward to a payday. And it's a good one, isn't it?" Better than Neeka's? Well, her former payday.

"Oh, yeah. Amazing. Azar promised to deliver Rathbone's head on a platter...and to facilitate your return to Ahdán. Speaking of, the Phoenix is alive again."

Neeka swallowed a screech of frustration. More trouble. Great. If something didn't break her way soon... "I've got to find those last bones and change the future," she said, forging ahead. Because what else could she do? Give up?

"You mean you aren't planning to visit your consort to prevent him from hunting you down?"

Shivers cascaded over her. An embarrassment to the nth degree. But it wasn't her fault. The promise he'd made was just so danged sexy. Judging by the heat in his mátia, he intended to do things. Sensual things. An outcome she must guard against.

Cherry Bomb could make mincemeat of her insides with only a few words. As he'd proven on several occasions. Let him have another go at her? No! Never again. He'd abandoned her, ending any hope of a romance between them. His loss.

Granted, he'd come back. Fed her his blood. Allowed himself to be captured.

Softening again?

No! *Walk away from me, don't bother crawling back.* Why would he crawl after her, anyway? He had his precious Lore.

Neeka bared her claws. Speaking of the monster-spawning goddess... Something prodded the edge of her memory bank. Something she had forgotten or missed in the visions. But what?

"I need to calm down and clear my head so I can get my vision on."

"I know," Taliyah replied. "That's why I'm here."

"Uh, I hate to shatter your illusions, babes, but you aren't a source of tranquility." T-bone was a force of nature.

The General rolled her eyes. "Fine. I'm really here to offer you a harsh truth no one else is brave enough to share. You don't want to face our prisoner, but you must. He's your tranquility now. It's the only reason he's still alive. Although, say the word, and I'll have him beheaded posthaste."

The threat sparked an unexpected growl, startling her. She pressed her fingers against her lips. "This means nothing."

Another eye roll from Taliyah. "You're already ultraprotective of him."

Maybe she was, but only instinctively, not willingly. There was a difference. "For the benefit of harpykind and the benefit of harpykind alone, I'll visit him. After I shower. And don the sexiest clothes I own. But I won't enjoy a second of our inter- action, and I will expect payment from the Astra. Everything Rathbone promised me, and more. Lots more. For starters, Azar must fire Grenwich and join Team Neeks."

Her friend grinned. "I was hoping you'd say that. Be right back." She vanished.

Three minutes on the dot later, a scowling Azar appeared.

He grabbed Neeka by the throat and squeezed while back- ing her against a wall. Her wings buzzed with aggression, the urge to defend and fight nearly too strong to tamp down. But tamp down she did.

"Let me guess," she offered drily. "You're here to tell me you accept my offer, and I'll regret it if I actually betray you."

"No," he said with a clipped shake of his head. "I *know* you'll betray me to protect your king. A harpy always chooses her con- sort. I'm here to give you *my* terms. I won't utilize your mother as long as you remain faithful. In return, you will bring me the remaining bones, along with the orb. Otherwise, the king dies."

25

Heart pounding with the precision of a war drum, Neeka approached Rathbone's cell. A seven-by-seven space at the end of a long corridor. Thick metal bars secured the front while a trio of stone walls completed the enclosure. Already his incredible scent infused the air, rich and spicy, chasing away any vestiges of past tortures.

Ian, the Astra standing guard outside the cell, barely blipped on her radar as she stopped at the bars. Her gaze never veered from Rathbone. He sat leaning against the wall with his knees drawn up, the mátia staring at her intently...

Shivers tumbled over her spine, but oh, she hated when he watched her like this—because she loved it so much. When you spent the bulk of your life desperate to be seen rather than dismissed, such unwavering attention became your kryptonite.

"You came. And dressed for seduction, I see." He dragged his gaze over her, his pupils spilling partway over glittering irises. A triumphant eclipse.

So she'd decided to wear a slinky halter top and short shorts. So what? He could take his ego and shove it. "Who says the outfit is for you?"

His nostrils flared. A sign of jealousy? Hope sparked—and died. No way she was going down that road with him again. "Where's the orb?" she demanded, despite their rapt audience.

"Somewhere else," he offered silkily.

She worked her jaw. "Why did you come to Harpina?" He'd known the danger and the likely outcome. "Did you realize you were doomed without me and wish to win me back to your side?"

"Were you ever really on my side?" he asked with a gentle expression, ignoring her question.

"I was always on your side. I just didn't know it."

He arched a brow. "Why did you fight my aid when you needed it most? Aid is aid."

Lies! Aid was connection, and she needed no more ties to him.

Taking a page from his playbook, she responded with another question. "Do you believe I told the truth about Lore and the outcome of her resurrection?"

"Though I'm having trouble wrapping my head around it, yes."

Oh, that burned! After everything Neeka had—wait. "What? You do?" She grabbed the bars and leaned in. "What convinced you?"

What are you doing? Falling for his sexy act all over again? *Be tougher!* She straightened, saying, "Never mind. It doesn't matter. FYI, I plan to use the elixir on someone else, overriding my connection to you." Hey! Not a bad idea. She just needed to get past his kingdom's defenses to retrieve her property. Why, why, why had instinct prompted her to leave the powerful, life-changing liquid in his whiskey and not keep it with her?

His eyelids slitted. He slowly stood, his impressive body eating up the space. "I suggest you *don't* do that, Neeka."

Her stomach fluttered. "I'll do whatever I please, *Rathbone.*"

He stalked closer, and she imagined his boots thumped against the dirt-laden floor in a mimic of her heartbeat. Ian made no comment, just watched and listened with unabashed interest.

She raised her chin. "Why did you come to Harpina?" she repeated. "Why did you allow yourself to be imprisoned?"

"Why else?" Wrapping his fingers around the bars, he studied her. "You might be *my* fated one."

Shock nearly unhinged her jaw. "Me?" she squeaked, thumping her rioting chest to be sure. "Not Lore?"

"Not Lore," he echoed, stretching an arm through two bars to gently trace two fingertips along the seam of her lips. His thumb stopped to plump the bottom.

Her cells caught fire, torching already cracked defenses.

Perhaps this was what her father had meant? Neeka would find her consort in the flames of passion.

Without conscious thought, she sucked his thumb into her mouth and nipped the pad, drawing a single bead of blood. Oh! Her lids sank as the potency of his power hit. Delicious. Heady. An addiction waiting to happen.

His pupils completely swallowed his irises. Raw possessiveness radiated from him. "I'm keeping you," he vowed, cupping her cheek. "I'll never let you go."

He...no. She shook her head to clear her line of sight. No way he'd said those words. Just no way. "Come again?"

"I'm keeping you." He moved his hold to her nape, gripping a fistful of her hair, as if to prove his claim. "We are together now."

A thousand flutters, in a thousand different places stole her breath. He made a future as a couple sound so easy. Just boom, done. "What makes you think I'm yours? Has there been a sign?"

"No, but I don't need one."

Just like he hadn't needed a sign with Lore? Ugh. "We can't work. We don't trust each other."

"Trust will come with time and effort. I'll even make the first gesture. As of this moment, my stable is officially closed."

"You'd do that for me?" she replied with her driest tone. But inside...

Do not soften. Don't you dare! He wasn't the party who'd been left for dead.

"My kingdom is your kingdom," he continued, petting her nape now and giving her the hard sell. "I'll ensure your throne is bigger than mine with a design patterned after our bedroom walls."

Oh! He just had to go and sweeten the deal. But. Despite his pretty words, he hadn't morphed into a good bet. She needed to guard her heart.

What if she—a vision consumed her in an instant, and she gasped.

Neeka lost sight of Rathbone, an ancient temple taking his place. Mother-of-pearl covered the columns, walls, and floor from top to bottom, shining with radiance. There was no dais, no altars, or royal seats, just emptiness. A starlit midnight sky stretched as far as her gaze could track.

What was this place? Why was she seeing it? She scanned from left to right, her brow furrowing. What was *that*?

Neeka pushed deeper into the vision, zooming in on two bones. A metatarsal and a femur. Both bore a carving. Oh, oh, oh! The final pieces of the Lore puzzle.

If you wish to save everyone, Neeka, you need only—

The whisper wafted a second time. Was there a connection between the speaker and this place?

The temple began to fade, a large shadow growing in the background. Wait! She wasn't done here. Wasn't even sure where here was. Neeka did her best to memorize as many details as possible. An outline of Grenwich! She stood off to the side.

Her mother noticed her and reared back, startled. So. They

were both surprised to see the other. This couldn't be a typical vision, then. So what was it? A summoning?

Whatever the answer, the competition was on. Who would reach the temple first?

The second Neeka blinked, the temple details erased. "No," she bellowed, spying a smoldering Rathbone. He hadn't released her.

"What did you see?" he asked, infinitely tender as he continued petting her.

Gah! No time for this. She backed away from his cage. From him. "I must go." Where, where? She couldn't visualize the temple, so she couldn't push the image into a flasher's mind and teleport.

His lightning-fast reflexes worked in his favor. He snagged her by the nape, stopping her in her tracks. With an insistent tug, he brought her an inch from the bars. "What did you see?"

"A temple and my mother," she replied, because what else could she do? "I'm going to find it first." But where to start? Back to the beginning? The Hall of Secrets, where she'd first heard that whisper? "You're staying here like a good little prisoner."

"No. Wherever you go, I will be accompanying you."

Ha! "I'm the seer in this relationship, and I say you're staying put. Not that we have a relationship," she added in a rush, her cheeks heating.

"We have a relationship all right," he said, and he didn't do it with resignation or dismay but fierce determination. "And I will catch up to you shortly. Before I go, I plan to ensure the Astra understand me better."

She didn't mean to, but she grabbed his shoulders through the bars, rose to her tiptoes, and kissed him. "Be alive when I return or heads will roll."

"Carrot," he said, letting her go, "you can check me for injuries in five minutes. That's all I require to find you."

No way he could escape the Astra, even with his shifting ability. They'd nixed the ability with that cuff.

She pressed another swift kiss to his lips before spinning and racing off to prepare for victory.

Rathbone stood rooted in place as Neeka disappeared around a corner. They hadn't solved anything, but he wasn't letting her leave this palace without him.

"Are you in love with the oracle?" his guard asked, appearing perplexed. Ian was Roc's younger and more powerful brother. The original Astra Commander who'd lost his position when he'd refused to sacrifice his virgin bride.

An excellent question. Neeka was flighty and forgetful upon occasion and treacherous always. But she was also soft and warm and eager to unveil her brilliant smile. A true partner willing to step up and do whatever proved necessary to get a job done. Take a blow and stay down? Not his carrot. She raised her chin and forged ahead. He'd hurt her deeply, yet she'd still come to him. Still protected him, in her own way.

Love or not, he'd meant what he'd said. He was keeping her. Woe to anyone who attempted to separate them.

"It's my guess you Astra are impervious to whatever substance you add to your metal. A substance you use to weaken prisoners and prevent them from flashing and even shifting. Am I right? Let's find out." As he spoke, he transformed into Roc's image without problem. Since he'd been Roc before, he carried the male within his genetic makeup now. With a slight pull, the metal split from his wrist. "Oh, yes, I'm right."

Ian tilted his head to the side, scanning up and down, as if he couldn't believe what he was seeing.

Rathbone grinned, but not with amusement. A bubbling well of fury-tinged determination powered the action. "Tell Azar the next time he sees me, he dies." That said, he teleported through–

out the palace until he found Neeka in a bedroom, bent over a bed, shoving piles of jewelry into a bag.

Shedding Roc's image in favor of his own, Rathbone appeared directly behind her. He gripped her by the waist and spun her, towering over her much shorter frame. "The King of Agonies reporting for his injury check, ma'am."

She yelped, taking a swing at him. Rathbone ducked, hooked his arms around her thighs and yanked her feet out from under her. Her shriek nearly broke his ears as she fell onto the mattress.

He sprang up, pinning her. "What else did you see in your vision?" he repeated, as if their conversation had never lagged.

"Oh! You are so annoying. But there's no time to flirt." She beat at his chest with her fists without any real heat. "I saw Lore's remaining bones, okay? They're somewhere I've never been and can't picture, so I don't know how to get there. But I do know where I can snatch a clue."

"What do you plan to do with the bones?" What did *he* plan to do with them?

"I'm still figuring things out."

He scrubbed a hand over his face, a new habit. One he expected to perform on a daily basis as Neeka's consort. Being her male had changed things for him. All his childhood, he'd yearned to belong. Now he did. The most cuddly, devious harpy had picked him as her partner. A title he wore with pride. She lit a fire inside him no other could quench.

"Where do you wish to go?" he asked.

"With you? Nowhere." Her gaze darted. Searching for someone, anyone else to transport her? Too bad.

He pinched her chin, forcing her attention on him. "With me or *you* go nowhere."

Frustration pulsed from her. "I'm returning to Nova, okay? To save a few minutes, I need to avoid Kanta and his theatrics. Azar can flash me straight to the red door. Speaking of the Astra, he's using you as an insurance policy. I have to give him the orb and remaining bones or he'll kill you, blah, blah, blah."

"We go together, even if we go with Azar," he announced, ignoring the insurance police nonsense. "That's how things will be from now on."

"No way. You and Azar will be all over each other, and I'll be the third wheel," she grated up at him. "Again."

"I told you. You are the *only* wheel, carrot."

"And for another thing—" Wait. "The only wheel?" she eked out. "You're ditching Lore, not just the stable?"

"Ditched, past tense," he stated, and her lips parted. "I crave you and no other."

As she floundered for a response, a new voice sounded. "Tsk, tsk. I'm highly disappointed in you, Rathbone. I came to give you one last chance and you're moving on."

Lore. His head whipped up. Smirking at him, she floated beside the bed. "How are you here? There are no bones."

"I never needed them," the goddess said with a smirk.

Neeka followed his line of sight, jolted, and hissed. He sat up, allowing his oracle to do the same, freeing her wings. Never again would he leave her in a position of vulnerability.

In that moment, everything he'd felt for Lore was just dead. There was nothing. Not even a spark of attraction.

"I'm actually relieved by this turn of events," Lore said, a little gleeful now. "At last I can tell you how much I've dreaded each of our encounters. How I've longed for the day you learned the truth, so I could rub it in your ugly face. What a fool you've been, thinking someone like me would want someone like you."

Her words were a gut-punch that sparked an avalanche of pain. He almost couldn't process the changes in her. Who was this female before him? "You are everything Styx accused you of." That much was clear.

She smiled now, a cold display of perfect teeth. "I did worse. I played the part he wished me to play until I had no more use for him. Then I played the part *you* wished, baby boy. Helpless, subservient, and eager to please." She pretended to gag. "Such a needy royal. You should be embarrassed."

Rathbone came to his feet with a quiet snarl, intending to— do something. What, he didn't yet know. "Why me?" he grated.

"Why not?" She hiked her shoulders in a negligent shrug, a sheen of translucent scales seeming to ripple under her skin. "You were the right man at the wrong time. Measures had to be taken to ensure your continued cooperation, so, I ensured it."

All the centuries he'd wasted on this female. All the guilt and shame he'd carried. The torment he'd endured. For nothing! His hands fisted. "And you don't need my cooperation now? You think you've won?"

"I know I have." A laughing Lore vanished.

He stood in place, panting, soon to come out of his skin. Until soft arms wrapped around him from behind.

Neeka rested her cheek on his shoulder and sculpted her body to his. "That had to hurt, and I'm sorry. I'd comfort you more, which wouldn't mean we're together or anything, because we're not. But. We are roughly ten seconds from an Astra invasion. Nine. Probably best to avoid Azar now. So, if you're to be my travel buddy, you've got to flash us to the spot I insert into your mind. Eight."

Insert? He drew her around to face him. "How will you—"

"Six. I'll explain later." She closed her eyes and inhaled slowly... "Five."

The image of an unfamiliar red door popped into his head, jolting him. She'd linked their minds, pushing a thought into his awareness without triggering his defenses? A dangerous skill to possess.

"Four. Go, go, go," she cried. "Three. Two."

Rathbone grabbed her backpack and flashed his female to the red door.

26

Here we go again.

Neeka stood before the red door, her stomach churning. If this didn't work... This had better work. If she lost her memory afterward... She had better not lose her memory afterward.

There was an amazing, potentially tragic decision that required addressing. To accept Rathbone or forever ditch him, that was the question.

With his total rejection of Lore and his newfound devotion to Neeka, she was willing to reconsider a future together. But she refused—refused!—to forget all the bad and the ugly that had transpired between them until they'd addressed everything, and he'd earned back her trust. And what if he decided *Neeka* wasn't his fated? Would she get the ax too?

In the name of calm, she drew in a deep breath. "Stay here," she told him twisting the knob and stepping forward. She braced for the coming onslaught—

Her companion gripped her chin and forced her attention on him. "That's not happening." He slung his arm around her waist to further punctuate his words. "We do this together. You are mine, and I am yours. I will see to your protection."

Argh! The man was proving to be a huge distraction she couldn't afford. How was she supposed to not melt into a puddle of goo when he went around making primal declarations about her. *Her.* The Unwanted.

"Lookit. I'm not sure you can handle the Hall—no, you know what? Never mind. It's your anguish." There wasn't time for an argument. Not with Grenwich on the hunt and the Astra once again on their tail. Neeka had to win this round. Had to save Rathbone, the harpies, and the Astra, or die trying. "Whatever happens, flash us to safety in five minutes." She doubted she could withstand much more of the barrage. "By the way, I might pass out and wake with no memory again. Do everything in your power to help me remember as quickly as possible." Please!

"Oh, I'll make you remember," he told her, his expression fierce. "Then you and I will come to an agreement about things."

Things. Aka their relationship. She gave her bottom lip a nervous swipe with her tongue and nodded. Then, she forced herself to focus and soared into the Hall.

To his credit, Rathbone remained at her side. Just as before, too many voices vied for her attention. Whisper piled upon whisper, quickly becoming a roar. Sharp pain sliced through her temples, and she cried out.

Keeping her mind fixed on the mother-of-pearl temple proved difficult, but she did it, motoring forward with Rathbone and absorbing as much information as possible. Maybe too much. Dizziness invaded, and she wobbled on her feet.

Her breathing quickened. So did his. Never had she been so grateful for his presence. His strength fed her own, keeping her upright.

Just as requested, he flashed them to safety at the five-minute mark. He dropped the backpack as Neeka collapsed, sagging against him. Though he dripped with sweat and wheezed his breaths, he caught her.

"What *was* that?" he demanded between panting breaths. "Other than something we will never do again."

"The Hall of Secrets. Mysteries spoken of throughout the ages collect there," she muttered, nuzzling her cheek against his pec. The rapid-fire pounding of his heartbeat helped ground her in the moment. "A way to download a lot of information fast. The problem is sorting through it afterward. Something I need to do but can't until I calm." Where were they, anyway?

Unwilling to disrupt her current position, she scanned her new surroundings while enfolded in his embrace. Ohhh. His bedroom. He'd brought her back to the Realm of Agonies, then. Home. Well, his home, not hers. Except it kind of might be hers now?

I'll never let you go.

Flutters teased her belly. She didn't mean to, but she curled her sharpening claws into his shoulders. A clear command for him to stay put. Had she truly decided to give him another chance?

"I think I know a way to calm you," he said, tilting her face toward his. "Can you predict what it is?"

Her pulse leaped. When his heated gaze dipped to her mouth, she shivered. Oh, yes. She could guess.

Pretending to misunderstand, she asked, "Are you referring to that chat of agreement you promised me?"

"I'm referring to sex."

His frankness ended her charade. Very well. "I didn't tell you this, but my instinct insists sex with you will forever change my life. Out with the old, and in with the new."

"Your instinct is both right and wrong," he responded without hesitation. "I've already changed your life. Today we start fresh."

Oh. Ooh. She went from terrified by the change to intrigued.

"I'm conserving my energy for my next vision, so if I even considered saying yes, which I'm not, you'd have to agree to do all the work."

"When you enjoy your job, carrot, it isn't work." He traced the pads of his thumbs over her cheeks, leaving a trail of fire. "Never again will I allow harm to come to you. I give you my word."

Goose bumps broke out, and her heart raced faster. She was more tempted to say yes by the second. Beyond tempted. Until she'd rendered a final decision about their relationship, however, she should say no. So that was what she'd say.

She opened her mouth to do it. To put a stop to the conversation. "I'm a maybe," she said, surprising herself. "Give me the hard sell."

His pupils expanded. Bending his head, he brushed the tip of his nose against hers. "For the time being, we're stuck, yes?"

Breath hitched in her lungs. Her favorite spots tingled. "Not stuck per se. But yes, also stuck."

Another brush of their noses. So gentle. Pure seduction. "And you remember me? No memory loss?"

"No loss," she admitted as tremors spread to her legs. She leaned her weight into him, letting him keep her upright.

"Then you remember how you react to my touch." A husky statement accompanied by a soft caress of her jawline.

Her blood heated. "A little? I mean, it's been so long. Days!" Actively participating in her downfall now? What was this male doing to her?

"A reminder probably wouldn't be amiss." He raked a glittering gaze over her body, and she nearly caved then and there. "But where should I start?"

Oh, sweet goodness. He was good at this. Very good. The snake in the garden, offering her an apple.

Common sense attempted a final stand. "You're my consort, but not my consort. And I'm definitely not your queen."

He arched a dark brow. "Would you like to be?"

What! He hadn't…no way he'd just…he…they…she… *what?*

"As my queen," he added, "you'll be rich beyond your wildest imagination."

Reeling… "You're resorting to bribery, Wrath Boned?"

"Whatever it takes, carrot" he told her, unabashed.

She nibbled on her bottom lip. "How rich?"

"Enormously."

Weakening her resistance at every turn! "The fact that you have sunk to such depths…"

He shrugged. "I do what I must to get what I want."

More vulnerable by the second, she searched his magnificent black diamond eyes. "You must want me desperately."

"More than I've ever wanted anything."

Six words. One powerful knockout punch. Common sense went down for the count. Defense after defense followed, crashing and shattering until only ravenous hunger remained. This powerful royal desired her above all others. Her. The Unwanted. Scratch that. The Wanted. She'd officially scored a new name.

He palmed her backside and eased her hips forward, grinding his erection between her legs. "Is that a yes?"

Clinging to him, no longer able to stand on her own, she rasped, "Yes."

Rathbone swooped low, claiming her lips with his own. There was no stopping her reaction. She surrendered to her need, kissing him back and pouring her body over his. She yearned for him and longed for this.

Pulling at her clothes, he backed her across the room. Her knees buckled as soon as they bumped into the bed. Down she tumbled, crashing onto the mattress but not bouncing because he followed her down, never breaking the kiss.

Needing skin-to-skin contact, she ripped at his leathers. The second he was naked, she wrapped her fingers around his pierced length. Such delicious heat paired with hotter metal! As if he'd had been forged in flames.

He touched and kissed her *everywhere*, traveling from top to bottom and visiting every inch in between, and he wasn't gentle about it. He squeezed and kneaded, pinched, and caressed, branding her on a cellular level. Drunk on pleasure, Neeka writhed and strained against him.

"Yes! More!" she cried, arching her hips. Grinding on his fingers. His mouth. Seeking a measure of relief as pressure built and built and built and—ah! Yes, yes, yes. "Right there, right there, right there."

He did something with his tongue, and she garbled a stream of nonsense. The ecstasy! Too much. Not enough.

"Be a good boy and get me to the finish line," she commanded between moans and sawing breaths.

"Greedy little harpy." He lifted, chuckling against her lips, his warm breath fanning her chin. "Are you fertile?"

"No." She had months to go before harpy mating season. Right? Argh! She didn't know anything anymore, couldn't think.

"Do it then. Take what you need from me."

Yes! She would ride him. Would take everything... Neeka nipped his lower lip with her small harpy fangs. When the sweetness of his blood and power hit her tongue, she cried out, as if she'd been tagged by a sexually charged Taser. Sensations heightened in a nanosecond. Aches and tingles and emptiness, oh my.

Groaning, she flipped him to his back and rose over him to straddle his thighs. Rathbone stretched out beneath her. Propped on a mound of pillows, he was a buffet of masculine deliciousness. Glorious in his passion, with his silken hair mussed. His dark irises flashed with internal flames. Kiss-puffed lips glistened with her essence. His crimson skin was aglow, his muscles bulging with strength and sinew. Such a beautiful male.

Her wings buzzed as she slid up and down his length without

initiating penetration. She watched him, loving that he watched her right back. In fact, *all* of him watched her, seeming riveted by the sight of her. Pleasure spiking, she snapped her hips.

He hissed and bared his teeth. "Having fun?" He palmed her breasts. Kneaded. Circled his thumbs around her nipples.

"Yes." Up, down. "No." Up, down. "Maybe?" Not even this play, as incredible as it was, pushed her over the edge. "I want... I need..."

"More." He flipped her to her back, pinning her wings. Hovering over her, shockingly intense, he unveiled a slow grin. His gaze grew hotter, hotter still, scorching her. "Prepare yourself. You're about to feel me in the marrow of your bones."

Shivers rained over her.

He dipped his head and got to work. The things he did... Sometimes infinitely tender, often deliciously firm, always blatantly possessive. If Neeka had been intoxicated before, she was bombed now. Rapture hit in waves, growing intensity. Every crest inched her closer to the brink.

Oh! "Where did you learn..." Silly question. His stable. "Your tongue is...your fingers..."

He shot up, putting his face over hers. His rumpled hair and strained but satisfied grin melted her. "I studied." Back down he went.

Rathbone whipped her to a fevered pitch. Until she panted every breath, cried out incoherently and pleaded for mercy.

"Now you're ready." He returned to his back and positioned her atop him. "Do it," he repeated, a command this time. He gripped her hips and squeezed. "No more waiting. Put me inside you."

Yes. Yes, yes, yes. Shaking, soaked and aching, she set the tip of his length at her opening. Sweat trickled from his temples. Strain etched each of his features.

Slowly, with her world spinning out of control, Neeka sank upon him. Every inch she accepted brought a new flood of bliss.

The stretch! The fullness! The intensity! Those piercings! The fact that he never looked away from her, never shoved her down, just held on tight and waited for her to adjust...

He groaned and growled beneath her, the vibrations of sound shooting to her core. Ahhh! She slid the rest of the way down, suddenly fully seated on him, unable to catch her breath.

There. It was done and couldn't be undone. Whatever happened from here, happened.

Worth it.

"Never leave me, oracle," he grated.

She almost echoed him with a vow of "Never." Somehow, she gathered the strength to smother the word with a moan. This was...she had... He rocked, and the piercings vibrated. Yes! "More."

He rocked again, vibrating harder, and she lost her ability to think.

"More," she repeated. Must have more. When he gave a gentler rock, she shook her head. "Harder."

He did it even gentler.

Teasing her? "You are...in trouble," she rasped between panting breaths.

His pupils flared. "Commit to me, carrot."

"No." She lifted up and slid down, taking over. "But I will give you more of me," she purred with a teasing roll of her hips. Mmm. Even better. Now she was tormenting them both. "I adore how you look at me. You *see.*"

Rathbone bared his teeth, the cords at the side of his neck pulling taut, revealing the depths of his strain. "I want all of you, Neeka."

"Yes, well, we don't always get what we want, do we?" Up, down. Again. Again. So close, so close. Almost...

He pressed his thumb against the heart of her need. Just like that, Neeka rocketed straight into an orgasm, coming on him with a shriek.

The warrior king required no further prompting. He clasped her hips and lifted her to his tip, then slammed her down while thrusting upward. Lifted, slammed, thrust. Again and again, picking up the pace. Her climax crested into another, rolling on and on and on. Swell after swell of ecstasy, drowning her. But oh, what a way to go.

Hammering inside her, he gripped her by the nape and yanked her mouth to his. They kissed as if they couldn't breathe without each other, the wild dance of their tongues frantic. Still her orgasm rolled on.

Rathbone arched his spine, thrusting one last time, coming with what she assumed was a wall-rattling roar. His pleasure heightened her own, and Neeka exploded to new heights, reaching for the stars.

He collapsed onto the mattress, and she sagged over him. She was panting, but so was he. He held on tight, as if he expected her to try and leave and he couldn't bear the thought.

Leave? Impossible. *Welcome to your new world.*

Contentment infiltrated her cells, another round of vulnerability on its heels. For the first time in centuries, she'd given herself to a male. Risked her heart. Her future.

Perhaps the feeling went both ways?

She peeked up at him.

"No vision?" he asked, petting her hair. His sharp features were relaxed in a way she'd never seen, giving him a boyish air.

Her chest clenched. "Not yet." What would happen if she failed to have one in time? "What if we visited the Hall of Secrets for nothing?" Her contentment dissolved. "What if Grenwich has already found the temple?"

"Guess I'll have to relax you again," Rathbone said with a smirk, and she barked out a laugh.

Well, it wasn't the worst idea. "Fine, but I refuse to cuddle with you after. And I'm definitely not sharing my secrets and sleeping in your arms." A girl needed boundaries.

He pursed his lips in a hurry. "You *will* cuddle with me and share your secrets, oracle, and you *will* sleep in my arms."

"Ha! Try and make me. See what happens." She was the one who did the smirking as she propped her elbows on his ribs and rested her chin in her palms. "Now, since I just won our first argument as a non-couple, we might as well change the subject. What do you wish to do about Lore?"

To her surprise, he remained relaxed, gently smoothing a lock of hair behind her ear. "Share a secret with me, and I'll consider telling you."

She rolled her eyes, but honestly, his insistence tickled all the right buttons. "Okay, here's a secret from my most secure vault. Though you've received several clues, you've probably failed to guess how much I like unfried, sugarless vegetables. I also prefer granny panties to thongs and tennis shoes to heels." Once she started, she couldn't stop. "I hate chocolate. I talk to my reflection, and she talks back. She told me to stay away from you. And I'm not a stalker or anything, but a part of me thinks we should wear matching tracksuits. Is that weird?"

"Yes. Good thing I have a weird girl fetish." His teasing, affectionate expression left her quivering. But it wasn't long before he grew serious. "Your secrets did the trick. You asked about Lore. This is my answer. We'll talk to Daisy about destroying the orb, ensuring Azar isn't able to resurrect her."

"Who's Daisy? Never mind. We can't destroy the orb, even if we find a way to destroy the orb. I'll explain in a sec. First, I require confirmation. You're saying you're okay with killing Lore?" she asked, needing to be sure. "You're sure?"

"To save you, I will do anything." Infinitely tender, he kissed her lips. "I'm sure."

That was...wow. Maybe the world's most romantic gesture. Maybe he was forever. She softened against him. "I've changed the future, Rathbone." But was it for better or worse?

"That's good. Tell me why we can't destroy the orb," he insisted.

Right. "We can't prevent Azar from winning his blessing task. Before you rage about it, don't. I promised Taliyah. That's how I earned the antidote for your spear-to-eyes poisoning. Which happened before Azar threatened to kill you if I didn't hand over the orb, so there might be some wiggle room for causing a few injuries."

"You promised to help the Astra. I did not. Trust me, love, I'm happy to do the dirty work for us."

Whoa. Hold up. Had he just called her...love?

"Um. Great!" she squeaked. *Get your head in the game, girl.* "We're about to have our first fight after halfway making up. If you're going to keep me, and I'm not saying you get to, my debts are your debts. That's nonnegotiable."

Would he pull away from her now?

He tightened his grip. "If your debt is my debt, my son is your son, and *that* is nonnegotiable."

Ridiculous tears welled. Neeka the Wanted...a stepmother... to a maddening eternal teenager? Talk about a bucket list item she hadn't known she longed to experience.

"You plan to find Maximus and take him from Hera?" she asked.

"I do. And I will. I'll figure out how to reverse whatever she's done to him, too."

"Oh, Wrath Boned, that's wonderful," Neeka said, hugging him. "With you at his side, he'll become a well-adjusted menace to society in no time."

Rathbone returned the hug. A weary sigh escaped him. "Very well. If you devise a plan to bring Lore to life and save the Astra without endangering your life, I'll aid you in your quest. But if you can't, I'll take care of matters my way. Do you agree?"

"Yes!"

"Good. Now, let's get back to relaxing you..."

27

Rathbone kept a sleeping Neeka nestled against his side, both intoxicated with satisfaction and somehow stone-cold sober. For the first time in centuries, perhaps his entire life, he truly lived. A bright future awaited him. Or a nightmare.

His chest constricted. Why did his oracle continue to fight their connection? Did a part of her sense their doom? *Were* they doomed?

He no longer put any stock in Erebus's warning that Neeka must die for Rathbone to survive. As if he had a life without her.

Protective instincts pitched at even the thought of her harm, and he tightened his hold on her. He believed the god had lied. According to Neeka, Erebus partnered with Lore, a world-class deceiver, and the two sought the destruction of the Astra. They must have known Rathbone was past the point of being swayed, so why attempt to plant such a nefarious seed? They must have a purpose.

Once again, Lore was multiple steps ahead of him.

He huffed. Such prolonged stupidity. So many eyes, yet he'd failed to see the truth. He'd let pride blind him to the goddess's trickery, exactly as Hades once prophesied.

Now, he must defeat her without endangering the Astra, who'd done him a favor when he'd killed her all those centuries ago. Rathbone scrubbed a hand over his face. See! A habit. But what was he supposed to do?

His oracle had received no new visions of the final bones before she'd passed out from pleasure, and he couldn't say he was sorry by the lack. He wasn't ready to leave this room, much less let her go.

I am hers, and she is mine.

With what felt like a feline grin, he reached for his nightstand drawer. While he savored this delightful perk of being mated, he'd munch on a few cookies, watch a season of soaps. His go-to. Maybe he'd fetch Daisy from the Realm of the Forgotten and surprise Neeka with "sister" time. Even though the harpy had forgotten said sister. Speaking of, he should tattoo Neeka with a key to the realm. To all realms he accessed.

A yawn cracked his jaw, and he paused. A yawn? He was tired? No way. He hadn't slept since his childhood. He—

"Hades," Neeka muttered, stirring in his arms. "Yesss."

His brow furrowed. Was his female having a sex dream about his uncle? Because there would be hell to pay!

"Hades," she said with a bit more force. "Hades, Hades, Hades."

A growl brewed. "Neeka. Carrot. I need you to wake up."

Her eyelids popped open, and she rocketed into a sitting potion, shouting, "Hades!"

Rathbone rolled her to her back, not letting himself get distracted by the tousled black curls framing a delicate face with glittering amber irises, flushed cheeks, and kiss-puffed lips. "What about Hades?"

"I need to speak with him," she said, panting and agitated. "Now."

"Why?"

"Because he—I." She turned pensive and grimaced. "I'm not sure. I just know I need to speak with him as soon as possible. I think he knows something about the missing bones. What if he has them? What if he betrayed you?"

"He didn't." Rathbone was certain of it. Not because he trusted the male implicitly, which he did. But because his uncle lived for bragging.

"Okay, so, he didn't betray you," she persisted. "But. If I'm drawn to him, there's a reason. He probably knows something without knowing he knows it."

"That is…possible." But he was still smarting about the possibility of a sex dream, all right? Hades was a powerful force of nature. Neeka might still consider herself a single female.

"Good," she said. "That means we're visiting Hades as soon as I'm presentable." She ruffled Rathbone's hair, gave him a swift kiss, then another, and sprang to her feet, deliciously naked. "Up, up," she said, clapping. "We leave in ten-ish. Wear something nice." Avoiding his gaze, she strutted over and picked up the backpack he'd dropped. "Getting ready together is too intimate. I'll return when I'm done. And I won't miss you while I'm gone. Not the slightest bit."

Rathbone flashed into the hallway, directly in front of her. She didn't notice and smacked into him. As he caught her, she flipped up her gaze, meeting his. "I've been inside you, carrot. Nothing is too intimate now. But you *will* miss me," he commanded. To guarantee it, he seized her lips in a fierce kiss.

Just as she melted in his arms, he lifted his head, ending the exchange. Desire glazed her irises, and passion deepened the color in her cheeks.

He gave her backside a teasing squeeze. "See? You're missing me already," he boasted, strutting to his bedroom. He kicked the door shut behind him, right in her stunned face.

Amusement blended with anticipation. As soon as they returned, he would install her in his room. Before the end of the day, her clothing would hang in his closet alongside his.

She banged on his door, calling, "Is the missing mutual?"

"It is," he called back, even though he knew she couldn't hear him.

He hurried through a shower, then donned a pair of leathers and combat boots. His version of "nice."

He was preparing to find her when she sailed into the bedroom. His heart stuttered against his ribs the moment he spotted her. This female...oh, this female. Both savage and sweet, and exquisite beyond measure.

She wore the uniform of a decorated harpy soldier—a metal breastplate, pleated leather skirt and a dozen different weapon sheaths. But the metal was white, the leather pink, and the weapon handles bejeweled.

My savage gum drop queen.

"How am I supposed to function with a never-ending hard-on?" he asked, and he meant it.

She flushed and pretended to fluff hair she'd twisted into a series of elaborate knots. "Learn."

He almost grinned. Oh, but he liked her confident like this. He liked her, period.

Rathbone gathered her close and flashed her to Hades's palace. They found the king in his throne room, perched atop his golden chair, presiding over a case between two citizens. A cat sat in his lap, and a raccoon played with the hem of a robe worn by the old man with a clipboard standing next to the throne. Pippen, Hades's most trusted servant. His *only* trusted servant. Rathbone had no idea what the spirit had done to earn such a rare gift.

The mirror hung on the wall behind the king, as if presiding over *him*.

"May we interrupt?" Rathbone called, leading Neeka forward with an arm wrapped around her waist. Fear tinged the air, the usual reaction to seeing him in the kingdom. "Let me rephrase. We're interrupting."

Hades studied their placement and smirked. "If I'm about to hear how right I was and wrong you were, you may."

"Your Majesty," the defendant rushed out, nervously shuffling his feet. "Please give me a chance to—"

"Guilty," Hades interjected, waving Rathbone forward. Armed guards hauled the protesting defendant away. "Everyone out."

The rest of the crowd followed the same path as if their feet were on fire, disappearing beyond a set of double doors. Everyone but the old man and the animals exited.

In his element, the king reclined, resting an elbow on the chair's arm, and rubbing two fingers over his mouth. "My, my. Aren't we cozy together."

"We are." Rathbone gave Neeka a little squeeze. "Go ahead."

Her gaze remained riveted on the mirror, her expression glazing. "I remember now," she breathed out. "If you wish to save everyone, Neeka, you need only speak with the girl in the mirror."

Rathbone blinked. The Goddess of Many Futures. She appeared in the glass, a delicate female with long, curling white hair, eyes like a starlit night, and dark skin. She peered at Neeka, both hands pressed against the glass.

Hades glowered. "That isn't happening. *No one* speaks with Siobhan."

"Let me," the oracle demanded, unintimidated. "The fate of the world depends on it."

"Not my world."

She turned to Rathbone, flattening her palms on his pectorals and batting her lashes at him, expectant. "Go back to the palace and fetch my dueling pistols I'm stealing from you. Don't worry. I'll win."

Muscles hardened, and blood heated. He clasped her waist and squeezed. "You cannot challenge Hades. He's our ally."

She slithered against him, saying, "Then he should have let me talk with the goddess."

He glanced at his uncle, who gave a succinct shake of his head. Rathbone sighed and flashed Neeka to his bedroom. "I will bargain with him." He tossed her onto the bed. "After we negotiate terms."

"Do you think I'll lose a challenge?" she asked, eagerly stripping out of her breastplate.

"I think I love him and want to keep him around."

"Fine. But you're gonna owe me so big." She shimmied out of the skirt. "More than just terms. I'm expecting more jewelry. And gold coins with my image."

"You'll have them." Rathbone kicked off his boots and unzipped his leathers. "But you are not issuing a challenge to him, Neeka, and neither am I. That's final. He's more than my ally. He's raised me after my mother abandoned me."

"Gah! You can't just drop an information bomb like that while I'm so hot for you. I can't concentrate properly, so I can't react properly." With her thumbs hooked at the sides of her panties, she slid the material down her legs.

"I'll remind you. Now, about our terms." He climbed onto the bed and pinned her with his weight. "I'll return to bargain with him as soon as you admit you're mine."

Neeka petted Rathbone's chest. He looked so cute when he snored, his hair mussed and his mátia closed. A startling contrast to the animal who'd taken her to bed. Oh, how she lov—liked the many sides of this complicated male.

Though she wanted to do nothing more than cuddle with

him, she forced herself to carefully maneuver from the mattress and rise. He didn't want her challenging Hades—his beloved uncle/father!—so, she wouldn't. But she couldn't not speak with Siobhan. And deep down Neeka knew. Hades wouldn't bend on this, no matter what treasure Rathbone offered him. That left one option: sneaking into Hades's palace.

The second she'd spotted the mirror, she'd remembered the words she'd heard in the Hall of Secrets. Though the speaker, whoever it was, could be luring her into a trap. Always a possibility. Also worth the risk. And this wasn't a betrayal of Rathbone's trust. Neither Rathbone nor Hades would ever learn of her actions. So. No harm, no foul.

Fine! It was a betrayal. Wrong on every level. But she was still going to do it. Because priorities! Save her consort and harpykind or assuage Rathbone's feelings? As quietly as possible, she dressed in her uniform, then strapped on as many daggers as she could hold and tiptoed from the bedroom. Without the ability to flash, she'd have to go on foot. And she'd have to go fast, or Rathbone would catch her. He'd have something to say about her no harm, no foul sentiment.

Wings rippling, Neeka cast the arresting male a final glance. Her chest compressed.

I do this to save him. Not herself. Not the worlds. Him. Was there any better reason?

She hurried from the palace, entering a deserted nightscape teeming with overgrown trees, vines, and bushes. She hacked and chopped through them, tacking the scent of crisp, fresh water. Her mind whirled. If she and the Scarlet Tornado actually ended up making a go of things after this, she was totally taking over the landscaping of their kingdom. Because dang. This sucked.

By the time she reached the outer edge of the overgrowth, coming upon a charred wasteland and the head of a river, she was panting and beating herself up. Perhaps she and Rathbone *could* make a relationship work? He seemed to really, truly want her. Like, big time. To keep. Forever. And dang it, she wanted him, too. Like, big time. To keep. Forever.

He fit her, as if his intensity, ferocity, and charm had been tailor-made from a blueprint of her most secret desires. How he looked at her...smelled...moved... She shivered with desire.

Trust was important to him. As it should be. Trust was important to her, too. A need like no other. With it came security, one of life's greatest treasures. She'd broken Rathbone's once, but he'd given her a second chance. Could she allow herself to hurt him the same way twice? Besides, his loyalty to his uncle should be rewarded, not punished.

Neeka skidded to a stop, narrowly avoiding an eruption of fire. The flames burst through cracks in the dirt. What was she even doing? Betraying Rathbone by doing the one thing he'd asked her not to? No, she couldn't, wouldn't do it.

Resolved, she spun, intending to head home. A vibration in the ground jolted her, and she turned, ready to strike. A flash of red stopped her.

Maximus! His mouth was open with a war cry as he rushed toward her, a hammer raised over his head. Bloody cuts marred his upper body and face.

He stumbled to a halt as soon as he clocked her identity. "You." The arm with the hammer fell to his side, as if too heavy to hold up. "You're the wench with my father."

She winced and waved. "Hi. The name is Neeka the... Wanted." The boy looked like he'd been shoved through a wringer and beaten with a stick. What had he suffered to get here? For that matter, *how* had he gotten here? "Your dad and I are friends." They were, weren't they? Rathbone was tough but fair, insistent but generous. At least he was with her. "What are you doing here? Shouldn't you be in hiding out with your grandmother?"

Maximus bared his teeth. "I came to meet my father, and

that's what I'll do. I won't be stopped. Not by you. Not by anyone!"

"Hey," she said, showing him her hands, palms out, "I won't stop such a laudable endeavor. Do you know what that means? Laudable?" She was going to rock being a stepmother. "Why don't I take you to him?" Rathbone would be over the moon!

As the kid's eyes brightened, she added, "Here's the thing. If you pat my rear or compliment my boobs, I will break your face. Understand?"

"I understand it's Tuesday," he remarked, regaining his former sass. "Why are you wearing a top?"

"Hey! You don't speak to your future stepmother with that mouth." She jammed her fists on her hips. "How did you escape Hera?"

"What? Like it was hard."

Were the two males really clones? Because wow. Neeka—hot prickles seared her nape, a sensation she knew well. Tension descended from her head to her toes, turning her muscles into stone. Ahdán neared.

Heart jumping, she withdrew two daggers from their sheaths. Scanning the area, she told Maximus, "Listen up, kid. Run as fast as you can. The palace is beyond the thicket. Shout for your father and tell him the oracle's ex-husband is here." She didn't need Rathbone's help; she just needed the boy safe.

Maximus nodded and shot toward the thicket, but he stopped before reaching the foliage and gaped upward. Ahdán hovered in the sky, flapping wings of fire. The flames spread to his entire body, turning the surrounding area into a smoke-filled oven.

Neeka groaned. She wouldn't emerge unscathed from the coming battle, that much she comprehended. "Go!" she shouted, waving Maximus on. He did not obey. Argh! To Ahdán, she called, "Here for another round of divorce court, baby?"

"Here to settle this between us once and for all, wife."

"You're planning to die permanently then?"

Her ex threw back his head, releasing what must be his "power squawk." Smiling with icy delight, he revealed a syringe in his hand. A snippet she'd heard in the Hall of Secrets teased her mind...

Give her the remaining doses at once. If she dies, she dies. If she survives, she'll be able to withstand your fire and you can bed her anytime you wish.

Dread slapped Neeka. Ahdán intended to force her metamorphosis to Phoenix or kill her, and all it'd take was a single needle prick. Oh...crap.

28

Rathbone awoke with a jolt. *Something is wrong.* The knowledge burned through any vestiges of slumber, bringing instant clarity. He was in his bedroom, and Neeka was gone.

He pursed his lips. Where was she? Was her absence the source of the problem? Had he grown accustomed to having her cuddled in his arms after a single night?

He flashed to his feet and dressed. Sunlight streamed through the balcony window, highlighting a chamber he once believed he'd designed for Lore. She might have liked the gold furnishings, but she would've disdained the vivid color scheme, preferring a plainer palette. As she'd proven, she lacked the taste to appreciate the intricacy of the mosaic. If he'd truly known the goddess—the version of her she'd pretended to be, at least—he would've realized this space reflected his tastes…and Neeka's.

Had he understood he belonged with the harpy, even before he'd met her?

As he flashed throughout the palace, on the hunt, eager to see her, to speak with her, to be near her and breathing her in, he imagined her redecorating every room to her specifications. Possessiveness grabbed him by the throat and refused to let go. Not just directed at the female herself, but the future they could—would—have together. He couldn't wait to have pink walls, unnecessary beaded pillows, and velvet recliners she'd never allow him to utilize.

The scent of sweet almonds and tart cherries drew him closer and closer. Muscles heated and hardened as he tracked her outside. A waft of smoke invaded his nostrils, and he stiffened. Fire? *My female is in danger.*

Rathbone balled his fists, urgency lashing him. He flashed into the cloud of gloom, materializing as a bird, scanning every direction at once. He squawked a denial. Neeka and Maximus, who lunged to strike at her ex. The very warrior Rathbone had killed on day one. The ill-timed and poorly executed assault failed, allowing the Phoenix to deliver a strike of his own. Neeka threw herself in front of the boy, taking the blow. Soot now streaked her breastplate.

Rathbone dove down, down, shifting into a dragon. But the oracle got swept up in a vicious battle with the Phoenix, and though blood poured from multiple wounds and she wobbled on her feet, she held her own. Protective instincts saturated everything, demanding immediate action but he pulled back, flying a circle around the pair.

The warrioress lacked self-assurance in some areas. If Rathbone stepped in and took over, he might bruise her hard-won confidence.

As he watched, wonder and pride filled him. She took as many hits as necessary to protect Maximus. Again and again, the Phoenix made a play for the boy, but the oracle always stopped him.

Rathbone scanned, aggression rippled through his feathers as he searched for any traps the Phoenix might have planted.

What do we have here? Phantoms blocked every path of escape, forming a circle around the combat zone. The apparitions were as bad as demons, able to embody at will and constantly starved for immortal souls. Created by Erebus, they remained subject to his will, able to do what he ordered and nothing else.

These particular phantoms were females dressed in black widow's weeds. Their milky-white eyes surveyed the battle as they walked in a circle, chanting with monotone voices. "Watch the brawl, hurt anyone who interferes, give Rathbone the message, return to Father. Watch the brawl, hurt anyone who interferes, give Rathbone the message, return to Father."

Erebus had another message for him, did he?

Anytime Neeka, Maximus, or the Phoenix got too close to the group of phantoms, they erupted into shrieking war machines.

Rathbone flew a circle around the phantoms. Sensing him, they tilted their heads in unison to follow him as he circled above.

Still monotone, they said, "Last chance to save yourself. Kill the oracle or suffer the consequences. The choice is yours."

Rathbone blew a stream of fire on the entire pack. Even doused in flames, burning to ash, the females walked and chanted. Those specks of ash vanished before ever hitting the ground.

"Let me handle this, Maximus," Neeka snapped, saving the boy from a fiery wing. When she tripped and crashed, she sprang up quickly. Fresh blood trickled into her eyes, blurring her vision.

"If you were any good at battle," the teenager snapped back while leaping to a stand, "the bad guy would be dead already."

She wasn't in a spot to read his lips. Was too busy huffing and puffing, kicking a fallen syringe when the Phoenix reached for it. As it soared across the clearing, landing with a thump near a tree, she proclaimed, "You are *so* grounded when this is over."

"And *you* are tiring, wife," the Phoenix said. "Surrender now.

Take the injection like a good little submissive. Perhaps I'll show you mercy. Eventually."

"This is an A and B conversation between family, Dan, so why don't you C your way out." Going on the offensive, she threw herself into the Phoenix and swung her body behind his, clawing out his throat.

The lord healed swiftly. So swiftly he maintained his stance, reaching back to grip Neeka by the nape and yanking her overhead. As she landed with a heavy thud, Rathbone spotted her melted, blistered flesh, and the sight nearly undid him.

"The remaining doses, administered at once," the Phoenix promised with a toothy grin, earning her fiercest glare. She wasn't healed yet, her flesh rejuvenating slower than usual. Too slow. She needed Rathbone's blood.

The Phoenix dragged her across the clearing, heading for the syringe. "We'll know if you survive in a matter of minutes."

Rathbone flicked his tail. *Step in?*

With a screech, Neeka ripped a wing from the male's back while kicking his feet together. She hit the ground, and the howling Phoenix toppled beside her. *Good girl.*

"Weapon me, Red," she called as she clambered to her feet.

With pleasure. Rathbone flashed midflight, appearing in her grip as a spear. The same spear the dragon shifter Kanta had used on Rathbone.

Neeka offered her opponent a delighted grin of her own.

Maximus raced their way with his claws bared. The Phoenix lunged for him. The oracle spun into the boy's path and shoved the spear through her ex's chest cavity. Flames scorched Rathbone, but he endured, ejecting metal spikes into the Phoenix's bloodstream. The same metal the dragon shifter had wielded against Rathbone.

The Phoenix jerked, roaring up at the sky as his fire died. His knees buckled, and he crumpled into the dirt, where he twitched.

"I did it! I'm incredible! I'm amazing!" Wheezing her breaths, Neeka stomped on the syringe, breaking the glass. Golden liquid spilled over the dirt, smoke curling into the air.

She returned to the writhing Phoenix, yanked the spear free with the last of her strength, and swung it. Rathbone transformed into a sword midway, removing the other man's head. Not a permanent death for a Phoenix, but a good start.

Rathbone shifted into his normal form just as Neeka crumpled. He caught her against his chest and eased her down.

As he bit into his free arm, drawing blood, then shoved the wound against her mouth, Maximus approached.

"Is she okay?" the boy asked, hesitant.

"She will be." Rathbone kissed her temple. "Take as much as you need, love."

She drank greedily, gulping mouthfuls, and contentment infused him. This was a version of his dream he hadn't computed until now. Nourishing his warrior woman, giving everything she needed.

He studied the boy, who stared at him, wide-eyed. A handsome lad, no doubt about it, with untapped potential. "I expect a full accounting. How and why are you both here? How did you get through the realm's boundaries unscathed?"

"What boundaries?" Maximus demanded. "I flashed in without problem. But then, I'm me." He rolled back his shoulders.

The barrier sensed the boy's connection to Rathbone and allowed him to pass without incident?

Neeka freed her mouth from his flesh and lifted her head, crying, "Don't be mad!" A flurry of movement, she twisted and wound herself around Rathbone, clinging to him like a vine. "I did it. I'm guilty. My plan was to sneak into Hades's palace and visit with the goddess in the mirror without anyone else in the know. But I didn't do it!"

"I see. Go on."

"I changed my mind because I couldn't bring myself to betray your trust," she told him in a rush. "I had just turned around when I smacked into Maximus. Then Ahdán showed up. Then you arrived, helped me save the day, and forgave me." She peeked at him through her thick fan of lashes. "Right? You forgive me?"

Infinitely tender, he kissed the racing pulse at the base of her neck. Whether she realized it or not, she'd chosen him over everything else. How could he be angry about that?

"Will you talk with me when you have a knowing from now on?" he asked. "*Before* you act?"

She nodded with enthusiasm. "I will, oracle's honor."

"Then I'll admit there's nothing to forgive. But I'll still let you show me how apologetic you are at home. I'm sweet like that."

"Wait. So you aren't mad?"

"Not mad," he confirmed.

"Dang. I really like you."

He chuckled. "I really like you, too."

Blasting pure defiance, Maximus bellowed, "I hate you both. I'm going to live with you, anyway, and let you train me to be undefeatable. What's for dinner?"

"I guess I have a consort and stepson now." Neeka crouched on the railing of a balcony, eating her version of popcorn, her attention on the ground below. She'd hung a mirror on the wall to her left, allowing her to converse with her reflection while watching Rathbone and Maximus enjoy a get-to-know-you sesh and trained. Though the sight of father and son working together gave her all the feels, the interaction wasn't going well.

The pair had begun an hour ago; as soon as they'd returned to the palace, in fact. Maximus took every bit of instruction as a criticism, frustrating Rathbone.

"You also have an ex-husband who's gonna rot in an Underworld prison until Rathbone is able to kill him for good," Reflection replied. "Oh, and don't forget the grumpy harpy housemate."

"As if I could." She and her handsome consort had fetched Daisy after they'd gotten Maximus settled. Neeka had forgotten her, but Rathbone hadn't. "She kicked me out of her room to play with gadgets and gizmos. Who does that?"

"You when you're making jewelry."

Anyway. "What am I going to do about Lore and the Astra?"

"Relax and let our brilliance play out?"

Neeka winced as Maximus took a swing at Rathbone, missed, and tripped over his own feet. He came up swinging, missed again, and shouted vile insults. Rathbone just stood there, accepting the abuse.

When the kid quieted, the King of Agonies asked, "We'll take a break, and you can tell me why you ceased aging."

Ohhhh. Yes, please do. She returned her gaze to the boy, her superior harpy eyesight allowing her to easily read his lips.

"Hera paid a sorceress. Said she'd keep me at peak stupidity, so I'd impregnate anyone willing to climb into my bed. Which you would've figured out already if you had cared enough to visit."

Rathbone flinched. "I was unaware of your existence."

"Excuses!" Maximus took another swing. And missed. The cursing started up again.

"Did you do it? Impregnate anyone?"

"Not for lack of trying," the kids replied, smug. "My little swimmers are too powerful. Eggs get ravaged."

"Boo! Hiss!" Neeka threw a handful of lightly salted corn kernels at her family. "That's disgusting, young man."

Rathbone pinched the bridge of his nose. "Break time is over. The urge to hit you is too strong."

Okay, back to business. "What should we offer Hades in exchange for a hobnob with Siobhan?" she asked Reflection.

"So relaxing is nixed? Just like that? Okay."

"What about a coupon for one free makeover?"

"Maybe?" Reflection spread her arms. "I've tried reaching out, hoping to bypass Hades altogether, but it's been a no go. I mean, she's in a mirror, and I'm in a mirror, so there's got to be a way to intersect."

If you wish to save everyone, Neeka, you need only speak with the girl in the mirror. Did Siobhan have a bead on the missing bones? Or something else? Did she *own* the bones? And dang it, who had spoken those words to Neeka in the first place, and why? How was the deaf girl supposed to make a voice identification?

"Maybe a coupon to find Hades his one true love, too," she mused.

Cherry... Crimson... Scarlet Avenger handed his son a dagger and demonstrated a basic move, his muscles rippling. Mmm. Maybe relaxing wasn't a bad idea. "I'm gonna get me some of that first."

Professor Hotness glanced up, as if he'd heard her words, and winked. She preened and waved like a schoolgirl with a crush.

"I miss single Neeka. She was enamored of me," Reflection muttered.

A soft smile played at the corners of Neeka's mouth. The expression on Rathbone's face—she snorted. He looked as if he'd sucked on a lemon as Maximus continued punching the blade through the air, grinning like a toddler with a new toy.

The desire to be with them proved too strong to ignore. "Excuse me a bit," she said, setting her bowl aside.

Wings stiffening, she prepared to drop and join the festivities. A vision stopped her, barging into her mind without warning. She jerked as the world around her faded...hmm. The landscape remained mostly the same, with only slight differences.

She saw the field beneath the balcony, where Rathbone and Maximus were practicing. Except, in the vision, Rathbone wasn't there; Maximus stood alone, staring with horror at... She tracked the line of his gaze and gasped. He watched Rathbone and Neeka.

A wealth of arrows protruded from future Neeka's chest. Her

consort held her limp form in his arms, feeding her blood and shouting commands at her.

Her heart thudded. Not because of her multitude of injuries, but Rathbone. He was so absorbed by her condition, he didn't notice Azar. The Astra materialized behind Maximus and captured the kid in a choke hold.

Azar called, "There's nothing you can do to keep me from your kingdom, Majesty. No place you or those you protect are safe."

Future Rathbone's head whipped up. Aggression radiated from him as he clocked the danger to his son.

"You have twenty-four hours to give me the orb, or I will execute the lad," Azar continued. "I look forward to hearing from you." He flashed away, taking his prize with him.

The vision morphed, whisking days ahead, revealing—No! No, no, no. Tremors cascaded through Neeka's limbs. Maximus lay on a stone altar, a gaping hole in his chest. Azar towered on one side of him, resolved, and Rathbone towered on the other, grief-stricken. Tears streaked his cheeks, and the sight nearly broke her.

"You should have given me what I sought," the Astra said.

Lore appeared at his side and draped a hand over his strong shoulder. Her touch was solid; she was a spirit no longer.

They'd brought her to life before the final ceremony in this timeline? Good to know.

"As you can see, we acquired the orb anyway." Lore smiled smugly at Rathbone before whispering to Azar, "Tell him he can watch my triumph in three days. We have a surprise for him."

"You can watch Lore's triumph in three days," the Astra parroted. "We have a surprise for you."

Lore controlled him so completely? How? And who had found the last bones? How had Azar acquired the orb, if not Rathbone?

"You will not win this," the king spat at the goddess. He

grabbed at her, claws bared, and Neeka jolted. Chains circled his wrists. She'd changed things, but not enough.

The vision morphed again, skipping ahead once again, depositing her in the harpy throne room. Azar walked in with a flesh and blood Lore, who took her place on the dais, made her victory speech, then unbridled her evil.

Three visions in one. Not uncommon and always spurred for the same reason. One event was tied to another. Prevent the first, and you prevented the others. Yay. On the flip side, the final path had begun to solidify, soon to be unchangeable. Every decision executed from this point forward set the dominos in place.

The vision ended, and trepidation pierced Neeka. "Save Maximus," she tried to scream in real life. Pinpricks of scorching pain penetrated her chest. Ow! Ow, ow, ow. Hot liquid rushed up her throat, gushing from the corners of her mouth. Her world tilted until she flipped end over end, her body weightless.

Falling?

Impact! Organs popped like balloons. Agony. So much worse than ever before. She moaned and writhed, fighting to see past a blurry haze. Where was she? What had happened?

Something warm and soft cupped her cheek, and she went still. Her world continued to spin, scattering her thoughts. Rathbone. Maximus. Azar and Lore. The vision!

She blinked rapidly and met Rathbone's gaze. His mouth was moving, his expression tinged with desperate concern. "Save Maximus," she commanded with the last of her strength. *Don't be too late, don't be too late.*

His head whipped up, fury radiating from him, just as it had done during her premonition.

Dread punched her. Was she already too late?

She followed his gaze, ignoring the influx of pain, and groaned. Sure enough. The Astra had arrived in reality and now imprisoned the teenager with his arms.

"You have twenty-four hours to give me the orb, or I will

execute your son. I look forward to hearing from you." With a nod in their direction, Azar vanished, taking a struggling Maximus with him.

Rathbone yanked an arrow from Neeka, demanding, "What did you see? Tell me!"

Despite the pain, she remained lucid. She knew she couldn't not divulge the truth, the full truth, and only the truth. "If you fail to give the Astra what he seeks, he acquires the orb another way and Maximus dies. Lore still wins." And dang it, this looked bad—for Neeka. Like she'd set everything up for another perfect betrayal. Distract Rathbone with the old get-arrowed-and-fall bit while the Astra collected Maximus, then hang back and persuade the king to risk the end of the world to save the boy. "By giving him the orb, we help Lore destroy us all, anyway."

He drew in a deep breath, then pulled out another arrow. "I'm the only one able to dismantle the orb."

"Not according to my vision," she muttered. The absolute worst thing she could say in her own defense, and yet, truth was truth.

A vein pulsed in the center of his forehead. "Very well. I'll give the Astra what he seeks. I'll also convene with Hades and convince him to let you speak with Siobhan. We will find the remaining bones, ensuring Azar cannot resurrect Lore, even with the orb."

A great plan. So why was her stomach churning and her instinct burning?

29

"Tell me what payment you seek." Rathbone stood in Hades's throne room, Neeka at his side. "Let my female converse with the goddess in your mirror, and I'll pay your price, whatever it is." Why waste precious minutes arguing over semantics when Rathbone was willing to give up everything he owned?

And there would be an argument if he attempted to bargain. He and Hades were family, yes, but business was business. There was no way Hades would allow the two females to interact out of the goodness of his heart.

"Um. Maybe I should do the talking," Neeka said from the corner of her mouth. She probably thought she whispered, but she did not. Her words echoed from the walls. "You kind of suck at negotiating."

"She isn't wrong." Hades pet the cat in his lap. "Why pay for this? And you know I'll make you pay dearly."

Rathbone snorted. "Offer an answer free of charge? Hardly."

"Perhaps the answer is my payment."

"Perhaps isn't good enough. Verbally accept my offer, and I'll explain everything." Hades might not do something out of the goodness of his heart, but he often did things for the sake of his rampant curiosity. The only ace Rathbone currently possessed.

"Does this have anything to do with rumors about your secret son?" Hades asked. He kissed the cat's face and held it out for Pippen to collect.

The servant claimed the feline, who clawed his arms into a bloody mess before diving to the floor. Pippen revealed no reaction.

"Maximus is your great-nephew," Neeka piped up. "Family is supposed to help family, I'm told."

"I am my family, and I help me," Hades said.

Rathbone measured his breaths. He hadn't given the Astra the orb—yet—but a countdown clock consumed his mind. An ominous ticktock he couldn't escape. Only twenty hours, seventeen minutes, and forty-three seconds remained. Forty-two. Forty-one. Enough time for Neeka to chat with Siobhan, learn what she needed to learn, find what she needed to find, and hopefully spark a vision.

Unless she was aiding the Astra and setting Rathbone up for further failure? The thought *had* crossed his mind a time or twelve. Look how susceptible he'd been to Lore's lies and schemes. To those of Neeka herself. But they'd been on different terms then. And his oracle wasn't his former wife. One lacked integrity. The other wouldn't violate hers for any reason.

No, Neeka wasn't aiding the Astra.

"What if I demand the Kingdom of Agonies instead, hmm?" the king asked.

Rathbone flinched inside. This, he'd suspected. If he agreed to do it, if he handed over the kingdom he'd fought so hard to acquire, Hades would accept, no doubt about it. Would Neeka be disappointed and therefore less likely to become his queen?

I'll win her another kingdom. "Verbally accept my offer," he said, "and Agonies is yours."

The king double blinked, a sign of his unparalleled shock. He looked to Neeka as his cat jumped to the top of his throne and perched. "You wouldn't mind losing your new kingdom?"

She shrugged. "Who says we won't win it back?"

Hades was the one to snort this time. "As if I'd want your hovel of a realm. The renovation alone would empty my treasury. No, I desire something that will cost you far more. An admission that I was right all those eons ago when I told you about Lore's trickery."

"Don't you dare!" Neeka spun in front of Rathbone. Her dark eyes glittered with cunning rather than concern. "Let me challenge him to a duel. Or kill him outright here and now. Or tell him about the vision I just had of his future. But your dignity is mine."

As she spoke, Rathbone watched her *and* Hades. The male projected only amusement until she mentioned the vision. Then he went still.

Rathbone almost smiled. Brilliant Neeka. She'd offered bait and hooked a big fish. Two fish, actually. He was curious to hear about the vision himself. "Very well, love. I'll keep my dignity."

"Thank goodness!" She kissed him before facing the king. "Well? Your move."

Hades tapped his claws against the chair arms. "I'll hear the vision, and in return, I'll grant you a one minute chat with my mirror. Two if I like what you have to say. The interaction will occur here, and I will bear witness."

"Five minutes," Neeka proclaimed. "Because you're going to hate what I have to say."

There was no stopping Rathbone's smile now.

Glowering and stiff, Hades nodded. "Done. Five minutes with the mirror in exchange for a detailed accounting of both your vision and your coming interaction with my goddess."

Behind him, soldiers rushed over. Using ropes and pulleys, they lowered the mirror and secured it upright.

"Leave us," he commanded when they finished.

The soldiers zoomed out. Pippen and his clipboard stayed behind.

"I'll cancel the rest of your appointments for the day, Majesty," the servant said, his tone as efficient as his manner. "I'll also cancel your afternoon orgy and pencil in a good long pout in case the young lady is correct."

Hades scowled. "Very good, Pippen. Now, let us proceed."

Neeka waited for Rathbone's nod before telling the other male, "Most of my visions are clips of reality. Sometimes they are symbolic. I'll let you decide which this is." She inhaled, exhaled. "You stand at a crossroads. One fork leads into a violent storm, where hail pelts an overgrown jungle with traps hidden throughout. But, beyond the storm and the jungle, a paradise awaits. A beautiful black female with white hair beckons you over. You go to her, overcoming many injuries along the way. She cuts out her heart and gifts it to you."

"And the other fork?" Hades demanded. Did he realize he was now white-knuckling the arms of his throne?

"A paradise that leads to a hellscape. Along the path, the sun is shining, flowers are blooming, and birds are singing. But a storm rages at the end, where the same female awaits, beckoning you. Once again, you go to her. When you reach her, you are without wounds. Until she claws out your heart and eats it."

With clenched teeth, the king asked, "And which do I choose?"

"Both. And neither."

Hades huffed. "That tells me nothing."

"And yet it tells you everything," she offered, all innocence.

"Get specific or you won't earn an interaction with my mirror," the male snapped.

"False! I've already earned it with specifics. Did I or did I not tell you how much you'd hate what I had to say?" She scratched her chin and looked to Rathbone. "Did I?"

"You did," he said with a nod. How effortlessly she improved any situation.

"See?" She rubbed her hands together and faced Hades anew. "So go ahead and start the clock."

Neeka blazed up the royal dais, her wings buzzing when she spied her own reflection. How did you summon a cursed goddess?

With time of the essence, Neeka knocked on the glass. "Siobhan. Yo. Get up here, girl."

"Careful," Hades snarled behind her. She watched his mouth in the glass. "Do that again, and I will remove your fist."

"Don't threaten her," Rathbone snarled back, at the king's side. The two males flanked her.

She looked good leading muscle. But this was a professional business meeting, not an audition for bodyguards. "Look," she said to the girl in the mirror. "I'm on a clock here. Someone at some point in history told me to speak with you. I think you're the solution to my problem. Are you?"

A wave descended over the glass, as if it had liquefied. Then another wave came. And another. Her brows knit together. Slowly she reached out. Contact. Her fingers sank—a clawed hand shot out to clasp onto her wrist and yank her through.

The throne room vanished and hazy smoke billowed in front of her. She glanced over her shoulder, wondering if she'd see Rathbone and Hades. If they could see her. No sign of the other world. Dang. What if she was stuck? Had she walked into a trap?

"Hello?" she called.

The vapor sucked together, producing a woman who appeared both modern and old-fashioned. Oh! Oh! She was *the* woman. A black beauty with long white hair in tangles. She wore a Victorian gown of jet, with a beaded corset and a flared skirt. Tattered threads hung from the wrist cuffs and hem.

"You're late," she admonished, red flickering inside her irises.

"And you're Siobhan, Goddess of Many Futures?"

"I am." She turned on her high heels and glanced over her shoulder, motioning Neeka to follow. "Come. You'll understand when we reach our destination."

As the goddess glided forward, eerily graceful, Neeka took note of her surroundings. Mother-of-pearl, everywhere. On the walls, the columns, and the floor. A galaxy of stars stretched overhead. The temple from the vision!

Fangs sharpening, claws elongating, she rushed after Siobhan— Um. The goddess stopped as a second female emerged from a thicker haze of smoke. Neeka swallowed a groan. Oh, yeah. She'd walked into a trap. But she didn't backtrack. She was here, there was hope.

"Hello, Unwanted," her mother said.

"How did you get in here?" she demanded. "The mirror is the only way in, and it's guarded twenty-four seven by Hades."

"Wrong. And right." Her mother remained smug and irritating. "There are two mirrors. Hades has one, but someone else has the other…"

"And who is this someone else?" Azar? Had he not fired the treacherous Grenwich? Or was the mystery person paying her fee now?

"That isn't information you'll receive at this time." Siobhan motioned to Grenwich. "Proceed. I don't like having visitors. The sooner you finish the better."

"I'm already done, and I've never been happier." Grenwich unfolded a white cloth she held, revealing the final bones. "You've lost, Neeka, your suffering assured."

Neeka winced. The word daggers cut deep, leaving gaping wounds. Rather than coddle the bleeders, as she'd done in the past, she strapped on big girl panties and forged ahead. "You should have run while you had the chance."

A smiling Lore materialized at Grenwich's side. "Why run when I'm here to take out the trash?"

Dang. Neeka should have known they'd partnered up. Like called to like. "Only two against me? Or are you more than an unwitting hostess?" she demanded of Siobhan.

Unperturbed, the goddess grinned with cold evil. "Tell Hades I'm coming for him."

Okay. "Two possibly three against me." Neeka met Lore's gaze. "And you expect to win?"

"Oh, there are more with us."

The veil of smoke thinned behind Lore and Grenwich, revealing a cluster of hybrids. They possessed the head of a wolf, the body of an ultramuscular human, with scales instead of skin, and two sets of arms. There were ten in total, and they stared at Neeka as if they could already taste her marrow. Her stomach flip-flopped.

"Meet my first attempt at motherhood." Lore flipped her hair over one shoulder. "They are unable to embody, but the same will not be true of my next brood." Smiling, she smoothed a hand over her flat stomach. "They are ready to secure their new kingdom for their baby brothers."

Neeka exaggerated a gag. "Yes, I see the resemblance." How to handle this? Like Hades at the crossroads, she must make a choice.

Did some part of Rathbone still love his ex? Would he resent Neeka if she harmed the goddess?

Was this the damage to her life? And what about her mother? Could she physically harm the woman who'd birthed her?

Grenwich noticed her indecision. "Walk away."

"I have no wish to kill you now," Lore said. "You have more to do for me."

For her? Neeka cut off a rebuke. "All right. I'll go," she offered pleasantly. "After." As cold as ice, she struck, raking her claws across Lore's trachea, then her mother's.

As the two toppled, Neeka snatched the cloth containing the bones and jetted off. The stable members were too concerned for their mother to compute what had transpired.

Her wings flapped overtime, increasing Neeka's speed. She intended to dive into the sky. Hopefully, she'd fly out of the glass and land with ease in the other world. If not, well, she'd figured it out.

Halfway there the hybrids caught up with her. Like a whirling, screeching tornado, they trapped her in a tangle of chaos and pain. Because they were spirits, the same as Lore, they swiped their claws *through* her body, cutting her spirit, making her feel as if she'd been dipped in acid and rolled in salt. Panic attempted to derail her defenses as she struggled to protect herself.

Weakness invaded her limbs, and she collapsed to the ground, cracking the mother-of-pearl and dropping the cloth. A gnarled claw-tipped foot kicked it from her sight line. No! As she continued to fight the interminable stream of blows, she crawled forward and patted the floor. Thankfully, her attackers paused periodically to lick bits and pieces of her spirit from their talons. But the anguish! The helplessness.

Through sheer will alone, she continued her search. No sign of the bones. Come on, come on...

The monsters started up again, delivering injury after injury. Her vision hazed. When she couldn't crawl any longer, she scooted, wriggled, and slithered—and fell right out of the mirror. She slammed into Rathbone and Hades and rolled down the dais steps.

"Nooo!" The bones. She'd left them behind. A treasure for Grenwich to nab.

"You are injured." Remaining on the floor, Rathbone yanked

her close, bit his wrist and placed the wound over her mouth. "What happened?" Strain etched deep grooves around his eyes.

"It was a setup," she said after swallowing a mouthful of liquid power. She fought to catch her breath. "Lore controls ten adult hybrids, and my mother aids her. They have the remaining bones now." Tears blurred Neeka's vision. How miserably she'd failed. "If we give Azar the orb, he'll resurrect Lore before the ceremony. Maximus might survive, but no one else will."

That was the true horror. Whatever road they traveled, they ended up in the same place: doomed.

Hades flashed in front of her, knocking Rathbone out of the way. "Yes, but what did my goddess say?" he demanded.

"Oh, um, she's coming for you or whatever."

Rathbone shoved the other male away and pulled Neeka onto his lap. "I'll present the Astra with a deal he cannot refuse."

"Which is?"

"I'll shift into Lore. I will be her in every way that matters. There will be no need for her to revive. He'll kill me and win his task against Erebus."

"What? No. *You* won't revive."

On cue, a new vision opened in her mind. The throne room ceremony. She saw Rathbone shift into Lore. Saw Azar claw out his heart while muttering words Neeka didn't understand. Saw Rathbone fall and never get up, and Chaos announce the Astra the winners of the task.

"No!" she shouted, jolting into the present. "Unacceptable. Promise me you won't do that, Rathbone. Please. I'll agree to be your queen if you'll swear not to do it. I require you in *this* form."

His expression softened, and he brushed a lock of hair behind her ear. "You were right about the shadow monsters. We can't allow Lore to birth them. If they were to harm you… " He shook his head. "That's a future I will never allow."

He jerked, his nostrils flaring with his next inhalation. "I now understand the warning Erebus issued. But it won't stop me. I caused this situation, and I will end it. To keep you safe, I will give up anything. Even my life."

30

Azar stared at the femur in his clasp, not wanting to ponder how he'd gotten it and desperate to destroy it. With this bone and its companion added to his collection, he needed only the orb to bestow flesh and blood upon Lore. An orb he was set to obtain within a matter of minutes.

Defenses cracked inside him. The King of Agonies wouldn't allow his son to die as a prisoner of the Astra. An admirable trait, but one that endangered everyone Azar loved. Because, as soon as Rathbone complied, and he would, their doom was assured. But then, their doom would be assured even if the king refused.

Azar squeezed his eyes shut, hating himself. The highest law of the Astra: if you did not guard it, you could not keep it. He hadn't guarded his brethren. Or himself.

How had he allowed his life to reach this point? Now there was nothing anyone could do to save themselves. Or stop him. Unless...

Perhaps a hope or two remained. The oracle, and Silver.

Azar glanced at his prisoner. Maximus sat secured to a chair at the end of the conference table, glaring at him. The boy wore Silver's metal; there was no way he could escape. If there were something Azar could use to bind Lore...

He flashed to Silver's bedroom, making use of the male's open invitation. The warlord lounged on a chaise, sketching designs for his next project. He'd shaved the sides of his head and bound his long black hair in braids.

As the metalworker, he made their weapons. Among other things. Of all Astra, Azar had the strongest bond with Silver, the gruffest of the nine. He was a soldier who never allowed his emotions to get in his way. Never deviated from an order or wavered during a mission.

"The crimson king won't escape us again," Silver vowed without glancing up. "I'll make sure of it."

"His capture matters little." Only the orb counted at this point.

"Nevertheless, I will bind him tighter than I bind my concubine."

"You and your challenges." Azar hesitated before asking what he'd come to ask. "Is there a way to undo an ancient binding spell between two immortals?" No one knew the rules of anything, and how to bend them, better than Silver.

The metalworker, also known as the Fiery One, placed his book on the cushion and sat up. Rare amusement glittered in eyes the same color as his name. "You thinking to cut ties between the king and the goddess?"

Guilt spread its poison across his mind, leaving a thick layer of infection. "I've considered it." But that wasn't his endgame. The two were no longer tethered. He didn't let himself consider the real reason he'd asked.

"There's an elixir touted to create a union stronger than fated mates, but I've heard the side effects are devastating. I can research what that means."

"Thank you." But he doubted it would do what he needed.

"I wonder if I can forge a collar with some kind of bond-breaking alloy," Silver muttered, picking up his sketchbook and drawing.

"I must go," Azar grated. Yes, he truly hated himself.

Silver didn't hear him, just continued drawing. Azar flashed to the conference room.

A grinning Lore greeted him. She perched atop the long rectangular table, swinging her legs, stunningly beautiful in a recreation of the dress she'd died in: a black-and-white Victorian-era ball gown.

His nerve endings awoke for her, singing. His blood heated. He swallowed a rebuke.

Maximus remained in his chair, shackled and gagged.

"Did you miss me?" she purred, crooking her finger at Azar. "Being away from me, even for a few minutes, must be awful for you."

He dug in his heels, staying put. For three seconds. In the end, he stepped between her legs.

"I love your resistance." Chuckling, she ghosted her fingers along his jaw. Though she was in spirit form, he felt the tingle of her touch. "The time has come, darling. I need you fully on my side, not deluding yourself with thoughts of victory."

He knew of what she referred. Of course he knew. He'd just tried to take measures against it. But even then, he'd separated himself from the truth. "Don't do this, goddess."

"Oh, I'm doing it." Tone indulgent but firm, she said, "Be my good Astra. Put the bone in its sheath, stop trying to forget, and let yourself remember the horrific thing you did."

An order he could not refuse. Because she owned him and had from the beginning.

He placed his bounty with the others: in a sheath that hung

from the back of his waist. Seconds later, the floodgates in his mind opened, and *the memory* overtook him. The day he'd killed Lore. She'd seemed to know why he'd appeared. Had tearfully begged him not to kill her. To let her live for the first time. But he'd ripped out her heart in the way of the ancients anyway.

Afterward, he'd replayed the interaction on repeat, unable to boot her image from his thoughts. He'd heard the tale of her bones and hunted down the skull. She'd appeared to him the day he'd found it, still acting like a damsel in distress. In fact, she'd appeared to him every day after for months, and his hand had burned to make stardust for her.

He remembered how he'd grown to believe he loved her. How, when she'd pretended to fade, he'd done the unthinkable… Had sung the song she'd taught him, thinking to share his strength with her by joining their spirits. In actuality, he'd bound his will to hers. Her plan all along.

From there, she'd ordered him to keep everything about her a secret. She'd ceased to visit him, only to reappear with a new attitude and a fresh order just before the assigning of his blessing task. Throw her skull into the sea.

He'd been compelled to obey. Exactly as he was compelled to obey *every* order she issued. Even if it meant betraying his brethren. Males he respected and loved.

"That's my sweet Astra," she cooed. "I do adore seeing revulsion overtake your pretty face. By the way, you will stand there, be still and quiet from now until the meeting with Rathbone ends. You may not speak telepathically with the Astra or leave this room."

Acid poured through his veins. "What is Erebus paying you?" Only the Deathless would have plotted something to make an Astra this miserable before ruining his life.

"He's not paying me anything." She stood and moved away from him, then angled to the side as Erebus materialized. "He's my true fated mate."

Azar didn't jolt—on the outside. Lore and Erebus, lovers. Of course. Erebus and his Blade of Destiny always knew who to target.

Erebus closed the distance, the hem of his dark robe swaying at his feet. Rage slashed at Azar's calm veneer. He could only stand there, silent and immobile, as his greatest enemy stopped directly in front of him. Mistress's orders.

"You're right, goddess." Erebus wrapped an arm around Lore's waist and kissed her temple. The creator of phantoms had ways of touching spirits that others did not. "His look of revulsion is priceless." Another kiss, this one directly on her lips, while staring at Azar.

He wished he wasn't bothered by the sight of the two together.

"We'll get to see it again soon." She giggled, resting her head on Erebus's shoulder and petting his chest.

Interesting. Azar recognized that high-pitched grating sound for what it was: fake. Did she play Erebus, too?

He almost—almost—laughed.

"As you can guess, I've always had an ace," the god said, smug in his ignorance. "I bided my time, awaiting the day you would help me devastate the Astra. Finally, that day has come. Or it will. At the final ceremony, your brothers-in-arms will realize the depths of your betrayal, and each of you will die in anguish."

Lore nuzzled her cheek against Erebus's chest. "Speak, Azar. Give us your thoughts."

"Someone will defeat you, even if I can't." The statement ripped from his throat.

"No, darling." Lore winced for his benefit. "They won't. Every piece is now in place."

"Well, not every piece," Erebus said, gleeful. "Shall we do it now or later?"

"Yes! Now!" she squealed, clapping and regarding the male as if he'd hung the moon. "Please."

"Very well. Give the order."

Gaze upon Azar, she smiled and commanded, "Accept the orb from Rathbone and kill the oracle while she's here. Make it hurt."

Azar shuddered internally. *So my downfall begins.* If Neeka the Unwanted aided the Astra, as she'd vowed to the General, she was now their only hope of survival.

Erebus kissed the crown of Lore's head. "I'll take my leave before the red beast arrives. Know that I'll miss you every second I'm gone." He winked at Azar as if they merely played a game before vanishing, leaving him with a toxic mix of rage, guilt, shame, and Lore the Incomparable, the source of his nightmares.

Rathbone and the oracle arrived only moments later, and they looked as happy as Azar felt. Especially when they noticed the female gloating at his side.

"Well?" Lore prompted. "Do you have something for us or not?"

"The orb." Rathbone tossed the small bulb Azar's way.

With lightning-fast reflexes, he caught the thing. He felt no satisfaction, only doom. Though he squeezed with every ounce of his strength, the object of his demise failed to shatter.

"Take the boy." He kept his gaze on Neeka, projecting a single thought. *Don't step within my strike zone.* Lore had given the order, and Azar would obey it. The outcome depended on the oracle. "He's yours."

"Hello, Neeka." Lore offered the other female a finger wave. "How wonderful. You've recovered from playtime with my boys."

Neeka smiled sweetly. "I've seen you die."

Lore made a pft sound, and Azar held his breath. Had she spoken true?

Maximus struggled in his seat, rattling his chains. The gag in his mouth muffled his words, but he clearly attempted to convey a message.

Rathbone flashed over, discarding the gag and chains one after the other, leaving the oracle a perfect target.

"—hurt Neeka," the boy erupted the moment his mouth was free.

Too late. Azar was already in motion. He tossed a toxin-laced dagger at Neeka. She was fast, but not fast enough. Especially because she'd frozen, her gaze faraway, as if she were stuck in a vision.

Rathbone appeared directly in front of her, taking the blade in his chest.

The king was powerful, amazingly so, but the toxin proved stronger. His knees buckled. He collapsed against Neeka, who snapped into the present. She struggled under the royal's weight while baring her fangs at the goddess.

"Well?" Lore prompted, giving Azar a little push. "Finish him off, then obey my previous order."

Azar fought the command with his considerable strength… but still he stepped forward, intending to deliver the final blow to both the red king and the oracle.

Maximus appeared behind the oracle, wrapped his arms around both her and the king, then flashed the pair away.

More guilt and shame barreled through Azar. There was a chance Rathbone might recover since he'd received the antidote not too long ago. There was also a chance he would not.

"Don't follow them," Lore said, and the compulsion to kill the oracle died. "The ceremony kicks off in three days. They'll be dead soon enough." She rubbed her hands together. "Show me the orb."

He ground his molars and held out his hand. "No one but Rathbone can lift the protective barrier."

"That's not true. Long ago, Erebus paid the barrier's creator to bind the orb to me, not Rathbone. The protective layer disappears when my spirit reconnects with my bones." A smile lifted the corners of her mouth. "Flash me to a large, abandoned location."

Though confused, he obeyed. They landed in a small, private world he'd created centuries ago. A lush paradise without inhabitants. The sunlit jungle teeming with flowers surrounded them.

She was too absorbed with the orb to notice. Lore waved her hand through its center and jolted. "Oh, yeah. We're in business."

The orb brightened until there was an explosion of light, blinding in its intensity. Birds took flight. A strong gust of wind hit him, and he stumbled back. When his eyes readjusted, he saw the golden throne set in a sea of marble title, with Lore's bones positioned on it.

"Do it," she said, excitement dripping from her voice. "Bring me to life."

Don't. Do not! But his feet drove him forward of their own accord. He knelt and removed the remaining pieces from the sheath. Reached out. Trembling, he set two of the bones in their proper place. *Click. Click.*

He shook as he withdrew the last. Shook harder as he joined it to the others...

Click.

The entire skeleton jerked. Soft, haunting music rose from each piece, blending together to create a breathtaking melody he heard deep in his marrow. The symbols turned bloodred and glowed almost as bright as the orb. Muscle and tendons began to grow. Veins wove together. Organs formed, and flesh melded like a woven tapestry until a dark-haired beauty sat naked upon the throne.

Moaning, Lore stretched. Her lids closed as she cupped her breasts. Sunlight paid her great homage. "This is magnificent." Giddy, she kicked her legs and shook her arms. "It's everything I remember and more."

A growl thundered in his chest. How was she so beautiful?

How could Azar long for a female like her? A seductress he despised. And yet, he did long for her. Greatly. "You let yourself die for Erebus." He stepped forward, drawn closer. "Would he have done the same for you?"

"Tsk-tsk. Trying to sow dissent in my *relationship*." She air quoted the final word, quirking her lips in a smile and utterly unafraid. "Ah. I get it. Does the Astra still believe I'm fated to be his?" She faked a pout. "I didn't meet Erebus until after I died."

"Are you using him, too?" he asked, taking another step in her direction. Inner shake. What was he doing? Urging her on?

He eased backward.

Noticing his retreat, she wagged a finger at him. "Aah, aah, aah, Astra. Come here. I'm going to fix your little obsession problem and prove how much I don't desire you."

He approached as commanded, his combat boots leaving scuffs in the floor. Far too soon, he stood a mere whisper away. Now wasn't the time to kiss her, but to spew vitriol at her. He had plenty on tap.

"What do you want me to do?" he grated instead. At one time, he'd prayed for this moment. The time he'd get to hold her in his arms.

All confidence and swagger, she reclined in the throne, kicking out her legs to display their length. "Kiss me."

"Yes." His hatred turned inward as he dropped to his knees without a fight, leaned in and pressed his lips to hers, thrusting his tongue past her teeth. Tasting the female he'd dreamed of bedding and killing for centuries.

She bit his tongue, wrenched free, and slapped his face, as if he hadn't done exactly what she'd stipulated. But she was panting, her smile gone without a trace.

He bent his head and kissed her a second time. She let him do it for a fleeting moment before biting and slapping him once more.

He lifted his head, meeting her gaze. She hissed at him. He

growled. Then down he went again. He kissed her with all the ferocity that bubbled inside him—and she kissed him back. A hard tangle of lips and tongue. They ate at each other.

His fingers wandered, exploring dips and curves. Moaning, she molded herself into him. But seconds later, she wrenched away, shouting, "Stop! No! B-back off. Immediately!"

Raising his palms in a gesture of innocence, he flashed backward, putting distance between them.

His heart thudded as she rose to shaky legs. She had desired him. True desire, nothing feigned. And his hands. They burned. Blistered, surely. Frowning, he looked down. His skin…sparkled. He had produced stardust. For *her*. Lore.

Incredulity hit him. Wonder and rage, too.

She noticed the stardust and gaped. "I…have things to do. I'll… I'll see you soon. For the ceremony." She looked anywhere but him. "Where can I score a gown? Never mind. I'll find one on my own." Blushing like a nervous schoolgirl, she teleported.

Azar stood in place, unsure what to think. Or what to do. But he had three days to figure it out.

31

"Is he going to be okay? He's going to be okay, right?" Maximus babbled the questions as he helped Neeka secure Rathbone and his two tons of muscle in bed. Thankfully, the kid had whisked them straight to the Kingdom of Agonies without incident, the realm defenses standing down, allowing him entry.

"He's going to be amazing, and that's my money-back guarantee." Yes, Rathbone currently thrashed and snarled, trapped in the throes of terrible pain, but what better place to recover than their home with Nurse Neeka on the case? And he *would* recover, thanks to the antidote already coursing through his veins. He wouldn't need another dose. Her last vision promised. Besides, she would never allow any other outcome.

A grin teased her lips. He'd been willing to die for Neeka, and it was the most adorable, romantic gesture ever. The big lug had done the impossible and fallen in love with the Wanted. Her. Not Lore. Her.

"But of course," she added, "we're all dying in three days unless I figure out a solution to our Lore problem." Because there was no way Neeka was letting Rathbone shift into the goddess. They had a future to enjoy as a couple. A family.

Maximus scowled at her. "You were *not* smiling when you said that."

"Well, it's hard to be upset when I know I'm heading to pound town as soon as your dad wakes up." She wiggled her brows. "That means we're going to have sex, in case you didn't catch my meaning. He's very good with his hands, your dad," she added to be contrary. "And his mouth."

Maximus pretended to dry heave. "Congrats, you just made dying in three days a relief."

"What? You're the one who told me to take my shirt off two seconds after meeting me. I thought you were on board with frank speech."

"I'll be out completing my bucket list. Do try to be quiet." He stomped past the door, gone.

Alone with her male, Neeka fit the covers over Rathbone's big, beautiful body and caressed his brow. "You better scream your love for me at the ceremony and not her. Because you do love me," she told him, in case he hadn't yet realized it.

He didn't awaken, but his thrashing eased.

Prickles erupted on the back of her neck, and they weren't the good kind. On instant alert, she spun, claws bared, ready to attack and defend. A female appeared, an ivory ball gown clinging to sensuous curves—Lore in the flesh, no longer confined to her spirit.

She was uninjured and unbound, and Neeka didn't have to wonder how she'd bypassed the realm's defenses. Long ago, Rathbone had tailored the place to her.

Dread slithered around Neeka. One of the three linked visions had come to pass, making the future of doom less likely to undergo change.

The goddess offered a smug smile. Glitter sparkled on her jawline as if—Neeka sucked in a breath.

"Stardust," Lore confirmed with bite.

Azar had already marked her. The dread tightened its hold, cutting off Neeka's airway. There was no way the Astra would harm her now. Not for any reason.

"Don't worry," the goddess said, adopting a breezy tone. "I'm not here to kill you. It's much more fun to make others do my dirty work, then watch them agonize over their actions. I'm merely here to check on our king."

"My king," Neeka grated. *All mine.*

"Possessive of him, I see." Her uninvited guest sauntered about the room, trailing her fingertips over this and that. "Well, one woman's trash is another's treasure, I suppose."

She ran her tongue over her teeth. "Why are you like this? Shouldn't you be sweet? Aren't you the epitome of desire?"

"I am indeed. But if you're not careful, your desires can turn against you."

It sucked that the incubator of evil wasn't wrong. "I suggest you say what you came to say and go," she snapped. "Being a spirit saved you from my wrath. But you aren't a spirit anymore. We can throw down." Though she would have to abandon her post at Rathbone's side to fight. Should she?

"I hope you do attack me," Lore said with a grin, as if she recognized something Neeka did not. "After our little Q and A session. You do have questions for me, do you not?"

Oh, she had questions all right. "How did you open the orb without Rathbone?" What had she missed?

"Oh. That. Daisy is on my payroll. Erebus predicted you would utilize her and we acted. I'm surprised you didn't realize the truth from the start."

"Me too," she admitted. No wonder Daisy had bargained to stay with them. How better to spy? But why *hadn't* Neeka realized the truth? She'd experienced zero twinges of warning. "How did you enslave Azar?"

"Easily. I convinced him we were life mates, the same way I convinced Rathbone and Styx and each male before them. The Astra was such delectable putty in my hands, willing to do anything I suggested. Even perform an ancient ritual to join our lives. But, oops, that isn't what I taught him to do. I tricked him into binding his will to mine."

So evil! And kind of brilliant. "Okay, you can go now." Giving the monster-spawner other opportunities to brag wasn't on today's to do list. "I have no more questions."

"Well, then. Before I head off to prepare for the arrival of my dearlings," Lore said, making her way to the wet bar, where she poured two glasses of whiskey, "let's toast to my victory."

"No!" Oh, no, no, no. The elixir! The concoction able to create a bond so strong it eclipsed that of fated ones. Days ago, instinct had led Neeka to pour the stuff into the decanter. "Don't drink that." She had no idea how the concoction worked, what side effects she would unleash upon herself, or what it would do to her connection with Rathbone.

As she rushed over, an extra smug Lore downed her glass, emptying the contents. "Mmm. Tasty." The goddess licked a final droplet from the rim.

Neeka's stomach sank. Why, why, why had instinct led her to partake? Now the elixir had a grip on them both.

How soon would the bond kick in?

She grew stiffer as seconds bled together and nothing happened. Not to Neeka, and not to her companion. Confusion set in. Had she missed an ingredient? Was the recipe a dud?

Wait. The recipe said to drink and bake. But for how long? Days? Weeks? Months? When would a connection to the goddess attempt to override her connection to Rathbone?

"The dominos are in place," she muttered. What was done was done, and there was no reversing time and changing it. But maybe this didn't have to be a bad thing. Lore would experience an unshakable bond, too. What if Neeka convinced her to accept a second death, without birthing the horde. Azar would win his task—not that he deserved it—and no one would become dinner.

Heart thudding, she swiped up the second glass and saluted the goddess. "Here's to your downfall." She drained the concoction. Two doses. Perhaps her side of the bond would prove stronger than Lore's, allowing her to better control the goddess.

Lore snorted. "Whatever strategy you think you've conjured will fail. I've thought of everything."

A panting Rathbone jolted upright. His gaze landed on them without preamble, as if he'd tracked them while sleeping. Flash. He materialized between them, his big body a tower of menace as he captured Lore by the throat. He stood in profile, allowing Neeka to (mostly) read his lips. "I'll meal with you wind the time combs," he spat at the goddess.

Or maybe he'd said, "I'll deal with you when the time comes." Possibly?

Lore laughed, even as her skin turned blue and blood leaked from the corners of her mouth. "Enjoy the next few days. They are your last," she said before flashing away.

Rathbone spun, facing Neeka fully. His entire countenance transformed from wrathful to sensual in a blink. "I believe you mentioned something about sexing me once I awoke. Yes, I heard you."

"I did mention sexing. But I should probably tell you what happened." With a baker's clock ticking in the back of her mind, she wound her arms around her male and tried to forget the coming battle, if only for a little while. If there were anything left for her to do, she wouldn't remember while stressing. But. She had a confession to make. She'd promised him honesty, and she intended to deliver. "Do you recall the elixir I told you about? The one meant to override your bond with your mate?"

"Yes." He cupped her backside and brushed the tip of his nose against hers. "Why?"

"Don't be mad!" Despite his groan, she rushed to continue. "I drank it days ago, before we reached our agreement, and Lore... she drank it today. I don't feel any different, and she didn't seem to either, but that's because it requires baking."

He stiffened. Drew in a calming breath. Held it. As he released it, tension seeped from him. He kneaded her giving flesh. "I appreciate you telling me, and I think I have a solution. Devote ourselves to strengthening *our* bond so *nothing* can override it."

He kissed her softly, and dang it, she melted against him. "That is the cheesiest, most romantic thing anyone has ever said to me," she told him.

"I think I heard it on a soap."

She laughed, her blood heating. This male. Oh, this male. Imperfectly perfect for her. She craved a future with him. "I refuse to let you become Lore and sacrifice your life to pay my debt to Taliyah," she said, toying with his hair.

"I will be Azar at the ceremony. I'll kill Lore on his behalf, freeing you from any unnatural bond while certifying the Astra's win. Of course, I'll have to hobble Azar beforehand, so he doesn't interfere, but you did mention something about wiggle room."

Oooh. "Rathbone, you beautiful, brilliant beast, you, that just might work!" Bright rays of hope beamed light into shadowy corners of her mind. They could actually pull off the big V. "You'll have to chain me up in case the elixir kicks in. And provide me with the world's most romantic gesture to make up for it."

"Deal." He lifted her off her feet, grinding his erection against her core as she wound her legs around him. "And now that the king and his chosen queen have reached an accord, we will celebrate."

"I'm intrigued. How do we celebrate in the Realm of Agonies?"

"With orgasms."

She chuckled. "I approve. But you can't just bestow such an important title upon me. There's got to be a ceremony or something."

"I beg to differ. I'm sovereign, my word law, and I say Neeka the Wanted is my queen. Therefore, you are my queen."

Tears of joy welled, blurring her vision. "Well. In that case, I guess I'm your queen."

They shared a soft smile.

"I once told you that I'd give you a grand love story," she bragged, "and that's exactly what I've done."

"It is indeed."

Rathbone dipped his head and pressed his mouth to hers, thrilling as Neeka opened for him and thrust her tongue against his. He fed her passion and adoration, giving her his promises, hopes, and tomorrows in return.

She tore at his clothes. "Guess what? We have more to celebrate than originally agreed upon," she rasped against his lips. "I'm Neeka the Wanted, and I'm all in. I'm yours, and you are mine. I admit it. We're a couple. The harpy-oracle and the red king. You're my consort. We're a family. Together forever. No takebacks." Had she covered all the bases?

He went still. "You want me as your one and only?" The consort she wouldn't share for any reason.

"I do."

Here it was. Everything he'd ever desired, his for the taking. And take it he would. He would brand her. Hear her cries of ecstasy. Show her how much she meant to him. Prove how important she was. How necessary.

"Yes. You are mine, and I am yours. Nothing will separate us." With a hoarse growl, he flashed her to the bed, sliced through her clothes, and pinned her to the mattress with his body.

The kiss deepened, every thrust of their tongues a meeting

of souls. He draped an arm over her head and angled her chin with the other, caging her in. Absolutely nothing in the vast eons of his life had ever felt this right. *Born for her.*

They strained together. Breathed for the other. He poured himself into each caress. Touched and tasted every inch of her. Pushed his control to its limit. Their moans blended, creating an exquisite symphony he yearned to hear for the rest of eternity.

"What are you doing to me?" she cried.

He lifted his head. "Whatever I want."

The air electrified when he spotted the fever flush deepening the hue of her skin. "So you're addicting me to your body, so I'll always crave more."

He kissed her, licking into her mouth. There was no greater prize than this female. "Exactly."

She moaned. "Get inside me. Please!"

"Mmm, but I like this word on your lips." He positioned himself at her opening and hooked an arm beneath her knee. With his gaze locked on hers, he thrust.

Her spine arched, exposing her vulnerable neck, and she screamed. He rode her climax to its end, then reached between them to ignite a second. And when he came with a roar, rapture like he'd never known consumed him. An unparalleled bliss that arrowed straight to the center of his being, changing his molecular makeup without a shift.

He wasn't a puzzle with missing pieces anymore. He'd been completed, and the future had never been brighter.

32

Hand in hand, Neeka and a shirtless Rathbone exited the bedroom. After hours of incredible lovemaking and whispered pillow talk, her heart was as full as her agenda. Nothing had happened with Lore—yet—so they might as well check on Maximus and confront Daisy while they had the chance.

The orb-making harpy had betrayed them from the beginning. A taste of Neeka's own medicine, yes. But. If you didn't work with them, you worked against them, and Rathbone had very strict rules about how to repay those who sought their doom. As the new Queen of Agonies, she must fully support her man in his endeavors.

"After this, you wanna spend the next two days in bed? I've decided to write a book, but I need to do some research first," she said.

He brought her knuckles to his lips and kissed. "Is this book a romance?"

"No sir. It's nonfiction. I'm calling it *The Cuddle Sutra.*"

"I will do this," he said with a nod, "but in return you will marathon my soaps and discuss the plots with me. In detail."

"Fine. But I expect a meal before, during, and after intermission." Smiling, she rested her head on his shoulder for a moment. "Let me handle Daisy, okay? Not to hurt your feelings or anything, but you aren't the greatest when it comes to dealing with enemy harpies. We can be a wee bit...quirky." Not to mention the fact that her instinct hadn't changed. Deep down, a part of Neeka believed she and Daisy were still meant to be good friends. Since Neeka couldn't be friends with a traitor to harpykind, Daisy must be on the up and up. Somehow.

Did that mean her actions would go unpunished? Not even a little.

He arched a brow at "wee bit." "I think I deal with you just fine."

"Yes, but that's because I'm oblivious to your flaws, since you're my consort and all."

"I have no flaws."

"No more than five. Ten. Probably closer to fifteen." She beamed a toothy grin at him. "I find your ego charming."

"Before the end of the day, I will hear everything you find charming about me."

"I'll need at least a week."

He squeezed her hand and kissed her forehead. Neeka grinned wider. Oh, how she loved her life.

They discovered both of their targets in a sitting room. Daisy lounged in a velvet settee, reading a book in her underwear and tube socks, with empty snack cartons piled around her. An orange corn chip hung from the ends of her hair.

Maximus sat across from her, staring hard. His clawed hands white-knuckled his knees. "I must have you," he blurted out.

Daisy belched in her hand and flipped a page without glancing up. "No."

"I'll give you jewels."

"Dude," the harpy replied. "You're embarrassing yourself."

Neeka released Rathbone to palm two daggers. "How dare you tell my stepson the truth, you lying liar!"

The boy tore his attention from the harpy, flashed to his feet facing Neeka and Rathbone, and growled. Actually growled, baring his teeth and everything. "We're busy, and you're interrupting," he snapped. He waved them off. "Go."

"That isn't how you speak to your par—elders," Rathbone snapped back.

Daisy flipped another page in her book. "Put the weapons away. You're not going to kill or imprison me. I've glimpsed my future, remember. Besides, you realize I did what I had to do for reasons. Also, you vowed to protect me while I'm living with you."

"Our vow was conditional," Neeka retorted. "You got a place to stay and in exchange, Rathbone controlled the orb. And FYI. I would never kill or imprison another harpy. I'm only going to rip out your guts and fly them like a flag while I sing about being a champion."

"I will pay my future wife's debts," Maximus proclaimed, holding his head high.

Rathbone scrubbed a hand over his face.

"I'm not your future wife, kid," Daisy replied. Page flip. "I met the condition, Unwanted. Rathbone was able to control the orb, but so was Lore."

"She's the Wanted," Rathbone stated at the same time Neeka said, "I'm the Wanted. And stop making perfect sense! It's annoying."

"I'm not a kid." Maximus punched a fist into his open palm. "I'm older than you are, harpy."

"Then grow up!"

As the different arguments rolled on, Neeka lost sight of the conversation. But that was okay. The most amazing contentment spread through her. These people were her family. With all their faults, weaknesses, and mistakes. The holidays were going to be oh, so fun.

More and more mátia on Rathbone's chest glanced her way and stayed put. Soon, Rathbone himself was peering at her, each of his irises glowing with an assortment of colors. Oh, wow. She marveled at the beauty.

"Rathbone, did you know your mátia is changing colors?" she asked.

Her beautiful crimson consort looked himself over and floundered. "I don't understand."

"They look the same to me," Maximus said.

So only she and Rathbone could see the switch? "It's never happened before?" she asked.

"Not to my knowledge." He canted his head. "Do you think…"

"Oh, yeah." It was a sign she belonged with him. Forever!

She stepped into him, gliding her palms up his chest. "The queen is ready to retire for the—" Flash. Rathbone tumbled her into bed. "Day," she finished with a laugh.

"One step ahead of you, oracle," he said before kissing her.

Neeka spent the next two days relishing all things Rathbone. If they weren't making love, they were listening to Maximus drone on and on about Daisy, who rebuffed him at every turn.

Though Neeka hadn't viewed a new vision, she'd pondered the others. Noted the smallest details. She'd also returned to her beach hideaway with Rathbone to collect the vial of Azar's blood. In her spare time, she exchanged carry pigeon messages with Hades, brainstorming contingency plans for the upcoming event.

Still nothing had happened with Lore. Neeka was beginning to think she'd screwed up the elixir somehow. Nothing required this much baking.

When the morning of the ceremony finally dawned, she and Rathbone shared a passionate embrace before he did as prearranged and chained her to their bed. At least she hadn't gotten this wrong. At some point, they'd changed the future for the better. She knew it. Even without a vision, she knew it.

"You will be protected at all times," he assured her. "Hades's men surround the realm and the palace and Hades himself is standing guard at your door even now."

Said door swung open and Hades peeked inside the room to say, "Hades is listening to everything you're discussing, so keep things PG." The door shut, then opened again. "That means perfectly graphic, in case it wasn't clear," he added, and Rathbone rolled his eyes.

"I hate missing seeing you in action," she pouted. And yes, she remained a bit leery. She hadn't attended the ceremony in her visions, either. What if—no. No going there today. They'd schemed, plotted, and bargained. They'd taken precautions. In none of the visions had Rathbone shifted into Azar. This was new. A twist she hadn't foreseen. "You're going to save the day, I just know it." Right? That's what she felt the strongest, yes? "You'll take Azar out of commission, assume his identity, and slay Lore before the shadow monsters are freed."

"Exactly. But first, I'm off to collect the necessary tools." He bent down to cup her jaw and softly kiss her lips. When he lifted his face from hers, he studied her for several beats while tracing the pads of his thumbs over her cheekbones. "If you want to watch, Peer through me. Or save your strength and I'll tell you all about it after I've gotten inside you. Twice. The festivities kick off in an hour."

Despite Hades's nearness, she was vulnerable while chained. Peering would drain her, leaving her doubly vulnerable. "Whatever you do, stay safe and return to me."

"Always." Rathbone kissed her again, then he was gone.

Ugh. She missed him already. And dang it, she regretted the

need for chains. She should be by his side, aiding him. Predicting moves and taking names. Why, why, why had instinct led her in this direction?

Hey! What was that strange tugging sensation in her chest?

She grimaced as the sensation amplified until—Neeka's body shot off the mattress, pulling her chains taut. Uh-oh. The straining metal cut into her wrists and ankles. Deep. Deeper. Pain arced through her limbs.

What was happening? She opened her mouth to scream for Hades, but the words coagulated in her throat. Odd thoughts bombarded her head.

Almost time. Untapped power awaits me. First Harpina, then the Realm of Agonies, then Nova. No one can stop me. Fools all! So why am I so unhappy? What will it take to feel joy?

Sparks erupted throughout her body, and she wheezed. Flames grew beneath the surface of her skin, licking at her insides, burning, scorching, blistering. Literally! Glowing embers began to spark from her pores. No, not embers. Not fire, either. She was breaking apart and fading.

No, no, no. This wasn't—she couldn't—the bedroom vanished, an unfamiliar throne room taking its place. Dark stone walls surrounded her, with a single row of torches stretching on all sides. A mirror as large as the one Hades owned hung from a vaulted ceiling.

As her hysteria dulled, she grew confused. What in the world? She perched on a throne made of fossilized hearts. Lore's children lounged at her feet, gazing at her with adoration. She soaked up the attention, charging like a battery.

Neeka reared back, getting into fight mode—except, she didn't move an inch. She remained reclined on the throne of hearts, drumming the seat's arms with the tips of too long, pointy nails. She now wore a black ball gown suitable for a storybook evil queen, and she had white skin. What the—*what*?

"That's right. Love me, my darlings." Lore's voice echoed

through the room, and shockingly, Neeka heard her. Such a soft, melodious voice. "Fuel me. I know you are upset I'm flesh and blood while you remain in spirit form, able to touch me no longer. But those I'm soon to birth will move between spirit and natural, solidifying and misting at will. They will be your bridge to do the same."

Their adoration intensified, and Lore moaned.

"Yes, yes. Just like that, my lovelies. I must be as strong as possible."

More odd thoughts drifted through Neeka's mind. *What is wrong with me? Why do I feel the oracle?*

She thought of herself as 'the oracle' now? Or... Huh. Had she forced a Peer without knowing it? Although, this felt like so much more than an inner eye connection. This felt as if she'd become a part of Lore.

Oh...crap. Guess they were done baking. Had the elixir *combined* them? Was that how it tied two people together?

The other woman gasped. "Combined us? Elixir? What did you do?" Lore screeched, upsetting her audience. Their scales spiked with aggression. "I will rip you out of me if I must!"

Neeka heard her voice as well as her thoughts, and apparently the goddess heard Neeka's thoughts too. But why was Neeka trapped inside Lore and not the other way around? Neeka had drunk two glasses, the goddess one; she should be the carrier, not the carried.

"Ah, I see what you did," Lore intoned. "Details are unrolling from your chaotic mind. How do you function like this?" She rubbed her temples. "Obviously, you are the weaker vessel."

Hardly! But why would her foresight lead her to do this? To condemn herself to such a horrendous future? She and Rathbone had worked up the most amazing plan.

Gah! *Don't think about the plan.*

Of course, now she could think of nothing *but* the plan.

Anger drained from Lore, and she snorted. "I doubt Rathbone

will be so eager to become Azar and kill me when he learns I carry his beloved."

Neeka beat her fists into the goddess's mind to no avail. She must escape. Must get to Rathbone.

"Hmmm. I wonder if I have access to your foresight. When you have a vison, will I?" A tinkling laugh escaped the treacherous female. "I like this very much. Maybe I'll keep you around for a while." To the hell spawn who prowled at her feet, she said, "I'll return with our army. Finally the goddess of desire will have *her* desires met. Power beyond imagining. Worlds at my feet, no one strong enough to steal what belongs to me." She stood and flashed to a spacious bedroom in the harpy palace. Azar's bedroom. A part of Lore was overjoyed to be there. Neeka felt her excitement.

The Astra pumped iron on a bench, sweat pouring over his bulging muscles. He didn't glance at Lore as she leaned against the side of the machine, but he definitely noticed her presence. He compressed his lips as hatred and longing pulsed from him.

Where was Rathbone?

"Hello, handsome." Lore stared at his mouth for seconds longer than polite, her blood rushing hot. "Are you ready for our big day?"

"You genuinely desire him," Neeka gasped out. *How can I use this information to my advantage?*

"You can't," Lore snapped, no longer quite so happy.

"Can't what?" Azar demanded, placing the bar in its perch and sitting up.

Scowling, she said, "Just thought you should know the oracle is a part of me now. We drank an elixir, and it combined us. I can hear her thoughts. Rathbone plans to shift into you and kill me. Be a dear and hobble him."

Surprise glistened in the warlord's extraordinary irises.

Neeka fought with all her might to seize the reins of control.

She grappled. Clawed. Kicked and screamed. The exertion depleted her—and empowered her hostess.

"Mmm, yes," Lore said with a delighted moan. "Keep doing that."

Neeka deflated, shocked. She'd failed?

Azar wiped a rag over his sweat-dampened brow, his palms already glittering with stardust. "Erebus isn't your fated. I am. He's done something to convince you—"

"Why are you focusing on what doesn't matter?" Neeka shrieked, and the words escaped her host's mouth.

She gasped, and the goddess went stiff.

Oh, oh, oh! What had allowed her to succeed? Not her strength, because she currently had none. She tried to control Lore's words a second time but...

"Of course he isn't," Lore said, herself once again. She opened her mouth to say more but closed it. Opened. Closed. Indecision plagued her, confusing Neeka. But that indecision hardened into resolve with a single thought: *For my freedom.* "He'll experience the same fate as you the second I'm done with him. By the way, just because I'm yours doesn't mean you're mine. Defeated foes aren't my type."

He stared at her without a change in his expression before issuing a clipped nod.

And with that, Neeka felt as if the final piece of the elaborate puzzle fell into place. Whatever he'd decided had etched everything in stone. Dread swamped her. The future was now set, the dominos already in motion.

An upheaval erupted in the hallway, voices exploding through the air. Azar stiffened. Lore rubbed her hands together as the word *Rathbone* reached her ears.

Neeka groaned. The King of Agonies had arrived.

Rathbone stormed the harpy palace. He could've started with stealth, secretly removing Azar from play and taking over his identity, but he didn't know Astra customs. This was an official ceremony with set rules; he would've gotten caught or caused disqualification.

Instead, he'd chosen another route. The plan rolled through his mind. Tattle-tale on Azar. If the other Astra refused to subdue the warlord, saving Rathbone the time and trouble, he'd go with Plan B.

Harpies catcalled. As soon as the Astra army learned of his arrival, they began to appear and attack. He did not go down. "Azar believes Lore is his fated," he shouted, throwing off a warlord. "He's already revived her."

Someone launched a punch. He transformed into a primordial panther and bit off the male's hand, then returned to his true form. Blood dripped from his mouth. "Azar! Show yourself, coward, and admit the truth."

Finally, the Memory Keeper arrived, appearing grimmer than usual.

"Tell them," Rathbone demanded.

The warlord stared at him, ice cold. "He's correct. I have already revived her."

Okay. That had been a wee bit easier than expected. He pointed at Azar but addressed the others. "According to Neeka's visions, he's under Lore's command. He can't kill her. He'll help her slaughter you and the harpies. If you want to win, you'll let me become him. I'll kill Lore and hand your victory."

The Astra attacked as a unit. They weren't going to listen to him, the enemy. Very well. He'd stopped fighting, allowing the warlords to wrestle him to the ground and bind his wrists with chains. His ticket to the ceremony.

"I thought you'd learned your lesson about this," Rathbone taunted. "Imprisoning me isn't one of your talents."

The brute with a half shaved head hauled him to his feet, snapping, "I might not have a soulbond-breaking collar, but the new cuffs will do for now. You won't be getting out of these. I made sure of it."

"You need me," Rathbone told them, trying again. "Neeka assured me I'll be Azar in every way that matters." If it would've worked with Lore, it would work for the Astra.

"You don't understand," Shaved said, unbending. "We love him. We'll bet on him every time."

Rathbone's gaze shot to Azar, who flinched the slightest bit.

"Where is she?" The question came from the General. The group of harpies parted, revealing the pale-haired Taliyah as she strode closer. "Where's Neeka."

"Safe," Rathbone said.

"What does that mean?" she demanded. "I want to see her. Hear the outcome from her mouth, not yours."

"Too bad. She and Lore partook of an elixir meant to create a tie stronger than mates. Neeka won't be going near her. But go ahead. Try to breach my palace defenses again. You won't bypass Hades, her personal guard, without my approval."

"Azar?" the General demanded. "Say something."

"Shifting into me won't do you any good," Azar told him. "The elixir has already done its job. Lore and Neeka have become one being."

No. No. Horror froze him in place. That couldn't be right. One being? That was— No. No! "You're lying," Rathbone snarled, lunging for the male. Shaved held him back. "This is you, trying to save your fated." He sprang forward, intending to tackle Azar and knock the truth out of him, but the chains sent an electric pulse through his body, and he dropped.

"You were never going to win," Azar said as Rathbone twitched, unable to move otherwise. "Love is weakness."

33

Lore hummed happily as she studied herself in a full-length mirror. Her beaded gown boasted a plunging neckline and a slitted skirt, the perfect style for her perfect hourglass figure. "I know all about your newest plan," she told Neeka, fluffing curled hair. "You're conserving your strength to try and take control of my body at the first opportunity."

"Our body," Neeka snapped. "Ours." And she wasn't not saving her strength. She was busy pondering. How had she taken over Lore's mouth? Because, if she could take over the goddess's mouth, she could take over her body. And if she could take over her body, she could walk into Azar's sword, granting everyone but herself and Lore a happily ever after. But she was okay with that. To save Rathbone, she'd give up anything, even her life. "I am you and you are me."

"So you wouldn't care if I—excuse me, we—climbed into bed with Rathbone?" Lore asked.

"Go ahead. Try," she said with a laugh. "I'd appreciate a front row seat to your rejection."

The goddess humphed. "As if anyone can turn me down."

Think! If Neeka didn't do something soon, she'd have a front row seat to the destruction of harpykind. And if Rathbone was in the throne room, bound by chains? Hope was lost, the vision set, all of her efforts in vain.

"All your efforts *were* in vain," Lore echoed.

"Why are you doing this?" she demanded. "Why do you hate Rathbone and the Astra so much?"

"I don't hate them. I only used Rathbone to flee a precarious situation after my former lover wised up."

"Practicing your victory speech, my love?" The familiar male voice startled both Lore and Neeka. As the other woman turned, heart drumming, she caught a glimpse of Erebus the Deathless and groaned. "You are ravishing."

"Darling!" Lore rushed to him to throw her arms around him. "How I missed you."

Disdain rose in Neeka—no, in Lore. It filled her belly and spilled into the rest of her. Did Erebus have any idea the goddess used him too?

He cupped her cheeks and held her gaze, searching. He frowned. "You seem different. Nervous?"

Erebus didn't sense Neeka was squatting inside his lady love? He hadn't expected it? Word hadn't yet spread to him? Interesting.

"I'm wonderful," Lore said, grinning, soaking up his admiration. "This is the day we've been waiting for."

"That it is. The ceremony is soon to begin." He kissed her brow. "Once it concludes, I will ascend into a god of gods, and you will become my cherished queen."

"Your queen," she echoed. Her disdain sharpened, but her sweet disposition never wavered. "The only thing I've ever wanted."

"I'll be waiting for you with bated breath." He was gone a second later, leaving them alone.

Lore released a growl she'd held back. "He is such a bore. They all are. I'm doing you a favor, allowing you to tag along today and experience my greatness firsthand."

"You're the bore. World takeovers? Yawn. You are an average supervillain at best."

"Maybe. But we all have our reasons." A note of sadness seeped into her voice.

"Are you seriously trying to elicit sympathy right now?" Neeka probed her host's mind for what those reasons might be but alas, the goddess was much better at hiding her thoughts.

"Stop that," Lore snapped. "You aren't worthy of my secrets."

With a fortifying breath, the goddess flashed to Azar's bedroom again, landing directly behind him. The warlord stood statue still while receiving a lecture from his Commander. Weapons were strapped all over him. He'd dressed for war.

Both males pegged her arrival, as evidenced by their bristling, but neither acknowledged her verbally. Treating her as insignificant?

Lore pressed her palms against Azar's shoulder blades, her thoughts flying straight to a kiss the two had shared. How good he'd tasted. How ferocious he'd been. How hot. The power he'd exuded.

His muscles jerked upon contact, and the goddess chuckled, loving it.

Roc simply continued his lecture.

"You still have a shot with Azar," Neeka pointed out, willing to utilize any advantage. "It isn't too late. Don't let those monsters you're brewing eat everyone. Let him slay you to win his war. You'll revive again, thanks to the Song of Life, we'll find a way to extract me, and boom, happily-ever-after for everyone. You get more kisses and stardust. The works."

"*We* are brewing the monsters," Lore said, interrupting Roc, who went quiet at last. "The two of us together. And I don't want a shot with Azar."

"I despise you," Neeka grated.

"It's mutual, I assure you."

"Since you are so eager to participate, face me, female," Roc commanded.

"Certainly, oh great one," Lore said, stepping around Azar. She grinned as she linked her arm through the Astra's. "Are you as excited as I am?"

A muscle jumped beneath Roc's eye, reminding Neeka of Rathbone, and the time he'd pretended to be the Commander. "My Cherry Bomb. I miss him." The words left Lore's mouth, and they both gasped.

Think of Rathbone and take over? Was that the key?

Rathbone, Rathbone, Rathbone. But... Nope. She didn't speak aloud again, and Lore relaxed.

The Commander stared hard for a long while before refocusing on the Memory Keeper. "Assure me you will do what you must."

"I will do what I must," the soldier vowed, yet all kinds of sorrow dripped from his tone.

Roc cast a narrowed glance to Lore, huffed, and nodded. "I'll see you in the throne room. Five minutes." He flashed away.

"Don't worry. I'll end you quick, I promise," the goddess told Azar, turning her body into his. She rested her head on his shoulder, saying, "Pet my hair until it's time to leave and say nothing."

He wrapped one arm around her and used the other to pet her hair as ordered, the action stiff and formal. Lore tried not to enjoy it but couldn't help herself. Meanwhile, Neeka wrapped her mental arms around Rathbone, clinging to her king.

"What happened with Rathbone?" the goddess asked. When he remained silent, she sighed. "You may speak."

"He is chained in the dungeon."

Neeka cried out. "No!"

Lore gave a little hum of delight. "Telepathically tell one of your Astra buddies to bring him to the throne room. I want him there."

"No," Neeka croaked. Here she was, living the behind-the-scenes activities of her vision, bringing the future of doom to life bit by bit.

"It's done," Azar said with a nod.

"Good. Now, be my dear and escort me to the throne room. The time has come, and I'm eager to finish this."

He hesitated, strain contorting his features. Then he flashed her just outside the throne room, the entrance within reach.

Neeka kicked up a fuss inside Lore's mind, making no progress.

Head high, Azar pushed open the doors and led his companion inside. In the center of the room was a newly built dais. On it was Lore's throne, minus Rathbone's flooring.

A crowd awaited them, just as she'd foreseen. Roc and Taliyah, side by side on their thrones. Chaos, Erebus, and Grenwich stood on Taliyah's other side. The remaining Astra stood next to their Commander. The best warriors in the harpy army filled the space behind them. And there was Rathbone, chained to a wall.

Neeka whimpered. They'd lost.

Hades stood beside him at least.

Lore laughed, calling, "Hello, Rathbone. Chains suit you." Azar helped her ease into her throne and stepped to the side, remaining near her, awaiting her next order. She took a beat, letting everyone else look their fill.

The crowd said nothing.

Finally, the goddess began. "Azar is my puppet," she called, "and soon, the rest of you will be food." Cupping the side of her mouth, she told them, "You should have listened to the King of Agonies." She soaked up their reactions. Everything from rage to uncertainty. "Let's give them a preview of the feats to come, Azar. Bow before me."

Still the masses kept quiet, every eye riveted on the Memory Keeper.

Though his strain magnified, muscles and veins bulging, Azar sank to his knees and inclined his head.

The throng of harpies erupted with comments and questions while the Astra army maintained the gag order. Some couldn't mask their shock, however, as if only then realizing the truth of Neeka and Rathbone's prediction.

"Do not do this," Azar whispered to Lore. "Please, do not do this." Dark irises beseeched her. Untold agonies steeped in their depths.

Lore stared at the Astra, a lump growing in her throat, startling Neeka.

She pounced. "It's not too late to forge a life with him."

"No one asked for your commentary," Lore softly snapped.

Rathbone fought confinement, shouting, "I love you! There's got to be another way. Please."

Neeka startled anew. Uh, no way he loved Lore. Just no way. He was gaga for Neeka, and she knew it. Zero doubts. So why would he ever—ohhhh. He knew Neeka inhabited the goddess. Knew her plan to die and save the day. And oh, how sweet it was to realize he'd shouted romantic confessions at her in the vision, not Lore.

He was always meant to be with *Neeka*.

Her heart swelled. *I was meant to be with you, too, Wrath Boned.*

"Shut up," Lore muttered to Neeka, rubbing her temples. "Just shut up. I can't concentrate, and I need to concentrate."

No, no, no! Neeka knew what came next, despite the many alterations. Small differences that led to the same result.

I'll teach her a lesson. "Cut out his tongue," Lore commanded Azar.

That.

The Astra straightened, unsheathed a dagger and stomped over. Hades readied for battle.

"Stop Azar," Neeka shouted, the words flying from her host's mouth.

The Astra stopped. Another change. This one emboldened Neeka.

"Shut up," Lore repeated.

"You shut up," Neeka retorted, and again, she hijacked their voice.

"Azar! Do it!"

"Azar, stop!"

Okay, these differences weren't so small. Neeka could win this!

Lore flashed in front of Rathbone and unsheathed a blade. Hades stood down, allowing the goddess to strike before Neeka registered that she'd moved. Rathbone's tongue plopped to the floor.

Hades glanced at his nephew, saying, "Told you."

"That's better," Lore said as Neeka shrieked. Except, Rathbone didn't seem to notice the wound. As blood poured from his mouth, he smiled. It unnerved Lore, who shuddered.

Neeka calmed, her heart swelling. This was a romantic gesture if ever she'd seen one! He was telling her how much he adored and trusted her. How much he believed in her. She tumbled straight into love. Totally, completely, utterly.

Lore centered and returned to the throne, where she licked the blade and cast it to the floor. "To keep things interesting, I'll wait to run out the clock before I continue, assuring your defeat. We have, what? Two minutes remaining?"

"Marvelous. Marvelous indeed." Erebus started clapping. He looked around, asking, "Shall we proclaim me the winner yet?"

No response from the opposing team. Neeka prepared for the war of her life, gearing up.

"Azar," Lore snapped, sensing her intentions and needing a distraction.

He flashed to her side, wrenching a new round of shock from his brethren.

"I'm already bored, and you owe me a kiss," the goddess announced. "Give it to me."

A vein bulged in his forehead. "It didn't have to be this way," he grated, shooting out his hand and clasped the back of her nape. His grip was firm, but his fingers shook.

She narrowed her eyes, too, a cauldron of emotions bubbling over. Hints of trepidation, longing, and anger. "You have your orders."

He yanked Lore close for a kiss. His palm burned her flesh. As Lore returned his passion, her resolve weakened, and Neeka strengthened. One minute remained on the clock. Now or never. She seized her chance.

"Kill me," she commanded Azar, the words echoing from the throne room walls.

Silence. Then chaos. "No!" Rathbone shouted, his denial gutting her. Had to be this way. "Don't you dare."

Lore grappled for control. "Do me no harm."

"Kill me," Neeka repeated as Rathbone's curses and threats intensified. Seconds ticked away.

Azar reared back and shook his head. His defenses toppled, nothing shielding the lust in his expression. "I don't want to do it."

Lore attempted to gain control again, but again, she was weakening. Neeka drew from her bubbling well of love and waged the final battle. "Ready your sword, soldier," she shouted at Azar. "Take my head, then my heart. Separate my bones. Do whatever is necessary to ensure I never rise again. Do it now!"

Groaning, Lore covered her lips with her hand. But it was too late. Neeka retained the helm as Azar lifted his sword. He was fighting the compulsion but losing.

"I will bring you back," Rathbone vowed.

She raised her chin, calling, "I love you, too, Red." As Lore contended for dominance, Neeka dropped to her knees. "Do it, Azar."

The midnight hour rang out.

He swung the sword. *Whoosh.* Darkness came, bringing silence. Neeka died, taking Lore with her.

Rathbone watched as his female lost her head, then her heart. A ragged roar escaped him. Erebus cursed louder. He'd lost this round.

The Astra and harpies cheered. They'd won without lifting a finger.

Hades removed the chains Rathbone had failed to shed on his own. He sprang over and collected Lore's headless body. Neeka's shell. Tears welled as the General rushed over to crouch beside him.

His oracle was gone. His fated. The one he couldn't live without. But not for long.

"Get me a chisel," he commanded the General. He would bind Neeka's spirit to the bones. He just needed time to figure out a better plan.

"On it." She vanished in a puff of smoke, and from his post, Hades groaned.

"Have you learned nothing?" the god called.

Wait. Why was the body so hot? Rathbone frowned. His skin blistered. Flames erupted from Neeka's—Lore's pores. He released her and eased back. The inferno spread, burning away the body... Dark smoke collected around the bones, creating a curtain.

Rathbone waited, daring to hope. His oracle was very good at pre-planning. Taliyah arrived with the desired item as the fire died and the curtain thinned...

He sagged with relief. A naked, smoldering Neeka stirred and stretched, as if waking from a peaceful nap. With a grunt, he scooped her up and yanked her against his chest.

"You're alive," he said, pulling back just enough to let her read his lips. "And you are fully Phoenix apparently, after only four doses of the toxin."

Head falling back, she laughed. "I saw you through the flames and it was glorious! But how? Why? Because I didn't arrange this."

"I gave her six doses of the Phoenix toxin as a child," Grenwich announced, approaching their side. Neeka hadn't noticed her yet. "Her father predicted her death the day of her birth, and I took measures to prevent it. There was no other way to trick Erebus into using me and choosing her. Tell her."

He did, and Neeka swung her attention to her mother. "Are you saying you have treated me as an enemy to...protect me?" she asked, dumbfounded.

"Yes and no. I don't want you dead. How then will you feel pain?"

The tracker offered the question so casually, it took him a moment to catch up and decide he had a cell with his harpy-Phoenix-in-law's name on it.

"Worst mother *ever*," Neeka stated as Grenwich strode away.

Rathbone flashed Neeka to their bed. As she wound her arms around him, he peppered her face with kisses, saying between each, "I love you. Adore you. Cherish you. But I am going to punish you for dying." Each of his irises lit up with colors.

"I love you, too," she said, laughing up at him. "I'll take whatever you'll give me."

"Uh, I guess I should go?" The question came from Maximus, who was in the process of loading himself with Rathbone's weapons. "I was preparing to save you both, so, thanks for nothing. You guys are gross." He stomped from the room.

"I'm going to figure out how to age him," Neeka promised as Rathbone kissed a path down the elegant length of her throat.

"I know you will. You can do anything. Even tame the untamable Crimson Thunder."

"I can, can't I?" she said, cupping his jaw and pressing her lips to his. She might not know what tomorrow held—yet—but she knew her future had never seemed brighter.

Azar stood in the throne room, unmoving. Lore, his gravita, was dead once again. Shock locked him in place as he stared at her bones. The ash had collected, and each piece had been rebuilt. If something wasn't done, she would soon develop flesh.

He'd hated her, but... he wanted her back.

Chaos declared him the winner. Erebus fumed and flashed off. Taliyah cleared the harpies from the room but stayed behind with the Astra. They hadn't left the dais. None of them had spoken a word.

Then Roc commanded, "Silver, when Azar is ready, scatter the bones across the galaxies. But do not wait too long. She is not to revive under any circumstances."

Silver nodded, his manner as cold as the metal he worked with. There was no task too gruesome for the male and no chance anyone could stop him from completing a duty.

Somehow, Azar gathered the strength to tear his gaze from the body and focus on his comrades. Roc seemed pleased. Halo and Roux, the other mated Astra, projected understanding. Sparrow, who never lost his calm, looked strained. Bleu and Ian conveyed confusion. Vasili was focused and alert, an unusual occurrence. Azar loved them, yet he'd nearly killed them all.

"I don't know what happened behind the scenes." The Commander closed the distance and patted his shoulder. "And I don't need to. I have experienced the allure of a gravita."

Absolution. Exactly what Azar did not deserve. Still, he nodded.

"Go," Roc called to one and all. "Celebrate the win but remain on guard. Soon another among us will face Erebus. He has planned ahead. Expect the unexpected and trust only your brethren."

"Or you will pay dearly for it," Azar croaked.

They left the room, one by one. All but Silver, who remained behind, at Azar's side. "You hoped to break your own soul-bond." A statement.

"Yes." Freed from Lore compulsion, he could answer honestly.

"I'm working on something. If, after we ascend, you want to try again, I'll have a way." Silver showed mercy and let the subject drop there. "Erebus knew he was going to lose today. I think he wanted to."

Ignoring the raw pain in his chest, he demanded, "Explain." Because Azar had observed the opposite.

"He sent phantoms to me this morning. They delivered a message. I'm next, special horrors await me, and I shouldn't tell the Memory Keeper he'll get another chance to shine."

Azar went cold. "He's going to pit us against each other?"

"That is my guess."

"I will not turn against you." Not ever again. Lesson learned. "I might want her back, but I will never accept her as mine. Will never give her an opportunity to spawn her eaters."

Silver studied his face for a long while before holding out his hand. "Brothers until the end."

He accepted, clasping tightly. "Brothers until the end."

★ ★ ★ ★ ★